THE
THROWBACK
LIST

THE THROWBACK LIST

LILY ANDERSON

HYPERION AVENUE

Los Angeles New York

First Edition, October 2021
10 9 8 7 6 5 4 3 2 1
FAC-020093-21232

Printed in the United States of America

This book is set in Garth Graphic Pro, Core Circus, Proxima, Zapf/Monotype,
Born Ready, Century Gothic, Janda, Lumios Marker/Fontspring
Designed by Torborg Davern

Library of Congress Control Number: 2021934796
ISBN 978-1-368-05193-4

Reinforced binding

For everyone who didn't have a home to go back to.
I see you. I am you.

What is life but a series of inspired follies?
The difficulty is to find them to do.
Never lose a chance: it doesn't come every day.

FROM *PYGMALION*,
BY GEORGE BERNARD SHAW

one

Palo Alto, California

JO

Jo Freeman stepped off the elevator with "Lose Control" stuck in her head. That morning's exercise coach—Salvador of Confident Kickboxing—put a song on the playlist for every heavy bag in the room, and Jo had found herself hitting in the Missy Elliott zone.

"Take your anthem with you into the world today! Use your big-bitch energy!" Salvador called after them as the class split up to go to their various Silicon Valley desk jobs.

Normally Jo left her buy-in at the door, discarding all the silly mantras and platitudes inside her gym du jour. But today, she could feel the "Lose Control" beat keeping her hips loose as she took long strides past the reception desk at Quandt Corporation's Palo Alto headquarters.

Work, wait. Work work work wait, Jo's heartbeat chanted in time with the music in her head.

If she was still thinking about kickboxing two hours after taking off her gloves, Salvador deserved five stars and a tip. She slipped her phone out of her tote and popped open the Gym Class app.

Once Jo got the promotion that she'd spent the last five years strategizing for, Confident Kickboxing could become her regular gym. As grateful as she was for the free subscription to Gym Class—a Q-Co work perk—she was getting tired of being an exercise vagabond. Lurking in six a.m. classes with strangers. Never knowing where the parking was.

When she finally got to update her business cards to say *Director of Digital Strategy*, she was going to buy that loft downtown—a huge upgrade from the college-kid-infested apartment building she'd lived in since she was one of the students—and then she was going to buy an annual pass to a gym. She could even get gym buddies. It'd been a minute since she'd had nonwork friends.

"Johanna?" College Kevin called after her as she passed him on her way to her cube. He skittered around the standing desk of shame that Jo herself had spent eight months chained to when she had been Q-Co's Stanford intern. Back in the day, the standing desk of shame had also come with a heavy phone headset that made Jo look like she was taking drive-thru orders. College Kevin wore AirPods all day that may or may not have been playing music.

Jo glanced slightly past Kevin's head toward Gia's office. Behind the glass partition, her friend-slash-mentor was sitting barefoot on top of her desk, the receiver of her office landline tucked under her chin as she gesticulated wildly with one hand and cut a Starbucks Pink Drink with diet Red Bull in the other.

"Is Gia talking to . . . the other guys?" Jo asked College Kevin, knowing he wasn't allowed to tell her. Even Gia, a girl who'd once been fired as a pharmaceutical rep for being "too fun," hadn't officially spilled the beans on the rumored merger. But Jo had worked for the Q long enough to know when change was in the air. And Gia working her ass off at nine a.m. was a big change. Client relations usually didn't start until lunch.

College Kevin squirmed. "Devo wants to see you."

Work work work, wait.

"Great," Jo said. She gave him a smile that he couldn't see with his eyes focused on the toes of his shoes. "I'm on my way."

Her phone trembled in her hands as she pulled up the interoffice messenger.

TODAY'S THE DAY!! she shot off to Gia, whose mouse clicked twice before the read receipt came through.

Gia sent back a thumbs-up, then noticed Jo through the glass and waved. Jo mimed walking toward Devo's office with a giddy *Oh my God, can you believe today's the day* smile. In return, she got a distracted IRL thumbs-up. Gia's eyes looked tired. Or possibly just lacking concealer. Jo felt bad for even noticing—there was too much pressure for women in the office to adhere to a problematically narrow beauty standard; she herself was guilty of daily flat-iron on top of her Brazilian blowout just to keep her natural 3C curls straight and glossy. Meanwhile College Kevin's hair was unbrushed.

After work, she comforted herself, *I'll invite Gia out for celebratory drinks and I'll let her vent about all the secret merger stress. We'll finally be equals.*

Without Gia, Jo would never have considered a career in social media. She'd never been a *Do it for the 'gram* type of person. But

3

Gia—a Portlander who had moved six hundred miles to avoid getting sucked into her family business—had seen Jo's résumé back in her standing-desk days and spotted their similarities.

If you've spent your whole life giving your parents' business free promo, you have more job experience than anyone else your age, she'd told Intern!Jo. *Just do the job you're already trained for.*

And that job was digital public relations. Jo switched her major from English to communications, took a summer intensive in photography so her student loans would cover a camera and Photoshop, and she offered to run Q-Co's Facebook from the standing desk. She tripled their followers and got a forty-hours-a-week and a job title: social media coordinator.

Now twenty-six-year-old Jo was on step three of the four-step career plan she and Gia had mapped out:

0. *Internship (unpaid foot in the door)*
1. *Social Media Coordinator*
2. *Social Media Manager*
3. *Content Strategist and Influencer Relations Manager*
4. *Director of Digital Strategy by thirty*

All it had cost her were her weeknights and her social life—both largely disposable since most of her college friends left town for grad school or love or cheaper rent. It had been a few months since she'd dusted off her dating apps, and she hadn't been home to see her parents in ages. But it would all be worth it when she became the first Black woman on the management team.

A biracial, bisexual girl-boss in Silicon Valley? Gia would say to hype Jo up when she got discouraged. *You know that is 30 Under 30 bait! The second you get promoted, I will call my* Forbes *contact.*

Jo wasn't in it for the 30 Under 30 lists—although she wouldn't mind having something cool to post about while everyone back home was getting married or having babies. She just wanted to reap what she'd sown. After five years of planting all of her hard work into Q-Co and their fancy fitness trackers, she was ready to harvest a real life for herself.

It was only what she deserved. She did more than talk the talk; she even wore the product. Today: a small silver ring on her index finger tracked her mounting heartbeat as she strode into the boss's office.

Devo—Devon Quandt Jr., operations manager and son of the founder—had a small water feature built into the longest wall of his office so that it was eternally raining on his mounted classics degree. The noise made Jo want to stuff erasers in her ears. It was expensive and wasteful water torture.

Devo himself was expensive and wasteful, sitting sideways in his ergonomic office chair.

No one else on the first floor had an ergonomic chair. But no one else's dad had successfully opened three start-ups and left them the last one to babysit.

"I see you, Johanna," Devo sang throatily, like a cartoon frog. *"I see you."*

"Pretty sure that *Sweeney Todd* isn't workplace appropriate, Devo," Jo said. She sat in the non-ergo chair across from him. "That song is about a stalker and a pedophile."

"I didn't realize you were a theater buff," Devo said, twirling in his chair before resting his elbows on his desk.

"I'm a woman of the world," Jo said. Devo didn't care that her childhood best friend had been a theater geek. "You wanted to see me?"

"Right!" Devo clapped his hand on his desk, momentarily focused on something other than humming stray bits of Sondheim. "I'm gonna need you to sign a little NDA, 'kay?"

Jo made herself smile with all of her teeth as he pulled a tablet seemingly from thin air and spun it to face her. A stylus was pressed into her hand while she read through the company's most basic nondisclosure agreement. There were no dollar signs or *Welcome to your new life!* notes of congratulation mixed in among the legalese.

She signed it and forced herself to sit back again. "What's up?"

"Well..." Devo leaned forward into the space Jo had vacated. "You may have heard some rumors..." He trailed off, waiting for her to jump in.

"Devo," Jo said, knuckles cracking as she made fists in her lap. "Don't make me guess. Please. I don't like guessing."

"Fine," he said, sulking, shoulders falling down to the desktop. "It's all true. We're being acquired by HeartChart. They're moving us to their office in the city. I say *us*, but I mean... Well, I don't mean *you*."

Jo stared at him. Her brain was doing its damnedest to hold on to the words, but she couldn't quite make herself believe them enough to stick. For a moment, she couldn't help but imagine everyone lined up in the school gym, Challenge Day style. *Everyone who has a job step forward.* The air left her lungs like it'd been punched out.

"You aren't—" Jo shook her head and coughed a laugh. "That can't be how you'd fire someone, right?"

Devo's lips pulled back into a *yikes* face.

This was why Gia hadn't smiled at her. If Jo had really been getting promoted today, Gia would have known first and Gia had a terrible poker face.

"You can't fire me," she said, entering bargaining as quickly as possible. Quandt Corporation simply couldn't run without her. The higher-ups still needed her help with the new copier, and College Kevin was useless with technology bigger than a phone. "I have spent every weeknight for two years cycling through seven social media accounts! Facebook, Instagram, Twitter, Snapchat, TikTok! All the stupid new ones that no one uses! I had us on Mastodon! I write the copy! I take the pictures! I got us viral movement on a picture of a fucking nose ring! Our accounts are my babies. I watch them morning, noon, and night."

"But that's it, Jo," Devo said, sitting up again and twisting his chair from side to side. "They aren't our accounts anymore. They're HeartChart's. Well, they're no one's. We'll be starting all-new campaigns when we relaunch, so take screenshots of your babies before they go off to boarding school or whatever—I'm sorry, I really wasn't following the baby metaphor. Do you think you just stare at babies all day or . . . Never mind."

He had her sign a termination form and gave her a boiled-chicken handshake. Jo didn't wipe her palm on her slacks out of a habitual politeness. But by the time she made it to the door—crushed under the weight of a new, shittier reality—she was ready to throw politeness out a window. This was the last time she would ever be in this office, on this floor, in front of this skid mark of nepotism. . . .

Devo said, "Oh, wait, Jo—"

Optimism flicked on like a light switch in her chest, making her pause. She turned back, brows high and hopeful. "Yeah?"

"Your Gym Class subscription is a company perk, so it'll expire after you check out with HR, 'kay?"

Sandy Point, Oregon

TWO MONTHS LATER.

Rock bottom smelled like the briny dumpster that was the ocean.

Jo's childhood bedroom was childhood small, about the same size as the office she'd cleaned out back in Palo Alto. The walls, small rug, and bedding on the teeny-tiny twin mattress were all hot pink and charcoal gray. The combination might have seemed like haute couture to tweenage Johanna—at the time she also envisioned her prom dress and wedding in the same color scheme—but it made her adult eyes want to bleed.

Home sweet home.

It took three rounds of wrestling to get the cork out of what Jo had decided to refer to as her *first* bottle of wine, a surprisingly decent Malbec. Especially considering it was also the only Malbec at Fred Meyer. Jo had doubted department-store wine, and she was being proven wrong.

Finally, a single win for Jo Freeman. *Woo.*

Sitting on the edge of her tiny bed, she dusted sand off her feet. Her entire hometown was covered in a fine eponymous dust of windblown sand, and the inside of the Freeman house was absolutely no exception.

Jo couldn't believe she was back in a town that didn't even have sidewalks.

Separated from Portland by two hours of forest, Sandy Point, Oregon, was the town people stopped in when they got winded on the way to see the *Goonies* house in Astoria or where they went to walk off all the ice cream and cheese they ate in Tillamook. It wasn't as quaint a seaside as Seaside, and it was too far north to have any of the famous sand dunes.

Sandy Point only existed because of a roadside attraction that had closed a hundred years ago. The Waterfront Cove resort had been torn down and replaced with a subdivision of McMansions that towered over the otherwise modest neighborhoods. With four thousand residents, it was too populated to be considered cute-small yet remained too small to be convenient. There was one post office, one grocery store, and a boardwalk instead of a downtown. The only doubles were nautical bars and empty vacation rentals.

Cloudy moonlight made the dry-erase-board wall at the head of her twin bed gleam. Arced across the white acrylic were the words *Welcome Home, Jojo!!!* in huge letters. She wiped them away with the back of her arm, impatient to start a list of things to dive for in the garage. So far, only the boxes marked *Wardrobe* had made it upstairs.

Comforter, she wrote. She looked around the room critically. On the other side of the window, the ocean droned on. *Noise machine.*

It felt good to list. Like complaining to a friend after a long hard day.

Essential oil diffuse—

Overused after a decade of neglect, the marker promptly expired. Jo pitched it aside and reached over to the desk. The single drawer rattled open. Inside were all the ingredients to conjure her teenage self: gel pens, Post-its, digital camera cords, a gunky lip-gloss tube, and a slim journal with a wraparound vintage map of the world as its cover.

The inside cover had Jo's unchanged handwriting: *If lost, please return to Johanna Jordan Freeman, 22 South Jetty Avenue, Sandy Point, Oregon.*

She flipped to the first page. The left-hand margin was studded with scraps, evidence of ripped-out pages. The lists inside the world journal had been too important to be anything short of perfect. These were Jo's original road maps.

Jo Freeman's Battle Plan to GTFO of Sandy Point FOREVER
○ *Take eight AP classes*
○ *Take extension courses at Ocean Park Community College*
○ *Become president of the honor society*
○ *Become editor-in-chief of the Sandy Point High yearbook*
○ *Get into Stanford*

Check check check, she thought. All tasks she had accomplished almost a decade ago.

Except for becoming president of the honor society. Jo had only wanted that because her ex-girlfriend Wren had held the office when she was a senior at Point High; Jo's campaign had been a brief reason for them to talk again while Wren was away at college. Once Jo had lost the race to Bianca Boria, she and Wren had lapsed into a forever silence.

She took the journal back to her bed, squishing herself against the window and drawing long pulls from the Malbec bottle. A month ago, this list would have immediately gone up on all of her social media under the hashtag #DopeSinceDayOne. Proof that she had accomplished everything she'd ever dreamed of.

But she hadn't, really. Because all she ever wanted was to stay gone.

She closed her eyes and tipped another gulp of wine into her mouth. Wiping away an errant drop, she bounced the back of her head against the whiteboard wall.

After her layoff, she had spent over a month scrambling to find work. Calling all of her contacts. Haunting job sites instead of sleeping.

But no one needed a social media director. Or even a slightly overqualified marketing assistant. She could temp or she could leave California. Neither would pay the bills that had started to pile up. After PG&E sent their final notice with her service shut-off date, she broke down and called her mom.

"Mom." Jo had hated how weak she sounded. It would have been easier if she could have started on equal footing and called her mom Deb. Instead, she felt herself de-age, confessing in a brittle, babyish voice, "Mom, I got laid off."

"Oh, honey, I'm so sorry." Waves and teaspoons crashed behind Deb. Her footsteps took her farther away from the noise. Jo imagined her mother stepping into the back room of her shop, the one recently converted to a prep kitchen. "You're gonna bounce back in an instant. Right now, you need to take yourself out for some fun self-care. A mani-pedi or a nice lunch at that—"

"It's been a month," Jo whispered. "Almost two."

"Oh," her mom said, clearly injured and determined not to acknowledge the hurt. "You tell me what you need."

Jo had squeezed her eyes until she saw flashbulb swirls. "I need to store some stuff in your garage for a little while. Just. Everything I own."

"And do you think you're gonna need to come with that stuff?"

"Yeah," she said. The finality of it crushed her. "I should probably come, too."

Tonight, after twelve hours of driving—but only six hours of crying—Jo arrived home to the same elaborate dinner her mom used to make for Jo's birthday every year. Beef ribs, Grandma

Freeman's recipe for mac and cheese, and a two-tier German chocolate cake. And with the spread, a gift: a pineapple necklace with a card saying *What doesn't kill you makes you stronger!*

Like it was a party. Like her failure was worth a feast.

When Jo recoiled at the spread without meaning to, her teenage sister beat their mom to a hug. Eden hugged Jo with loose arms like Jo was someone at a networking event with whom Eden would rather shake hands.

"Mom and Dad closed the store for this," Eden hissed in her ear, her loose curls scratching against Jo's cheek. "Be nice, please."

A senior in high school now, Eden was too young to remember when Mr. and Mrs. Freeman had zero days off. For most of Jo's life, they'd been too busy keeping their various businesses and side hustles afloat. For reasons beyond Jo's understanding, the change from consignment store to art gallery to tea-and-surf shop seemed to be paying off for her parents.

She had been younger than Eden when she wrote out the battle plan to GTFO. The map journal had homework assignments, shopping lists, and names for the paint-your-own-pottery place her parents had debated opening. She got lost in a pro/con list about whether or not to wear pants to homecoming—*Is being subversive really just begging for my classmates to acknowledge my queerness?* asked the con list. "Yes," she told her younger self. "Do it anyway"— and relived the drama of deciding to drop out of the yearbook prank. How had life felt so big back then? How could anyone feel like Sandy Point was big enough to breathe in?

The end of the journal and the end of the Malbec bottle occurred around the same time, which was enough like kismet that Jo decided she deserved another slice of leftover German chocolate cake.

Chocolate and wine are perfect together, she thought. *I'm basically a sommelier.*

Definitely a drunk thought. Drunk mission accomplished.

The last page of the map journal was another list—longer than the others, reaching every corner of the page and continuing onto the endpapers.

- TP Bianca's house
- ~~Be in a play with Autumn~~ Perform onstage
- Get ~~nose~~ ~~TONGUE~~ ~~eyebrow~~ belly button pierced
- Surf the Point
- Host a dinner party
- ~~Plan~~ ~~Do~~ Redo the yearbook prank
- Have a ~~paintball~~ glitter fight
- Eat the giant sundae at Frosty's
- Get a pet
- Learn a whole dance routine
- ~~Smoke~~ ~~eat brownies~~ Get stoned
- Try everything on the menu at TGI Friday's
- Do a keg stand
- Play hide-and-seek in public
- Pose like a ~~Suicide Girl~~ pinup girl
- Break ~~a jack-o'-lantern~~ something with a sledgehammer
- Climb the giant anchor on the boardwalk (and survive!!)
- Get a ~~perfect~~ high score at the boardwalk arcade
- Host a bonfire party ~~where everyone brings a picture to burn~~
- Eat breakfast at ~~sunrise~~ midnight
- Dig up the time capsule

Something this messy would never have been allowed if there'd been a page left to rip out. The inks didn't match, so Jo knew it was a first draft. Some items were written in blue, some with a glittery silver gel pen that wasn't her handwriting at all, but Autumn Kelly's.

It was strange to be able to recognize the handwriting of someone she hadn't seen in almost a decade. But could you ever really forget your old best friend, even when passed notes gave way to internet likes?

The last item on the list sparked Jo's memory. *Dig up the time capsule.*

After reading about the idea in a rainy-day activity book when they were eleven, she and Autumn filled a metal tackle box with pictures and toys and letters to their future selves. Having buried it behind the doghouse in the Kellys' backyard, they agreed to dig it up again after they had done everything worth doing in Sandy Point.

It wasn't supposed to be a long list. Sandy Point wasn't a big town and nothing much ever happened there. They consulted Autumn's older brother for dumb townie traditions like climbing the anchor or surfing to the Point. They searched the internet for ideas like "glitter fight."

Throughout junior high and high school, they brainstormed the list whenever conversation dipped. And then suddenly it was nearly senior year and they hadn't done a single thing.

The list became official in the back of the map journal. It would be how she and Autumn would spend the end of high school, celebrating the end of childhood by doing every fun thing their town had to offer. Things they'd need to know how to do before college. Things they couldn't get anywhere else.

Senior year, Jo split her time between yearbook and working at her parents' store while Autumn became fully enmeshed in Point

High Theater—playing both Dorothy in *The Wizard of Oz* and Ado Annie in *Oklahoma!*

They got distracted. They grew apart. They were childhood best friends and their childhood had already ended.

Jo half tumbled down the stairs toward the beacon that was her *Welcome Home from Your Real Life* cake—inscription not included. She took the journal with her and reread the final list. She couldn't tick off a single item. Thus far, her life had been void of pets, dinner parties, and sledgehammers.

Seventeen-year-old me would think I was so *boring.*

She tried not to be offended by the thought. After all, Present!Jo hated Teen!Jo's bedding, hometown, and wardrobe. If any of Teen!Jo's ruffled plaid shirts or colorful flip-flops were still around, Present!Jo would throw them into the ocean.

And yet.

The battle plan had been so clear about who Jo wanted to grow up to be. Someone who made 30 Under 30 lists. Independent, educated, physically fit, head-bitch-in-charge Jo Freeman.

Now, unemployed with zero prospects, Jo had bounced all the way back to the starting line, and she couldn't even live up to her younger self's dream of doing a keg stand.

She wasn't even sure where kegs came from. Bars? Breweries?

Peeling the foil away from her cake, Jo pulled off a bite with her thumb and forefinger, too glum to bother with a fork. The coconut frosting was an adrenaline burst of sugar and fat. She could have cut a piece and taken it back upstairs to her appointment with Second Bottle of Malbec, but something stopped her.

At the end of the long galley kitchen, past the shelving covered in decades of forgotten juicers and George Foreman grills, was a window. It faced the front yard of the house next door.

Bianca Boria's house.

Bianca Boria had been Jo's pace car in high school. If Jo did well, Bianca did better. If Jo worked hard, Bianca worked harder.

While Jo did everything with sweat in her eyes and the wind in her hair, Bianca glided past her with an easy smile. When people talked shit about her single mom and tattooed grandparents, she didn't even flinch. She wore a bikini on social media and captioned it *Fat Doesn't Mean Ugly*, single-handedly bringing body positivity to Point High. She was president of the honor society *and* prom queen, a feat that rocked the core of their teen social hierarchy.

It's like living next door to a unicorn, Jo thought. *Or a princess. Or a . . . princess unicorn? Nope. That's the wine talking.*

Like any self-respecting marketing professional, Jo wasn't unfamiliar with the art of internet stalking. She knew that Bianca still lived next door—although her mother had moved out—and she was married to a guy whose name Jo didn't recognize from the yearbook. Jo had tried scrolling through their wedding album—Bianca had worn the poofiest Cinderella dress imaginable—but had been too weirded out when she saw Autumn Kelly as the maid of honor.

Autumn and Bianca must have become friends in college. Basically anyone going to college after Point High went to Oregon State.

Seeing Autumn weepily help Bianca into a wedding dress had flared an uncomfortably territorial feeling in the back of Jo's mind. She hadn't been able to enjoy peering into Bianca's account since.

But now, *TP Bianca's house* was staring up at her from the top of the list. She took another pinch of cake. Popped it into her mouth.

Mashed it into the roof of her mouth. Tried again. Chewed it like a sober girl.

She went searching for toilet paper.

There was a roll hidden behind eight cans of baked beans from the hall-closet emergency kit and then three rolls from the bathroom that she and Eden now shared upstairs. Jo grabbed her phone and ran out the front door.

Freezing in the pitch-dark, she loped across the sandy driveway toward the yellow glow of Bianca Boria's porch light. Unlike the Freemans' house with its dehydrated wood shingles responsible for a million childhood splinters, Bianca's house was bright white with a pastel-blue door and a yard full of matching hydrangea plants.

Right in front, nearest to Jo's house, there was the biggest tree in the neighborhood. An Oregon maple.

Supplies set down in the grass, Jo threw a roll of toilet paper at the tree. It bounced off a branch and fell to the ground, dribbling back toward her across the perfectly trimmed grass.

"Oh. Fuck," she said out loud, genuinely surprised.

She hadn't come out here to fail at TP-ing. It wasn't a par game. It was a skill test. She squared her shoulders. Picking up the failed throw, she quickly unwrapped as much of the paper as she could while having a decent handful left on the roll to hold on to. She tossed it again. The little tail flapped between branches while the rest fell to the ground.

Success was a rush even better than a tipsy mouthful of German chocolate cake.

She launched more toilet-paper rolls, delighting in the way they floated in the darkness like ghosts. Soon she didn't feel the cold. Bianca's lawn rinsed the sand from her feet.

If she'd still been wearing a Q-Co tracker—rather than leaving all of them in a toilet at HQ after cleaning out her desk—it would have shown her pulse rate up in the heart-eyes emoji range.

Behind the warm glow of exertion and wine, she imagined TP-ing becoming the next fitness craze. All-black athleisure, ski masks, the pseudo-nemesis of your choosing's house, a coach in your earpiece screaming something motivational.

Until losing her Gym Class app, Jo never realized how much she would miss the aggressive affirmations. How did people get out of bed without being called a sweat goddess at five thirty every morning?

With the tree covered, Jo reached for her phone and took a few pictures of her work. The shot would have been better with her camera and tripod, but they were in boxes in the garage. The picture was just a souvenir, proof to her younger self that she was capable of hitting a goal. Even a stupid one.

Through her phone lens, she saw that a single roll of toilet paper had fallen to the ground between two tree roots. Determined to leave no roll behind, she scooped it up. Looking for the perfect place to launch it, she ran around the tree, smiling as beatifically as Bianca Boria crushing her GPA. Running the student council. Getting married at twenty-five with the only best friend Jo had ever had by her side . . .

"Johanna?"

Bianca Boria stood directly beneath the porch light. For a moment, Jo was positive that Bianca was wearing a long-sleeved evening gown, red-carpet-ready in the middle of the night, but as her eyes adjusted, she realized it was a large plush bathrobe. Bianca's dark hair was pulled up in a high, elegant bun that had never known frizz. Her skin was clear.

Jo looked at the last roll weighing down her right hand. She threw it.

It bonked Bianca in the nose.

Jo ran home and didn't look back.

✓ *TP Bianca's house*

two

AUTUMN

"Jo Freeman TP'd my tree," Bee said on speakerphone.

"You're joking!" Dripping on the bath mat and half in the shower, Autumn hopped on one foot toward the sink. Blotting the towel into her eyes to better see the screen, she saw that it wasn't even six in the morning—too early to be a goof. "Jo doesn't even live here. She lives in California."

"When I caught her, she beaned me in the face with a roll of toilet paper," Bee said. She took a loud slurp of coffee. "At midnight! I'd already taken off my eyebrows."

Autumn's brain whirled through a dizzying number of images and questions and old rotten hurts. She sat down too fast on the toilet seat and slid sideways on her wet skin. "That's just so too weird, Bee."

"Thank you! I needed to hear it from you since she's your—"

"Estranged bestie?"

"Oh good. I was afraid you were going to be dramatic about this," Bee said drolly. "You're not *estranged*. That's for families."

"Best friends should count as family. I spent way more time with Jo than I ever did with any of my cousins. They're all gun-toting skiers in Bend." Autumn grabbed her pajama shirt from the floor and used it to dry sections of her long red-brown hair. Upside down, she twisted her face toward the phone. "How else should I think of Jo? She was the Elphaba to my Glinda for ten years and then she just stopped talking to me, which I guess still makes us Act Two Elphie and Glinda—"

"I understand how much you like *Wicked*, but I really don't like you comparing a Black woman to a green one."

"Note taken!" Autumn said. She flipped her hair up and, grabbing a brush from the counter, tore through the tangles. "I haven't seen Jo in years and years. She basically stopped coming home after college. Are you sure it was her?"

"I'm pretty sure I can recognize my own neighbors. I've only lived next door to the Freemans since the second grade," Bee said, over the sound of running water and dishware clinking. "Of course, I don't think I've actually talked to Jo since college. I ran into her in Fred Meyer around Christmastime. I remember because she said 'Merry Christmas, Bianca' and I wasn't really listening because I was looking at wreaths. So what came out of my mouth was *Yerp-yup!*"

"Yerp-yup?" Autumn laughed. "What were you trying to say?"

"No idea. It haunts me. Once every six months, I just wake up in the middle of the night and think to myself, *Yerp-yup.* Anyway." Autumn pictured her friend recentering herself by smoothing the air in a long swipe. Bee was a hand talker, which seemed like a dangerous quality in someone who wielded needles for a living. "Last night, I was two seconds away from finally falling asleep when Lita comes to the bottom of the stairs, screaming about a burglar. Birdy slept through the whole thing—"

"Comforting!"

"I know, right? But it wasn't a burglar. It was Johanna Freeman. So now I'm trying to solve the case of why did my tree get TP'd."

"Definitely not a Nancy Drew I'd read," Autumn said. She wound dental tape between her fingers so she could floss her veneers—a *good luck in Hollywood* present from her parents, facilitated by Bee's now-husband, Dr. Bobby Birdy, one of Sandy Point's two orthodontists. "Does the toilet paper have *yerp-yup* written on it?"

"Ha-ha," Bee said, not entertained. "Could you be slightly more helpful? You know Jo better than I ever did. She and I aren't even social media mutuals. You guys were best friends for a decade. She dated your boss!"

"Wren isn't my boss," Autumn said. "I go days without seeing her. She's normally too busy to even eat lunch with me. I've started playing sudoku like a real loner."

"Isn't her sister one of your students?"

The dental tape squeaked between her molars. "Wren only has brothers."

"No. Jo!"

Eden Freeman was one of the seniors in Point High's drama program. Going into her first year of teaching, Autumn had been worried that it would be awkward having Jo's sister in her class— Eden had been the first baby Autumn ever held. But Eden never talked about her older sister. And Autumn never mentioned Eden being in diapers. A fair trade.

"Eden was little when we all graduated," Autumn said. "I don't think she and her sister ever had a chance to get super close. As far as I know, Jo has been living in California for almost a decade. When I moved to LA, I asked if she was close enough to get coffee.

But she was hours up north, which is still miles from here." She flung the dental tape into the wastebasket and heard the expectant silence on the other end of the phone. Sometimes Bianca was a dog with a bone. Autumn sighed, taking a moment to arrange her scraps of knowledge into a picture of a friend lost. "Jo kind of always hated Sandy Point. She literally counted down the days until she could move away, starting the first day of senior year."

"What? Like a Christmas paper chain?"

"No, she wrote it on the whiteboard wall over her bed. But that's how much she would never be in Oregon in the middle of a Monday night. Normally she's getting tagged in pictures in, like, a wine bar with people all older than her or at someone's wedding reception. And she's wearing black or gray, never a color, and keeps pretending to be surprised when people tell her she looks like Meghan Markle but also never cuts her hair so that she looks *less* like Meghan Markle."

Jo's resemblance to Meghan Markle was undeniable. In fact, the last time Autumn had tried reaching out to Jo was around the time Prince Harry and Meghan moved to the United States.

Can't wait to see the 'bloids accidentally pay millions for pictures of you getting coffee and going to the gym! Have you considered this as a new revenue stream?

Jo sent back a single laughing emoji.

That was when Autumn realized that they had become strangers. She wasn't even worth words to Jo anymore.

Autumn didn't want to think about Jo. It was too early to get sad wondering why her oldest friend had dropped her after graduation. She stood up, adding with forced cheerfulness, "At least she didn't TP the shop. Can you imagine what Lita would do?"

"If anyone touched the shop, Lita would set them on fire. Or tell me to. Thankfully she doesn't care as much about the house." Bee let out a long sigh. "Soon I must blend her breakfast."

Autumn opened the bathroom door. Steam dissipated around her while she went from one end of the cottage to the other in less than a dozen wet footprints. She lived in an old fishing cottage owned by her father's wife, Ginger Jay. Ginger had bought it to convert into a vacation rental but hadn't gotten around to it. It was on the forest side of town, as far away from the ocean as you could be. The snap-together laminate floor Autumn had installed was a huge improvement over the stinky old carpet that had come with the place—although, sometimes, she could still catch a whiff of cigarettes and surfperch stuck inside the wood paneling. Every wall was wood paneled. Autumn considered herself lucky it wasn't on the ceiling.

"How many days until your honeymoon?" she asked, knowing this would cheer Bee up. Bee and Birdy hadn't had a chance to take a honeymoon last year because they'd been busy taking care of Lita. While the wedding had been beautiful and perfect, Autumn knew Bee had been disappointed to have to go back to work the next day.

"One hundred and eleven days to go!" Bee said. "Oh, speaking of vacations, Nana Birdy is getting a preliminary head count for this year's Birdy Bash."

On top of a bookcase that sagged under the weight of a rainbow of scrapbooks and cracked script binders, there was a sepia photo of Autumn, Bee, and Birdy dressed up at the Old West picture booth at Knott's Berry Farm. In the picture, all three of them wore boysenberry-beer-stained smiles, feather boas, and rented corsets. "What could possibly top our adventure to the berriest place on earth?"

"This year, the rumor is we're going to the Dave and Buster's resort in Indiana. All the *Dance Dance Revolution* you've ever wanted, in one place."

"A bar-cade resort? Count me in!" Autumn rummaged through one of the open dresser drawers and found a crumpled pair of pajama jeans. Today, she needed full range of motion. She was teaching the Broadway Club the *9 to 5* choreography Pat Markey had called *needlessly complicated* for the Senior Showcase. The choir teacher unsurprisingly preferred her musicals more stationary. Which wouldn't have been a problem for Autumn if only Mrs. Markey would agree that the choir teacher's opinion on good theater shouldn't count more than the theater teacher's. Unfortunately the Point High drama program had always been a two-party system, and Autumn had been appointed to the losing side.

She shimmied herself into her pajama jeans. "What time is it right now? I have to finish getting ready by six. If I'm even a second late, Florencio will leave me behind. I learned that when I tried to do my makeup at home last time."

"He's a terrible chauffeur but a good brother," Bee said.

"Yeah, yeah. He's a peach. Everyone loves him. Ask me how many boxes he's packed."

"He has three jobs, sweets," Bianca reminded her.

"Three *part-time* jobs. Three parts don't necessarily make a whole!" Autumn countered. "And he hasn't helped with anything on Main Street. Not a box! Not a bag! There's already a sign in the yard!"

"We have to have a sign in the yard and staged pictures of the interior online before tourists start showing up for summer if we intend to sell this year," Ginger Jay had told Autumn—to tell her mom. "No one buys beach houses when it's ugly outside."

25

Personally, Autumn thought that Sandy Point was prettiest when dusted with winter snow—when the ocean rushed up to meet white powder. The beaches in LA had been crowded like amusement parks. The traffic packed down the sand so much it was hard as asphalt.

"It's five fifty-three. Do you want me to meet you at the house sometime this week?" Bee asked. "I could help any night I'm not on Lita's dinner duty."

"That's okay. You have your own family to help," Autumn said. Bee had never seen the Main Street house in its glory days, when the bright green walls were filled with life and love and laughter, just as her mom's Hobby Lobby plaques demanded. Before it became a storage space on a floodplain. "Send me a picture of your TP tree! Love you, bye!"

Autumn had enough time to throw on shoes and put a breakfast banana in her bag before she heard the telltale rumble of her brother's Jeep out front.

The final drive from Los Angeles to Sandy Point had mortally wounded Autumn's car, so as long as it wasn't snowing, she normally rode to work on a beach cruiser scavenged from her parents' garage. She loved Sandy Point at sunrise—the nippy wind that smelled like salt and pine, the buildings and signs unchanged since the day she was born. But today she had to bring a box too big to fit in her bicycle basket—the T-shirts for the Broadway Club to go along with their increasingly elaborate spring carnival performance.

With the box safely situated in the backseat, Autumn climbed up into the passenger seat beside Florencio. Seat belt clicked, the Jeep jumped away from the curb, speeding off like they were racing someone up the empty street. Their mother liked to say that Florencio drove like there was cake and ice cream at the finish line.

Cindy Kelly had an adorably G-rated imagination.

The sun wouldn't rise until after the zero-period bell, but the dashboard lights illuminated the dark circles under Florencio's eyes and the hollow shadows of his deep brown jaw. He pointed at the cup holders between Autumn and him where two environmentally unfriendly cups of coffee sat steaming.

"Both of these are mine," he croaked. "Don't get any ideas."

"I'll try to resist," Autumn said. After a stint working as a barista in LA, she'd lost the acquired taste for Rotten Robbie's gas-station joe. "Did you sleep at all? You sound like my janky garbage disposal."

Flo burped hazelnut battery acid. "I slept literally . . . some. We had a match last night, but I went into Days to close."

Short, buff, and covered in Filipino and Celtic tattoos, Florencio was the chillest dude who happened to be indistinguishable from a CrossFit douchebag. Looking at him, people never guessed that he regularly cried watching the teams he coached win tournaments. Although it was the most likely explanation as to why his eyes looked so puffy this morning.

Florencio coached wrestling all day, but his gig at the middle school was unpaid since the dry-cleaner's fire that had taken out the team's sponsor. So, at night, he ran the blender at Days Bar & Grill and told girls on Tinder that he was a bartender.

"I have Mom's camping cot at the theater," Autumn offered. "I brought it over for double show days. Or when I have a meeting an hour after school and don't want to ride my bike all the way home. It's in the prop closet, if you want to catch a nap later."

"No time." Flo yawned wide. "Only coffee."

The Jeep chugged up the hill, toward the streetlamps of the nicer neighborhoods.

"Mom and I were talking about going crabbing soon," Autumn said. Casual, offhand, not even looking at him. "You know, like we used to when we were kids?"

Florencio grunted in the affirmative.

"I was thinking we could do the crab boil on the beach. We'd get steamed artichokes for you because you hate corn, duh, and we could bring Rooster with us!" Autumn put extra sparkle in her voice, a spoonful of sugar. "All we have to do is pick up the crab rings and camping pot from Main Street and—"

"No," Flo said.

"Dad and Ginger said they would be totally down to get everyone together and officially bury the hatchet."

"No!"

"It's your family, too, Florencio!" she snapped, her hands balled into fists in her lap.

He took his eyes off the road long enough to glare at her. The Kelly siblings may not have been related by blood, but Florencio had been adopted two full years before Mrs. Kelly got pregnant with Autumn. There had never been any doubt between them that he was the firstborn, even if he'd been born to parents in the Philippines and raised by white, mostly Irish Oregonians.

"I know it's my family," Flo said, turning back to the road with a sniff. "That doesn't mean where the Chief buries his hatchets is any of my business."

It always came back to that.

Chuck and Cindy Kelly had announced their divorce three years ago, just after Autumn moved to LA. The paperwork had been filed in secret. Lots of things had apparently been done in secret. Less than six months later, the Chief and Ginger Jay dropped professional pictures of their boat elopement to Facebook. Autumn met her father's mistress as his wife.

It wasn't that Autumn was a huge fan of adultery—or Ginger Jay—but she had spent the last couple of years coming to terms with her family changing. She was ready for them to move on. Make new memories. Start new traditions. This year, Cindy Kelly had even started acknowledging Ginger Jay in public. It had recently been reported that the two of them spoke in line at the grocery store with zero bloodshed.

Florencio, on the other hand, was a thirty-year-old man giving his father the silent treatment. For three years—through marriages, breakups, holidays, and beach-opening celebrations—Autumn's father and brother had avoided each other. The two of them could even ignore each other in the same room. Standing in line at the post office. Sitting in the audience for Autumn's sparsely attended directorial debut. Autumn had once watched them eat breakfast seated at opposite ends of the counter at the Surfside Café, their sour looks as identical as the Celtic knots and crosses tattooed on their forearms. It was totally out of control.

Autumn knew that Chuck Kelly hadn't handled the end of his marriage well, but she couldn't quite say that he deserved losing a son over it.

She cleared her throat, trying again for civilized conversation. "Bee called this morning."

"Early of her," Flo noted.

"She said Jo Freeman toilet-papered her maple tree."

Flo's eyebrows went up. Autumn could tell he was tired because they only made it halfway up his forehead before he seemed to lose the energy to continue, but even he couldn't resist the lure of townie gossip. "Really?"

"Super weird, right?" Autumn said with a pang of guilt. If it turned out that it was really Eden, she'd feel so stupid for mentioning Jo at all. The sisters did look alike, enough that in the middle of the night Bee easily could have mistaken one for the other. It was more likely Eden doing some senior prank than Jo back from her fancy life in Silicon Valley.

"Do you think it's about you?" Flo asked. His jaw cracked with a yawn. "BFFs fighting over who gets you forever?"

"No way," Autumn said as they pulled into the empty Point High parking lot. "I'm sure that Jo forgot about all of us years ago."

When the lunch bell rang, Autumn was surprised to find her classroom totally empty—well, her side of the classroom. The drama room was split in half with an accordion wall, like a line of tape down the middle of a sitcom bedroom. Autumn had been expecting the Broadway Club to come flooding in the second the lunch period started so that they could tear into the cardboard box of T-shirts. For weeks, the small group of sophomores had been hounding her to track the shipment, even having her mirror her FedEx account to the SMART Board.

Autumn debated whether or not to dawdle. She didn't want to disappoint her students if she showed up late, but she also had a grocery-store salad waiting in the staff room. She checked her phone, hoping to catch her sole work friend not in an administrative meeting.

The accordion wall screeched aside, making Autumn jump as Pat Markey burst in with a cry of "Oh, Autumn! There you are!"

Papery white from head to Skechers and wrapped in many kinds of fleece—including the ever-present green zippered vest with *Mrs. Markey* embroidered in gold thread on the left side—Point High's choir teacher had never surrendered to living in a beach town.

"Hi, Pat. I'm right where you left me," Autumn said, frowning at the chaos of music stands and risers on the choir side of the room. She didn't understand how someone as fussy as Pat could also be such a slob. "Are you ready to talk about next year's show? The kids are dying to vote, and I had a couple of ideas with more name recognition—"

"Yes, I saw the note," Pat said with a dismissive flap toward the many reminder Post-its on Autumn's desk.

Nobody is nosier than a teacher, Autumn's mom had warned her when the school year started—she taught middle school science across the street. *Don't leave anything out you don't want the world to find out about!*

Pat puffed up like a pigeon. "We can't put up anything as spicy as *Spring Awakening* or *Rent*—"

"Schools all over the country do those shows," Autumn protested.

"That may be, my dear, but no one in Sandy Point is going to attend a performance where teens sing songs with swearing and sexual content."

No one in Sandy Point had attended the closing performance of the fall musical either. Autumn had never seen a show flop as hard as *Bugsy Malone.* She had taken for granted that the cast members' friends and family would attend both performances. Having the curtain come up on an empty audience had crushed her students. Not that Pat had seen the problem. She had rushed the kids out to put on the show. For nobody.

31

Pat Markey wasn't a performer.

One day she will retire and I'll actually get to do all of my job, Autumn reminded herself.

Autumn had thought of Point High throughout grad school. As she learned what made a good teacher, she realized that what she wanted to give her students was what she had been given by her old drama teacher, George Hearn—"not *that* George Hearn!" he'd say at the start of every school year; Autumn was the only person who ever laughed.

Autumn's time as one of Mr. Hearn's drama disciples had been the happiest and most hopeful part of her life. Standing in a noisy ensemble of friends was the safest place in the world. Every rehearsal had been so much fun. Every show had felt like high art. The Point High auditorium had been a haven in which to sing and talk and laugh at full volume, every day.

Grad school was only ever supposed to be a cover for her acting career, an excuse to move to the big city with a scholarship to foot the bill. When Autumn got to Hollywood, she'd assumed that it would be a matter of weeks until she got discovered and promptly sold back all of her textbooks. And while she had found an agent and raced all over LA for auditions, she never booked a single gig. She did become a very in-demand substitute teacher for kindergarten through twelfth grade. At the end of her two-year program, she had a second degree in theater in a town full of film studios.

Her mom drove south to her graduation—traveling alone for the first time—and brought all the latest gossip from Sandy Point. Florencio was coaching wrestling at multiple schools. Bianca was taking over as the manager of her family business. Mr. Hearn was retiring and looking for someone to replace him as the drama chair.

When she needed somewhere to belong, Point High theater called her home.

During Autumn's job interview, as she expounded on her dream of creating a theater program that would draw in kids from all over Tillamook County, no one had mentioned that Pat Markey wouldn't be stepping down.

Ten years ago, Mrs. Markey—*Pat*, Autumn reminded herself; they were coworkers now—had been Point High's choir teacher. She helped Mr. Hearn—who had never learned to read music—by playing the piano for musical rehearsals. But as Mr. Hearn got older, he kept up with the graded work—theater history, Shakespeare, one-act plays—and Pat took over directing the annual school shows: the fall-semester musical and the end-of-the-year Senior Showcase. And she had zero intention of relinquishing them to Autumn. The best she could offer was a chance to co-direct. As long as Autumn understood that her place was behind, not beside, Pat.

"What I came to discuss with you, *on my lunch break*," Pat said, as though it were not everybody's lunch break, "is that while I think it is wonderful that you are having headshots done for the students, that is the sort of thing one would want to notify parents of in advance. To give them a chance to opt out, you see? You can't just have people take you at your word that your friends are trustworthy, my dear. Permission slips exist for a reason."

"Permission slips?" Autumn asked, feeling like an echo. "For headshots?"

"It does show excellent initiative," Pat continued, punching the air. "I wouldn't have trusted the students to take their own pictures for the program. And it is nice to see that we have so many talented alums. It seems like yesterday you girls were in my algebra class.

But next time perhaps we could send an email introducing Jo to parents before she sets up shop at the auditorium."

"Jo?!"

Racing across campus without outright running made Autumn look like a speed walker with a wedgie, but being a teacher meant upholding the rules even when she would rather lose her shit.

Jo couldn't possibly be at Sandy Point High. Not on campus. In the middle of the day. On a Tuesday. No one dropped out of the sky on a Tuesday morning.

Bee's voice echoed through her head. *Jo Freeman TP'd my tree.* She started jogging.

All the drama students were hanging from the railing on the switchback ramp that led up to the auditorium's back door.

"The photo shoot's not for the Broadway Club!" one of the seniors was shouting at the underclassmen. "It's just for seniors!"

"That's bullshit!" one of the (four) Broadway Club members yelled back. "Miss Kelly, tell them that's bullshit!"

"It's not for anyone!" Autumn called as she passed them. "Everybody go back to the cafeteria!"

Cries of protest followed her around the corner, where a tripod topped with a white umbrella was set up next to the wrought-iron memorial bench. Eden Freeman was seated stiffly on the edge of the bench in front of her sister's huge camera.

Jo really was in Sandy Point. Wearing all black, with straight hair and heavy mascara.

Neither sister noticed Autumn until she stamped her foot. "Excuse me!"

Unlike the Kelly siblings, Jo and Eden were very visibly related. Both were gangly limbed and jumped like yanked marionettes at the sound of Autumn's voice.

"Autumn! Hey! How cool is it that you're the drama teacher?" Jo said, taking a step in front of her sister. She started going in for a hug before she caught sight of Autumn's face.

With a student present, Autumn wasn't allowed to say: *Oh yeah, Johanna Jordan Freeman. That's right. I am fucking pissed right now* and *I remember your middle name.* So she let her glare say it. As a naturally friendly-looking person, Autumn had spent years practicing mean faces in the mirror. A great actor had full control over their expressions.

Jo dropped her hug arms. Good.

Autumn turned the glare on the younger Freeman. "Eden, you are excused. Go tell everyone that there is no photo shoot."

"But, Miss Kelly!" Eden said. "If Jo takes everyone's headshots, then we don't have to use selfies for the Senior Showcase program! And we'd have headshots to use for college, too. We'd look so much more professional!"

"That *might* have been cool," Autumn said, annoyance slipping into her tone. "If we had signed permission slips. Or if we'd talked about how you choose the right outfit for headshots. It would be super professional if Jo had a visitor's pass! If you had done all the steps that it requires to bring a stranger on campus to take pictures of minors, it could have been really cool!"

"She's not a stranger!" Eden protested. "She's your best friend!"

Autumn couldn't bring herself to look at Jo. The denial there would be needlessly hurtful.

"I'm not signing any fourth-period tardies," Autumn said tightly. "Tell everyone the photo shoot is off and clear them out."

With a frustrated growl and a heel spin—she was a drama kid, after all—Eden stormed away. Autumn watched her leave, wishing she had been able to play the cool teacher that rewarded out-of-the-box thinking. Not the kind of teacher who parroted Mrs. Markey. She wanted to be Miss Honey, not the Trunchbull.

"Sorry. Last night, she found me hunting for my comforter and saw the box with all my photography stuff in it," Jo said, sitting down on the bench and packing her camera in a bulky zippered bag. She was wearing black slacks and a black silk top, as though dressed for a very slinky funeral. "To be fair, I was *not* sober when she asked me to do headshots and was way too hungover to disappoint her six reminder texts this morning. I can take headshots. I used to take yours."

Autumn couldn't stop herself from remembering running around the boardwalk looking for the best lighting or the strangest props to pose with. Jo used a kazoo to make her laugh when she started to get too posed in the photos. All so Autumn could audition for *Seussical* in McMinnville—a whole hour and a half away. What goofs they had been.

No. She had to fight the nostalgia.

Think of the laughing emoji! she coached herself. *Vague! Impersonal!*

"You should have asked me if it was okay." Autumn crossed her arms and brought her voice down to a whisper. Teaching had conditioned her to bring all of her anger down to a volume that couldn't be eavesdropped on. "God, Jo, do you have any clue how stupid this makes me look? I *work* here, if you hadn't noticed. You don't see me busting into your fancy office and redoing projects, do you?"

Jo's hands stilled inside her camera bag as she grimaced at the ground.

"What?" Autumn asked too sharply. "Are you still hungover?"

She had never seen Jo get drunk. Not really. Florencio had given them a six-pack of Mike's Hard Lemonade for senior skip day, but they only managed to get giggly before the malt-liquor headaches set in.

"Just a little dehydrated," Jo said, looking up blithely. "But I'm back in town for a while, if you do need my help with anything. I could come back and take pictures once there are permission slips. Or run a social media campaign for your next show. Start a hashtag. I've got hashtag experience."

"We don't need your help, Jo." Autumn's jaw locked. She was positive that she was now going to cry. That was going to make her look like such a baby. She had really enjoyed having the upper hand for once. "Why would you think you could just forget about people and then show up out of nowhere?"

A wrinkle cut across Jo's forehead. "I didn't forget about you—"

"You don't call or text or answer Snapchat messages—"

"No one really uses Snapchat anymore," Jo said, missing the point.

"I don't care about what's cool in social media!" Autumn interrupted. "Why don't you go home and help my actual best friend, Bianca, who called me this morning begging to know why you vandalized her house."

Jo's chin tucked back into her neck. She was a lot less duchess-like when she was miffed. "Vandalized? It's toilet paper, Autumn. I didn't key her car."

"You littered, violently!" Autumn said in a whisper-scream. "Just from an environmental point of view, it sucks! You should be cleaning it up! Right now! You should clean up all the trash on your street as penance!"

"I thought I was doing a nice thing by coming here," Jo said. "For my sister. For you."

"Well, you were wrong!" Autumn said. "What you do here matters. People can see you. People have to deal with you. You aren't invisible. When you ghost people, they know."

Jo swallowed, the muscles in her neck flexing against the silver chain around her throat. Autumn noticed the necklace for the first time. It was a silver pineapple with a diamond in its crown.

When Autumn was in the second grade, her best friend, Johanna, had eaten a slice of Mrs. Kelly's famous pineapple upside-down cake, not knowing that she was allergic. Jo's throat closed instantly. When the ambulance pulled up, her cheeks were starting to turn gray-blue. Huge brown eyes searched for Autumn, wild and scared. Autumn had thought she looked like Bambi's mom as she smoothed Jo's frizzy hair and whispered promises to her.

"If you live, Jo, I'll give you all my birthday presents."

"If you live, Jo, we can wear matching Carmen Sandiego Halloween costumes like you wanted."

"If you live, Jo, I'll make sure you never, ever have to touch that stupid evil fruit ever again for the rest of your life."

And now there it was, dangling below Jo's collarbone.

Damn it, Autumn, act like you don't care. Act like an educator and not a little kid. Act like none of this matters.

But the part of her that was still Jo Freeman's best friend forever just wanted to cry.

"You can't be on campus without a visitor's badge," she told Jo in a strangled voice. "There are a million signs about it in the main building." She stared up at the sky, hoping to keep the beading tears inside her eyes. "Go home, Jo."

three

BIANCA

At least once a month, Bianca had a nightmare that the doorknob to the downstairs bedroom broke off in her hand. Or there was a dead bolt she didn't have the key for. Or a fire she was powerless to put out. Regardless of the fantastical emergency, trapped inside the room were her mom, Tito, and Lita, making lists of things that only she could take care of while she tried to claw her way through the wood grain on the door.

It would kill her grandmother to know that Bianca had regular nightmares about her. So, before she knocked on Lita's door, Bee pasted on the pleasant smile she used to practice in the mirror before Sandy Point High pep rallies. No teeth, eyebrows up. What Autumn referred to as her "commercial headshot" face.

Bianca thought of it as "faking."

She knocked on the door and sang in nonthreatening singsong, "Lita, buenas tardes. ¿Está bien?"

Since Tito died, Bianca used her scant Spanish like a desperate breath on cooling embers.

"No, no." There was a ruffle of blankets that sounded like sails caught in a breeze. A grunt. "Too early. I just lay down."

Bee tapped the face of her smartwatch: 11:47. She was already two minutes behind schedule. Persistence was key. Lita was at her most agitated when being woken up from a nap. Bee dropped the singsong but kept the smile. Lita would sense a frown and Bianca would lose. "Lita, it's time for lunch. Can I come in?"

"Yeah, yeah."

Bee opened the door before Lita changed her mind. Despite having the entire living room at her disposal, Lita had the large flat-screen TV mounted above her dresser on, playing a recorded Santana concert.

"Lunchtime," she said aloud with forced brightness, before Lita could open her mouth to complain about her touching the remote control.

Somehow even minimally invasive brain surgery couldn't make Lita less observant. Her eyes narrowed at Bee as she swung her legs heavily over the side of her bed. Lita preferred to have something else to keep her attention while getting dressed. Bee preferred Lita's attention on one of the few conversations she would have that day not with the TV.

"What would you like for lunch?" Bee asked, taking both of Lita's hands and helping her to her feet. The mermaid waving the Puerto Rican flag on Lita's forearm did the smiling for both of them. The mermaid looked exactly like Rosie Perez, but predated the actor by at least five years. "I was thinking about putting together a spinach salad for myself. We have some nice strawberries."

Lita let go of her hands and took a pained step toward the dresser. "Is Birdy having pizza bagels?"

Bee wanted to lie, but also knew that they would pass the oven she had preheated per Birdy's request.

Lita took her silence as an answer.

"Then I want pizza bagels."

Bee checked the smoothie cup on the nightstand. There were some flecks of spinach clinging to the plastic sides, but, for once, Lita might have consumed the entire thing. Or she had decided it was worth the energy to dump the blueberry protein goo in the toilet, which would require her using her bedroom walker. Either way, she'd done more before lunch than normal. It wouldn't hurt to have a treat. Even if that treat had zero nutritional value.

"Fine," Bee acquiesced. "Pajama time is over, though."

When Bianca and her mom decided to move Lita back into the house, the doctors helped plan her daily routine down to the minute. Since she spent most of her time inside, they were firm about her changing from pajamas to real clothes every day. No question. Now, when she looked down, she could tell whether it was day or night depending on her outfit.

It did require Bee's mom keeping a key to the house so that she could be on nighttime duty if Bee needed to be at the shop past seven. It was a small price to pay to keep Lita calm. Autumn often told Bee that she would never let *her* mother have a key to her house, but Autumn had been raised with an inflated sense of privacy.

Besides, Bee's mom couldn't be more of a cock block than Lita, who had stood at the bottom of the stairs screaming, "Burglar!" at midnight—far past her bedtime—and all because of a noise that ended up being Jo Freeman TP-ing the maple tree.

With a wave of dread, Bee recalled the toilet paper swaying in the tree. The morning had been lost to sorting out the tattoo shop's new digital appointment book. Bee had forgotten to clean up the yard. That was bound to steal twenty minutes of her lunchtime.

Today would have been a perfect time for that magic wand she spent her whole life hounding Santa for to finally show up.

While it would have been much easier to dress Lita in adaptive senior clothing, she refused to give up her old wardrobe. And since Bee was the ungrateful brat who moved Lita out of her apartment over the Salty Dog tattoo parlor, Bee didn't argue much. Lita picked out one of Tito's old Harley-Davidson T-shirts and a pair of pajama jeans she'd gotten for Christmas from Autumn.

"The front door at the shop is flaking," Bee said casually, topping off Lita's outfit with the Velcro house slippers that had replaced her fall-risk chanclas. "It needs a touch-up. I found a great match. It's called Rusty Anchor Red, isn't that perfect?"

Lita's foot went limp. Bee didn't have to look up to feel the disapproval aimed at the victory rolls she had painstakingly pinned from 6:20 to 6:27 this morning.

"Muñeca, what am I going to say?"

Bee stood up. "Lita."

"What am I going to say?"

"You're going to say 'Don't be fancy,' but—"

Lita wasn't listening. She was listing. "Don't be fancy! No glitter. No sparkles. No permanent-makeup artists. No new paint."

Tito was gone, but his many catchphrases echoed on behind him forever. *Don't be fancy* had been his most frequently offered advice. Bianca had never once found it helpful.

"I would argue none of those things are particularly fancy, but new paint especially—"

"Soon you'll want the artists to deliver their pieces in thirty minutes or less," Lita grumbled. "This isn't your square pizza."

In college, Bianca had managed a chain storefront called Square Slice Pizza. It wasn't a cool job. For three and a half years she wore a baseball cap to work and all of her bras smelled like marinara, but the job gave her full benefits for the first time in her life and enough money to not have four roommates.

Every single day she regretted telling her family about it.

The front door closed with a thunk that rattled the windows of Lita's bedroom. "Honeys, I'm home!" Birdy called. It had only been a couple hours since he left for work, but the sound of his voice was immediately welcome to Bee.

Even if it did mean that it was noon already. Shit.

"We're back here!" she cried. "Be right out!"

Bianca didn't ask if Lita wanted to walk to the living room because yes, she *wanted* to, but her tiny steps telegraphed that her knees were bothering her more than usual. Bee hoped that didn't mean there was rain coming. That would turn the TP tree into a mess that would take more time to clean than she had to spare.

She motioned for Lita to take a seat on her four-wheeled walker. Too distracted by the horror that was the idea of new paint, Lita forgot to argue and plopped herself down.

"My husband, your grandfather," she said, starting with Tito's official title. "Picked that particular shade of red by comparing it to the ink on his first tattoo."

"The rose he got for you, his Rosa, so he could think of you when he was with the navy."

"The rose he got for me!" Lita said, both agreeing with Bee and correcting her. "Now that he's gone, the rose is gone. The paint stays."

"I could literally take a picture on an app and get an exact—"

"Apps are definitely too fancy, Bianca."

Bee put her tongue between her molars and bit down hard so that she wouldn't blurt out that apps already controlled the Salty Dog's appointments, reviews, and most of the artists' designs.

One hundred and eleven days until I'm finally on my honeymoon. One hundred and eleven days until I take my first vacation with zero family members ever.

It would be just her and Birdy in a Hawaiian cabana for an entire week. Bee had purchased a different bathing suit for every day and zero sarongs.

One hundred and eleven days until it's us, the warm surf, and endless blended drinks.

She parked Lita in front of the dining room table, facing the TV, and kissed her cheek. "Okay, Lita. The shop is your baby. I'm just the nanny."

Lita patted her cheek, kissing her back and swatting her away. "Puerto Ricans don't have nannies. We have family."

"Tell that to J.Lo."

"I would. I have words for that Miss Jennifer." She sucked her teeth. "Who leaves Marc Anthony?"

"Someone who found a Yankee," Bee said.

"Mano!" Lita shouted to Birdy. "Come help me with her! She's being wrong again!"

Birdy walked into the dining room, wearing his Monday-through-Friday button-down-shirt-and-tie combo and holding a can of diet ginger ale. Six-two and heavyset, Birdy looked more like a football player than an orthodontist. It continually struck Bee as odd to see his large frame in her decidedly small house. He was twice the size of her late Tito, the only other man who had ever lived there.

"Sorry, Lita." Birdy shrugged. "I'm more of an Enrique guy."

Lita recoiled and stuck out her tongue. "Go get my pizza bagels."

"Hey," Birdy said, teasingly pointing at her. "We have to share those pizza bagels."

Lita sniffed. "Bianca can go get more with all the time she'll save not redecorating my tattoo parlor."

Birdy watched Bee with apologetic eyes as she squeezed by on her way to make herself a lunch plate.

"How about some music?" Birdy asked Lita. "What're you in the mood for? Springsteen? Bowie?"

"Fleetwood Mac," Lita said. "Something early. None of that *Rumours* shit."

"Something Stevie-less. I'm on it."

Bee pulled out a cookie sheet and lined up frozen discs that really didn't bear much resemblance to pizza or bagels. The living room filled with the familiar lunchtime patter. Lita told Birdy how much nicer her music would sound on vinyl. Birdy agreed but pointed out that the house didn't have the square footage to store every album in her encyclopedic memory, which was why they used the TV's Spotify app.

Lita never told Birdy that *he* was being too fancy, no matter how many apps he introduced. He got to be her bro, her mano.

With the music settled and pizza bagels bubbling, Birdy loudly announced his intention to get Lita a chocolate coconut water. As he came around the corner, he noticed the timer on the oven already ticking.

"Thank you," he told Bee softly. "You didn't have to do that."

He leaned down, setting a warm, wide hand on the back of Bee's neck as his lips met hers. The kiss woke up her blood like a static shock. Better than any of Bee's three cups of Folgers. It made her want to tug his tie off and rock his world with a *Cosmo*-style checklist of newlywed acrobatics before he went back to his office.

Lita humming along with "Rattlesnake Shake" reminded her how very impossible this dream was.

She extricated her mouth from Birdy's, leaving his cheeks flustered pink. She ran her thumb over his lower lip, wishing she had the time and privacy to make his whole body turn this color. It was too easy to scandalize him into a full blush. It made her feel more like a dangerous femme fatale than a short killjoy.

"You gotta stop looking at me like that," Birdy begged in a murmur.

Bee gently cuffed his chin. "I made a vow to never stop looking at you like this. Your brothers cried. Don't you remember? I was dressed like a very sexy cupcake."

"Like it was yesterday." He kissed her knuckles before pressing his cheek to the same spot. "Speaking of cool things that happen in July—"

"One hundred and eleven days!" She beamed at the top of his head. Until he raised it, wearing his hangdog apology face. Round, sad green eyes and a pouty lower lip tinged with her Bésame Red. Bee's stomach sank somewhere between the anchor tattoo on her left foot and the lighthouse on her right. "Oh. Oh no."

She could hear Tito calling down to her from heaven, *"You can't always get what you want!"*

"I got the call from Dr. Banns," Birdy said with a wince. "He's really doing it, honeybee. He's going to retire. And then the office is mine."

Counting back from ten, Bianca pictured the dentist office on Main Street. She knew all of its selling points: the natural light and high-tech dental equipment and proximity to the beach. Unlike

Birdy's current office, the Main Street location wasn't sandwiched between the ugliest of the local motels. And it would put Birdy's practice in the same part of town as the Salty Dog, rather than on the other side of the hill.

Not that they wouldn't both continue to come home for lunch to be with Lita.

But regardless of everything else, Birdy had moved to Sandy Point with the intention of being the sole orthodontist. The only game in town. And it was finally happening for him.

"This is why we made sure everything was refundable," he reminded her, nudging her arm so that she would make eye contact again. "Between the plane tickets and the resort fees, we should have enough for the deposit on the building. Dr. Banns is going to give me the official walk-through this evening, so I might be late. Is Bonnie on dinner duty?"

Bianca started to shake her head, but decided to spare her hair. "Mom has plans with Tony. I'm home for dinner. Cruz has a late appointment at the shop, so I'll go back after Lita's eaten to lock up."

"I know pushing the honeymoon again is inconvenient," Birdy said, guiltily twisting his black wedding band around and around. "But this is good news, Bee. Great news! Business is going to really explode. I'll have an endodontist in the building and a real lobby. And we have Birdy Bash to look forward to in November! It's not exactly summertime in Hawaii, but—"

"But it'll have to be good enough," she interrupted. If he started describing how going on a vacation with his army of siblings and great-aunts and third cousin Brewster "Squiggy" Birdy was anything like taking a private trip together, Bianca would scream. Just as loud and long as she possibly could, until she used up every molecule of air in her lungs.

Birdy watched her, waiting for more, expecting a fight that she didn't have time to have. How was it already 12:10? She had to give Lita her afternoon meds soon.

"I need to get the toilet paper out of the tree," Bee announced. "Lita's knee has been bugging her, and I'm afraid we're going to get some unscheduled rain."

"Lita's knees are never wrong," he said, continuing to search her face.

Not wanting him to find what he was looking for, Bee slipped over to the hall closet to retrieve the mop bucket and broom. She hoped the handle would be long enough to reach the top of the maple tree.

"You're on pizza bagel duty," she told him.

Birdy steepled his fingers and inclined his head to her with faux seriousness. "And it is an honor to serve. Pizza bagels."

He always tried to make Bee smile when she was upset. He thought that laughing could rinse away any lingering disappointment.

It didn't work so well when *he* was the one disappointing her.

"Just remember to turn off the oven this time," she said.

Bianca barely felt the mop bucket slapping against her leg as the front door closed behind her. Ignoring the paper fluttering on top of the tree, she checked the hydrangeas for any signs of harm. Thankfully, nothing appeared to be affected by Johanna Freeman's random act of vandalism except for the tree.

Leaving Bee extra time to mope.

I can't believe my honeymoon is canceled.

That wasn't true. She could believe it. She did believe it. In her heart, she knew that the real mistake was believing that her honeymoon was ever going to happen.

Her brain tormented her with all the useless things she'd

purchased for this canceled trip: six bikinis, two fancy dinner dresses, various floppy hats, and a variety of SPF-100 sunblock.

All useless in Sandy Point, where summers were almost never over seventy-five degrees.

To top it all off, she couldn't even repaint the door of her own business because when Lita found out—*and she would find out*—she would either yell until Bee cried or cry until Bee cried.

Either way, painting the door ended in tears.

Like the Salty Dog, the deed to 20 Jetty Avenue was in Lita's name. Bee had grown up in the little white house with her mom, Lita, and Tito. Her grandparents moved into the apartment over the shop when Bee was in the fifth grade in the name of "privacy."

Privacy being code for "not listening to Bee and Bonnie fight about tampons."

Tito died when Bee was in college. Two years later, Lita fell down the stairs in the shop. No one was sure how long she had lain broken behind the register before one of the artists had finally found her and called an ambulance. By then, the swelling in her face was horrific and the internal bleeding in her brain had to be surgically drained. Her broken leg hadn't set well and it was a miracle both of her hips were intact.

Bianca turned down her acceptance to a hospitality management grad program so she could come home and take over as the Salty Dog's manager while her mom took care of Lita.

Then Bonnie met Tony, and Bee ended up with both the business—minus their star artist—and Lita.

Bee didn't blame her mother for falling in love. After all, Bonnie spent Bee's entire childhood without a partner as she worked two jobs on top of apprenticing with Tito so that Bee could have things like SAT fees and food.

These days, Bonnie took special appointments, so the shop wasn't losing all the income she used to bring in. But she had the freedom to do things like spur-of-the-moment trips to Portland wineries and indoor rock climbing. If Bonnie had planned a trip to Hawaii, it would have gone off without a hitch, Bee was sure of it.

Things would have been so much easier if there had been even one more person in their family. A Boria cousin who could drop by to take Lita to lunch. A sibling who could help get her in and out of the shower. An uncle with a mommy complex who wanted to repay all the love Lita gave him as a child with a guesthouse and paid caretaker and endless bootlegs of Santana concerts.

Bee just wanted help.

A white Mini Cooper screeched up the street, nearly crashing into the U-Haul parked next door. Bianca recognized Johanna Freeman behind the wheel.

Jo jumped out of her adorable—and expensive—British car and ran toward Bee. "Bianca, stop!"

Over her shoulder, Bee checked the front window. The curtains were open, and Birdy was distracting Lita with a game of cards at the table. Good. The last thing Bee needed was Lita wheeling herself to the door, demanding that Jo speak up so that she could have the chisme firsthand.

"I was on my way to come clean up," Jo said, stepping awkwardly as her kitten heels sank in the grass. "I had to do a favor for my sister, and high school lunch is earlier than I remembered. But I'm here now, so please let me get all this"—she made a circular gesture at the tree—"out of your way."

Jo reached for the broom, but Bee stepped back and held it out of reach. She had spent all night in a spiral of *Why Does Jo Freeman Hate Me?* All of her dreams had been interrupted by memories of her and Johanna walking the same routes to school—never together—and vying for the same position in honor society and running into each other on the boardwalk where their families worked. Despite being neighbors, they had never been friends, but Bee had certainly never considered them enemies.

Until the toilet paper hit her in the face. After the TP gauntlet had been thrown, things felt suddenly personal. Acrimonious, even.

Bianca had to know why.

"Is this about Autumn? Are you mad at me because I stole your friend?"

"What? No!" Jo let out a startled laugh. "This isn't second grade. My friends can have friends."

"Are you really trying to convince me that you're too mature for petty vengeance? Here?" Bee folded her arms. "Under my quilted maple?"

They both looked up. There wasn't that much toilet paper, really. Less than a family pack. And Jo hadn't managed to wrap any of the rolls fully around the tree.

Amateur work, Birdy had said when he saw it this morning. *You should have seen some of the trees we used to hit back home. So much paper it looked like we'd mummified the lawn.*

"This isn't vengeance," Jo said quickly. "I didn't even mean for you to see it. I woke up to, like, twenty texts from my sister, and I had to rush out."

"But I saw the tree," Bee said. "Last night. When you threw toilet paper at me."

"You scared me!"

Bianca thought of Lita shrieking at the bottom of the stairs. "*I* scared *you*? You were the one running around in the dark!"

Jo gave the smallest eyebrow flick of acknowledgment. In daylight, her tall posture crossed the line into rigidity. Like there was an invisible hanger holding up the back of her silk shirt. "Wine might have been involved."

She reached out her arms again for the broom and bucket. Bee handed them over.

Using the broom handle, Jo flicked down one of the long strips of toilet paper. It fluttered easily into the bucket. She seemed pleased with this for a moment, but her face fell as she turned back to Bee, like she was surprised to find her still standing in her own yard.

"So, what?" Bianca asked, wrapping her arms around her waist. The self-hug made her feel brave enough to keep prodding this wound. "Did I ruin your family legacy of prom queens, too?"

Jo flicked down a second strip of TP and made a face over her shoulder. "What are you talking about?"

"Jen G is still pissed about prom. She won't even say hi to me at the grocery store. Which is extremely awkward seeing as how she's the head cashier now. Do you know what it's like to not be able to make pleasant chitchat while you buy bulk pizza bagels and diet soda? All I can do is stand there and watch her bag everything upside down out of spite."

"She's probably mad that people still don't know what the *G* stands for," Jo said, voice strained as she stood on her tiptoes to reach a TP tail. "You should try moving to another lane."

"It's Sandy Point. There's only one lane open unless it's the day before Thanksgiving. If you're going to be my neighbor again"—she thrust a finger at the U-Haul parked in the driveway—"I'd really like to know why you're mad at me. Is it honor society? Do you still think you deserved to be president because your girlfriend did it first?"

Jo and Bianca had both been members of the Point High honor society their junior and senior years. Probably because the same counselor sold it to them as a clear path from Sandy Point to college, somewhere else. The honor society collected all the type As—*A* as in achievement, awards, and Adderall—in one room only to dole out jobs for upcoming community service projects. All the projects were designed by the president.

Wren Vos had wasted the club members' talents on nonstop tutoring—on campus, at the middle school, at the library. No fund-raising or fun or socializing; only academic progress. The next year, Jo ran against Bee on a platform of more of the same, plus a readathon charity drive.

Bee offered the honor society the high school experience everyone wanted. Canned-food drives and safety patrol for the elementary school Halloween parade and decorating the school in homecoming colors. Basic. But the kind of basic that everyone actually wanted. She still offered to let Jo host the readathon. Jo declined.

"I'm not mad about high school, Bianca," Jo said. She took a few steps away under the guise of reaching a new piece of TP. "You were good at being president. Is that what you need to hear?"

"No, I need to hear you apologize!" The last word echoed like a command, bouncing off the Hammerbecks' porch across the street. "Because when you're sorry, you say so! You don't move forward like nothing happened! You say sorry and *then you fix it!*"

The sound of her own breathing was louder in Bee's ears than the sound of the ocean. Without turning around, she knew that

Lita had moved from the dining table to the front window. Lita was attracted to drama the way magpies were drawn to shiny things. She spent more time with daytime judge shows and telenovelas than people.

Chirrup-chirrup!

Jo and Bee both looked at Bee's wrist, where her smartwatch displayed fireworks and Lita's afternoon meds alarm.

Bee was running behind schedule. She didn't have time to indulge in pity parties with high school acquaintances.

"I have to go do fifteen other things before I can even go to work," she told Jo. "So you can leave the broom and the bucket on the porch when you're done."

Jo's posture slumped again. "Bianca—"

Bee held her hands up in surrender. "It's okay, Jo. I accept your lack of apology. You wouldn't know this about me, but that is what I am absolutely best at."

She could only storm as far as the front door before she had to stop and adjust her face back to faking it, so she could shoo Lita back to her lunch. Her meds had to be taken with food.

four

J O

In college, Jo worked as an office temp instead of coming home for summers. She had been determined to drown out her parents' businesses from her résumé. It helped prepare her for a life without summer vacation and covered the down payment on her Mini, but she never stopped having nightmares about needing to learn a new office culture by immersion.

It was the jargon that killed her—backronyms and mantras peddled by desperate management that she was supposed to automatically know and parrot. Like the company that wanted her to answer the phone, "This is Jo—that's *J-O*, let's go!"

Her family had become that office.

According to Eden's ongoing, grudging translation, in their house *refeasting* meant having leftovers for dinner, eating *in front of Netflix* meant in the living room using their laps instead of tables, and the *fie-fie* meant the wireless router.

To make things worse, it wasn't until Jo had her piping-hot

refeasting plate in hand that she realized that she had the lowest level of seating priority. Her parents were on the couch and Eden swooped into the armchair; she was already folding her spindly legs in the seat, holding her plate over her head to keep from spilling enchilada sauce on herself.

"What's the matter, Jojo bean?" her dad asked. Phil Freeman had a window-rattling deep voice that drew attention like a spotlight. "Are you lost?"

There is no third piece of furniture, Jo thought. *How can there only be a couch and a chair in this room?*

She tried to remember the last time all four of them had used the living room together. On a Christmas Eve or Christmas Day, Jo had sat on the floor between the tree and the fireplace. But now, in the off-season, the fireplace was an empty hole in the wall behind a metal grate.

The only seat left in the house was on the couch with her parents.

"Just not used to eating on the couch," she said, slowly taking the seat next to her dad.

"You didn't eat in front of the TV when you lived alone?" Eden asked in a disbelieving monotone.

Jo pictured her apartment. Through the Vaseline lens of perspective, it had been sheer bliss to eat takeout directly from the box, stretched out on her long leather sofa. Had she ever truly appreciated the feeling of complete and utter autonomy?

"I'm not used to it *here,*" Jo corrected. "We ate at the table last night."

"That was a celebration," her mom said, switching between remotes seemingly at random.

"We're standing on ceremony less day to day," her dad said.

"And the dining room doesn't have *Black Mirror*," Eden said.

"*Black Mirror!*" her mom cheered, waving the two remotes over her head.

"You guys are watching *Black Mirror* together?" Jo frowned over at her sister. "Isn't that a little mature?"

Eden thrust her chin forward, looking exactly like the little kid she didn't think she was. "Uh, okay, Grandma. I'm leaving for college in six months. I don't need you to monitor my TV."

"I'm not monitoring anything!" Jo said to her plate. She cut into an enchilada before adding, "But the first episode of that show is about a dude fucking a pig on live TV."

"It's political commentary!" Eden snapped.

"Is it, though?" Jo asked.

"Do you not want to watch *Black Mirror*, Jo?" Her mother's voice wobbled. "I suppose we could try the new Johnny Appleseed show."

"*That* show is supposed to be super horny," Eden said.

"It's fine," Jo said over the sound of her baby sister saying *horny* at dinnertime. "Just surprised. I can watch whatever."

"Thankfully, it's an anthology series, so we won't have to catch you up on anything," her dad said.

"Very unlike *Westworld*," Eden said.

"Oh man." Phil crowed with laughter and clapped Jo on the shoulder, making her choke on hot cheese. "We're gonna have to get you a timeline map to get you on board for *Westworld*."

"And a character bible," Deb added, beaming.

Jo stifled a groan. If she tried to make a list of things she had absolutely zero interest in, it was anything that required something that could be considered a character bible. She would have been more suited to rooting for everyone Black on competitive cooking shows. With a sectional couch.

The Freeman living room bore the brunt of Philip and Deb's various—loyalty wouldn't quite let Jo think of them as *failed*—businesses. The bronze replica rococo clock on the mantel was a relic from Another Man's Treasure, the consignment store they'd run when Jo was very young. As were the two blown-glass vases—whose lives, Jo was pretty sure, had started as bongs—which were being used to bookend stacks of Deb's creased-spine romance novels. The psychedelic Hawaiian sea-turtle painting watching over Eden's armchair was left over from their money-guzzling—and people repelling—art gallery, Freeman Fine Arts.

Even the long lumpy couch had been moved out of the back room to make space for a prep kitchen.

Jo barely had her mind wrapped around the idea that her parents ran a beach-themed tearoom. She was distantly aware that she was the only person in the family who'd never surfed—her parents both took up the hobby when Eden did. Jo, who had no use for the ocean or hot beverages, hadn't been down to the boardwalk since the store's sign changed to say *Surf & Saucer*.

And anyway, history had taught her not to get too attached to what was inside the shop. Better to love the unchangeable address.

Around her, the family talked in odd bursts about the bleak action on-screen. They threw out wild theories about the inevitable plot twist, then shushed one another when someone seemed to be getting too close. Deb covered her eyes a lot and hid behind her husband's shoulder. Eden ate dinner with her plate an inch under her chin. Phil tried to catch glimpses of the job websites Jo was scrolling through on her phone.

It was the third time her mother's guess for an actor on *Black Mirror* was "from that Helen Mirren movie" that Jo faked a text.

"Cool," she said to her own reflection in the cell-phone screen. "I'm gonna go meet up with some people."

Her skin went cold at the lie, but she pushed through the feeling. There had to be something in Sandy Point that was open after seven. And if not, then she would go on her new nightly stroll through the Fred Meyer.

"That's nice, Jo," her mom said, one eye on the TV. "Have you and Autumn had a chance to catch up at all?"

Yes, she hated seeing me so much that she cried. Jo had to keep herself from wincing at the memory. She'd spent all day drafting messages to Autumn apologizing for showing up unannounced. Every attempt felt either too cold or too clingy. She deleted them all.

"Some." She got up and prepared to bus her plate, balancing the silverware poorly.

"Tell her hey from the Freemans," Phil said. "Don't be a stranger, et cetera, et cetera."

They assumed she was leaving to see Autumn. Who else in Sandy Point did she know?

"You'll see her at the Senior Showcase, Dad," Eden said.

"That's months away," Phil said, grasping his heart. "We've got decades left until you graduate and run off to college, leaving us all alone."

"At least now you won't be alone." Eden held her empty plate up to Jo as she passed. "You'll have Johanna."

That was when Jo decided to google *bars in Sandy Point* like a goddamn adult.

Braving an unexpected rainstorm, Jo found herself in a familiar parking lot, at the corner of Wolcott Furniture Emporium and Wolcott Mattress Emporium. Before she got out of her Mini, she ducked her head to read the truncated sign over the door of the massive restaurant: DAYS.

The hottest karaoke bar and best burgers in Sandy Point—according to a shocking number of positive Yelp reviews—was the reanimated corpse of an abandoned TGI Friday's.

All the other bars in town were beach-themed—the Coastline Tavern, Harbor Cove, and, least clever, the Sand Bar. The only internet complaint about Days Bar & Grill was that it wasn't beachy enough. Making it ideal for Jo.

She stepped through the front door and into a nightclub-level wall of sound—blenders whirring, cocktails elaborately shaken, a screeching MIDI file blasting from the screens hung above the platform stage. People crowded into booths and perched on tall bar chairs and leaning around the bar were singing along with the performer of the moment, a red-faced guy wailing "I Believe in a Thing Called Love."

It felt like opening a door into the atonal beating heart of her hometown. Jo had never expected this town to have even a pulse, much less a nightlife.

Screens hung in every direction, flashing the lyrics to the current selection in a variety of unreadably bright colors on busy backgrounds. Along with half of the neon sign and the red vinyl booths, Days had also kept the TGI-fryer. The air was thick with old grease and the chemical hypersweetness of chocolate mudslide mix.

Jo claimed a seat at a mostly unpopulated end of the bar, a comfortable distance from the short stage. She scoped out the room for familiar faces. In a booth in a corner, two girls were sitting on the same side, feeding each other chicken strips. Jo squinted hard to see if she could recognize either of them. The idea of there being a queer population here without her made her heart leap. She recognized a couple of guys sharing a pitcher of beer in the front row as Thatcher Vos's soccer friends, although none of them had the same hairlines they'd had the day they all crowded into the Voses' living room and watched Abby Wambach's miracle score at the Women's World Cup. It was the only time Jo had ever seen her infamously reserved ex-girlfriend Wren cry. A girl in a Days T-shirt with *Barback* written across her shoulder blades dropped off a slim dinner menu and a binder of drinks. Jo chose the binder, where she learned that the Days definition of "mixed drink" mostly meant blended. Sandy Point's namesake cocktail included pineapple vodka and three kinds of ice cream and came with a genuine Sandy Point beach sand dollar, free with purchase.

Deciding to do as the Sandy Pointers did, she ordered an orange-cream vodka milk shake.

The bar cheered the chorus of "Call Me Maybe." Either Sandy Point had a ton of Carly Rae Jepsen stans or the combination of liquor and ice cream made for the most encouraging karaoke audience.

"Are they always this enthusiastic?" Jo asked the barback. "No one ever divas out and demands to sing alone?"

"Not on singalong night," the barback said, tucking her pen behind her ear. She examined Jo's face—likely for signs of an impending diva tantrum. "You from out of town?"

"Sort of. I haven't been here since the sign had all its letters."

The barback's eyelids twitched. She was tired of talking about the missing letters. "Participation is encouraged on Singalong Mondays," she said, talking faster as the song hurtled toward another chorus. "You gotta pick a song off the most-popular list."

She pointed out the flip menu of songs next to the napkin dispenser. "Then you put your name in with Alfie over by the jukebox. If you're in a hurry, he loves a bribe."

After a cursory glance at the most-popular-song list, Jo took out the journal while she waited for her drink. That morning, she had planned to share it with Autumn. She had pictured them sitting in the creaky folding chairs inside of the auditorium, like they'd done in high school at lunchtime, and looking at the list, flinting their memories together.

Instead, Jo had literally been asked to leave campus. Like a stranger. Worse than a stranger, because a stranger wouldn't have made Autumn cry just by existing.

"Is that Jo Freeman?"

Autumn's older brother appeared on the other side of the bar. Jo tried not to look surprised. Florencio Kelly was bad-boy hot with good-boy dimples. The addition of two sleeves of tattoos and thirty pounds of muscle only helped.

Florencio set Jo's orange booze-shake on a coaster and reached across the bar. Jo's heart fluttered as she gave him dap, a quiet nod of solidarity in an aggressively white town.

"Flo Kelly," she said warmly. Florencio had always been a weight on her Kinsey scale, the cutest dudebro in dudetown. "Weren't you bussing tables here when I left?"

His brows pulled into an ironic V. "There were jobs in between, but yeah, I've worked up the Days ladder."

He noticed the journal open in front of her and craned his neck to take a look. She clumsily swatted it into her purse, hoping her dazzling smile was distraction enough.

"How upwardly mobile of you," she noted. She dragged her straw in a thick circle before taking her first sip. The vodka went straight to her head, but she was too knocked down by the sugar to notice. It was the first drink she ever had that actually tasted like a hangover. "I thought you'd be fighting fires. How are Chief Chuck and Cindy?" she asked.

"Divorced."

The straw fell out of Jo's mouth. "No!"

Flo nodded in time to the music. "Yep. It's the Chief and Ginger now."

"I can't tell if that's a joke. Ginger like Ginger Rogers? Or Ginger like your new stepmother works at the strip club in Oceanside?"

"Ginger like Ginger Rogers," Flo said.

A pang of guilt hit Jo in the chest as she remembered the ghosting accusation. If she were really up-to-date on Autumn's life, wouldn't she know that her parents had split?

Glittering disco-ball lights danced against Flo's puckish smile. "Autumn said she didn't think she was gonna see you again." His gaze drifted over her head. "I guess she was wrong."

Turning, Jo instantly spotted Autumn's distinct shade of red hair near the door. "She must have underestimated my townie bias against tourist-trap nautical bars," she said, wondering if sending any—or all—of the texts she'd drafted earlier would have made her less nervous at seeing the only person in town she'd consider a friend. She raised her hand to wave, but Autumn abruptly turned away, greeting the approaching barback with a huge smile that felt pointedly not for Jo.

Jo thought of the map journal. *Perform onstage* was next on the list. It wouldn't be too hard with this audience. They'd do most of the heavy lifting by virtue of being collectively louder than the speakers. And Autumn wouldn't be able to avoid her if she was center stage with a microphone.

Abandoning the straw, Jo gulped down her drink until her brain froze. Sharp cold melted to liquid warmth as cheap vodka luged around her veins. Eyes watering, she checked the popular-song list again and stood up, resolute.

"You're going up there?" Flo asked, pointing to the stage. "You don't seem like a karaoke person."

"I've never done it. That doesn't mean I'm not hiding a secret talent for it."

She wasn't. She knew she wasn't. Jo didn't even sing in the shower on the chance the neighbors could hear. She reached into her purse and fished out her credit card. "Film me, will you? And have another drink waiting for me when I get back."

"One more Cream Dream for the lady."

"I won't pay for it if you call it that."

Leaving Flo laughing behind her, Jo threw her bag over her shoulder and leaped down from her stool. She strode across the restaurant, biting the skin on her lips as she went. This morning, she had embarrassed Autumn at work. She would embarrass herself to make up for it. An eye for an eye. A public shaming for a public shaming. Having no current place of employment, this very crowded bar would have to do.

Underneath a porkpie hat, Alfie at the jukebox frowned up at Jo. When she held up a folded dollar bill and asked to jump the line, he kept his hands folded over his stomach. "They won't listen to you, you understand? You want to jump the line just to stand onstage before anybody else?"

"I'm trying to catch someone before they leave. Number twenty-two, please," Jo replied, pointing to the list on the table in front of him.

"What a fucking song to have screamed at you," Alfie muttered, snatching the dollar out of her hands and shooing her onstage with it. "Yeah, yeah, go on, moneybags."

Jo's limbs felt like they'd been replaced with wet sand as she walked toward the taped X that marked center stage. The lyric screens all flipped from shrieking pink to lime green as her song choice came up on the screen. The opening chords landed at the same time as the audience made a collected grunt of reserved recognition. The intro was a thousand years long; the lyric screens all continued to broadcast the title: "Mamma Mia."

While the canned track plink-plonked the manic blinker sound of a digital marimba, Jo cleared her throat into the microphone and talked fast. "I want to dedicate this song to my friend Autumn Kelly. I shouldn't have dropped by on you earlier. I hope this makes up for— 'I was cheated by you!'"

Thin voice pushed to the limit, Jo sang and disco-danced to ABBA like she was in the Kelly family's living room instead of the gutted husk of a chain restaurant. *Mamma Mia!* had been Autumn's favorite musical throughout most of elementary school. She had watched it on a loop, and for at least two years, it was the only CD in the Kelly minivan stereo.

Jo knew every single word by heart.

The crowd made up for anything Jo lacked as a performer. They held notes too long and improvised half harmonies. When Jo quickly ran out of disco moves, she got helpful hints—like *macarena* and *running man* and one screamed *"Freebird!"*—from the former soccer players closest to the stage. When she busted out her running man, she finally heard the familiar whipcrack laugh that could only belong to her ride-or-die bestie.

"'I should not have let you go!'" Jo warbled the last note reaching out toward the audience. Squinting past the lyric screens and the flop sweat in her eyebrows, Jo could make out Autumn reaching back to her from the bar next to her brother. The song finally ended, and she staggered past a bewildered Alfie Jay.

"I got a video of it for you, Jo," Florencio assured her, waggling his phone. "But it feels more like blackmail."

"Johanna Jordan Freeman! Singing and dancing in public?" Autumn gasped, giving her a second round of applause. "What brought that on?"

Florencio pointed out the two booze shakes sitting in front of the stool Jo was dropping her purse on. "About half of a cocktail I'm no longer allowed to mention. I take it back, Jo. You are definitely a karaoke person. At least by Sandy Point standards."

"Wow. Literally the meanest compliment I have ever received," Jo said. Then, like a badly wrapped gift, she said to Autumn, "ABBA always makes me think of you. It's your entrance music."

Jo realized how long it must have been since she had seen her old friend smile because Autumn had honest-to-God new teeth. Bigger, whiter, straighter teeth like a local news weatherperson, and no gaps between them.

Jo tried not to look shocked. The gap in Autumn's teeth had been as foundational a part of her face as her freckles or her rusty-orange eyebrows. But the gap was gone, replaced by bright-white Chiclets.

"Did I ever tell you that I finally got to do *Mamma Mia!* at OSU?" Autumn asked. "It was freaking incredible. I was a total self-actualized Christine Baranski queen in high-waist, ruffled bell-bottoms." She gave a bounce of remembering and turned on a dime. "Flo, put in an order of mozzarella sticks for me, please? I am starving. My oven broke."

Her brother frowned at her. "You don't have an oven."

"No, I *had* a microwave that was my oven and now I have nothing. Except the promise of heavily discounted moz-sticks."

"I only discount the ones we drop on the floor first," Flo said.

"Whatever you have to do. I'm starving!" Autumn called after him before turning back to Jo with an ever-so-slightly more reserved smile.

Jo wasn't ready to go back to being strangers.

"Ice cream and liquor?" she offered. She slid the full orange milk shake in front of Autumn. "A very boozy apology for showing up unannounced today? I haven't been good at keeping in contact. With anyone, not just you. But I'm still sorry for being an accidental ghost."

"I accept your sorry-shake." Autumn took a sip of the drink, then recoiled at the flavor. "Woo! That is vodka-forward. Is this what fueled both karaoke and TP-ing in twenty-four hours?"

"You forgot trespassing on school grounds," Jo added with a nervous chuckle.

"Why do you think I'm so hungry?" Autumn asked. "I had to abandon my lunch when Pat Markey told me you were taking pictures of children."

Jo shook her head. "I shouldn't have let Eden convince me it was okay to drop by. Just because she sounds like an adult doesn't mean she knows anything."

"I understand that you thought you were helping. In the future, please consult other adults. In general, you should tell people what's going on with you," Autumn said. "For instance, why are you here? Don't you kind of hate it here? You know, in Oregon. Not Days."

Jo picked at her cuticles, focusing on them rather than Autumn's expectant face. "I got laid off and had to move home," she said.

Would it ever get any easier to say? Every time felt like she was taking out a Sharpie and scrawling *I Fucked Up* on her own forehead. "I got back yesterday. And the first thing I found in my room was the list of everything we wanted to do before we dug up the time capsule."

"Our time capsule!" Autumn blinked in genuine surprise. "That's where I left the replica *Annie* locket Santa got me! Ten paces from the back porch?"

"Five paces from the fence," Jo finished. "Behind the doghouse."

"Aww, I haven't thought about that in so long." Autumn sank down on her elbow, giving her milk shake a contemplative swirl. "What were we supposed to do before we dug it up? I mean, wasn't it just literally anything Florencio and his friends did, we wanted to do, too?"

Jo slid the map journal out of her purse and handed it over. "All the fun Sandy Point has to offer."

Autumn's eyes hungrily scanned each item on the list. "Oh, look, it has both of our handwriting! That's nice. Thank God TP-ing Bee's house was your idea, not mine. I feel guilty every time I remember that we used to call her 'Bianca the Bore-ia.' So mean!" She gazed at Jo with a curious scrunch in her nose. "You're going to do all of these?"

Jo opened her mouth to protest. She hadn't TP'd Bianca's house intending to work through the whole list.

But with a second item ticked off, the rest of the list looked more inviting. When else was she going to have the free time to learn a TikTok dance or stage herself an elaborate pinup-girl lingerie shoot?

Instead of more days like today, where she bounced around

town, her very existence getting in the way of everyone living their actual lives here, she could fill her time with something fun. The idea of a real, old-fashioned check-box to-do list was weirdly satisfying.

And it would be easy to document everything. She'd fished her camera out of the garage in time to commemorate the TP tree. If she gave everything else on the list professional lighting, some Photoshop tinkering, maybe a hashtag . . . It was basically a social media campaign. Except for herself instead of for a company that dumped her like her tenure there was a cache to be cleared.

"Yeah, I'm going to do all of them," Jo said, deciding then and there that it was true. She could see herself ticking off every box, feeling the rush of completing a huge project on her own. "I mean I can't pass up something to do in a town with nothing to do. There's still no gym here, right? And no Starbucks?"

"There's a Starbucks kiosk inside the Safeway now! You get used to it." Autumn dropped a sheepish smile into her straw. "I did."

"Right!" Jo wished that she had studied Autumn's social media to fill in the huge gaps of knowledge she had. It seemed rude to have to ask but ruder not to know. "How long were you in Los Angeles? You went to UCLA for grad school, didn't you? Eden said she applied because you went there."

"Oh, really?" Autumn looked surprised. "I would have gone to any school near Hollywood that gave me a scholarship. I just wanted to get discovered and drop out. But I fell in love with teaching instead. And I really missed it here."

"Here?" Jo spluttered. "You must mean Days specifically."

"No! Sandy Point!" Autumn laughed. "Here. *Home.* LA was never home. It was just a place I lived. It was like I was commuting a thousand miles away from my real life. So I got my teaching credential and left. I'm not the only one. Half the staff of Point High grew up here. Maybe more."

Stunned, Jo sat back. She could not imagine anyone purposefully choosing to live between nowhere and the ocean. Autumn had managed to get so far away—all the way to Los Angeles! And yet she chose to be here, in a town that got together on a weeknight to scream-sing top-40 hits.

"At least you ended up with a job," Jo said, struggling to find common ground. She rubbed at the music throb in her temple. "I did nothing but work, but when my old company goes public with their acquisition, none of the work I did will survive. I'll have literally nothing to show for the last ten years. I need a real job so I can get to my adult life, as soon as possible."

"Well, in the meantime," Autumn said breezily as her brother reappeared with a steaming basket of mozzarella sticks, "you can count these *free* mozzarella sticks—"

"You are paying for these, Autumn." Florencio frowned.

"—as your welcome basket. And your first step toward eating everything on the menu here." Autumn pointed to the item list in the back of the map journal.

"That is going to be a very different challenge now that there are only five appetizers and seventeen kinds of margaritas," Jo said.

"Jo is working on a bucket list we wrote in high school," Autumn told Florencio. "At the end we can dig up the time capsule in the backyard on Main Street. You'd better work quick, Jo. Ginger Jay wants the house picture-perfect and on the market before summer. May first, they're putting everything left behind in a big dumpster. So you've got about six weeks to get what you want out of there."

Jo got the feeling that somehow the intensity of that deadline wasn't just meant for her.

Florencio bristled as though considering having an opinion on the May first dumpster or, perhaps, Ginger Jay, but instead he set his decorated forearms on the bar and put his face closer to Jo.

"A bucket list, huh?" he asked, turning the full force of his sparkle on her. A cheap but effective distraction. A girl could lose a pinkie in those dimples. "Is that why you TP'd Bianca's house?"

"Yes! The list wanted me to!" Jo said. Then, hearing herself, she added, "The first item is 'TP Bianca's house.' Because in high school she was so annoyingly perfect—"

"That hasn't changed," Flo said. Autumn threw a cocktail napkin at him.

"I just wanted to muss up her shit. A little," Jo said. "I went to clean it up when I left Point High this morning, but I didn't quite beat Bianca to it. I thought she'd be at work. She has a house. She must have a job."

"She runs the tattoo shop on the boardwalk," Flo said. "They open late."

"I'll take your word for it," Jo said, inclining her head toward his heavily inked forearms. Flo obliged her by flexing them. A gift.

"Did you tell Bee you were sorry for vandalizing her house?" Autumn asked.

Jo opened her mouth to say, *Yes, of course.* Except that as she replayed the scene, she realized that no, she hadn't. She had felt sorry before Bianca screamed at her for not being sorry, and then all of her sorries sort of evaporated. She gave a sheepish wince at the Kelly siblings, who both threw up their hands at her.

"Jo!" Autumn chided.

"You vandalized her house and didn't apologize?" Florencio exclaimed, caught somewhere between laughing and shouting. "You've been back for two seconds, hometown hero!"

Guilt made Jo's stomach roil. It had been a long time since she had lived in a small enough community that word of what she did was instantly known by everyone. In Palo Alto, if she cut someone off on 101, she never had to think about it again. In Sandy Point, if she didn't greet the postman by name, everyone would know by dinner.

"She let me take over cleaning when I got there, but she followed me around, interrogating me." Jo thought of Bianca's meticulously styled hair sheepdogging her around the yard.

"Did she ask, 'Why did you do this?' and you said, 'A list told me to'?" Autumn asked. "Because then I would understand why she was mad."

"No, I said I wasn't mad about high school, then she told me I wasn't sorry enough and stormed off. But! Did I mention how clean the tree is? Spotless."

"Fifty percent right is still half-wrong," Florencio said. "That's an *F*, Freeman."

"You're a wrestling coach," Autumn scoffed. "Your grades aren't real. You don't know the pain of report card season."

"Because all of my students are winners," Flo said with a cavalier flick of his head.

"Coach?" Jo gasped. She didn't know how many wrestling matches she and Autumn had gone to as Florencio's own personal cheer squad, armed with elaborate signs made out of Mrs. Kelly's infinite craft supplies. "Coach Kelly! You didn't tell me that you had your own honorific. Your dad must be so proud."

"Must be," Flo said, noncommittal. He craned his neck to catch a better look at the journal. "You never did any of this? Climbing the anchor! Kegs and bonfires! This is like everything I did in high school."

"No shit." Jo laughed. "Where do you think we got the ideas?"

"Aww, remember when I thought you were cool, Flo?" Autumn asked.

"I don't miss it," her brother said. "You were little stalkers. Autumn followed me the night when I went to climb the anchor."

Autumn tipped her nose up in a proud smile. "And then I climbed it faster."

Florencio turned his attention back to Jo. "So why didn't you?"

"I was in a different neighborhood. I couldn't just sneak down to the boardwalk in the middle of the night," Jo said. "We had to plan anything that required sneaking out."

"Sure, but the rest of this," Flo said. He swept a hand over the list. "What did you do in high school if you weren't surfing or smoking weed?"

"Studying," Jo said at the same time that Autumn giggled and said, "Wren Vos."

Flushing, Jo thought of her ex-girlfriend longboarding by, pockets heavy with paperbacks, long blond princess hair whipping in the wind.

"That's right!" Flo laughed. "You dated the Vos sister for a minute."

"A minute and a half," Jo said. "Two years."

"Have you seen her?" Autumn asked.

Jo shook her head. "Not in the last ten years. She thought social media was participation in a surveillance state, remember? We lost touch." She tucked her hair behind her ears, fingers twitching. "I lost touch with everyone."

Jo was coming to realize that it had been a long time since she'd let herself have a social life. Talking to influencers expecting goody boxes or coworkers shit-talking their man-child boss wasn't the same as having fun with other people. It wasn't the same as being known.

She really hadn't done anything fun in a long time. Not fun that wasn't work. She had really liked her job and found it enjoyable to be good at it, but it wasn't glitter-fight fun. Pointless fun was rare.

If she was going to do this list, she would have to commit to every step. That would mean a lot of time on the boardwalk. Coming and going. It would be a good idea to make sure that the next-door neighbor wasn't holding a grudge.

As she looked down at the list, her gaze caught upon *Get belly button pierced*. "Does Bianca's tattoo parlor do piercings?"

"Bee does them herself," Autumn said. Then, in a conspiratorial whisper, added, "She can't draw. But she *can* run a business. She has a degree in it and everything."

Jo bit into a mozzarella stick. "Do you think letting her stab me with needles sounds like the start of a good apology?"

Autumn smiled with all of her new teeth. "That sounds like a great apology."

By the next morning, the whiteboard wall had a list of project-title ideas. She needed something that would work as both a brand and a hashtag. Something that wasn't already crowded on social media. Autumn had suggested "The Way Back List," but Jo found it already in use by a Floridian teen working on her own bucket list. "The Home Again List" sounded too much like a community-sponsored program. "The Time Capsule Project" put too much pressure on the time capsule itself to be interesting—Jo was pretty sure it was mostly dollar-store trinkets and letters written on binder paper. After ten more false starts—all of them a mishmash of vaguely nostalgic words: *hometown, ten years later, return*—she finally landed on one that worked.

She dusted off her Instagram, uploading her first post since leaving California.

♡ ◯ ◁

PhotogFreeman: Sorry I've been so quiet on here recently! Life has been hella busy and is about to get even more exciting. I'm embarking on a new project, starting today! I'd like to introduce you to the Throwback List.

Would high school you be proud of who you are now? When I found this list of everything I wanted to do before the end of high school, it was ten years later and I hadn't done a single thing on it! Now I am going to check off every single item, no matter how terrifying or silly or impractical (wow, that's a lot of TGI Fridays!).

What task on my list would you be most scared of? Sound off in the comments!

#TheThrowbackList

✓ *TP Bianca's house*
✓ *Perform onstage*

five

BIANCA

Dear Bianca,

I hope you can forgive me for yesterday. I'd love the chance to apologize in person. Do you have any appointments available for a navel piercing this week or next?

Best,
Jo Freeman

"She vandalizes my house then has the audacity to ask *me* for a piercing appointment?" Bianca shouted at her computer in the Salty Dog Tuesday afternoon. "She didn't even have the decency to call! An email! Does she think I don't know she lives next door?"

Dear Jo,

Think nothing of it. This week, I could schedule you for Thursday afternoon or Friday morning.

Cordially,

Bianca Boria-Birdy

General Manager & Body Piercer at the Salty Dog

"I bet she's never been inside a tattoo shop in her life. She's going to find every single flaw," Bee said, at home, hacking apart a head of lettuce. "She thinks she is so cool and metropolitan because she lived in California. It's only a state, people. If she'd moved somewhere less flashy, maybe she'd still be there. She could afford rent in Idaho, I bet. No one moves in with their parents because they *want* to."

Bianca,

Thursday afternoon would be perfect. Would it be okay with you if Autumn joined us? She offered to take pictures of the process for my Instagram, but I thought I should ask if she could tag along. I don't want to be rude.

Thanks,

Jo

"It's rude for her to not ask permission to take pictures inside my shop," Bee said, Wednesday morning at the kitchen sink. Wet spread across her side as she scratched shampoo into Lita's scalp. "I bet she won't even go through with the piercing. She'll wimp out at the last second. But not before Autumn takes a bunch of pictures of her in the chair."

"Pictures are good for business," Lita intoned, eyes closed. "Tell her to put them on the Yelp reviews. My husband, your grandfather, he loved the Yelp reviews."

Jo,

Of course, Autumn is always welcome. Accommodating her after-school club schedule, how does Thursday at 5 p.m. sound to both of you?

Regards,
Bianca Boria-Birdy
General Manager & Body Piercer at the Salty Dog

Bianca,

We're on! Thanks again!

Jo

"Now I'll just be the fat suburban friend," Bee said, crashing Dez and Dede's smoke break mid-Wednesday, holding a Safeway latte instead of a cigarette. "And, yes, that's what I am. But I don't want to feel like that's all I am!"

"It isn't! You're a boss, Boss!" squeaked Dede.

> **AUTUMN:** Aww, yay! Thanks for scheduling an appointment for Jo! See you Thursday for sure!

"Autumn's *real* best friend is back, and already everything is changing," Bee told Birdy as he got into bed Wednesday night. "I didn't hear from her *at all* on Monday. After I told her that Jo was rude to me, they went and had drinks at singalong night! And they're going to come into the shop together tomorrow! So the duchess can look down that bump in her nose at my ancestral business."

"Is Meghan Markle still a duchess?" Birdy asked now, slipping his reading glasses on as he reached for his e-reader.

"Of course she is," Bianca snapped. "Just like Diana will always be the people's princess."

"Fair enough," Birdy said. "And this girl you're talking about *isn't* Meghan Markle but is just some girl you went to high school with? The mysterious daughter of Phil and Deb next door?"

"If *mysterious* is code for 'snobby robot.'"

"I'm not in the habit of speaking in code, honey," he said, patting her arm.

Bee yanked the patted arm back. "I can't lose my one friend, Birdy." When his face fell into an offended frown, she amended her statement. "My one friend other than you. Not that I want to share you either."

"That's very only-child of you."

Bianca gasped. "Birdy!"

"It's true!" He laughed. "I know you think you've outsmarted it or you're immune because of your *Gilmore Girls* situation with your mom."

"Rory Gilmore is the ultimate only child. I would never steal a boat."

"But you do expect your friend to pick up the phone. Every time."

"I wouldn't call her if I didn't know she was free."

"That attention to detail is endearing and not at all scary. But you are an only child, honeybee. Growing up alone means that you weren't raised to share anything. Except your personal space."

Unlike Birdy and his two brothers—all known as Birdy in their social circles—Bee's childhood hadn't been an endless stream of Tom Sawyer–esque hijinks. While the Birdy Brothers were flexing their white privilege and running amok in suburban Ohio, Bianca had been following the rules to keep the Boria name squeaky clean.

She hadn't been friendless. She just liked her friends the way Lita liked a dinner plate—in distinct, separate quadrants. School friends stayed at school. Work friends within a block of work. Family friends were rare—and usually guest tattoo artists who fell back into work-friend territory.

A best friend had to be able to move in all those spheres with her. More than that, they had to be someone she could talk to day or night, but who wouldn't get mad if she disappeared on family business. Someone who she could travel with but who would understand how far in advance all trips would need to be planned. Someone who could enjoy both working and playing hard. Someone who wasn't pushing diets, religion, or pyramid schemes, which ruled out most of the people she was Facebook friends with.

When she re-met Autumn at OSU their freshman year, she found the first person who ever ticked all the boxes. Finding Birdy shortly after had felt like lightning striking twice.

Except tonight, when she was pissed at both of them.

"What did Lita have to say about it?" Birdy asked.

Bee punched her pillow into shape. "That Autumn is a social butterfly who needs to flap her wings."

"Is she wrong?" Birdy had learned to ask questions rather than outright agree with someone on the opposing team. It had been an important lesson for him to grasp before he'd been upgraded from boyfriend to husband. "Don't you think Autumn's used to having more than one friend? What about all those people she used to hang out with in LA?"

"Some friends," Bee sneered. "They all dropped her the second she moved back here. That girl she lived with didn't even invite her to her wedding!" She tugged a wrinkle out of the duvet. "I don't want Jo to hurt her. It's that old best-friend thing."

That untouchable thing, she mentally added. It was something that Autumn and Jo had that Bee couldn't reach: shared history. Sure, Autumn and Bianca had grown up in the same town, attended the same schools. But they'd been in different classes, different social clubs, cared about different school functions.

Jo had deep-sunk roots in Autumn's life. Bee couldn't trust that Jo wouldn't rip them all out again.

"I was there the first time, too," she said. "They were like the best friends in a toy commercial. Linked arms and finishing each other's—"

"Sandwiches?" Birdy asked innocently.

"Please don't be cute when I'm ranting." She frowned at him. "Autumn puts a lot more faith in Jo than I would. I don't want to see her get her hopes up."

"You gotta trust people, wifey," Birdy said with a yawn. He placed a clumsy peck on her cheek before disappearing behind his e-reader. "They won't all disappoint you."

Not using one of her many useless swimsuits to strangle him made Bianca the queen of restraint. She had an inbox full of disappointments as honeymoon refund confirmations continued to pour in.

Bee slept between long, imagined fights with Jo and Autumn. Twice she woke up, sure she could hear Lita yelling downstairs, only to find her snoring peacefully when she got up to check. The second time, Lita woke up long enough to swear at her for shuffling around like a hungry ghost.

By the time Bee made it to the shop Thursday afternoon, she had been up since predawn and was on her fourth hairstyle—she'd hated the first two and had briefly fallen asleep on the third. She walked into the tattoo parlor with her travel mug already half-empty and her hair up in a try-hard ponytail.

The Salty Dog sat atop the Park Place of the Sandy Point Monopoly board—right at the end of boardwalk—in the last building facing the beach next to the big parking lot. It was sunny inside, thanks to the picture windows at each station. Each black foam-padded chair faced the ocean lapping at the sand.

The navy had dropped Bee's Tito in Washington state. Once he was discharged, he and Lita moved a couple hours south to Sandy Point, where he'd set up an open-air stall on the other end of the boardwalk. The building they were in now was the culmination of the Boria family dream—beachfront body art, sending people back to shore with permanent memories of the sea.

Between the buzz of the needles and the crash of waves outside, the shop was certainly more relaxed than most of the other tattoo parlors Bianca scoped out.

"Morning, all!" Bee called as the warped door jangled behind her. She forced it to latch with a practiced tug.

There was a chorus of "Morning!" from around the shop, even though everybody knew it was afternoon.

Jogging up the stairs behind the counter, Bee could see that most of her artists were in a lull, waiting for either appointments or walk-ins. Except for Dez, grinding out an image on the leg of a customer with the salt-crusted hair of their usual clientele.

Kooks pay the bills was a classic Tito aphorism—less popular than the others because it sounded vaguely like an old-timey racial slur. Kooks were newbie surfers. The whole boardwalk catered to them.

Surfers came to town, braved the icy waves, and passed the Salty Dog on the way to their car. Nine times out of ten, they wandered in, rinsed off in the surf shower Lita had installed in the customer bathrooms, and got inked with whatever wave, surfboard, or *Live like you're dying* flash art the artists dreamed up.

The artists called the room upstairs the manager's office, but to Bee it would always be Tito and Lita's apartment. Even now that it was empty. It was a waste of money to have a room in the shop nobody utilized, but going into the upstairs room broke Bee's heart. The discolored patches of floor where her grandparents' furniture had been. The phantom cologne and hair pomade in the air. The broken rubber on the threshold that Lita had tripped over, leading to the fall down the stairs that changed all of their lives.

The only furniture left in the room was a shoji screen against the windows and a dusty oak desk with a tall red candle in a glass jar adorned with Our Lady of Guadalupe. From inside the desk drawer, Bee pulled out a fireplace lighter and lit the wick.

"Buenos días, Tito," she murmured to the flame. She imagined him greeting her in return, calling her muñeca and reminding her to sanitize the doorknobs.

She left the lighter and her purse in the drawer and retrieved her work tablet from its dock in the kitchenette.

"Who's got news?" she asked the artists as she descended the stairs. She climbed onto the too-tall chair behind the front counter and opened the appointment book on her tablet for the first time in ages. Piercing regulars went to Mo, while Bee took the rare walk-in.

Piercing wasn't a passion of hers, as evidenced by her personal lack of body jewelry other than in her ears. The only reason she had apprenticed with Mo was because it felt ridiculous to manage a business where she couldn't do *any* of the work herself.

As a Boria, you either needed the artistic talent to tattoo, like Tito and Bonnie, or the stomach to pierce and keep track of the money, like Lita and Bianca.

It was very different from the life of resorts and cozy inns Bee had imagined for herself while applying to grad school for hospitality management. If she were managing a B and B somewhere, she certainly wouldn't be counting down the hours to stabbing a big-ass needle in Johanna Freeman.

What was that? An upside.

Mo, the Salty Dog's key holder, wandered over, holding a steaming mug. They brushed their white-blond flop of hair to one eye. "Got a résumé. Some girl," they said, offhand. The building could be burning and Mo would saunter off with a mumble. It came in handy with the occasional nightmare customer. "Does permanent makeup. Told her we didn't want any."

"What?" Bianca dug through the single drawer under the counter. She scooped up the résumé and starting reading. "Why?"

"Lita said no makeup."

There was no one left in the shop who referred to Lita by her given name, Rosa. No one under fifty was allowed to. Mo and Cruz were both in their forties and the last artists hired by Tito. Bonnie had poached thirty-three-year-old Dez from a scuzzy Portland parlor. Lita had okayed Dede as an apprentice from her hospital bed, then yelled at Bianca for letting a future employee see her with her brain-surgery bandaging on. Still, the shop had needed Dede's young energy, and even Lita knew that nothing said young blood like dimple piercings and a Nicktoons chest piece.

"No face art, no makeup, no checks," Cruz said. "We know the rules."

"Nothing that goes bad the next day," chanted Dez and Dede from their shared station. Bee was almost surprised the guy getting tattooed didn't chime in.

Tito hadn't died as much as he'd scattered into sound bites all over Bee's life. It was just rare for it to be a sound bite she wanted to hear.

"Yes. Even so, don't run off people who might want to work here. They might also, you know, want tattoos," Bianca told the crew at large. "Friendly keeps people coming back for those longer sessions. Don't you all work on commission?"

She got to work with the usual pre-appointment sterilizing, guided by the chirps and bleeps of her smartwatch. All week, she had scrubbed, swabbed, and dusted to avoid being nervous today. She knew the store was clean. She knew everything was in its place. If she started re-cleaning, she'd get sweaty, and she had spent too long doing her hair to ruin it again. She spent the afternoon inventorying biohazard bags and boxes of gauze.

At exactly five, Jo appeared in the front window, where she was quickly met and hugged by Autumn.

Bee tried not to feel jealous. It would only prove Birdy right.

Sharing friends is normal, she told her pouting inner child. *Great, even. When the people you love are happy, you have more reasons to be happy, too.*

I'll believe it when I see it, said her inner child.

Brat, Bee chided herself.

The bell on the door clanged as Jo and Autumn stepped inside.

"Hey?!" the three of them said in the questioning soprano of three people unsure as to how cool the next hour was going to be. Autumn rushed in to give Bee a hug hello. Jo offered a handshake that was unsurprisingly firm.

"Thanks so much for fitting me in," Jo said, peering around the mostly empty shop. Somewhere in the distance, Mo's tattoo machine hummed. "Sorry, again, about TP-ing your tree."

"Of course, no problem," Bee said, bristling at the *again* when there had been no original apology. She didn't trust that this scene wasn't being directed by Autumn. Her friend's increasingly wide smile was too proud.

"We didn't have a chance to really catch up the other day," Jo continued. "I'm working a project while I'm in town."

"Like an ad campaign?" Bee asked. She'd never had a firm grasp of what Jo did in California. Deb Freeman said that Jo tweeted for a living, but that seemed at odds with her charcoal-gray slacks. Who wore business casual when they didn't have to?

"It's more like a photo essay," Jo said. "Based on a list Autumn and I made in high school—"

"I told you that we had a time capsule buried behind the dog-house on Main Street, didn't I?" Autumn asked Bee, whose brain sputtered for a moment over not being included in the *we* described.

"It'll help keep my social media active while I'm between jobs," Jo explained. "It looks bad for a social media strategist to abandon her personal accounts. Not very strategic. And more followers looks good on a résumé, as stupid as that sounds."

Oh, Bianca thought. *Unemployment boredom.*

That made more sense. Last year, when Autumn was adjusting

back to Sandy Point after Los Angeles, she'd been so bored—and so caffeinated—that she ended up ripping all the carpet out of her cottage in one night. Bee and Birdy had helped lift the stinky old shag into the dumpster behind Days, then drove the two hours with her to the closest Home Depot to pick out prefab flooring and a table saw. All in all, one weird Sunday.

"So, you want to put a picture of my house on your Instagram?" Bee asked Jo.

"Just the tree!" Jo said. "Nothing identifiable about the house. I'll give you right of refusal on the photo before it goes live."

"I guess?" Bee said, feeling as though she was being backed into a corner where she wasn't allowed to be mad anymore. "Why don't we get started with picking your jewelry?"

She pulled out the tray of ball-closure navel rings from the lit display counter. Various colorful cubic zirconias glittered up from the tray, in the shape of bows, crowns, flowers, and one seahorse eyeball.

"They're all surgical-grade metal," she assured Jo. "Nothing that'll turn your belly button green in the morning."

"Oh my gosh, didn't you have a mood ring that turned your finger green once?" Autumn asked Jo.

"Where did we win those? Oaks Park?" Jo gasped at the reclaimed memory. "I was desperate for a butterfly ring to tell me my own feelings."

"You could get a butterfly piercing to match," Bee said, pointing to a particularly ugly butterfly in the tray. It had sharp blue wings and wiggly antennae.

"I'm not as wild about bugs as I used to be," Jo said, appraising the tray. She aimed a finger at a plain silver-and-faux-diamond ring. "This one."

The three of them wandered over to the farthest chair in the shop. Outside the picture window, waves broke in green-blue sheets. The rhythm reminded Bee how to breathe.

"I've got my phone, and I am ready to take pictures," Autumn said. "I'll try to make them angular and arty like yours, Jo."

"Oh. No. I brought my camera. Can I show you how to—" Jo took her camera out of her giant purse and started clicking through settings.

Bee felt a guilty sort of relief as it became clear that Jo and Autumn didn't have an easy patter. No sentence finishing. No shorthand. Just the intensity of two people trying as hard as they could. Both of their rigid spines and unblinking eyes screamed, *LOOK AT HOW ACTIVELY I CAN LISTEN!* Like a first date happening on a prank show. Like best friends who didn't actually know each other.

Once Autumn had a basic understanding of how to line up the shot within the viewfinder grid, Jo shimmied down the chair and pulled her shirt up to the unsurprisingly gray cups of her bra.

Black latex gloves snapped into place, Bianca sterilized Jo's navel with a swab of surgical wash.

Jo's stomach jumped.

"I read online that tattoo parlors have topical anesthetic," she said, the quaver in her voice bouncing between the frosted-glass partitions that walled in Bee's station.

"For a six-hour tattoo sitting, maybe." Bee laughed. Then, seeing the tension in Jo's neck, she asked, "Are you not good with pain?"

"I'm not sure," Jo said stiffly.

Bee set a consoling hand on top of the goose bumps on Jo's shoulder. "Well, this is as good a way as any to find out. It would take longer to totally numb out your patch of skin here than it would to just pop the needle in and out. Quicker than getting your blood drawn, I promise."

"Bee almost became a phlebotomist," Autumn reassured Jo.

"Really? You wanted to draw blood all day?" Jo made a face. One big eyeball examined Bee. "Why didn't you?"

"My family said it was a waste of my valedictory honors to go to community college," Bee said tightly. The emotional scab itched. Her family had demanded she go off to college only to demand that she come right back home when she was done. "But if I hadn't gone to OSU, I wouldn't have run into Autumn in line for our hall's bathroom. She tried to pay me twenty bucks to cut in front of me."

"And you said no because you'd had three cups of cocoa." Autumn lowered the camera enough to smile at Bee. "Aww, I love that our friendship meet-cute includes our tiny bladders."

"And my super-cool bedtime cocoa habit." Bee made a mark where she wanted the exit hole of the piercing on Jo's belly.

Jo gulped. "You see a lot of tummies in here, Bianca?"

"Not really. The belly ring isn't as popular as it was ten years ago." The second the words were out of her mouth, she remembered herself and gasped. She clapped her hands over her mouth, willing the condescension back in.

Autumn's jaw dropped. "Bee!"

But Jo's body made an arc like a wave. Knees up, mouth open, she let out a laugh that drowned out the ocean. "Clap back, Bianca Boria-Birdy! Tell me how you really feel. Don't hold back."

"Oh my God, Johanna, I am so sorry," Bee said, her pulse wild even as Jo continued to snort. "We don't know each other well enough—and I would never treat a customer—"

"No, for real, I get it," Jo said, swiping tears from her eyes. "It's hella funny, though. Trust that it will be the insta caption. I just won't add that the literal owner of the shop said it."

Bee breathed again.

"It's okay, she's the manager," Autumn said, talking fast. "The shop is still owned by Lita."

"Oh, right," Jo said. Soberly, she added to Bee, "I heard about your grandfather. I'm really sorry."

"Thanks," Bee said, recentering herself in the memory of Tito. Inside the Salty Dog, she didn't have room to be, well, salty with customers.

She helped Jo readjust on the chair before reaching over to the instrument table. Wielding her forceps, she pinched Jo's belly-button skin.

"Breathe in." She waited for Jo's abs to contract before jabbing the needle through. The camera shutter clicked. "And out." Jo complied and Bee hit the needle with a cork. The ring slid easily into place. With more surgical-wash-soaked Q-tips, she swabbed the top and bottom of the ring.

"Done. And barely any blood," she told Jo. "Keep it clean and stay out of the ocean for at least six months. Maybe four if you wear a waterproof bandage."

Jo's nose wrinkled. "Learning to surf is next on my list. I guess I don't have to go in order...."

"The list just says *learn to surf*," Autumn said. "Maybe you could couch-surf!"

Jo started to laugh but clutched invisible pearls instead. "Ew. You're serious. Whose couch would I surf on? I'm miserable enough crashing in my old room."

Autumn's eyebrows went up; somehow she was uninjured. Bee

was sure if *she* ew-ed something Autumn said, there would be a fight. With Jo, she smiled extra hard. "I have a couch, Flo has a couch..." She tried to catch Bee's eye. Bianca refused to participate. Autumn clapped, changing tactics. "Or we could get a thrift store couch and race them down the hill whilst surfing them."

"The *whilst* really sells it," Jo said with a chuckle. She hopped down off the chair and adjusted her clothing. "But I need Flo's generosity for how many different booze milk shakes I'm gonna try. I'm unemployed, remember? My credit cards are already crying."

"Have you applied for anything in town?" Autumn asked Jo.

"At one of your many start-ups in need of a marketing manager?" Jo asked.

Bee snapped off her latex gloves. "Surfside Café needs a server."

"Oh yeah!" Autumn said. "They fired Burps When He Yawns guy!"

"Finally," Bee agreed. "He should not work morning shifts. That sound makes it impossible to eat eggs."

"I haven't hit food-service desperate yet," Jo said, in the tone of someone who had never in her life considered service of any kind. She had no idea what it was like to work elbow to elbow on an assembly line, making sure that every slumber party in town got its cheese pizza. "I don't think Sandy Point can afford me."

Anyone can afford you when you're unemployed, Bee thought. She chided herself for being uncharitable. Jo had gone to the same university as Olympians and Nobel laureates. She probably found her feces too fragrant for food service.

Whoops. Uncharitable again.

"Let me run and grab you a bottle of surgical wash and the aftercare sheet," Bee said. "I'll be right back."

She had started toward the downstairs storage closet when she saw Cruz behind the counter with the store's iPad. The landline receiver was tucked under his chin, the cord wound around his index finger. He was speaking in Spanish too quickly and too softly for Bianca to catch every word—he'd grown up fluent and she'd grown up with a mother who'd patently refused to learn—but she knew enough from Lita and Tito to understand:

"She's getting her hands dirty for once. Yeah, yeah, tomorrow Dez will bring in good money, but Pizza Girl has a—" He spotted Bee watching him and muttered a hurried goodbye.

"Who was that?" she asked, dreading that she already knew the answer. The only people who cared about the shop's inner workings *and* made fun of her for working in the quick-service industry were her own family.

Cruz immediately put his hands up. "Bianca. Did your friends leave already?"

"Why are you reading my calendar into the phone? Who are you reading my calendar to, Cruz?"

"No one, I swear. It's not what you're thinking—"

"Yeah? Did I get a new stalker? Are you reporting on me to a murderer or— Ha!" She boxed him out and pushed the History button on the phone. At the top of the call list was the name *LITA CELL. Speed dial 4.* "Cruz, how could you? She's not the boss anymore."

"She was curious about the appointments we had on file for the month," Cruz said, his shoulders coming up to hide his ears like he was afraid Bee might take a swing. He'd grown up with older sisters. "It wasn't supposed to rain this week! Lita's worried we might not get the pre-tourist-season bump that we normally do."

The pre-tourist-season bump that I could have brought in with new paint or a permanent-makeup artist? Bee mentally screamed. But it wasn't Cruz's fault that her grandmother was all Lita all the time.

"Really, Bee, I don't hear from her that often. She's too busy watching soaps. And, besides, Mo's her favorite. They're the one planning that flash event."

Dread rose in her stomach. "Flash event?"

"Red and white and blue designs going on sale, first come, first served." He searched for recognition on her face. "The Fourth of July thing?"

"The Fourth of July thing that they were planning to host in secret while I was on my honeymoon?"

Cruz's horror dawned as Bee whipped the phone out of her back pocket. Thumbs flying, she sent out a text to the Salty Dog employee thread—the one that *didn't* include her mother or grandmother.

> **BIANCA:** Memo: orders/ideas/events that come from any Boria but the one who signs your checks are NOT OFFICIAL and should not be treated as such.

She started to type *I know she's a scary old lady, but you can't follow her every whim!* but thought better of it. She would rather die than have someone accurately diagnose her hypocrisy, thanks.

Her brain tried to spin out an argument with Lita. Marching into her bedroom. Turning off the TV. Folding her arms with disapproval.

Lita would ask whose back that shop had been built on. Bianca, after all, was only acting manager. Lita was the owner. Lita would win. She always won. All Bee could do was try to hold back the drowning tide of demands and traditions.

She washed her hands in hot water, rinsed them in cold, then pressed the tips of her fingers under her eyes. She waited for her core temperature to cool from hopping mad to sociably chill.

Belatedly remembering to grab the bottle of wash, Bee came around the corner. Her ponytail bobbed cheerfully behind her, doing the lion's share of making her look more chipper than she felt.

"Good! You're back," Autumn said the moment Bianca turned the corner. "One of the next things on Jo's list is tackling the Sunday Sundae Surprise from Frosty's. And *I* thought, 'Duh, what better way to make new friends and re-meet old friends than to share, like, a metric shitload of ice cream?' This weekend! Florencio already said he was in—he's never had the Sunday Surprise either. Jo has to meet Birdy!" Autumn clutched Jo's forearm. "Birdy's the absolute best. You'll like him, I swear."

Bianca's instinct was to decline. With a laugh and a *Hell no*. She wasn't sure that she needed to spend more time in Autumn and Jo's friendship reboot. Or eat a sundae that was advertised in the Frosty's window as *a whale of a treat*. Besides, on weekends, she normally focused all of her attention on Lita.

Well. If Lita could have friends and secret plans, then so could Bianca.

COMPLETED ITEMS

- ✓ TP Bianca's house
- ✓ Perform onstage
- ✓ Get belly button pierced

TO BE COMPLETED

- ○ Surf the Point
- ○ Host a dinner party
- ○ Have a glitter fight
- ○ Try everything on the menu at ~~TGIFridays~~ Days
- ○ Do a keg stand
- ○ Play hide-and-seek in public
- ○ Break something with a sledgehammer
- ○ Climb the giant anchor on the boardwalk (and survive)
- ○ Get a high score at the boardwalk arcade
- ○ Eat the giant sundae at Frosty's
- ○ Redo the yearbook prank
- ○ Pose like a pinup girl
- ○ Get a pet
- ○ Learn an entire dance routine
- ○ Eat breakfast at midnight
- ○ Get stoned
- ○ Have a bonfire
- ○ Dig up the time capsule

six

JO

While her sister was hogging the upstairs bathroom, Jo grumbled her way down the stairs to the half-bath to wash her stomach again. She winced as the saltwater solution touched the open wound above her navel. Twenty-four hours into having a glittery belly button and Jo was still mostly on the fence about it. Possibly because she'd yet to take a cute after-photo. Self-portraits had never been her strong suit, but taking an attractive picture of her midriff in her childhood bedroom might prove impossible. She'd at least have to throw out the furry pillows first.

In the living room, Phil Freeman was stretched out on the armchair under the turtle painting watching some miserable Nordic crime drama with a landscape not unlike Sandy Point's. Apparently the Surf & Saucer closed after lunch, making both of Jo's parents almost unbearably present.

"You're going out again tonight?" he asked.

"Eden's going to help me check something off my list at Point High," Jo answered vaguely. She hadn't figured out how much input she should let her parents have about the Throwback List. They subscribed to her social media, so they saw the posts and wondered aloud about them over shared meals. Jo brushed off questions about it. Part of the list's appeal was that it was separate from life inside her family home.

"I hope it's not punching more holes into either of your bodies," Phil said with a huh-huh chuckle that meant *We both know this is no joke*. He crossed his ankles and tilted his head toward Jo. "The day you were born, the doctor assured us that you were good on holes. Didn't mention you needing any new ones at all."

Jo refused to touch the sore spot above her belly button. She didn't say, *Dude, even Beyoncé has a navel ring*. She did say, "Well, Dad, doctors rarely discuss how the patriarchy shapes beauty norms with new parents, but we could deep-dive into how my piercing will affect my personal sexual worth, if you want?" She flashed him a full-teeth smile, her own silent *That wasn't a joke either*.

Marching up the stairs, she called, "Eden! Let's go!" before finding her sister slouched moodily in the bathroom doorway. Like Jo, she wore head-to-toe shades of black. Unlike Jo, most of her outfit had come from the Hot Topic website. Her beanie had a Jack Skellington face on it. Less stealthy than Jo had hoped for.

"Why are you being mean to Dad?" Eden asked.

Jo rolled her eyes until she felt like her optic nerve was in actual danger of snapping. "I'm not mean. He won't talk to me like a person."

"No..." Eden said, cocking her head in the exact same way their father had. "He's talking to you like your dad?"

Jo exhaled through her nose. "I haven't had parents in a long time, Eden. It's not like riding a bike."

"You've always had parents, you weirdo," Eden scoffed. "You don't become an orphan when you go to college."

Reaching out and smushing her sister's cheeks together into a chipmunk pucker, Jo crooned, "Oh, my sweet summer child. Yes. You really fucking do." She released her sister's squirming face. "Are you ready to go?"

Eden grabbed a bulging backpack from her bedroom. Less enthusiastic than before being face-smushed, she said, "Ready."

Jo took the stairs down two at a time, practicing her quiet pranking walk. Eden clattered behind her.

"Home by nine," Phil called after them.

Jo skidded to a stop with the doorknob in her hand. "What the—"

"Not you," he said. He pointed at Eden. "But her, yes."

"*This* he's strict about," Jo muttered, once there were two closed doors between her mouth and her father's ears. The air inside the Mini Cooper was frigid. She blew into her hands to warm them before touching the steering wheel. She prayed that it wouldn't unexpectedly rain for a second time this week. "The pig-fucking TV show is political commentary but hanging with me is 'home by nine.'"

"I help open the store on Saturdays," Eden said, buckling her seat belt. "I overslept *one time* and he's been the most paranoid about it since."

Jo turned the ignition over, glancing at her sister in disbelief. When she'd been a high school senior, she put in at least twenty-five hours a week at Freeman Fine Arts, going in every day after school and serving canapés at exhibit-opening galas. "You only work one day a week?"

"Saturdays. Mom needs to do all the accounting. Otherwise it comes home."

"So what?"

"Sooo, work stays at work?" Eden said.

How am I even related to you three? Jo thought.

Point High was dark out front, but the parking lot was packed for softball opening day. The stadium lights were on but invisible against the golden-hour light. The bleachers were noisy.

Jo broke into a flop sweat as she and Eden stepped away from the sounds of the game. Striding into the dimly lit Point High main building like she belonged there, Jo tried to comfort herself by remembering what Autumn had told her as they'd game-planned this in the boardwalk parking lot yesterday—as long as she and Eden were in and out of the building before the end of the softball game, they should beat the custodian setting the security alarm.

Jo was a lot more nervous than she had been TP-ing Bianca's house. But less nervous than she had been with Bianca's forceps yanking at her skin.

Keeping that in perspective, she rolled her shoulder back and prepared to *redo the yearbook prank.*

Back in the day, all the student clubs pulled end-of-the-year pranks. Usually it was a harmless excuse to sneak around school grounds in the middle of the night. Jo's senior year, the football field had been so densely sporked that it crossed the invisible line between morale booster and grass-murdering nuisance. All school events were put on hold until the pranksters came forward. It fully soured the concept of pranking for Jo. She shut down the yearbook committee plan to move the vice principal's office into the center of the quad.

A choice she would rectify tonight.

The administrative offices were at the far end of the main building's rectangle, where all the windows and doors faced dark classrooms across the quad. The white cinder-block hallways echoed the Freeman girls' footsteps.

"Here," Eden said, stopping abruptly in front of an office door with a *vice principal* nameplate.

The original prank ten years ago had been aimed at Mr. Dawson—and the infamous shot-glass collection he kept mounted above his desk—but Autumn had informed Jo that he'd retired.

"There's a new vice principal this year," Autumn had assured Jo after her piercing appointment. They'd stood in the parking lot for twenty minutes, caught up in talking about ideas for the newly dubbed Throwback List. "She doesn't have a lot of stuff, and her office windows open onto the quad, so you'll only have to take the big pieces through the building. It's even easier than the original plan, I swear!"

Jo would have been far less nervous with a staff member present. She invited Autumn along, but Autumn was needed across campus at the PTA concession stand at the softball game. Because Autumn was a member of the PTA.

"And the vice principal isn't my boss, per se," Autumn had told Jo. "But she's not *not* my boss, you know?"

Jo was in no position to ask Autumn to put her job in danger. Hanging out twice in a week had been a nice surprise, but Jo didn't want Autumn to think she was being needy. Or competing with Bianca.

"It's unlocked!" Eden squeaked excitedly as she swung open the door.

The two of them stepped inside the underdressed office. There were plain white walls. A metal desk faced by two chairs. A filing cabinet. A tall rubber-tree plant that could have been real or fake. An ancient computer desktop. A short red bookcase. Jo aimed her Nikon around, making sure to get every detail.

Eden tossed her backpack aside and went behind the desk. She shoved open the large windows. The evening air was sharp and cold. Jo pulled her hat down over her ears. Eden picked up the computer chair and heaved it out the open window, into the quad.

The sound of the chair casters clattering on the pavement outside ended in a crash.

She beamed. "I've been looking forward to that."

"For fuck's sake, Eden," Jo said. "It's a prank, not a smash and grab!"

"The shortest distance between two points is a straight line!" Eden pointed out the window at the flagpole in the center of the quad where the chair had overturned. "And it landed perfectly center!"

Eden started clearing the desk while Jo started scooping books onto the floor. The covers were emblazoned with buzzwords like *Restorative Justice*, *Educational Leadership*, and *Principalship*, a word Jo had never seen before. The only two nonacademic texts stood out, their black-and-white covers nearly identical: Abby Wambach's memoir and Megan Rapinoe's. Jo couldn't stop herself from pulling down the latter. Stumbling upon gay nonfiction in the vice principal's office was just too exciting. It was the polar opposite of Mr. Dawson's horrid *I Got Crabs in Boston* shot glass.

"You're dead-ass reading right now!" Eden gasped. "Help me get this desk outside. Unless you want me to try to push it out the window, too?"

Jo set the book aside.

The metal desk was lighter than it looked—hooray—but awkwardly wide. They carried it at a scurry, down the hallway, hissing curses as the metal legs repeatedly clipped their shins.

Outside, they set the desk down beneath the flagpole, site of so many pep rallies. Eden righted the chair and slid it neatly into place. They moved the bookcase and chairs through the window. Eden carried the rubber-tree plant and desk lamp in one go.

But no matter what they did, they couldn't move the filing cabinet. It was too heavy, the metal sides impossible to grip. With the sisters' power combined, they could only manage to lift it off the floor an inch.

"Fuck." Jo shook the filing cabinet until the metal sides thundered. "We can't leave *one* piece behind! That ruins it! The only difference between a prank and a misdemeanor is *all the furniture* makes it outside."

"Start moving the floor stuff outside," Eden said. "I'll get a dolly from the attendance office for the filing cabinet."

Jo pulled the hat off her head and blotted her hairline with the satin lining. "Why would there be a dolly in the attendance office?"

"It's how they move the paper boxes," Eden said. "I used to be an office aide. Trust me."

"The last time you told me to trust you, I ended up getting thrown off campus."

"Yeah, but that was personal between you and Miss Kelly. Now that you've made up, do you think she'll let you do headshots? I don't like the ones we took on Tuesday."

"Eden. The dolly?"

"Fine, but I'm going to ask again later." Eden ran out into the hallway and around the corner.

Jo got all the books back on the small case and the computer monitor situated outside. She checked the Nikon reference photos. Adjusted the desk lamp's position.

As the sun started to fall, turning the sky pink, Eden rattled into view with an ancient brown metal hand truck with *PHS Office* written down the side in gold Sharpie.

"You're a hero," Jo said.

"You know my Venmo," Eden said.

They rocked the filing cabinet onto the dolly and pushed it out into the hallway. The cabinet rattled the whole way, metal on metal on metal. Jo steered it to the right of the desk, right next to the rubber plant. The hand truck scraped against the pavement unpleasantly as Jo pulled it away.

"Someone's coming!" Eden hissed.

"Remember the plan!" Jo whispered back.

"Right!" Eden yanked off her backpack, grabbed something inside, and thrust it at Jo. A visitors' sticker.

Jo slapped it over her heart, the scarlet apple printed on it garish against her formerly covert outfit. She could hear the footsteps approaching now, too, echoing up the hallway.

Before Jo could stop her, Eden leaped into the nearest cement planter, camouflaging herself behind a skinny sapling. Feeling remarkably like the last person to dibs a seat in the living room again, Jo was caught in the center of the quad. Nowhere to run. Nowhere to hide.

As the footsteps rounded the corner, she sat in the desk chair.

Eden swung the Nikon's lens, so that Jo distantly heard the paparazzi buzz of burst mode. And then Jo's first love stepped into the quad. With the cool blue eyes of a Siamese cat and a short asymmetrical haircut, her lips gave the slightest quirk as she said, "Hello, Johanna."

Wren Vos. Here in front of her. In a sweater vest. With a tie. If there had been elbow patches, Jo's underpants would have no choice but to up and quit.

More than anything, she wished that she hadn't chosen to wear a hat today. Later, she would burn this glorified bonnet.

"It is good to see you," Wren said, stepping forward and catching Jo's one hand with two. Somehow, the warmth of both Wren's hands on her felt more intimate than a hug.

Her palms started to sweat.

The back pocket of Jo's pants buzzed. Prying her eyes away from Wren—and her brown leather brogue-trim boots—Jo checked the text.

AUTUMN: 😄 SURPRISE! It's a mid-prank prank!

Wren turned her approving face to Eden. "Thanks for the heads-up, Eden."

"You're welcome, Ms. Vos," Eden said without taking her eyes off her older sister. Jo almost expected her to start making kissy faces at them, like she did when she was eight.

"Ms. Vos?" Jo cleared her throat, willing herself to look less stunned. "You *work* here?"

Wren's eyes sparkled. "Whose office do you think you're in?"

Jo looked around: the leadership library, the Abby Wambach memoir, the color-coordinated stack of Post-its. She hopped out of the desk chair, her face and neck flushed.

"Eden." She gave a panicked giggle. Oh no. If she started nervous laughing, she would never be able to stop. "You didn't tell me Wren was your vice principal."

"I didn't recognize her at first! It's not like they introduce principals by their first name," Eden protested. "I remembered Rapunzel hair. And the skateboard." She passed Jo the Nikon. "Don't you dare get rid of the pictures. I'm going to go out to the softball concession stand. Miss Kelly said I could have a Coke for helping double-cross you." She waved behind her. "Bye, Ms. Vos."

Wren inclined her head. "Bye, Eden."

Since Jo had moved back, it seemed like everywhere she turned, people were appearing in their next evolution. Autumn and her new teeth. Bianca and her flawless makeup. Her parents and their wrinkles. Eden not being in elementary school.

But Jo was blindsided by new, twenty-seven-year-old Wren. It was almost impossible to reconcile the short-haired, semi-suited woman in front of her with the sixteen-year-old skate punk Jo had fallen in love with.

The daughter of surfers, Teen!Wren rebelled by being firmly terrestrial. She wore Vans instead of Birks and rode a longboard with slick ease. She dressed in her brothers' hand-me-downs and beat all of their soccer records in one season.

Jo had fallen in love with her on sight. For months, during honor society meetings, Jo would lose hours just trying to glimpse the title of the books in Wren's pocket.

One day, a book fell out. *Orlando* by Virginia Woolf. Jo replaced it with *Passing* by Nella Larsen, which she happened to be reading. Wren said nothing for two days, then returned the book to Jo in the cafeteria and spoke to her directly for the first time. "So. What else are you reading?"

Jo traded her Maya Angelou for Sylvia Plath, Amy Tan for Steinbeck, and, regrettably, Ayn Rand for more Ayn Rand. Their own private—and admittedly pretentious—book club. When Wren had shown up with a book too large for her cargo pocket—*Fingersmith* by Sarah Waters—she traded it to Jo for a kiss before longboarding away.

They had gone from quiet acquaintances to girlfriends without pausing to learn each other's last name. Wren didn't risk losing things she wanted. Slowing down was for the weak.

You have to stop staring, Jo reminded herself. *It's making you look thirsty as fuck.*

She sat down on the edge of the desk, hands folded between her knees. "I can't believe you work here. You hate it here!"

Wren nodded, her hands tucked in her pockets. "True. I did my time as the token lesbian of Sandy Point. But I'm the youngest vice principal in the state. Not that it's a competition." A dimple appeared in her right cheek. "And, unless you want to fail, you can't be principal without being a VP. So. Here I am."

Jo smiled dazedly. "Here you are."

"I don't live here, of course," Wren said. "I commute from Forest Grove. This is around the time I'm normally packing up to leave, but Autumn proposed sticking around to see you. All I had to do was put my sensitive documents away. Didn't you find the office oddly neat? I thought it gave the whole thing away."

"I'm not an accomplished vandal," Jo admitted.

Wren sat down beside her. Jo caught of a whiff of juniper and beeswax and thyme—a scent as perfectly androgynous as Wren herself.

"This is the part where you pull a bottle of scotch out of your desk drawer," Jo prompted.

"Johanna," Wren said in the same tone she would have said *Oh, you.* "I'm an administrator, not Don Draper."

"Your shoes say otherwise."

"Thank you for noticing." Wren tapped the side of her foot against Jo's. Jo's pulse tripled. "So. How was Stanford?"

Wren had been the only other person in Sandy Point who had ever shared Jo's obsession with getting out. The battle plan in the map journal was based on Wren's template: honors classes, extra credit, community service, anything that could sway college admissions offices or scholarship boards.

They broke up when Wren left for college, the year age difference insurmountable. The few emails Jo got from Wren's college account were braggy and dismissive and had the overall vibe of *You had to be there but! you never will be.* In hindsight Jo was sure that was how she sounded writing from her dorm, too.

"Stanford was good," she told Wren. "The internship program pretty much changed my life. I ended up majoring in communications because of it."

"Communications?" Wren snorted. "Really?"

Jo glanced bashfully at her shoes. "It's more useful in public relations than an English degree. How was Reed?"

"Glorious. The most intellectually stimulated I've ever been. More heroin use than you'd expect."

"White boys will find opioids," Jo said.

Wren swept her hair back. In the pink light, her pale cheekbones glowed like moonstone. "Oh, here, when Autumn told me you were coming, I put this in the top drawer as a clue."

"You think I'm a snoop?" Jo asked as Wren leaned over and pulled open a drawer.

"I would have snooped," Wren said.

"I would have snooped if I'd known it was you," Jo admitted.

Wren handed Jo a grainy picture. Beneath dozens of fingerprint smudges, younger versions of Jo and Wren sat at a cafeteria table with a handwritten sign that read *Join the Best of the Best: National Honor Society!* Jo had braces and curly bangs. Wren had hair to her hips and an oversize *Zero Skateboards* hoodie. Their arms were hooked together, surely holding hands under the table. They seemed oblivious to the rest of the club gathered around and behind them—Chad Pendleton blinking, seniors whose names Jo had forgotten throwing up offensive fake gang signs, Bianca Boria with her hair in a simple French braid sitting primly in a plain white sweatshirt.

"Look at us!" Jo cackled, kicking her heels against the desk. "We were so scrubby! Who let me leave the house like that?"

"You're adorable," Wren said, reaching over to point at the photo. "Look. Your braces match your flip-flops."

Jo snorted. "The height of fashion."

"The new club found it in the library and lost their minds," Wren explained. "Now students keep challenging me to skate. They call me Principal Betty. And let me tell you: Skate tricks are much harder than I remembered."

"I wouldn't know. I never had the balance for it," Jo said. She handed the picture back. She would have loved to add it to the Throwback List, caption it something like *These baby gays would hate my current haircut.* But she was sure that Wren would never agree to it. Bianca Boria-Birdy probably wouldn't love it either.

"You aren't working right now," Wren said. It wasn't a question. Jo wondered if Autumn had filled her in or if Wren just still knew her well enough to assume.

"My company was acquired, but I wasn't part of the deal," Jo said. Quick like a Band-Aid this time. It helped. "I'm at my parents' house until I find a new job."

Wren considered this with a purse of her lips. "Back in California? It must be a pain to schedule job interviews from here. Unless you particularly love long drives?"

"I'm not looking to stay here. Obviously—" Jo said.

"Obviously," Wren agreed.

"—but I don't have anywhere in particular in mind. I'm applying mostly in Portland right now."

"How's your LinkedIn profile?" Wren asked.

"I've been tweaking it," Jo lied, guiltily flashing back to sitting on her bed at two in the morning deep into a mindless scroll of new bullet journal layouts. "I worked for one company for a long time, so it's hard to make all of my different promotions stand out."

Wren clapped her hands on her thighs. The sound made Jo's mouth snap shut. "I'm sure you've got it handled. But if you want another pair of eyes on it, let me know. We could grab dinner or drinks. Isn't it bizarre that we've never had a drink together? We mastered so many other milestones."

Jo's tongue stuck to the inside of her cheek. "You could slum it with me and the townies at Days sometime."

Wren's forehead creased. "I actually prefer my alcohol unblended, if you can believe it." She leaned over, grabbing a pen and paper from the drawer. She jotted something and handed it to Jo, her fingers warm and soft. "Here. I still have yours."

Looking down, Jo found Wren's phone number on an ice-blue Post-it. Under it, an address in a different zip code.

Wren smiled at her. "Why don't you visit me in civilization? We have coffee shops and bars that don't serve ice cream."

And, just like the old days, Jo would have followed her anywhere.

COMPLETED ITEMS

- ☑ TP Bianca's house
- ☑ Perform onstage
- ☑ Get belly button pierced
- ☑ Redo the yearbook prank

TO BE COMPLETED

- ☐ Surf the Point
- ☐ Host a dinner party
- ☐ Have a glitter fight
- ☐ Try everything on the menu at Days
- ☐ Do a keg stand
- ☐ Play hide-and-seek in public
- ☐ Break something with a sledgehammer
- ☐ Climb the giant anchor on the boardwalk (and survive)
- ☐ Get a high score at the boardwalk arcade
- ☐ Eat the giant sundae at Frosty's
- ☐ Pose like a pinup girl
- ☐ Get a pet
- ☐ Learn an entire dance routine
- ☐ Eat breakfast at midnight
- ☐ Get stoned
- ☐ Have a bonfire
- ☐ Dig up the time capsule

AUTUMN: Event reminder! This Sunday we will be taking on one of Sandy Point's most infamous challenges: Frosty's Sunday Sundae Surprise ! If we finish the whole thing in less than an hour, it's free!

BIANCA: And if we don't finish it?

AUTUMN: It's $50.

BIANCA: AUTUMN BREEZE KELLY

AUTUMN: We just won't fail! Winning is cheap!

seven

AUTUMN

"You and Wren went out?!" Autumn's shout carried all the way out to sea through the misty morning air.

Jo hid inside the collar of her coat as they continued up the boardwalk. "Not immediately! I had my sister with me, remember? Last night, I drove out to Forest Grove so we could go to her neighborhood bar. We caught up. Looked at my résumé. She made fun of me for having my Instagram followers on it. Then I drove home."

In the window of the Surf & Saucer Tearoom, Jo's mom waved.

"Ugh, mortifying," Jo said. She hurried away from her parents' shop, her footfalls hollow on the planks.

Autumn waved back to Deb enthusiastically over her shoulder before she caught up with Jo. She had always liked Phil and Deb Freeman. Their marriage was part of why she hadn't felt bone-deep shocked by her own parents' divorce. The Kellys may have been married for longer than the Freemans, but they could never have run a business together. After family vacations, they'd retreat to opposite ends of town—Mom to the craft store next to Fred Meyer,

Dad fishing in the cove. They were much better friends now that they saw each other sparingly.

Past the tourist center; the arcade; and Airborne, the wind-chime-and-kite store, at the farthest end of the boardwalk, where the wooden planks met the concrete of Main Street, there were the ice cream parlor and the anchor statue.

Staring up at the anchor's sharp angle, Jo adjusted the strap of her bag, making the camera tripod inside waggle against her shoulder. "How the fuck do people get up there without falling?"

"Balance," Autumn said, and her brain helpfully added a chime from *Sunday in the Park with George,* setting off a low-level ear-worm. She tipped her head back to look up at the anchor towering over the "blue, purple, yellow, red water." Including the cement stand it was built into, it was easily eight feet tall. "I used koala arms. I did a sort of hug-scoot-hug-scoot thing. But I was twelve and at peak monkey-bar strength, if you remember. Now." She gave a suggestive shimmy. "Tell me exactly how I pranked you into what the kids call 'backsliding.'"

Jo picked an invisible piece of lint from her wool sleeve. "We didn't have sex. I didn't even see her apartment. And there's no way the kids use slang from *How I Met Your Mother.*"

Autumn shook Jo's arm. "Oh my God, remember when we cared about *How I Met Your Mother?*"

"It's how I learned TV could betray me," Jo said. She wrapped her silky straight hair around her neck like a scarf. "Should we wait out here?"

"Too cold." Autumn shivered. "Let's go inside and order ice cream."

Leaving the statue behind, they went into Frosty's Franks & Treats.

Intended for sunnier weather and outdoor seating, Frosty's was the smallest restaurant on the boardwalk. Generally people went in for a scoop and a hot dog to eat as they walked down the boardwalk or up the beach. Inside there were only two tables and a large corner booth held for special occasions.

Taking down the Sunday Sundae Surprise counted as a special occasion at Frosty's. Especially in March.

"Anything for Phil and Deb's girl!" crowed the woman behind the counter, whom Autumn had only ever known as Mrs. Frosty, leading to a small period of her childhood when she and Flo believed that the owner of the ice cream shop was a cannibalistic snowman.

As Jo and Autumn slid into the corner booth, the door swept in a rush of nose-wrinklingly cold air. The Birdys walked in with Florencio. Birdy wore plaid shorts. Bee and Flo both wore hats, although Flo's wool beanie wasn't as high fashion as Bee's red beret and glossy black bumper bangs.

Bee overdressed when she was anxious. Today, her lipstick matched her hat, coat, and gloves, but not her shoes. Social anxiety of about seven out of ten, if Autumn had to guess. Fairly normal for Bee away from home, especially with Lita left behind.

"We did ride over together," Flo said as the three of them approached the booth. "But not in the order you'd expect."

"Hey, is it weird that my wife and Coach Kelly need so much alone time?" Birdy joked, scratching his head. Bee smacked him in the chest.

"Birdy, this is Jo Freeman," Bee said in a tone of voice that Autumn recognized as her friend's Mean Mommy tone. It meant *Best behavior in front of new people, please.* Autumn got Mean Mommy'd whenever she and Bee drank together and they started disagreeing about what constituted an inside voice. Those disagreements got shouty when clear liquor was involved—as they learned the hard way while crashing Birdy's bachelor party. The smell of vodka still made Autumn feel like she and Bee were going to rumble.

"Nice to meet you," Birdy said, reaching over the napkin dispenser to shake Jo's hand before pulling a chair up to the end of the table. "Dr. Bobby Birdy. Call me Birdy."

"Ms. Johanna Freeman." Jo smiled. "Call me Jo."

"Did you guys already order?" Flo asked, taking the seat next to Jo. He craned his neck to see the chalkboard menus above the counter. "I'm kind of feeling a hot dog."

"We ordered a family-size sundae, Coach," Jo said. "It comes with every flavor of ice cream."

"That's still zero dogs. The sign says treats *and* franks, Freeman!" Flo said.

"I wish they had coffee," Bee said with a shiver as she tugged off her gloves and stuck them in her pocket. "This is the earliest I have ever consumed ice cream."

"Ice cream brunch sounded whimsical at the time!" Autumn protested. "You all agreed to it!"

"It sounded whimsical at the time," Birdy mused, knocking his knuckles against the table.

"Sounds like a Lifetime movie," Jo said. *"It Sounded Whimsical at the Time: The Autumn Kelly Story."*

"Lindsay Lohan can play Autumn," Flo said.

"Rude! You know I'm an Ellie Kemper type." Autumn tossed her auburn hair over one shoulder. "A casting director once called me Kimmy Schmidt Goes to Yoga. It was...not a compliment."

"You were too good for Hollywood, sweets," Bee assured her.

Florencio turned his attention to Jo, beside him. "Alfie Jay wanted to know if you'd take pictures for the Days menu."

"The karaoke guy wants pictures of the food?" Jo asked.

"He's the owner," Florencio explained.

"He owns the restaurant and runs karaoke?" Jo asked.

"And he's our father's wife's ex-husband," Florencio said.

"And sometimes my mechanic," Autumn said.

"Didn't you ride a bike here?" Jo asked.

"The restaurant used to be Alfie Jay's Fridays before he lost his TGI-lawsuit," Flo explained to Jo, diverting attention from Autumn's continually dead Saturn. "He liked the pictures you tagged on Instagram. I told him you were planning to try every-thing, and he said he'd pay you to shoot the menu."

"I mean, I totally need the work, but I just put a bright back-ground behind everything. It's a basic food-blog trick," Jo said with a shrug. "I don't have actual food-staging experience."

"Then teach yourself how to do it! Use the internet! You're already taking pictures of everything you order," Autumn said enthusiastically. She loved seeing Jo's feed starting to fill up with glamour shots of town. No one ever took pretty pictures of Sandy Point, unless they were aiming at the ocean. The Throwback List had already showcased the art on the walls of the Salty Dog and the seafoam-green trim of Point High against the yellow sky. Glimpses of Sandy Point that used to exist only in Autumn's memory.

Jo started to scoot Florencio out of the booth. "That reminds me. I should set up the tripod. I got distracted chatting when I'm supposed to take pictures."

"Chatting was the point!" Autumn said, motioning for her to sit. She didn't want Jo to start hiding behind her camera when there were people around. Their whole senior year, after Wren went off to college, poor heartbroken Jo took pictures instead of talking to people. "It's totally okay to get distracted by friendship."

"Encouraged, even," Florencio said. Turning the full wattage of his smile on Mrs. Frosty as she processional-marched a punch bowl full of dessert to their table, he asked, "Ma'am, would you mind taking our picture so we can dig into our cold brunch?"

The resulting photos got a grudging approval from Jo. After ticking judgmentally through the camera roll twice, she turned the camera around to the table. "This is the post. Everyone's eyes are open and you can see the water behind us. I'll frame it out with a crop. Bianca, do you want me to tag your personal account or the Salty Dog's? Views have been really steady since I got some pity reposts from a few influencer contacts."

"I'd rather direct your thousands of followers at the shop, not me," Bee said, touching her roll of bangs as though it could have budged an inch.

"Do you think Frosty's has an Instagram?" Jo asked.

Bee shook her head. "They don't even have a website. The Salty Dog is one of the only places on the boardwalk that does. Other than your parents, obviously."

"This town is run worse than a roadside attraction," Jo said, stuffing the camera back in her bag. "Seriously. On my drive up from California, I saw a cement dinosaur with more current marketing tactics. I'm so tempted to just gift every business on the boardwalk a website with their address, phone number, and open hours. They can't expect everyone to walk up and check their business hours on the door. That's absurd."

"That's what people do," Autumn said. "It is a small town."

"A small town that relies on tourist revenue to exist," Jo huffed. "Some people like to plan their trips. Meals included."

"People end up here on their way somewhere else," Flo said. "Usually the *Goonies* house."

Birdy ducked his head and raised his hand. "Guilty."

Jo lifted her spoon in cheers. Everyone fumbled to keep up.

"To the list," toasted Jo.

"To friends," Autumn added.

"To life," said Florencio, proving that he did listen to his sister with a *Fiddler on the Roof* reference.

"L'chaim," said Birdy with a grin. As a gregarious giant, he had, of course, been enlisted to play Tevye back in Sweet Apple, Ohio.

"Well, if everyone is toasting..." Bee muttered before lifting her spoon the highest. "To free ice cream if we finish it within the hour."

Five long metal spoons clinked together.

Jo took the inaugural scoop, between the mint-chocolate-chip mountains and the hot-fudge river. Her lashes fluttered closed in decadent ecstasy. "This is a fucking delicious mistake."

Bee stiffened. "Food doesn't need moralistic judgments. That can be triggering to people, thanks."

Jo's eyes popped open. "Oh. No, sorry. Not calories. The hot fudge is going to melt everything way before our hour limit is up."

"Eat all the hot components first!" Autumn said, heaping her spoon with warm caramel and letting it ribbon onto her tongue.

Drawing the spoon out of her mouth, Jo examined the wall. "I'm almost positive that this is the exact same color my parents painted the inside of their house."

"It's probably the same paint," Bee said, also looking up at the wall. "Your mom and the owner's wife play Bunco together."

Jo looked baffled. "What the fuck is Bunco?"

"D and D for moms," Florencio said.

"Bingo with binge drinking," Autumn clarified. Some of the PTA moms played in the monthly Bunco night at Surf & Saucer. Autumn had yet to earn an invitation. Pat Markey definitely got to go. She always bragged about the crab dip she brought.

Bee shuddered. "It would take something way more fun than a dice game to convince me to party with the wine moms."

"More fun like death?" Jo asked.

Birdy scrunched up his face. "Is Apples to Apples still hot?"

"Two minutes in before you outed yourself as the oldest, Birdy!" Autumn teased.

"It's true." Birdy spread his hands in a shrug. "I didn't have a cell phone in high school. I'm old."

"Prehistoric," Bee joked.

Birdy put his arm around her, planting a kiss on her temple. Bee smiled but wriggled away to reach for a scoop of Marshmallow Fluff, which struck Autumn as odd. Normally Bee and Birdy were annoyingly affectionate whenever Lita wasn't around to shame them for it. Then again, if the group ended up paying for the sundae, their contribution would come out of the same bank account. Bee could get weird about nonessential spending.

"So, Jo," Birdy rhymed, carving a divot into the cheesecake side. "Bianca said you used to date Autumn and Flo's new boss."

"Not *my* boss," Florencio said. "I answer to the athletic director."

"But Wren is *a* boss," Autumn clarified. "She could boss at any moment. Her main focus is students, not staff."

Jo lowered her lashes, focusing on scooping a perfect bite. "Wren was my first girlfriend."

"First love," Autumn added.

"First everything." Jo hid her face behind the sundae. "I haven't heard from her in years. Hadn't."

Autumn stage-whispered to the rest of the table, "They went out last night."

Jo's lips curved up into the bashful smile of the seriously smitten. Autumn's plan was totally working.

Not that it had started as a plan. It started out as Pat Markey throwing her under the bus in front of the vice principal.

The staff lounge was at its busiest before the first bell as everyone crowded around the Keurig and teakettle, shaking out sugar packets and stuffing dollar bills into the Sunshine Committee jar when the French-vanilla creamer ran low.

Wren and Autumn hadn't been super close in high school—Jo had always been between them to keep conversation afloat, to connect the dots of their disparate interests—but working together for the last few months had forged a new bond, a double knot of acquaintanceship that felt almost like being friends. Wren rarely made it out of meetings in time for lunch, so they tried their best to catch up as they dressed their coffees.

Early Wednesday morning, Pat had sidled up to the two of them and said to Autumn: "I know that Eden Freeman didn't follow protocol for having her sister join us on campus, but I hope you will reach out to Jo and invite her back to finish taking headshots for the Senior Showcase. The students were so looking forward to their photo shoot with her when you ran her out on a rail."

Autumn had opened her mouth to protest that Pat had all but *told* her to send Jo away, but Wren spoke first, her face pert with interest.

"Johanna was here?"

When Autumn mentioned Jo taking down a list of old goals,

she had seen Wren's *teeth* in a smile. Normally Wren saved loud facial expressions for sports and academic progress.

That toothy smile was a declaration of love, Autumn was sure of it.

Wren and Jo had been bonkers about each other from the moment they met. Like Romeo and Juliet without the fourth or fifth act or Maureen and Joanne in *Rent* with two Joannes. The couple had been true high-school-sweetheart material, except for the single year between them. When Wren left for college, Jo had been absolutely disconsolate for most of twelfth grade.

If Autumn knew anything about Jo, she already had a pro/con list about staying in Sandy Point. Probably on the whiteboard in her bedroom.

Wren would be a big check in the pro-town column.

"It wasn't a date or anything," Jo protested. "We worked on my résumé. She reworded some of my LinkedIn profile. And she let me borrow a book so that we could discuss it the next time we get together."

"So there is a next time!" Autumn exclaimed.

"That is exactly what I think dating Wren Vos would be like," Bianca said, adjusting her beret to a jauntier tip. "Homework. That's how she ran the honor society, too."

"Homework is Jo foreplay," Autumn said.

Jo threw her head back, letting loose one of her Disney-villain laughs. "I've been gone for almost a decade. How can you still read me to filth?"

"Um, best friends *forever*." Autumn giggled, poking her friend in the ribs. Out of the corner of her eye, she could see Bianca turn away. She imagined tearing herself down the center, leaving two Autumns to converse at full speed with both friends without having to leave anyone out. Or bursting into a song that both Jo and Bee could sing, too, something that could convey all of their feelings in three scripted parts.

Offstage, no one ever fell into perfect, unrehearsed harmony. Jo was mostly tone-deaf anyway.

"You should have invited Wren along today," Birdy told Jo affably. "The more the merrier. Based on name alone, I already like her."

Jo gave a sheepish shake of her hair. "She commutes here five days a week. I didn't want to ask her to come back on a Sunday."

"'On an ordinary Sunday.'" Autumn hummed the last note of *Sunday in the Park* under her breath, hoping to clear the earworm.

"What is Wren Vos's apartment like?" Bianca asked Jo, one penciled-in eyebrow raised impishly. "Not to be super nosy—"

"But she can't help it. It's genetic," Birdy interrupted.

"My guess is white soundproof box," Flo said. His eyebrows drew together like Oscar the Grouch's. "Vos drinks Soylent."

"But Soylent Green is people!" Birdy said.

"We keep Ensure around for when Lita doesn't want to eat," Bee said dismissively. "It's the same as Soylent with less-cool packaging."

"And, Florencio," Jo said, hitting each syllable of Flo's name hard. "Didn't you used to drink your mom's Slim Fast for extra calories when you were trying to make weight in high school?"

Rubbing the heel of his hand bashfully over his eyes, Flo asked, "Who remembers shit like that?"

"Everyone!" Autumn laughed. "Especially Mom. Watching you pack on weight was why she stopped buying those shakes. She thought it was proof that they didn't work."

"When really it was proof that her growing son needed twice as much food," Flo said.

"Pobrecito," Bianca said, drawing a single tear down the side of her face. "Go ahead and eat all the ice cream you want now."

"Anyone else getting full?" Birdy asked, flipping a chocolate chip cookie into an untouched scoop of brownie-batter ice cream.

"Oh yeah," Bee and Jo said in unison.

"Don't you give in to that quitter's mentality!" Autumn said, pointing an accusing spoon at the assembled party. "We can't even see the bottom of the punch bowl yet!"

"I'm still thinking about that hot dog," Flo said.

"Here you go, Coach." Jo turned the bowl counterclockwise so that the rest of the cheesecake slice ended up in front of him. "It's cream cheese. Full of protein. Practically savory."

Frosty's got their second sale of the day as Dr. Wiley came in. The town pediatrician had the same gray ponytail she'd had the day she diagnosed Autumn's teddy bear with croup.

"Good morning!" Dr. Wiley announced to the room at large. She had the sort of voice that would have carried clear across the Pacific if the restaurant walls hadn't been in the way. "I'll have two franks to go!" She winked at the group. "Not exactly clean eating, but a nice happiness honeypot after a bummer sermon. Is that the Sunday Sundae Surprise you've got there?"

"It sure is!" Autumn said.

"Would you like some, Dr. Wiley?" Birdy asked. "We've got plenty!"

"A kind offer, but I will pass today. I'm afraid I know what the surprise is. I did hear that congratulations are in order to you, Dr. Birdy! We're excited to have you on Main Street!"

"I am excited to be had!" Birdy beamed, apple-cheeked. "Birdy Family Orthodontics, coming this summer! I've always wanted my own swinging bungalow."

"You got the office? I didn't know we were celebrating!" Florencio said. "Congratulations!"

"We might do our grand opening right after the Fourth of July parade," Birdy said. "We've got the perfect spot to give out toothbrushes and burgers to the town."

"Fourth of July weekend?" Autumn asked, aiming the question at Bee. "Won't you be in Hawaii?"

"Oh. We aren't going," Bee said, blinking a lot in a bad impression of airy. "We're upgrading lobby furniture."

"What?" Autumn lowered her voice and angled her face away from the group. "Since when?"

She couldn't possibly be this far out of the loop on Bianca's life. They talked practically every day. Bee had been running the countdown earlier this week, hadn't she?

"Birdy *Family* Orthodontics, eh?" Dr. Wiley asked with a mortifyingly conspicuous look at the second button of Bee's red coat. "Is the nest growing yet?"

Birdy cleared his throat. Bee all but shouted, "Ha! No! Nooo! Birdy's buying a second house; that is plenty of nest for us right now!"

Dr. Wiley took a step back from the table. "Oh well, welcome to the neighborhood regardless. I'll leave you all to your sundae!"

Waving one of her franks, Dr. Wiley closed the door with another gush of winter air.

"I like the phrase *happiness honeypot*," Jo noted to no one in particular. "Do you think it's trademarked?"

Bee seethed, wielding her spoon in her fist to stab apart a brownie. "I swear to God everyone in this town either wants to tell me that I'm practically still twelve or they want to know why I don't have kids yet."

"Getting a dog could push that off for a couple years," Florencio said. "That's what I did."

Autumn glared at him. "You gave your dog to Mom."

"I *share* my dog with Mom," he corrected. "She needed the company, not the vet bills. She's living on a limited income now."

"I can't have a dog," Bee said, loud enough to declare the route of conversation. "I have a business and a Lita."

"Thank you for leaving me off the list, sweetheart. I appreciate your reserve." Birdy leaned over to kiss the curve of her cheek. "But I would love a dog."

Bee leaned away, brushing aside an itch on her nose. "You'd love ten dogs."

Birdy's chest puffed out. "One for each kid."

"That sounds terrifying," Jo said.

"Unless you picture the kids riding the dogs," Autumn said, miming holding the reins to a galloping golden retriever. "Then it's *adorable*. Except in real life; then it's animal cruelty. Picture the dogs with robot bones."

"Birdy's a big family guy," Bee explained to Jo.

Birdy popped a gummy bear into his mouth. Autumn couldn't tell which part of the sundae had been hiding gummy candy. "My dad was the baker's dozen of his siblings. He and my mom started late and only got to three."

Jo's eyes bulged. "Holy shit! Roman Catholic? Mormon?"

"I think they prefer Latter-day Saints," Bee said.

"They do, but we aren't," Birdy said.

"Nana Birdy told me that Birdys just love babies," Autumn said, remembering last year's Birdy Bash trip to Orlando and subsequent cruise down to Bermuda. For Autumn, who grew up without cousins nearby, being absorbed into a family of fifty had been like stepping into a Cheaper by the Dozen film. Two solid weeks of overindulgence and PG-13 fun at top volume. Chaotic bliss.

Bianca sucked her teeth. "My vagina and I reserve the right to not love childbirth. Of course, we are *years* away from it being a problem. There is no way in hot hell that I am raising a kid and a Lita, thanks."

A second silence fell over the table, this one as dense and suffocating as a weighted velvet curtain to the face. Autumn may have been behind on the honeymoon news, but she knew for damn sure that the Boria-Birdy household hadn't made an official ruling on babies. Until now.

It seemed to catch Birdy by surprise, too. He kept searching for Bee's attention, but she was busy turning the sundae again—pausing only once she reached the maraschino cherry pile. She crushed a mouthful between her teeth as her smartwatch rang.

"My mom," she said with a weary flash of red-stained teeth as she slid out of the booth. "Excuse me."

Birdy watched her mutter into her wrist and walk away, his face tight. He sniffed and forced a jovial expression at the table. "I love that watch. It looks like she's talking to the *Enterprise*. So, Autumn, what happens if things don't work out between your boss and your bestie? You've got a union, right?"

The shift in conversation was so fast, Autumn felt dizzy. "What? Yeah, but—"

"No!" Bee snarled into her watch as she stepped outside. "Firm no!"

"Excuse me." Birdy tossed his chair back as he bounded after his wife.

"Ten bucks says they aren't coming back," Flo said.

"I'll take that action," Autumn said. Her tongue tried to anxiously wedge into the gap in her front teeth, only to bounce back against the cold smoothness of her veneers. She loved having straighter teeth in photos but missed the comfort of the gap that was no longer there.

"Weird news," Jo said, peeking under an orb of spumoni. "The bottom layer of the sundae is pie."

"Surprise!" Autumn shook two jazz hands.

COMPLETED ITEMS

- ☑ TP Bianca's house
- ☑ Perform onstage
- ☑ Get belly button pierced
- ☑ Redo the yearbook prank
- ☑ Eat the giant sundae at Frosty's

TO BE COMPLETED

- ○ Surf the Point
- ○ Host a dinner party
- ○ Have a glitter fight
- ○ Try everything on the menu at Days
- ○ Do a keg stand
- ○ Play hide-and-seek in public
- ○ Break something with a sledgehammer
- ○ Climb the giant anchor on the boardwalk (and survive)
- ○ Get a high score at the boardwalk arcade
- ○ Pose like a pinup girl
- ○ Get a pet
- ○ Learn an entire dance routine
- ○ Eat breakfast at midnight
- ○ Get stoned
- ○ Have a bonfire
- ○ Dig up the time capsule

eight

BIANCA

"I didn't know that Cruz moved into the apartment over Harbor Cove!" Bianca's mother followed her daughter through the house, still caught in the explanation she had started the second the front door opened. "You move outside of town, just five minutes away, and everyone stops telling you anything! How am I supposed to know where people live if they don't tell me?"

Where Lita and Bee were wide, Bonnie Boria was lithe—a sleeker version of her father. A strand of henna-black hair stuck to the new-to-her diamond on her left hand. She carelessly tore it away. "What's an alcoholic doing living over a bar?"

"I think you just answered your own question," Bee said, the ice cream in her stomach churning. When she had the time, she would feel awful about running away from brunch.

For now, Lita's screeching tantrum took precedence.

The downstairs bedroom was illuminated by curtains ripped to one side. The bedding had already been thrown into a heap, blankets shaken within an inch of their life, sheets untucked. In the center of it all, Lita raged.

"Who are you to say no?" Lita shouted, pushing over her laundry hamper. Dirty socks and wadded-up yoga pants rolled across the carpet.

"Mama," Bonnie said in a placating singsong that Bianca found annoying, so sure as shit Lita wasn't going to like it.

Bee stepped between her mother and grandmother, using the fullness of her hips to block her mother from entering the room and causing more damage. "Mom. I have this. It's me she's mad at. Go home. Tell Tony hi from us."

She could tell her mother wanted to argue, but Bee didn't have time to watch her mom debate between what was right and what was easiest.

Bianca set to work, hunching over to scoop up the mess as Lita made it.

"You are the child!" Lita continued, tearing the pillows from her bed. "I am the grown-up!"

"No," Bee said, soft but firm. "I am the grown-up *and* you are the grown-up. It's too many cooks in the kitchen."

"I don't want to go into your stupid kitchen. Keep it. Keep your pizza and your house and your fat husband. I wanted to go see my friend."

Lita kicked at a chenille blanket. Seeing a fall risk, Bee dove to grab it.

"You wanted to go someplace with *stairs*! Twenty stairs to get inside? No! Absolutely not! Cruz can come to you. You don't have to walk up to his teeny-tiny apartment to see him."

You couldn't, Bee didn't say. Because that was another fight.

Fights with Lita were Russian nesting dolls. Fights within complaints within advice within a longer-running tournament called Matriarch.

There couldn't be three cooks. How in the world could there be three moms?

The front door slammed shut.

Well. They were back down to two again.

"I wanted to go *anywhere*." Lita stressed the word, shaking her clawed hands in Bianca's face. "Outside. Inside. Somewhere else. Smell someone else's air. Someone else's nasty perfume plugs."

Bee collapsed on the corner of the bed, holding the hamper in front of her stomach. "I took the air freshener out of your bathroom, Lita. I have already apologized. But I'm not unplugging them from upstairs because you don't like them. You're not supposed to go up there at all. No stairs."

"What life is this?" Lita was shouting again, her tiny steps moving her furious and snail-like in the other direction. "Locked up, penned in. Chickens live better than I do now. I watched a whole movie about how worried everyone is about the chickens. What about me? Rosa, a grown woman? A human being! Is this my thanks for giving you and your mother my house?"

Seventeen years ago! Bianca mentally screamed.

"I didn't ask for your house, Lita. I was a little girl then."

Lita pinched at the air at ear height, a motion that would have made Bianca's child self scream and cry in fright. "You're still a little girl! A little brat! Leaving me here all day long!"

The sharp plastic cutouts of the hamper sank into the pale undersides of Bee's arms. *I'm doing my best. I'm doing my best. I'm doing my best.*

"Cruz was wrong to promise you a visit to his place," she said in between long, even breaths. "I made it very clear when I scheduled it with him that he was going to visit you here."

"Because you are not listening! I do not want to be here!" Lita said, clapping between the words, a move she had learned from TV. Bee was not a fan of anything that made Lita louder. "You don't want me to have friends. You forbid the artists from talking to me—"

"I forbade them from listening to you—"

"That's what I'm saying!"

Bee had to shout now, just to finish her point. Hamper falling aside, she stood for higher ground. "I forbade them from taking direction from you. You can't manage the store out from under me. But you can talk to them about anything else."

"As long as it is where you want, when you want. When you want to go play with your friends, then you send me your mother. Otherwise I'm alone."

"What more can I do, Lita? Put you in a geriatric play group?"

"Put that cruel tongue back in your mouth." This she didn't shout. This was a note played so gently that it slipped through the bars of Bianca's rib cage and found the tender meat of her heart.

This hurt.

"I'm sorry," she choked. Bianca's stomach turned to lead—ice cream and all—pulling her down toward the floor. "It's just. I don't. I can't."

Lita wouldn't look at her. "Go, go. You want to steal my turn to be sad? Go cry somewhere else. I'm crying in this room. My room. The only room I have left."

Bee swallowed her screams until she got upstairs and let them loose into the memory foam of Birdy's pillow. She found it trapped sound better than the couch cushions.

Across the hall, in the not-quite guest room that Bee still thought of as Mom's Room, she found Birdy hiding among his bachelor flotsam. Gaming consoles going back decades. Acoustic guitars he bought when he left Ohio to play on the beach at sunset. A *Warcraft* tapestry that was truly too ugly to live in any other room of the house.

Sitting on the futon he insisted was a daybed, Birdy watched his heavy black laptop boot up. The keyboard flashed menacingly red, then faintly blue.

Any greeting was stolen by a stream of curses coming up through the floor. Lita, swearing at the ceiling again. Bee couldn't hear the words, so she wasn't sure if they were aimed at her or just making a pit stop on their way up to Tito in heaven.

She leaned her head against the wall next to the framed photo of Birdy Bash '98—*the one with the Harlem Globetrotters*; Birdy family reunions were named like *Friends* episodes.

"And you want a baby," she said, monotone. She flipped the light switch. The curtains in here were Bonnie-purchased, royal purple and thick enough to block out the ocean.

Birdy refused to acknowledge the change of brightness. He barely raised his eyes from the screen. "And you want to wait until your grandmother can't know your baby?"

"That's cruel." She heard Lita's vocabulary in her mouth and wanted to rinse it out with corrosive soap. Her anger was beginning to crumble into a more tolerable weariness. The corners of her eyes twitched again. She closed them with a sigh. "She can't even walk up here to keep yelling at me. How was she going to go up to a third-story studio in the flats?"

Birdy's voice softened. "She'll calm down by dinner. Seeing Autumn makes her happy."

133

Bee's eyes popped open. "Family dinner. Five thirty." She flipped through her schedule on her smartwatch, until she found the slow-cooker app. Tonight's turkey chili had another four hours before it needed her attention again. Thank God. "I doubt Mom will be back. I was sharp with her."

"You were being efficient. She'll understand."

"That doesn't mean she won't sulk while she understands. If she doesn't come, there's no dessert."

"Blergh," Birdy huffed, puffing out his cheeks. "Please. The Sunday Sundae Surprise was meant for no fewer than twelve people."

Bee tugged on the ends of her hair. "Lita will be expecting dessert. I'll pick something up. Just in case."

She stepped out of her shoes, the black-and-white prison stripes of her socks cutting around stacks of board games they'd never played. She sat down on the other side of the futon, kicking her heels against the frame. "It wasn't this hard before, Birdy. When Tito was alive, she wasn't like this."

"She's angrier than she was then. So are you. The world is different. You're in a different place in it. Emotionally if not literally."

Bianca didn't let herself think about other houses. She didn't count how many bedrooms other people had or look at dream houses on HGTV.

But when she saw the nubby beige carpet now, she didn't see the familiar ground of her childhood. She saw the disappointment in Birdy's face as he'd realized it was in every room.

Who puts wall-to-wall carpet in a beach house?

Bee had never considered it odd before. Now she saw it as a sand trap that wasn't very pretty, especially the bald patches from where dried nail polish had been cut away over the years.

Bee had never even thought of her house as a beach house until Birdy moved in. She didn't think about the ocean much at all. It was part of the endless sky.

"Jo seems nice. I get why the Kelly kids like her so much."

Bee gave a grudging agreement.

"Can we talk about the baby thing now?" Birdy asked.

"I'm sorry," she snapped. "I'm already in a screaming fight with someone right now. Can you take a number?"

He inched away from her, looking hurt. "Not picking a fight with you, Bee. Just seemed pretty final for something we've literally never talked about."

"That's not true," she dissented. "We talked about talking about it."

It.

They weren't ready for a baby. They weren't even ready to *say* baby.

It had always been something to be dealt with in the future.

The first thing we'll do when we get back from our honeymoon is write out our five-year plan, Bee had promised once. *We'll take an extra day off and everything. I'll buy a fancy planner with stickers.*

Well, the honeymoon was canceled, and her decision was made.

At brunch, she hadn't even meant to say that she didn't want a baby right now. It was supposed to be a joke. Not a funny joke, sure, but a joke that would release some of the steam inside her. Instead, she found the truth of it as she was talking.

No babies. No pets. No more roommates. No more patients. She was not taking on any more dependents, thanks. Apply again later.

"It's not a priority right now, Bobby," she muttered, using the intimacy of his first name as a dead bolt on the conversation. In

Oregon, Bobby only existed behind closed doors. And if his pants were on, it was generally bad news.

"I hear you," he said.

A month of couple's counseling had been required before she agreed to set a wedding date. She had never been in love before. She had to make sure she wasn't buying a lemon. To date, it was the best money Bee had ever spent—including her Drybar Teasing Brush.

The futon groaned as he shifted away from her. "I told Benji and Blakely that I'd join them for a game. Okay?"

Bianca Boria-Birdy Grown Woman thought, *It will be good for him to work through his feelings with his brothers, however indirectly.*

Bianca Boria-Birdy Recently-Yelled-at Only Child thought, *You're going to play video games NOW?*

Both statements were allowed to be true at the same time.

Everyone to their separate corners: Birdy throwing his feelings into an MMORPG hole, Lita working herself up for a hate-nap, Bonnie driving back to Tony.

Bianca, alone.

It was time to scream into another pillow.

The fact was that the last two years had aged Lita more than the ten before. Losing her husband had hardened her. Losing her independence had shriveled her steps and stolen her patience. Last year, at Bianca's wedding in a rented mansion in Portland, Lita had become so frustrated by not being able to dance that she quit the reception entirely, demanding that Bonnie drive her the two hours back to Sandy Point. Bee and Birdy had cut their cake without any of Bee's family present.

Not that cake cutting was as important as her grandmother's

well-being. Bee was grateful that she had anybody present in the sea of Birdy relatives.

Maybe she had sheltered Lita too much. If Cruz and the other artists had seen her more since she moved out of the shop, they would understand why Bee was always running home, checking her watch, writing down reminders.

Maybe if they knew how hard it was, they could help instead of making more problems.

She couldn't decide whether to call Cruz or wait until they were at work together to go over the specifics of why today had failed. Was she supposed to approach him as his boss, disappointed that he couldn't follow a very simple instruction OR was she supposed to approach him as the granddaughter of an infirm old lady who wasn't as strong as he remembered?

Hungry for distraction, she opened Instagram.

Bianca was more curious about the Throwback List than she wanted to be. Probably because her name was at the top of it, the very first thing Jo had thought of. After a week of avoiding it, she finally gave in and searched for Jo's account.

She opened the picture of the TP tree. It wasn't that Bee didn't know what it would look like—true to her word, Jo messaged her the photo days ago—but she couldn't help but be curious about seeing her house through someone else's eyes.

Item one: TP Bianca's House.

I've been missing my GymClass app since moving home. Does anyone else think TP-ing people you were jealous of in high school could be the next exercise fad? #TheThrowbackList.

Jo Freeman had been jealous of *her*? The idea made Bee want to guffaw. Jo had grown up with everything Bee hadn't: two parents, a sibling, friends, relationships. Their high school year-books were full of Jo—in clubs, at events, with Autumn or Wren Vos. The only after-school events Bianca got to go to were honor society meetings. When she decided that she wanted to go to prom, she spent months justifying it to the council of elders that was Lita, Tito, and Bonnie. Even then, a new dress was vetoed because the shop's heater was on the fritz and it had been a particularly brisk May.

Jo's parents threw her and Autumn a sober afterparty at their then art gallery on the boardwalk. Bee hadn't even garnered an invite to it.

✓   *Item two: Get belly button pierced.*

Thanks so much to Bianca, my next-door neighbor and manager at the Salty Dog. First she put up with my hella petty first task (she was way more understanding than she had to be when I went to take the toilet paper out of her tree!) and now she's helping me conquer item number two: getting my belly button pierced!

Fun fact: Bee and I have known each other since second grade! I had no idea she had such steady hands. #TheThrowbackList.

Breaking the first rule of internet, Bee read the comments.

CUTE

You're so brave, I could never!

Now I want to see MY high school friends!

But we weren't friends in high school, Bee thought. *We're barely friends now.*

Not that it stopped Autumn from sending out a follow-up text to get everyone on board with the next list item.

AUTUMN: Introductory group text! Woo-hoo! What should our title be? The Sunday Sundae Surprised? I'm open to suggestions.

Also, all hands on deck for Jo's dinner party at Surf & Saucer next Friday! Who's in?

BIRDY: Frosty's Fallen Heroes Assemble! Sounds fun! Let us know if we can bring anything!

Bianca glared at the door. Birdy hadn't quite mastered the art of asking her if she wanted to socialize as much as he did. Possibly because he knew the answer was no.

BIANCA: If I can find a new Lita sitter, yes.

Bee wasn't wholly convinced that Jo wanted to be friends with her personally—rather than just as an Autumn tagalong. However, she was willing to participate out of curiosity or spite. Whichever ended up more applicable.

Besides, it had been a long time since she had multiple non-work, nonfamily plans in one week. It was a little like having a real social life.

nine

AUTUMN

"You're sure we shouldn't be worried about Bianca running off like that?" Jo asked.

"Oh no," Autumn said, zipping her puffy jacket to her neck. Her insides were frozen solid with ice cream. "Bee's always rushing to handle something. In college, she used to disappear every time someone called in sick to the pizza place she managed. Even in the middle of a party, if work called, she left. She's too responsible for her own good. I'm more worried about them moving their honeymoon again. Bee was really looking forward to Hawaii."

"Because she can't get enough of the same ocean in her front yard?" Jo asked.

Autumn shoved her shoulder. "Not everyone hates the beach, Jo. Have you learned to like seafood yet?"

Her friend snorted. "Nope. The only thing I like fishy is boys."

As they crossed the street, leaving the boardwalk behind them, Autumn's heart sang a brass-band version of "Fortuosity."

Florencio refusing to join them and the Birdys running off couldn't dampen the feeling of walking up Main Street, the ocean splashing behind her. This was the view she had imagined when she was homesick a thousand miles away in unknowably large Los Angeles. This was her favorite street in the world.

"It hasn't changed at all," Jo noticed.

"I know," Autumn said warmly.

Familiarity made her vision sharpen, annotating every house they passed. Dr. Wiley's navy-blue bungalow with a bright white ramp up to the door. The Nedelmans' gnarled tree cut in a U around the low-slung power lines. The wall of spiky shrubs in front of the office that would soon be Birdy's. The trout mailbox at the house with the missing shingles.

While many of the homes on the street had the same sharp roof and tall porch stairs, the red-and-white house that sat dead center was the only one with a picket fence. Weeds drooped between the white posts.

Ginger Jay had finally hammered one of her real-estate signs into the overgrown front lawn, her smiling face frozen under a threatening *COMING SOON*.

Jo paused, her head cocked toward the sign. "This is your dad's new wife? She looks familiar."

The porch stairs groaned under Autumn's footsteps. "She didn't use to have her picture on the signs. When we were in high school, she used—"

"Puppets!" Jo gasped, scampering up the stairs behind her. "The Chief is married to the Puppet Lady?!"

"Sandy Point's own," Autumn said. "He moved into her huge house in Waterfront Cove."

Jo's jaw dropped. "The Chief lives in the vacation houses? Tell me he's wearing bougie boat shoes and driving a Subaru. No! A Prius."

"He kept the truck and his boots, thank God, but he shaved off his mustache. His upper lip is *so* pale."

Autumn patted her pockets for her keys and pulled them out by the Fire Station 75 key chain her mom accidentally ordered in bulk triplicate one Christmas.

For a second, between the turn of the key and the click of the latch, Autumn would always forget this wasn't her home. The memory of it was a glowing beacon—the friendly noise of dogs and friends, the Chief in the kitchen, her mom's perfume everywhere.

The reality was colder. While the Main Street house had the bones of Autumn's favorite place—Kelly-green everything, family photos taken at the JCPenney in McMinnville, fish wallpaper in the bathroom—it had none of the warmth. Or electricity. No one wanted to pay the utilities on an abandoned house.

"Oh," Jo said, the syllable loaded with surprise and disappointment.

"I know," Autumn said, wrinkling her nose at the musty air. To the right, the living room was crowded with furniture—tables and piles of folding chairs—but no couches. The greige carpet was discolored where the curtainless windows let in too much light. Autumn toed aside a particularly thick dust bunny. "Mom and Dad both moved out when I was in LA. Dad first, obviously. Then Mom last year. They've been using the house for storage since."

They continued past the stairs, into the dining room off the kitchen. The Kelly-green walls were dingy, the matching green piano dusty. The floor was crowded with storage tubs and half-packed boxes of dishes.

"Mom couldn't take most of her entertaining stuff with her," Autumn said. "Actually, Florencio carried the china hutch *into* and *out of* the condo when Mom forgot to measure the walls. It was a whole thing. But when I told her we were stopping by today, she told me to tell you to 'grab whatever you want and welcome home and sorry about California.'" Her impression of Cindy Kelly was exaggeratedly simpering, bordering on drunk, but it made Jo laugh, so Autumn continued: "And remember! 'If your dishes are jazzy, nobody remembers the food!'"

Throughout Autumn's childhood, her mom had loved to entertain without a lick of knowledge in the kitchen. Instead of buying cookbooks or waiting for the Chief to be off shift, Cindy Kelly bought premade food and dumped it in ornate dishware. KFC out of crystal. Dips in ramekins. Entenmann's on a cake stand. Juice in champagne glasses. Autumn couldn't count how many times the all-green dining room table had been packed with friends or firefighters or the wrestling team eating chili out of a cabbage-shaped soup tureen.

Autumn peered into the nearest box. "Here are wineglasses! What else is on your list for the dinner party?"

"My mom said the shop already has silverware, plates, and water cups. But I'd love to get some of the covered casserole dishes. Especially the chicken dish—"

"Henrietta! Of course. That's at my house. I make Henrietta Casserole all the time." Technically anything served in Henrietta the chicken dish was Henrietta Casserole. The little-red-hen Dutch oven had been Florencio's favorite when he was young, so it used to come out a lot when there were new fancy foods to try.

"Friends are kind of important to a successful dinner party," Jo said, wringing her hands. "When we wrote the list, I'm sure we just meant the two of us eating mashed potatoes out of pretty bowls, but that wouldn't read super well on camera. Do you think everyone will be okay with pictures? I don't want them to feel like I tricked them into a photo shoot."

"I'll just add a note about pictures to the group thread!" Autumn said. She retrieved her phone in a flash. Visions of her friends being friends danced through her head like sitcom opening credits. Having a regular booth at Days for singalong night. Jo and Bianca and Autumn braiding each other's hair at a sleepover. Birdy and Florencio dancing in a fountain.

"Wait!" Jo said, chewing on her bottom lip. "Is this too desperate looking? Like texting right after you get home from a date? They just left Frosty's to deal with something, and we're already planning next week."

Autumn laughed. "Don't be silly. You can talk to your friends whenever, Jo. People like to be thought of. It's past time for us to have a group chat. The only way to make friends with people is to *be* friends with them. Trust me. Should we add Wren to the list? She would hate to be in a group thread, but I could grossly misuse our Slack chat for personal business."

"No! No, I'll invite her on my own," Jo said. Her eyes wandered around the room. She squeezed between stacks of Christmas china to inspect a box. "Is this really a box of just buttons?"

"Oh yeah. Mom's craft supplies are everywhere. Which is good news for the list! There's buttloads of stuff for you to use here. One of the closets should have all the glitter you need for the glitter fight. And, last time I checked, Flo's surfboard was in the garage. He refuses to come back here, as you may have noticed." Autumn gestured to empty brother-shaped air beside her. "He's been avoiding Dad for three-ish years now. Selling the house was Dad's idea, and Ginger's the one on the sign, so now he avoids the house, too. The thing is, the money would make sure Mom could stay in her condo, not just pay for the Chief's boat—"

"He wants to sell the house for a boat?" Jo asked, sounding exactly like Florencio.

"I know, I know. It's not great. But neither is a sad house that nobody uses! This place deserves to be more than just storage," Autumn said, tucking her phone back into her pocket. "Now, do you want to go upstairs and rummage through Flo's room like when we were kids?"

Jo's eyes sparkled. "Um, yes, of course I do."

Framed school photos of Florencio and gap-toothed Autumn watched as she and Jo thundered up the stairs. Flat cardboard boxes lined the upstairs hallway, waiting to be folded and filled. Both of Autumn's parents had started and abandoned the project multiple times. Rather than face the magnitude of it, Chuck Kelly had ordered a bulk pickup and told the family to claim what they wanted by May 1. After that, the newbie firefighters would make a hundred bucks throwing all the Kelly family memories into a dumpster in the driveway.

Florencio's room was the first off the stairs. The door, still papered with *Get Out* signs and caution tape, stood open. The walls were dark blue and white, except for the patch on the ceiling that was all Rihanna posters. The wall shelves were crowded with cobwebby plastic trophies and ribbons. The bed was made, as though her brother had just left for school, rather than moving out a decade ago to live with Melody, the girl he'd nearly married.

"I forgot about the sheer number of sports trophies. No wonder he dedicated his whole life to coaching," Jo said, craning her neck to see the tops of the shelves. "Can you recycle trophies?"

"He has more than enough room for them at his house," Autumn said, brushing clean the spines of a row of Star Trek novels. "He has an empty second bedroom. And a mostly empty first bedroom. His ex was an interior designer. She sort of un-designed the house when she left."

"Well, if he ever wants to wallpaper his ceiling with Rihanna again, he knows where to start." Jo squinted at the ceiling. "How did he even get those up there?"

"Don't be jealous," Autumn teased. "I remember watching the 'Umbrella' video with you."

Jo clutched her heart in a fake swoon. "Those legs! Did I want to be her? Did I want to have sex with her? Yes and yes. I'm not saying I wouldn't make a Rihanna shrine. Just not on the ceiling. It's less creepy in a frame. Or a Pinterest folder."

The more interesting things they remembered about Florencio's room were gone—the shoe box with weed and condoms under the bed, the dresser candy stash, the gym bag where bottles of shop-lifted liquor used to wait for the next jock party. The closet had golf clubs, moldy gym shoes, turn-of-the-century PlayStation controllers, and a Point High letterman jacket with *Kelly* embroidered on the breast.

"I would love to roll up to Days in this," Jo said, rubbing the leather arm of the jacket between her thumb and forefinger. She checked the label. "Oh my God, who let him order an XL? This is peak short-guy vanity. Even with his jacked arms, Flo's a medium."

"And in high school, he was totally a small. All of those trophies are for lightweight champ," Autumn said. "I'm sure Mom said he'd grow into it. She used to swear that Flo would get taller and I would get boobs. Obviously neither of those things is ever going to happen, but she still swears that we're both just late bloomers."

Autumn's room had only an empty bed frame, a bookcase she didn't have room for in her cottage, and her mother's StairMaster.

"What happened to your Broadway posters?" Jo asked, examining the orange-painted walls. Autumn could picture exactly where *Wicked, Sweet Charity,* and *Mamma Mia!* had hung over her bed.

"They're in my classroom!" Autumn said. "Well, my side of my classroom. The other half is Pat Markey's. She does *not* like my *Sweet Charity* poster. She says Fosse is too sexual for high schoolers. I think she might be anti-dancing, like the dad in *Footloose.*"

"It's so weird that our algebra teacher started directing the musical," Jo observed.

"To be fair, it was weirder when our choir teacher also taught algebra," Autumn said. "Sandy Point Unified School District gets real creative. My mom is teaching sixth-, seventh-, and eighth-grade science this year. It may drive her to finally retire. Pat, on the other hand, I think is only getting stronger over time."

"So, sharing a classroom with her isn't going great?"

Autumn had shared a room before—not on Main Street, unless Jo sleeping over for consecutive nights during summer vacation counted. In college, she'd lived in the dorms, then with three roomies off campus. In LA, she split an apartment with a group of struggling actors who worked at different Coffee Bean & Tea Leaf locations. All to say: she was no stranger to having a roommate.

Sharing a classroom with Pat was absolutely nothing like anything she had ever experienced before.

"First off, she still gets the class's attention by ringing that tiny bell. I hear it even when she's not ringing it now. And she starts every morning by singing the national anthem at the piano and expects everyone in our first-period classes to salute until she's done."

"What the fuck?" Jo laughed. "Have you considered taking a knee?"

"Of course I have!" Autumn said. "But she thinks she's my boss because she doesn't teach math anymore. When I got hired, she even made a new job title for herself: *senior* co-chair of the drama department."

"The last time I invented a job title, I ended up making myself redundant and getting fired," Jo said, folding her arms. "Maybe it's time for her to redundant herself into early retirement."

The ice cream in Autumn's stomach protested. She didn't want to be mean to Pat. In high school, Pat had given her so many of her fondest memories—standing beside her piano, singing "Over the Rainbow" for the first time, or clapping out the rhythm to the title song of *Oklahoma!* on the football field when the fire alarm interrupted rehearsal. Even at the beginning of this school year, she and Pat had a good time hammering out the cast list for *Bugsy Malone* together. "She's been doing her best to keep the theater department afloat all by herself for years. I guess Mr. Hearn needed a lot of help, so she's used to doing all the work." It just didn't seem like it was ever going to change. "She's not letting me touch the Senior Showcase at all." She grimaced, remembering Pat telling her that as a first-year teacher, Autumn just didn't have "the experience or emotional connection to the seniors" needed to direct the end-of-the-year performance.

I'm the only person left in the department who has been with these kids since their freshman year, Pat told her. *It really wouldn't be fair for someone else to decide the best showcase for their talents.*

"I started the school year with so many big ideas," Autumn told Jo. "I even pre-choreographed all the dances for the seniors over winter break, but Pat won't let me put them in her show. So now my Broadway Club is learning *A Chorus Line* for their performance at the spring carnival because it's the only place I don't have Pat overruling all my decisions."

Since the school district's curriculum largely ignored musical theater, Autumn had created the Broadway Club as a creative outlet for herself and her small group of like-minded sophomores. When Pat cut all of Autumn's choreography from the Senior Showcase— citing that it took up too much of their semester-long rehearsal period—the Broadway Club had been more than happy to learn all the dance numbers.

"Last year, they did *Doctor Doolittle* for the fall musical, and the kids say all Pat let them do was march. In circles. In lines. Just. Marching."

"That sounds like a nightmare," Jo said.

"Or like the part of *Sound of Music* where everyone's a Nazi," Autumn said. "Or the second act of *The Producers*, where everyone's a Nazi. Or *Cabaret*. Wow, Broadway really tried to warn us about white supremacy for years."

"While mostly centering white people, sure," Jo said, wandering over to the window that overlooked the backyard. She peered down for a second before her attention whipped back to Autumn. "What the fuck is all that?"

Autumn joined her, pressing her nose to the glass.

"Oh. Right. Mom's last dog, Lacy, ripped up all the grass," she said, her breath fogging the view. "I haven't been back there in a while. Dad covered the dead patches with decorative rocks."

Below them, the backyard glinted white, as what had to be

hundreds of pounds of pebbles stretched from porch to fence. There wasn't a stitch of grass left.

"And they got rid of the doghouse," Jo observed. She made a face at Autumn. "That complicates digging up the time capsule, huh?"

"We've got until May first to excavate the backyard," Autumn said, clapping her on the shoulder. "That's five whole weeks to build up your strength. By the time you get to the end of the list, you'll have new keg-stand and surfing muscles!"

JO: We are officially on for a dinner party at Surf & Saucer this Friday night at 6pm. Pictures will be taken before dinner, so please don't wear anything you don't want seen by the internet.

AUTUMN: PUT ON YOUR SUNDAY CLOTHES, PEOPLE!

BIRDY: Does that mean I should or should not go buy a tuxedo T-shirt?

BIANCA: That hilariously implies you don't already own a tuxedo T-shirt.

FLORENCIO: Need us to bring anything?

JO: Sure! I haven't picked appetizers or drinks yet.

AUTUMN: Google Doc sign-up sheet incoming!

ten

JO

Three days into her gig taking pictures of the Days menu, Jo was beginning to enjoy the crackle of terrestrial radio in the background. The guys in the kitchen spent the morning heating up the fryers and grooving to KDEP. The adult-contemporary channel was oddly saturated in 1D solo projects. Jo had no complaints.

Alfie Jay pushed his way out of the kitchen doors belly-first. With a serving tray hoisted expertly over his shoulder, he made his way over to the blinding light of Jo's makeshift studio setup.

"Pour vous, Madam Photographer," Alfie Jay announced in French about as authentic as a Fred Meyer baguette. He set the pan on the turquoise place mat that was serving as the new menu's backdrop. "One Sheet Load of Totchos."

To distinguish them from all the other local tater-tot nachos, Days served their tots on a half sheet pan. The stainless steel clashed with the gaudy gold—possibly real—Super Bowl ring Alfie wore.

"Jesus, Alfie, these portions are out of control," Jo said, choosing a particularly loaded tot from the back of the pile. Queso and potato scorched the insides of her mouth. She exhaled steam. "But those are perfect. Could you bring me a side of jalapeño slices? I want to tweeze them around to fill visual gaps."

Alfie doffed his Panama hat, briefly exposing a sweaty comb-over. "Oui, oui," he said.

Jo wondered if he'd spoken this much faux-fancy French to Ginger Jay and if that was what had sent her running to Chief Chuck's beefy arms.

"And another Perrier, please!" she called after him. It was an abuse of power—their agreement was for free food and drink while Jo worked and a lump sum for compiling the pictures onto a very basic website template at the end—but unlimited mineral water felt like a small taste of Silicon Valley here in the Point.

Although, come to think of it, her drink order could be why Alfie only spoke to her in garbled French. Apparently she was the only person in Sandy Point who didn't pronounce the *r* at the end of Perrier.

Once the jalapeños had been arranged and Jo had a fresh green bottle in hand, she took her time shooting the tray, pausing at intervals to adjust the angle of the tots.

The inside of her tote glowed blue as her phone blinked a notification. Jo set her camera down and cracked her knuckles. She ate one more tot from the back of the Sheet Load as she plugged her passcode in.

"You have one unheard message—" said the voicemail robot. There was a short inhale and then a soothing NPR announcer voice saying, *"Hello, Johanna, this is Trish Zavaglia from the Seattle*

City Orchestra. We would like to interview you for the social media strategist position you applied for on our website. If you could give me a call back at your earliest convenience . . ."

Jo choked on her Perrier.

Job applications had started to feel like a shitty hobby she had—a daily surrendering of her career history to every spam folder on the West Coast. She still hadn't heard back on jobs she'd applied to while living in her own apartment. Seattle City Orchestra was actually within driving distance. It was actually in a real city.

It was actually possible.

Reeling, Jo went out to the parking lot before she returned the call. For some reason, talking toward the ocean made her feel more calm. Maybe it was just being away from the smell of nacho cheese.

She came back to the totchos with a scheduled job interview. Friday morning, she wouldn't take pictures of the burger menu as planned. She was going to drive to Seattle. For a job interview. For a real job that could go on her real résumé. It was even her old title: social media strategist. She could live without *influencer relations manager* tacked on at the end. Or she could add it back on for a pay bump.

"Do you know much about orchestra music?" Alfie Jay asked her as he brought out a Cobb salad for Jo to have for lunch. He seemed to enjoy finding the non-seafood menu items for her to eat. Probably because it was expensive to waste shrimp on someone who gagged at the smell.

"Not a thing," Jo said. She barely even remembered applying to the job. Wren had convinced her on their nondate to expand her search to include lower Washington. "But I have two days and a four-hour drive to Seattle to figure it out."

The orchestra could hand her back the key to her adulthood. She could get on track with her old game plan again. She could still ascend to director of digital strategy in the next four years.

Her parents booked her a hotel room—which was low-key humiliating to accept, and even more so when it came with a warning not to overspend on room service. "We're already buying you food to eat at home," Phil said with his not-joking laugh. "Maybe bring a sandwich for the road."

Jo drove up to Washington the day before the interview, listening to playlists of classical-music podcasts, hoping to absorb the jargon, and Megan Thee Stallion, hoping to absorb the bad-bitch vibe.

She walked through Seattle trying to look at it through the rose-tinted glasses of a blind date. Could she fall in love with that coffee shop? This neighborhood? That mural? Could these be the sidewalks she rushed down looking for lunch? The receptionist she flirted with, the elevator she rode, the echoing hallways she worked like a runway?

The interview ran long—she managed to keep the panel talking and they asked about the Throwback List, that must be a good sign, right?—but then she was being thanked for her time and offered a round of inscrutable handshakes. She was ushered back into the lobby, where the cute receptionist asked how it went.

"Great!" Jo said, with a confidence she didn't actually feel. Admittedly her last job interview had mostly been a formality with Devo Quandt when she'd been promoted from the standing desk to a paid position. He hadn't even asked her about her job history, just told her that it might take a while for the office to stop calling her Intern Jo. Maybe it was a good sign that the orchestra panel had called her Ms. Freeman and assured her that she'd hear back from them soon.

Replaying her answers in her head on her walk back to the parking garage, she couldn't see any immediate reason for them *not* to hire her. They'd laughed at her joke about their competitors at the philharmonic only posting pictures in black and white. She had successfully named their last two concerts without referring to her notes. Now all she could do was wait for their call.

Buckled into her Mini, she jumped when she saw the clock. She was two hours behind the schedule she'd written in her bullet journal last night. Suddenly she was staring down the barrel of a six-person dinner party from the wrong side of the state line.

She didn't even have time to rinse the smell of hotel room bar soap from her skin. She drove directly from the orchestra to the boardwalk, arriving back in Sandy Point at eighty miles an hour. Ninety minutes until her guests were promised dinner.

The sand-dusted planks of the boardwalk crunched underfoot as Jo jogged from the parking lot. The salt air in her tight lungs made her feel sixteen years old and late for a shift at the art gallery. Teen!Jo was docked a dollar for being tardy—and she was often tardy, sitting at the other end of the boardwalk with Wren's Rapunzel hair wrapped around both of them.

She was so lost in the memory that she almost ran too far, expecting to see the kinetic pirate-ship sculpture that had tricked many a tourist into coming into Freeman Fine Arts. Instead, she found herself outside of the Surf & Saucer, where the window display was a surfboard covered in a massive lace doily. She took a deep breath before she stuck her key in the lock.

If a lace doily could hump a surfboard into submission, the end result would surely be her parents' odd hybrid tea-parlor surf-shop. Jo hoped she hadn't made a mistake trying to stage a photo shoot here.

One-Eighty Boardwalk Avenue, the building that Phil and Deb Freeman had spent their 401(k)s on, was a crowded, wood-paneled box that faced the ocean. The rough plank walls had once been rich brown, two shades darker than the back of Jo's hand. Now, thanks to a former HGTV host also named Jo, the walls were white shiplap.

Jo had a lot of snarky remarks about her parents whitewashing their business, but she was keeping them as a list in her bullet journal instead of saying them aloud. Having floated one by Eden on the way home from pranking Wren, she knew the reception would not be friendly. *Mom just likes easy-to-clean walls, okay?!*

Jo made multiple trips back to the parking lot to retrieve the boxes and bags of Kelly house treasures. Thanks to her interview, the week had slipped out of her fingers like sand in a windstorm. Now she had a whole dinner to cook and shoot, and she was sweating just from bringing in the dishware. She didn't know how the hell she was going to also socialize at the party.

Moving aside starfish-and-sand-dollar-pasted cake stands by the handful and worried that she'd already missed her window for calling the whole thing off, she found her phone and texted Autumn in a mild panic.

> **JO:** I just got back to town from my interview! Any chance you could help set up for tonight? My family is at the movies in Tillamook.
>
> **AUTUMN:** Sorry! Wren and I are at a PTA event for another hour.
>
> (Can you even picture me and baby Wren hanging with the wine moms??)

157

If you need-need help, I can totally send you Flo! He's already
home from work.

Jo blew out a breath before she responded. She didn't like needing anything. But imagining Wren *and* Bianca Boria showing up to
a dinner party with no dinner felt like handcrafting a nightmare
straight out of her Honor Society days.

JO: Yeah, I need-need.

AUTUMN: You got it!! 👍

Not long after, Flo appeared in the closed dining room with
wet hair and a metal coffee thermos. He immediately jumped in
to help Jo move a table.

"Coach! You're a hero and a half," Jo said.

"Happy to help," Flo said, showing no visible strain as they
dropped the table into place. He craned his head to look around.
"And it looks like most of the helping is—"

"Hiding the ugly shit, yes," Jo said. "But first, food prep."

She led him into the prep kitchen. The dishwasher pumped out
boiling steam as it sanitized plates from the lunch rush. "We don't
have clean dishes yet, but I do have—"

"A list?" Flo guessed into the rim of his thermos. He took a
long, pointed sip.

"You don't get any points for knowing the one thing about
me that even strangers know." Jo pulled out the pad of Post-its
she'd prefilled with recipes and reminders. She stuck them on the
fridge in order, overlapping them like pastel petals. "We're already

behind, so I need everything done from T-minus-three-hours to present. This job interview totally fucked my schedule."

1. REST CHEESES

She pulled open the fridge and piled precut fruit and fancy cheeses on the butcher-block counter.

"Your social media is falling behind because you might get a job?" Florencio asked in falsetto singsong. "Oh no."

"It's a social media job, Florencio," Jo said, thrusting a wedge of Brie into his hand. "If I can't keep up with my own brand, how am I gonna create one for the orchestra?"

He laughed, tossing the Brie into the cheese pile. "If you give the orchestra marketing momentum, you'll be burned as a witch." He scooched in close, the tattoos on his right arm brushing against Jo's sleeve as he reached into the fridge to help. She noticed that he often kept his right sleeve pushed up so the word *nature* was visible, printed down the length of his forearm. Above it, she recognized the flag of the Philippines from its eight-pointed star. Before it decorated his arm, the tricolor flag had been hung in Flo's bedroom on Main Street beneath his trophy collection.

2. DECANT WINES

Florencio popped the cork out of Jo's old friend Fred Meyer Malbec. "Vos is coming, huh? Autumn said that they were riding over together after Boosters Bingo."

"A group hang seemed like the lowest-pressure way to see her again," Jo admitted. She dragged her eyes away from Flo's biceps and back to his face. "We've only hung out once since I've been back. After Frosty's, everyone was so sure that I was feeling her, but I need more eyes to tell me where she's at."

"I'll be happy to give you an unbiased report," Florencio said. He had the same high-eyebrow active-listening face as Autumn. "I was already graduated when you guys dated the first time. To me, she's just Thatcher Vos's little sister."

"And your boss?"

"My administrator," Flo corrected. "My supervisor's supervisor, at best."

3. PRESSURE-COOK MEATBALLS

Following her mother's instructions to check behind the rice cooker, air fryer, and food processor, Jo found the pressure cooker. She set it down as soon as she picked it up, alarmed by the number of buttons staring back at her.

"How do I set this so that it doesn't explode?" she asked aloud, checking inside for a user's manual. There wasn't one. "Pressure cookers always explode on Food Network."

"You're scared of a slightly souped-up Crock-Pot? Move, Freeman." Flo slid in front of her, expertly pressing a series of buttons. The pot sounded like a furious digital cricket. "Can I get a recipe, or am I winging this?"

Jo pulled the recipe sticky note off the fridge mural. She stuck it on the wall at Florencio's eye level and got to work pulling ingredients out of the fridge. She lined up jars in front of him.

"You and Vos rekindling could be cute," Flo said. "Did you know my parents were high school sweethearts?"

Jo knew that he was referring to the Kellys. She didn't know anything about his birth parents except for what was represented on his left arm. The Filipino flag. Jasmine flowers. Words in Tagalog between lines and lines of black triangles.

"Your parents are the inspiration for this list item," she admitted,

rummaging around in the fridge for a missing basket of blackberries her father had sworn would be waiting for them. "They were
the only people I knew who had real dinner parties. They must
have had everyone in town over to eat at least once."

Reading the Post-it, Flo rearranged the ingredients into working
order. "Mom liked having an open door."

"I was always so happy crowded into the dining room, pulling
in chairs from all the other rooms so we could all eat together," Jo
said, picturing the house in its heyday, not as the cold gray storage
container she had seen last weekend. She threw a bag of herbs
onto the butcher block in case they were helpful. "Do you remember playing rock, paper, scissors to see who could eat alone in the
beanbags?"

"Remember?" Flo chuckled. He popped the top off a jelly jar.
"I was reigning champ. Undefeated."

"Other parents would have said that their kids could use the
special chairs. Especially since we all wanted them. But yours
made sure to keep it fair." She found the blackberries behind a
stack of many kinds of cream cheese. She took them over to the
sink, shaking the basket under the faucet, rinsing and checking for
mold spots with each bounce. "We would get so hyped hearing the
front door slam shut. The more times it closed, the crazier things
were gonna be."

"Because if there were over ten people," he said, playing along,
while into the pot, he threw jalapeños, jelly, and frozen meatballs
with the same offhand competence that he had making drinks at
Days, "the Chief went into the deep freezer for ice cream to get rid
of everyone. 'Take your Fudgsicles and go home!'"

Jo had always been allowed to stay, even when everyone else
got kicked out. Best-friend privileges. She held the damp basket of

berries out to Flo. "It was like any day at your house could turn into Thanksgiving. Non-genocide-related Thanksgiving."

He cocked an eyebrow and dumped the berries into the pressure cooker. "Can you separate Thanksgiving from the genocide?"

"I wonder that every November. It really needs rebranding. Otherwise we're all guilty of perpetuating the myth of the friendly colonizer."

Flo slammed the lid shut with a scoff. "No joke is safe around you, Freeman."

4. REARRANGE TABLES

In the dining area that had once been the local-pottery section of Freeman Fine Arts, Jo shoved aside all but one of the irritatingly round tables.

"It was a bummer to see the house on Main Street abandoned," she said. She set a cardboard box of wineglasses on the table and looked over her shoulder at Flo.

His eyes caught hers, unfooled. "I wouldn't know."

"Are you never going back? You're going to avoid it forever?"

"This from the girl who avoided her home state for—what was it? Five years? Isn't this the first time you've ever seen the new shop?" he asked, gesturing around at the room.

Jo held up her hands. "Hey, I'm not saying you can't avoid your parents. I'm just curious about why that means they have to hold on to your letterman jacket."

"You snooped through my room?" His face twisted in familiar annoyance. It made him look like the squawky kid she and Autumn used to spend the summer having water-balloon wars against, back when they were young enough to wrassle.

"If you don't want people to wander into your Rihanna jack shack, then don't abandon it!"

He rolled his eyes. "Now you just sound like Autumn."

"Hardly," Jo said. "Autumn would never say *jack shack*. Your mother would sense it and immediately collapse."

5. SET UP LIGHTING TREES

She spun in a circle, searching the netting-draped tables for her lighting equipment. "Do you see a gray tote full of umbrellas?"

Flo found the bag under a fallen surf doily. He helped Jo set up the lighting trees around the room.

"I'm not mad that Mommy and Daddy don't love each other anymore, you know," he grunted, unscrewing the lock on a tripod.

"So, you aren't avoiding the house because it represents all of your broken dreams?" Jo asked with a cheeky wince. "Because the optics—"

"Have you ever been cheated on?" he interrupted.

Jo tucked her chin back. "Um. No? Not to my knowledge."

"It sucks," Flo said. "It's basically the worst thing you could do to someone who loves you. And my dad, Chief Chuck Kelly—the fireman who can go out and chase down wildfires and run into burning buildings and never get sick when he sees blood—that guy? He's actually a fucking coward. I spent my whole life thinking he was some big hero, but when he wanted out of his relationship, he had to sneak around to do it. He couldn't be uncomfortable long enough to have an up-front conversation with my mom. And that hurt all of us. Broke our family up. I have to look out for my own feelings, Autumn's, Mom's. Why should Dad get my time, too? When your house is on fire, you don't save the arsonist."

Jo blinked at him. "That's actually kind of noble of you, Coach."

"Maybe I'm kind of noble. I've got a heart, you know. A big one."

Jo giggled. ""It doesn't matter which organ you brag about. It's just gonna sound like a dick euphemism." She deepened her voice and bowed her legs. "My massive brain. My huge, rock-hard liver."

"Is that what you think I sound like? Keanu Reeves?"

"My enlarged gallbladder knows kung fu," said Jo-as–Keanu Reeves.

6. HIDE BEACHY SHIT

"The list says beachy," Jo clarified. "But it means offensively ugly. I have to take pictures of this room. No fake Hummel figurines. No dried coral. Nothing branded *Sex Wax*."

"It's for foot traction," Flo said, idly knocking on a can of Sex Wax. He looked over his shoulder at Jo's silence. "On surfboards. Not beds."

"And I am not going to deal with a hundred comments of people needing *that* particular explanation. Put one of those towel ponchos on top of them."

He picked up one of the purple tie-dyed towels. "I thought you said nothing offensively ugly?"

She laughed, artfully stacking leftover teacups on the tables around the wide party table. "Thanks for your help tonight. I hope I'm not ruining your weekend."

"Not at all. A free meal, minus some prep work? Still nice. And you got the Birdys out of the house on a non-Sunday. That's a fucking miracle."

"It'll be a miracle if I can pull it off. It doesn't just have to go well. It has to photograph well."

Flo frowned at her. "Of course. The photographs. How else will strangers online know you're perfect?"

"It's not about perfect," she said, prickling in defense. "It's about proficiency. Besides, this is my parents' business. I want the organic advertising to look as good as possible. Which involves some editing of the decor."

7. UNPACK KELLY FAMILY HEIRLOOMS

"Henrietta Casserole!" Florencio cried as he withdrew the Dutch oven from a tote. The ceramic chicken clinked as Flo hugged it to his chest, the beak peeking out from the curve of his bicep. "Did you find this at Main Street?"

"No, Autumn dropped it by my house before she went to Bianca's for their family dinner."

"It's just 'family dinner.' On Sundays, Bee does a weekly dinner for whoever wants to come by. Like this"—he gestured at the dining area—"only not for internet strangers."

"It's not *for* the strangers," Jo stressed. "It's for us. The strangers will just appreciate the authenticity."

Underneath a heap of doilies made from fishing net, Jo's phone rang and vibrated across the table. She hauled it out gingerly and saw the caller ID: *Gia Nicotera, Quandt Co.*

"I have to take this," she told Flo.

"Go ahead. Pretty sure Henrietta and I can handle unpacking wineglasses. I am a bartender."

"There is no wine on the Days menu."

"No, but the new cotton-candy milk shake comes in a wineglass. The cotton-candy milk is too expensive for the normal-size pour."

"Remind me to order that."

Flo shot her a wink before she stepped out onto the boardwalk.

Answering the phone on an exhale, she said, "Gia, thank you so much for calling me back."

"Jojo, girl!" Gia squawked in her ear. "I am so so glad to hear from you! I swear I have been so salty about the way things went down for you here."

Gia was the sort of well-meaning white girl who only talked to Jo in a sassy *you're my only Black friend* clip. It's what kept them work friends and not real-world friends. They'd never seen each other farther than the wine bar across from Q-Co HQ. *Always in view of the Q.* Just like the slogan Jo introduced last spring. She wondered if it had been deleted yet.

"You're sweet," she said into the phone. "Hey, I wanted to give you a heads-up that I used you as a reference for a job interview I had this morning. I couldn't trust Devo would be coherent."

"Good call. Anything for you, honey. It breaks my heart seeing you wasted in *Goonies* boonies," Gia continued, popping gum in Jo's ear. She must have quit smoking again. She had quit two summers ago, and all the pencils in the office had turned up chewed to splinters. The woman's oral fixation was a menace. "I'm obsessed with your new project! The Throwback List! I can't believe no one else had snatched up that hashtag! And that sundae was total food torture porn."

Jo gazed down the boardwalk, toward the anchor in front of Frosty's. "You have no idea. How's the office?"

"Changing fast," Gia said in a cryptic whisper. "I'll let you know if I pull my parachute."

Gia's parachute was working for her family's liquor company. Her sisters were both brand representatives. They had the same hungry eyes and sharp ankles of pharmaceutical reps but spoke with a learned faux-Southern drawl for when bourbon sales were down. Once, on a visit to Palo Alto, they tag-teamed a sale at the wine bar across from Q-Co, a case of copper-distilled gin that smelled a bit like Wren Vos's cologne. Jo had been impressed with the pitch, less so with the gin.

"I'll continue my liquor research just in case. I could be your best employee, one cocktail at a time." Jo snorted, imagining drinking a cotton-candy milk shake as a tax write-off. "In the meantime, please hype me hard to whoever calls?"

"You know it, Jojo. Talk soon. Byezers."

Jo hadn't missed people saying *byezers*. She hung up.

Confession: I've never had a dinner party. Jo started composing the caption to the evening in her head as soon as people started arriving. She couldn't help it; the narrative was building with each photo she took. *Living far from home, I've even spent the last few holidays eating instant mashed potatoes, alone and working. I haven't been great at slowing down or keeping in touch. Tonight was about both.*

So that everyone could chill and be present, we put our phones away. But first, I took these mostly unstaged photos of obliging friends.

"Bianca Boria! How are you? It's been ages," Wren said pleasantly, reaching out to shake Bee's hand as the Birdys came into the Surf & Saucer.

"It's Bianca Boria-Birdy now," Bee corrected.

"Autumn told me you still live next door to Jo's parents."

Bee hugged her coat closer to her chest. "Oh, I moved and came back after college—"

Wren nodded. "Business school, right? You got your MBA?"

"No, I had to defer my acceptance when my grandmother got sick."

"I'm so sorry to hear that." Wren reached out, briefly clasping the shorter woman's shoulder. "I hope you find an online program that suits your needs."

"Um...thank you," Bee said awkwardly. Birdy cleared his throat. "Wren, this is my husband, Dr. Bobby—"

"Call me Birdy," Birdy said, shaking Wren's hand. "We're a real flock tonight. I hope Jo's not serving *wings*."

Wren's brows went up. "Bird pun. Funny. Can I get anyone a glass of wine? I brought a beautiful high-acidity Beaujolais."

"Sure," Bee said. "Hit us with some sour wine, Wren."

With music on and all the guests present, Jo took more pictures than she normally would. The Surf & Saucer speaker system was surprisingly decent, leaving Jo to wonder what her parents were playing all day in Bose surround sound. Probably nothing like the Solange-heavy sensibilities of their firstborn.

Wren poured the first glass of wine. Jo took extra care to aim her camera at Wren's eyes sliding to hers. When she caught the image in the display, it felt like evidence. Heat she could revisit.

With prodding, Autumn sat on top of the counter next to the dessert cheese plate. Knowing there'd be photos involved tonight, she had arrived in fake lashes. The tartan wool of her blanket scarf blended in nicely with the sprigs of rosemary Flo had used to keep the jams from running into the almonds. Jo hoped her parents wouldn't miss the herbs.

"One more," she lied to the crowd, shooing everyone to the seats they'd claimed with jackets folded over chair backs. "I'm gonna run around to different parts of the table and take a picture standing next to each of you."

"How long is the interval on the camera?" Autumn asked with a Tigger bounce in her chair.

"Thirty seconds."

"Perfect. Built for a game!" Autumn surveyed everyone at the table with a glint in her eye, the same look she used to get when it was her turn to tell the ghost story at a sleepover. "The name of the game is Ding. When you hear the buzzer, you have to change positions."

"Keep them classy and relatively believable!" Jo implored.

The buzzer dinged. Jo stood next to Autumn, bent down low, cheek to cheek. Eyes squeezed to only lashes and laugh lines.

The flash went off.

"Ding!" Autumn called.

Jo moved as briskly as her pencil skirt would allow. She already regretted not stopping by home to change out of her interview clothes. Silk seemed so stuffy in a group of wool and cotton. Plus, her booties made her tower over everyone except for Birdy.

Bee's *Diet Industry Dropout* shirt felt like it was daring Jo to crop it out of the shot. If she were working for Q-Co, she would have had to. It would offend investors and alienate influencers. Keeping it in frame could lose Jo old fitness followers, but it would underline her independence from the Q. Jo stood for the photo while Bee sat, so she could make the choice to crop or not to crop later.

The oven dinged. "That's for the bacon-wrapped dates I brought," Birdy said. "It's okay. They're on pretty low."

"You can photograph us together and then we'll get them out," Bee said, smoothing the red plaid of her suspender skirt with one hand and lifting a wineglass with the other. "We've had more than our share of Throwback List screen time."

"Speak for yourself, woman," Birdy said, adjusting his tie just before the flash went off. He leaped out of his seat and disappeared into the prep kitchen.

"New pose!" Autumn reminded everyone. "Ding!"

Jo posed with one hand on Florencio's shoulder. He crossed his eyes and stuck out his tongue to make her laugh but managed to conjure a smolder for the camera before the flash, leaving Jo alone in looking goofy. As she clattered around to the other side of the table, she flicked his ear and he pinched her elbow.

Chirrup-chirrup, Bianca's watch rang, faking everyone out. The camera flashed as they all were looking at the noise.

Bee coughed into her wine and waved her hands in the air. "Sorry, Lita's nighttime meds. It's fine. My mom has it. It's fine."

"New pose!" Autumn stressed. "Quickly, or we'll have two of everyone looking at Bee's watch."

"Sorry!" Bee said again, tapping her watch like she was signaling in Morse code.

Jo froze like an antelope in headlights as she turned to pose with Wren. Around her, she heard the scrape of chairs as everyone else changed positions. Birdy reappeared with a tray that smelled like caramelized sugar and pork.

"If you get to stand..." Wren said. She kicked her chair back. Having come from casual Friday, her Point High staff polo was tucked and belted into olive-green pants. She wrapped an arm around Jo's waist and tugged her close.

Jo felt dip-dyed in heat. She could have ascribed it to expensive wine on an empty stomach or stress, but staring at the dark flecks in Wren's blue eyes, she knew it was just plain hot-round-the-collar lust.

Oh, right, she thought, vision closing to a depth of field as far as Wren's unpierced ears. *Decisiveness was at the top of the Wren pro-list.*

Bianca moaned, "These dates are amazing."

Wren let go of Jo and reached across the table for a date. "Bacon wrapping is an overused fad now—like putting a fried egg on burgers, everyone in Portland was doing that for years—but it does taste good!"

"Thanks?" Birdy said.

With the clock ticking—literally, above the register and horrifically made of seashells—Jo hustled into the kitchen. Autumn trailed her.

"I'll help carry!" Autumn said, theatrically loud. Autumn loud. Once they'd cleared the corner into the prep kitchen, she squeezed Jo's forearms. "Um, sparks fly much?"

"God, is it that obvious?" Jo hissed, dipping into the fridge to cool her jets and grab the salad course.

"That you're having cheer sex?"

Jo lowered her voice, hoping that Autumn would get the hint and whisper. Shushing her could draw attention from the front room. "Is that a *Bring It On* reference?"

"Would you rather I say 'eye fucking'? Because it is sort of too blue for me."

"No, you're right. Cheer sex it is. I feel like I'm sixteen and have no chill at all right now." Safely out of view of everyone but Autumn, she adjusted her skirt hem, shirt hem, and cleavage. "Thank you for suggesting this," Jo said. She felt like she was smiling hard enough to leave permanent creases in her cheeks. "I really didn't think I'd be able to get it all done. But Flo is a prep machine. The pictures look good, Wren looks good, and if Bee's happy noises are to be believed, we have at least one edible dish."

"I'm sure everything will taste great," Autumn said, picking up two salads. "On with the show!"

Each dish set down in the center of the table was an item

crossed off the second-to-last to-do list and a weight off Jo's shoulders. Chilled spinach salads prepped by her dad, Bianca's recipe for sweet and spicy meatballs, and premade mashed potatoes in crystal bowls, Safeway mac and cheese in a floral casserole dish, and pressure-cooker coq au vin served in Henrietta.

She took the last pictures of the food while people served themselves. Untouched food wasn't as homey looking as something with a spoon divot or missing slice.

"Sit down and enjoy yourself, Jo," Autumn chided her. "You have enough pictures to prove that you threw a dinner party."

"And no photography while we're eating, please," Bianca said.

"Sorry, sorry," Jo said, tucking the camera bag into its case and sliding it under her chair. "I'm putting it away! Everyone is safe to eat."

They all clinked glasses of wine or water. Jo hadn't eaten a full meal since before her job interview in another state, so she tamped down any urge to toast and dug into her food.

Bianca's watch went off again, this time with a *bing-bong*, a sound Jo had never heard it make before. How many plates did Bianca have spinning at the same time?

"All the food is great, Jo," Autumn said, casting the reel for compliments so that Jo wouldn't have to go fishing on her own. Jo had forgotten how natural it was for Autumn to gas up everyone in a room. Every other theater kid Jo had ever known, her own sister included, preferred to hold on to the spotlight rather than share it.

"These meatballs are incredible," Birdy said, his attention on Bee typing into her wrist.

"Thank you," Florencio said, toasting his water. "I dumped the jelly on them myself."

"My parents have this amazing pressure cooker in the back," Jo said, hoping to pull Bee back to the dinner. "It cooked most of dinner in, like, half an hour. When I have my own place again, I gotta buy one. Now, someone pass me those bacon-wrapped dates, because the smell is making me actually drool."

"That's what an appetizer is supposed to do," Birdy said proudly as he passed her the platter. "It gets your salivary glands ready to feast!"

"Sounds like science to me." Autumn giggled.

"Is this the spinach salad from the Surf & Saucer menu?" Bianca asked.

"Probably. I've never actually eaten here before," Jo said, examining the spinach and dried cranberry on the chilled glass plate next to her water cup. "My dad prepped them while I was in Seattle."

"I think it's the spinach salad from the Phil plate," Bianca said. She coughed a nervous laugh. "Did you say you've never eaten here before?"

"Most of my meals in town have been Days comps," Jo said with a shrug.

"Have you seen that there's a lunch named after you?" Bianca asked.

"Yeah. I don't know how to feel about being cast as a mushroom-and-onion tart," Jo said. She had transcribed the menu when she built the website. "It's aggressively fungal."

"Think how Eden feels as curry cashew chicken salad," Bee said.

"Oh my God! Someone's a fan!" Wren laughed. "You have the menu memorized?"

"I work four doors down?" Bee said.

"It will make my whole life if I tell my mom that someone other than her thinks about the menu," Jo said. "She keeps threatening to get rid of the scones."

"Don't let her!" Florencio protested. "They're the only sweet non-ice-cream breakfast on the boardwalk!"

"This town needs donuts," Birdy said.

"And decent coffee," Wren said.

"But here, have some surfboards and tea," Jo said, gesturing around them with a shake of her head. She'd never understand her parents' business decisions.

Dinner never got as loud as the Kelly family meals that had inspired it, but there were fewer people and far less sugar in the drinks. They weren't little kids anymore, so perhaps it wasn't a problem that they were better listeners.

Between *mmm-mmm, good* noises and questions about how dishes were prepared, conversation kept up enough that Jo only had to deploy two of her emergency icebreakers—*If you could travel anywhere, where would you go?* and *What's everyone watching on TV?*

The first one was interesting as Autumn was detailing her dream Canadian vacation—the Green Gables museum and a famous theater company in Stratford, Ontario—but then Bianca said, "I hope to see Hawaii before I die," and conversation ground to a halt.

When the cheese-plate dessert was presented, Jo explained that it was an apology for forcing the Sunday Sundae Surprise on them.

"You guys tried to take down the Frosty's sundae?" Wren asked, wiggling her pinkie nail between her molars. "Didn't anyone ever tell you there's a pie at the bottom?"

"No," Bee said tightly. "It's a *surprise*."

"My parents bought us one whenever they had a new baby." Wren shuddered and pushed her plate away. "From October to

December, the pie on the bottom is pumpkin. You guys went late March, so my guess is that you found rhubarb?"

"By the power of Grayskull," Birdy whispered, awed. "She's Sherlock bloody Holmes."

"Nothing is as predictable as life in this fucking town," Wren said, swirling the wine in her glass. "As dull and reliable as the tides washing in and out, day after day."

"'Full of sound and fury, signifying nothing,'" quoted Autumn with a titter. She clapped her hands together twice, a cheerleader getting the crowd to adjust their focus. "Okay, friends—"

"Oh no." Florencio tipped his head back and groaned at the dusty ceiling fans. "We've finished dinner and now she's gonna try to sell us leggings again."

"Or nail stickers," Wren intoned.

"You aren't pyramid scheming again, are you?" Bianca whirled on Autumn, upsetting her wineglass. She clamped down on the top of the cup, catching it just after a single drop flew at her wrist.

"No! Geez, guys. Calm down," Autumn said, handing Bee an extra napkin. "I'm not selling anything. Except for local phenomenon the Throwback List! Did you guys see it on BuzzFeed?"

"It wasn't the Throwback List, really. Just the pictures of the Sunday Sundae Surprise," Jo said, hoping to brush the whole thing aside. She didn't want to say that she celebrated making it onto an aggregator website by having Taco Bell delivered to her hotel room. Not in front of Wren. "They love cutesy local shit. It got more eyes on my account, so I can't complain."

"Jo has a lot of list left to tackle," Autumn said to the table. "I call dibs on 'learn an entire dance routine,' but everything else is up for grabs."

"You have a plan for the dance routine?" Jo asked Autumn.

"Who else is going to teach you a whole dance number?" Autumn asked loftily. "I have dance numbers coming out of my butt. Pat won't let me put them in shows; please let me give them to you!"

"What do you mean 'Pat won't let you'?" Wren asked. "She's your co-chair, not your mother. You had dancing in the fall show."

"Not as much as I wanted," Autumn said. "But that's not the point. We're dividing up Throwback List tasks because everything is more fun with friends."

"You didn't make a printout of the list?" Flo asked his sister.

"He's right," Wren said. "If this were a staff meeting, you'd lose the room about now."

"There's the arcade, climbing the anchor, a glitter fight, a keg stand," Autumn recited from memory. Her obvious time investment was touching. Even Jo didn't have every item memorized. She kept forgetting about needing to get a pet. "Public hide-and-seek definitely needs more than just me. That would be the saddest."

"And I need a place to stage the pinup shoot," Jo said. "I can't think of anywhere I'd feel less sexy than my childhood bedroom. I need a blank wall and privacy."

Wren's fingertips settled in the curve of Jo's arm, holding her ever so lightly in place. Jo turned to look at her, watched the intake of breath between her pink lips—

"I have a blank wall!" Bianca blurted. The tip of her tongue was starting to turn wine-grape red. The last time Jo's mouth had been that color, she'd launched six rolls of toilet paper at the Boria-Birdy maple tree. "You could use the room upstairs at the shop. It's empty other than a desk and a candle."

"Lita's apartment?" Birdy asked.

"No one's using it! It has a ton of natural light, room for your umbrella thingies," Bianca said, swishing a hand dangerously close to the nearest lighting tree. "I think it'd be a great spot for a photo shoot. I could even help with your makeup, if you wanted, Jo."

"That would be amazing! I'd love to harness the power of your makeup skills," Jo said, surprised by the offer. She hadn't expected Bianca to help with any of the list items. She had sort of assumed Bianca wanted to stay at a distance from her, the in-person version of social media mutuals. Cool but not close. But one-on-one help could be like a real friend thing.

"Does the whole list have to be done in Sandy Point to count?" Wren asked, with a questioning pulse of pressure to Jo's arm. She withdrew her hand, stretching out to rest her heels against the nearest empty chair. Jo wondered if she still had a sweeper's quads under those sensible green trousers. "No offense to the townies, but I already commute to the anthill five days a week. Can I entice you to handstand on a microbrew keg in the real world, Johanna?"

Flo stood, reaching for his plate and Birdy's. "Everyone pass me your plates. Phil and Deb gotta serve breakfast out of here in the morning."

"Cleaning up after everyone else's good time is part of hosting," Jo protested. "Guests don't have to be busboys."

"Never let my grandmother hear that," Bee said. "I already have to beg her to put her breakfast cup in the sink. She loves to pretend she's a guest. Birdy, help Flo."

"On it," Birdy said, scooping up plates in a blur.

"Leave the wineglasses," Wren added.

"Check 'fill dishwasher' off the cleaning list on the fridge, Coach!" Jo called to Flo's retreating back.

"Add more tasks, got it!" he called back.

As the energy dipped, Bianca and Wren topped off their glasses with the last of the wine. Autumn filled a cardboard to-go container with leftover cheeses. Jo made a note in her phone to help her parents design to-go containers with the Surf & Saucer logo on them.

"We've never had a real pet store in town," Bianca said, stuck on the *get a pet* list item. "My Tito always said if one opened, I could have a bunny. But it never happened."

"My dad always said no mammals, no reptiles, no cages, no fur," Jo said as she started to disassemble the lighting trees. "Which leaves me with fish or rocks."

"Fish often require rocks," Wren noted.

"Oh!" Autumn yelped with a mouthful of cheese. She threw a hand over her mouth. "Come to the carnival at school next week! You could win a goldfish at the ring toss! And then you could see the Broadway Club performance and pick the dance you want to learn!"

"Perfect!" Jo said.

"I've never been to the spring carnival," Bianca mused.

"Really? How did you learn not to do meth if not from one of the four antidrug booths?" Wren asked, swirling the wine in her glass.

"Are you running a carnival booth?" Jo asked Wren, catching her eye from across the wide, round table. "Dunk the Vice Principal or one-on-one sports trivia?"

Wren's eyes crinkled at the corners. "Afraid not. The spring carnival is strictly volunteer based and the first day of a week of not having to commute here. I will be in Portland, celebrating the end of March Madness with rye and Reedies."

Bee loudly slurped the last of her wine.

"Behold the mighty beta males!" Birdy announced once the dishwasher was filled.

"Thank you both so much," Jo said. "Thank you *all* so much."

Autumn was present, so there was a round of hugs and handshakes before anyone started for the door. Living away from home, Jo had forgotten how often it was possible to be hugged. She felt out of practice. When she was faced with a bear hug, her arms naturally curled back, turning her into an awkward T. rex. She was grateful when Flo dapped her up. She was delighted when Wren hung back, holding the door open for everyone but staying firmly inside.

Autumn winked at Jo before the door closed behind her.

"Ready to tackle that last of the cleanup?" Wren asked when they were alone.

Jo flapped a hand over the mess. "I have to unhide all the beachy shit and move the tables back. You don't have to stay for that. If you don't want to. You don't live here."

A single blond hair fell into Wren's eyes as she shook her head. Back in time, Teen!Jo's heart fluttered at the very idea of Wren's jaw on constant display. "I'll stay a bit."

They stood at either end of a table, shuffling it into place. Inside her heeled booties, Jo's feet ached and she wished she had thought to bring flats with her. She couldn't stop thinking about Bianca's fake Yeezies. They looked like cozy sweaters for feet.

"So, your internet list," Wren said.

"The Throwback List," Jo corrected.

"Is it going to get you where you want to go?" Wren sat on the edge of the table, arms folded. "Is getting the high score at the arcade going to fix all of your problems?"

"Hey, the Seattle City Orchestra thought it was pretty cool," Jo said. "At my hiring panel, they told me the list highlighted my 'youthful exuberance.' No one ever thought of me as youthful before I posted pictures of trying to consume a comical amount of ice cream."

"Do you think you've got the job?" Wren asked.

"I think I've got a chance," Jo said. She laced her fingers together over her stomach. The lump of her navel piercing pressed between her middle and ring fingers. "But it would almost suck to have to leave again so fast."

"Before you have a chance to finish your list?" Wren asked.

"Before I get to spend enough time with everyone I want to." She bit her lip and took a step toward Wren. "We've only been alone for, like, ten minutes in ten years."

She left the overstatement between them. Wren only liked hyperbole when it was flirtatious; otherwise she had to pounce on the correction.

"And only ten seconds tonight," Wren said, a smile lighting up her eyes. Snaking her arms around Jo's waist, she drew the two of them close, hips locking together. "You throw a good party, Johanna. Crowded, though."

The tips of their noses touched. Date sugar from Wren's lips warmed to melting against hers.

"Then maybe you should take me home," Jo murmured.

Wren skimmed her hands down the sides of Jo's waist, pushing the silk roughly over her skin as she dropped a husky whisper in Jo's ear. "Maybe I should take you in the back and then take you home."

Jo kissed her, a hard and emphatic yes.

COMPLETED ITEMS

- ✓ TP Bianca's house
- ✓ Perform onstage
- ✓ Get belly button pierced
- ✓ Redo the yearbook prank
- ✓ Eat the giant sundae at Frosty's
- ✓ Host a dinner party

TO BE COMPLETED

- ○ Surf the Point
- ○ Have a glitter fight
- ○ Get stoned
- ○ Try everything on the menu at Days
- ○ Do a keg stand
- ○ Play hide-and-seek in public
- ○ Break something with a sledgehammer
- ○ Climb the giant anchor on the boardwalk (and survive)
- ○ Get a high score at the boardwalk arcade
- ○ Pose like a pinup girl
- ○ Get a pet
- ○ Learn an entire dance routine
- ○ Eat breakfast at midnight
- ○ Have a bonfire
- ○ Dig up the time capsule

JO: I don't own heels high enough for the pinup shoot. Does anyone else have tall shoes?

BIANCA: Tons!

JO: Thank goodness! Can you bring red or black heels to the shoot?

AUTUMN: Bee, tell her what size you wear.

BIANCA: 6?

AUTUMN: Jo, what size shoe are you?

JO: 9.5

BIANCA: I'll ask my artists if they have tall shoes.

eleven

BIANCA

Birdy was walking on sunshine. Having refunded their honeymoon reservations, he had finalized the deal for Dr. Banns's office and was drowning in furniture catalogs and paint samples.

At six in the morning, Bianca's alarm had been closely followed by Birdy shoving his cell phone under her nose, showing her blindingly white paint.

"What do you want to hear this morning, abuelita?" he asked as Lita and Bee made it into the living room. "I want something dance-able, something upbeat. AC/DC? Creedence? Ooh, lemme play you 'Mambo Number Five.' Have you heard 'Mambo Number Five,' Rosa?"

"Someone is feeling cheeky this morning," Lita said, watching as Birdy high-stepped around her rollator with the TV remote in his hand. She looked at Bianca. "Did you do this to him?"

"No!" Bianca said, scandalized. She set the rollator's parking brake. "This is the joy of choosing the right shade of eggshell paint."

Lita remained confused but blew it off. "Mano, you are too young for my name."

"Lo siento, señora," Birdy said, dramatically hangdog.

"Play your mambo, ridiculous eggshell boy." Lita affectionately patted his arm before scowling at Bee. "I do not want a smoothie this morning."

"Too bad," Bee said, getting up from the couch and starting toward the kitchen. "Smoothies are what I have the ingredients for."

"I want pancakes." Lita raised her voice to Bee's back.

"I don't have pancakes, Lita," Bee called back in a singsong.

"Then find me someone who does." Lita caught the melody easily then dropped it. "You are not the only person in the world."

"Never said I was," Bee said under her breath, covering the backtalk with the slam of a cabinet door as she took down the sugar shaker for her coffee. It had to be stored above Lita height or she would pour it into her smoothies until they started to crust over.

"She is not plotting against you, honeybee," Birdy said, coming around the corner from the dining room. "She just wants to live her life."

Bee rested her back against the counter. "She can't live that life, Birdy."

"Why?" he asked. Reaching over her head, he pulled down her favorite mug, a Cedar Point souvenir bought to commemorate her first trip to Ohio. It clinked against the coffeepot. "Because she's disabled now?"

"What? No, of course not. That's not what I—"

"But," he said, voice firm even as he poured creamer into the coffee and twirled it with a teaspoon, "it is what you implied. It's true that she can't live the life she used to live. She can't go up to her apartment. She can't work twelve-hour days at the shop. But she could have friends. Or maybe she can't. We haven't tried. You get to try having friends. Shouldn't she get to try something, too?"

He handed her the coffee. The first sip helped soothe her resentment. The cup was perfectly tailored to her tastes.

She exhaled into the coconut-scented steam. "I don't want to burden other people with her schedule."

"You mean you don't trust people to do it," Birdy said, quickly adding, "and that's okay! You're the sole arbiter of that schedule. But you could let us try."

Bianca didn't know who this imaginary "us" was. Her mother certainly didn't want to help more than she already had to, and fiancé-Tony's time was an uncrossed boundary. But it was early and Birdy was eager for conversation, so Bianca played along with the hypothetical.

"What if they screw it up? What if she skips her nap and then can't sleep for three days? Or if she forgets a pill and her feet swell up and get stuck in her shoes. Like that time you put her in boots."

Bianca often had nightmares about the rose-embroidered cowboy boots Lita had purchased the year line-dance fever hit Sandy Point. What was left of them—a shameful pile of scissor-shredded leather—lived in a box in the top of Lita's closet. Higher out of reach than the sugar shaker. Even Bianca would need a step stool to face the boot remains. Not that she ever wanted to see them again. She just wasn't allowed to throw them away.

Lita would know.

"How about this?" Birdy asked. He rubbed his hands together, a gambler scenting a bet. "Write down everything that could go wrong. All of it. Make a Lita bible. *The Care and Keeping of Rosa Boria.*"

Bee took a long drink of coffee to make sure he was done

LILY ANDERSON

talking, a trick learned from being friends with Autumn. "Who would read that?"

"The other people who love her."

"And when would I write it?"

"Now. Let me take her to Surfside for breakfast."

She set the mug down. "Just the two of you?"

"If all else fails, I can carry her across the street to Dr. Wiley."

"Dr. Wiley is a pediatrician."

"You're the one who said she was an overgrown toddler."

She shook her head. "I think she said that about me."

"I think I said it about me that time I trimmed my bush too close."

"Birdy!"

He playfully pinched her hip. "Go. Take the morning off. You're hanging out with Jo before lunch?"

"She's coming by the shop to do her photo shoot. I'm just doing her makeup."

A promise born out of too much Malbec was a promise nonetheless. During the dinner party, Bianca would have promised anything to put an end to Wren Vos's hometown bashing. It was just like high school—Wren turning her nose up at anything that could be considered townie, assuming the whole world was better than Sandy Point. It was so much more irritating now that she had a fancy job title given to her by the very town she snubbed.

Birdy caught her mouth in a surprise kiss. "Have fun. Take dirty pictures."

"Pinups are barely dirty. Besides, I'm not the subject."

"But you sure could be. . . ." He stroked up her forearm and waggled his eyebrows before turning on his heel, back to the living room. "Lita! Let's get your dancing shoes on, girl. I'm taking you for pancakes! We'll listen to 'Mambo Number Five' on the way!"

Bee flipped through her smartwatch, forwarding alarms to Birdy's phone before silencing them for the morning. She touched the kissed patch of her lips and smiled.

Birdy had finally managed to contaminate her with some of his hopeful happiness.

"I can't get over the size of this room," Jo said, staring up at the lights recessed into the high ceiling as she finished setting up the lighting equipment Bianca recognized from the dinner party: gigantic white umbrellas and reflective tarps. "Is that a kitchen back there?"

"A kitchenette. Just a sink and a dishwasher. Very Tito priorities. He never wanted to wash a dish after the navy. Said he was too old for KP duty." Bee closed the door that looked out over the shop. "I checked in Dede's station and behind the counter, but I don't see the shoes she said she was going to drop by for you. Do you want me to text her?"

Tapping the screen of her watch, Bee checked the time. Bonnie had an appointment this morning, and Bee was praying that she would beat the client to the shop. It was too awkward to try to enforce her tardiness policy on her own mother.

Jo shook her head. "No, no. Don't worry about it. They were more for confidence than anything else." She positioned her ever-present camera stand in front of the longest, blankest wall. Where Lita's framed Santana posters used to hang over the awful floral couch. "Bianca, you could rent this out!"

"The only entrance is inside the store. No one but family could live in here. I should clean it out and put one of the artists up here, but no one wants to leave their view downstairs." She pointed toward the four-panel room divider that covered the window, giving privacy to the empty room. "It faces Main Street, not the ocean."

Jo raised her eyebrows significantly. "Then you should hire someone who doesn't care about the ocean but who would love to have crown molding."

"My grandfather would be so honored that you noticed. He installed that himself before he and Lita moved in up here. He thought it made it feel more like a home and less like an office."

Jo fiddled with the height of her tripod before nervously glancing over her shoulder. "Are you sure it's okay that I hog this space for an hour or two? No one is going to want to use the bathroom while I'm in my undies?"

"No one. The shop isn't even open today. My mom has a special appointment, but she's using one of the downstairs stations."

If she ever gets here. Bee checked her watch again.

With the lighting trees in place and blazing false daylight at them, Jo moved to sit.

"Not to sound like a creep," Bee said, looking at Jo's loose sweater and slacks, "but you're probably gonna want to change your clothes before hair and makeup, not after."

"Right, right," Jo said. She stood and kicked off her shoes. "I brought something for this."

Bianca barely had time to avert her eyes before Jo had her clothes off, briefly revealing the tobacco-colored lace chosen for the shoot. From inside her gray tote, she fished out a wrinkled khaki trench coat.

"Are you planning on becoming the town flasher after this?" Bianca asked.

Jo sheepishly slid on the trench coat, belting it loosely around her waist. "No one in my family had a bathrobe."

"You should have asked me!" Bianca said. "Everyone in my house has a robe."

"I really don't know if either of my parents wears pajamas. They both appear fully dressed every morning. Always have," Jo said. She swept her hair back without even glimpsing a mirror— *How in the world?* Bianca thought—and sat down on top of the desk.

Bee had one of the instrument trays from downstairs. On it, she set out clean makeup brushes and the various cosmetics she and Jo had compiled to match the reference photo displayed on Jo's phone.

Ignoring how odd it was to be so close to a face that until recently she had only associated with resentment, Bee dappled Jo in primers.

It's not flip-flopping to get to know someone, she assured the part of her that felt disloyal to her younger self.

"Wow, being in my underwear is so much weirder than I thought it would be," Jo said, aiming her gaze at the kitchenette rather than staring directly into Bee's eyes. "I really didn't think it would bother me. I've worn less clothes to the beach."

"Less clothes than a trench coat?" Bee teased. "I would hope so."

She started sponging foundation onto Jo's cheeks. Jo flinched at the cold liquid.

"S-sorry," Jo stammered, wiping her palms on her thighs. "This is the most nervous I've been doing a list item."

"Really?" Bee held the sponge away from Jo's face. "Because I was there when you saw the piercing needle."

"Yeah, but that was done by you," Jo protested, biting her lower lip. "You're Bianca Boria—"

"Bianca Boria-Birdy." Bee was used to correcting people. No one in town ever called her Mrs. Birdy. Sometimes people called Birdy Dr. Boria. Lita called him Mr. Bianca when he took what she considered the wrong side in a fight.

"—you're effortless," Jo continued, talking too fast to leave Bee room to argue—or ask for elaboration. "What if I can't make myself look normal on camera? I never take self-portraits with my actual camera. I like selfies because there's a built-in mirror. I can control my whole situation."

Bee continued blending foundation into Jo's skin. The woman didn't even need it. Her color was already even, her skin unbothered by bumps or scars or scraggly mustache hairs. "You're a pretty girl who exercises for fun, Jo. What could go wrong?"

"My face is going to do that thing where it slides right off my head," Jo groaned.

"Excuse me?" Bee asked.

"I make this specific, awful face when I'm uncomfortable in a picture," Jo said. "So many of the dinner-party photos I didn't post look just like this."

She made the face. It did appear as though her smile were attempting a getaway.

Bianca had to hold in a giggle. It would be so rude to laugh directly into Jo's face.

"See!" Jo cried. "It's bad."

"Stop squirming or you're gonna crease your foundation," Bee warned. She held Jo's jaw still between her thumb and forefinger. "You control the list. If you take the pictures and you hate them, you'll delete them. Or find a different way to represent it for the internet. The important thing isn't how you sell it, it's that you're trying stuff that scares you."

"That is literally the opposite of how I have been thinking about this," Jo mused to the back wall. "I start with the plan for the post and then work backward."

Bianca shook her head too hard and had to push her head scarf back into place. "That means you're prioritizing the consumption. You're more than your social media."

Jo cut her eyes at her. "Yeah, but outside of social media, I'm just a grown woman living with her parents. The Throwback List is the only thing keeping me sane." She wrung her hands in her lap. "I really do appreciate your help today. Just let me know what you think a fair price is for makeup services."

Bee scoffed as she leaned over to her instrument table, loading her favorite fluffy brush with eyeshadow. "You don't have a job, Jo."

"That doesn't mean you should give me free labor. You are the only person I'd trust with sharp implements near my eyes. You've got professionally steady hands and technique. I have neither. Before homecoming once, I poked Autumn in the eye trying to help her put on fake lashes. I haven't even looked at lash glue since."

"Most people don't let it dry on the strip long enough before they apply. Rookie mistake."

"I poked her in the *eye*. With a finger that I have to keep on my hand *forever*. Ugh, it was disgusting. Squishy."

"Don't make me flinch while I am this close to your face." Bee motioned for Jo to close her eyes. Sweeping arcs created shadow, deepened her lids, brightened the deep set of her eyes.

"Your eyes are less hooded than Meghan Markle's," she observed.

"I know! And I'm, like, *so much younger* than her," Jo said, peeking out of one eye. "I keep almost cutting bangs so that people will stop comparing us, but there's nothing that screams *life crisis* like new bangs."

Bee agreed. That's why her bangs were just artfully rolled and pinned long hair.

"This is the first time I've ever had another woman of color do my makeup," Jo said. "It is cool that I don't have to tell you not to use pale concealer on me. I don't know what it is about having vaguely Anglo features that makes girls at MAC counters want to cover me in buff beige powder. I eventually just gave up. I was tired of paying to come out like a ghost."

"Do people try to guess your race to your face?" Bee asked Jo.

"Daily. You?"

Bee pointed at herself. "Hello, I am also ambiguously brown. My ancestors are from an American territory, and no one has ever said, *'Oh you're Puerto Rican!'*" She set to work on Jo's other eye. "My grandparents wouldn't think that was a bad thing. The point of living here was to blend in. Not to stand out. My mom never even learned Spanish."

"It's supposed to be safer to assimilate," Jo said. "They never think about how it means you're supposed to disappear."

"White people don't dream about blending in." Bee sighed. "The American dream is being loudly and defiantly yourself. For better or worse."

"But first you have to decide what the *you* things are." Jo wrung her hands in her lap. Bee had to tip her chin up again when she tried looking down. "After the dinner party, Wren asked me what the list was getting me."

"Shocking," Bee said drolly. She was zero percent surprised that Wren Vos could only quantify things in terms of what they earned her. Judging from the dinner party, Wren appeared to be the same hipster snob Bee remembered from high school. The kind of person who even hated the things she liked. Like the bacon-wrapped dates that she insulted *and* bogarted.

"I mean, I mostly just wanted something to do," Jo said. "But I like testing the boundaries of what I am. When I first read the list, every single item felt so far away from me. But I haven't hated any of it so far. I've been uncomfortable, I've been frantic—"

"You've been surprised by pie underneath ice cream."

"Never forget," Jo concurred. She picked up the end of her coat sash and wound it around her knuckles like a boxer. "I haven't flaked on anything yet. But I might just be saying that so I don't chicken out of taking a picture of myself in my underwear."

"It's hard to try new things," Bianca said. "What if you suck at them? We're a culture obsessed with winning."

"I like blaming the culture for it. It makes me feel better than saying that I'm a competitive bitch." Her eyes slid up to Bee's. "You posed in a bikini in high school. Were you nervous?"

Bianca rarely thought about the Fat Doesn't Mean Ugly picture she had been known for in high school. It had even made it into the yearbook, not to commemorate any kind of body positivity but on the *Beach Weather* page that showcased the various ways people dressed on the beach through the year. From Bianca's gingham bikini to Vince Rice's snowsuit during that year's freak blizzard.

"I wasn't nervous. I was pissed off," Bianca explained. "It was the summer before senior year, and I wanted a new bathing suit.

And that already started a fight about my weight because I couldn't get one in town unless I wanted to get an old-lady suit with a swim skirt. I was seventeen and wanted to feel cute. I couldn't even wear lipstick."

"Seriously? You weren't allowed? But you love makeup."

Bee threw a guilty glance at the red candle, burning in Tito's memory. "My family was obsessed with the idea of me not growing up too fast. They thought lipstick was too sexual."

"I'd argue, but you're literally dressing me up so I can take my clothes off."

"You already took your clothes off. You're clinging to a coat." Bee chuckled. "I fought so hard to get that particular gingham bathing suit. It was the first vintage-looking piece of clothing I ever bought. I found it for cheap online and convinced my mom to buy it. And then Tito saw it come out of the box in two pieces and flipped out. He loved me, but he hated my body. That's a weird thing to say, but it was equally weird that he had an opinion. Some people just hate fatness. He was sort of offended by it. People in his family weren't fat. I'm built like Lita, but she didn't gain weight until she had my mom. I've been fat the whole time.

"When Tito saw the bikini, he said that I was going to humiliate myself putting my stomach on display. Like people can't see the curve of my body underneath clothes. Like a bikini was going to reveal some great and terrible truth of my fatness. So I put the bikini on and went down to the beach to ask a tourist to take a picture of me on my phone. I posted it on Facebook because my whole family was watching what I was doing online. I just wanted to prove that it wouldn't change anything. It was like wearing lipstick. It wasn't like the first time I wore makeup to school, my virginity fell off. People could always see me, no matter how much my family thought I should be hiding."

"Your super-courageous act of body positivity was motivated by spite?" Jo asked.

"I'm mostly powered by spite. And coffee."

Jo smiled. "I can't think of where else I would have been inspired to do my own pinup shoot. It must have been something I wanted to do because you did it."

Bee hardly counted standing in a bathing suit as posing as a pinup. In the picture in question, she was a chubby teenager in a plain ponytail.

"Because if the fat girl could do it, why not you?" she asked, too sharp.

Jo gently pulled her head back, out of Bee's grip. Her filled eyebrows formed a concerned V. "No, not at all. If you did it, then it was probably worth doing. You never bothered with the low-level bullshit everyone else did."

"You mean 'having fun'?" Bee asked ironically. "Are you sure you weren't influenced by a real pinup? Like Bettie Page?"

"I was never interested in Bettie Page," Jo said, putting her face back into Bianca's care. "I prefer my porn gayer and less old-timey."

"I didn't ask if you like Bettie Page recreationally!" Bee giggled, swatting at Jo's shoulder. "I mean that she's most people's first pinup. She was mine, and I hardly want to bang girls at all." Jo gave her a significant blink and Bianca laughed. "I live in the same world as Lizzo. Come on!"

Jo cackled, almost ruining her blush as her neck snapped back like a Pez dispenser. Happy Jo was the Tin Man with all of his joints oiled.

The lip pencil stole the conversation for a moment as Bianca focused on tracing a clean line around Jo's mouth. It was hard to push her ego down enough to make space for the revelations of the last minute.

Jo Freeman had put items on her bucket list to emulate her.

The TP making number one made more sense. Even so, Bee couldn't yet feel the truth of the moment in her bones.

Jo Freeman really had been jealous of her once.

The stairs creaked with body weight. Bianca dropped the lip pencil onto the instrument table with a clang. She raced toward the door as Jo tightened the sash of her coat. The door opened just enough to let through a *Shining*-level amount of Bonnie Boria's appalled bug eyes before Bianca wedged her body behind the knob to keep it from opening farther.

"Mom!" she shouted, pushing forward to move her mother out of the way. She closed the door behind her, standing on the landing above her mother. She adjusted her head scarf imperiously. "Do you need something?"

"What are you doing in there?" Bonnie asked. "Is it true you're having a naked photo shoot?"

Bee looked over the railing of the stairs, seeing Dede standing at the counter with a pair of red high heels.

"I promised I'd bring shoes, but I forgot last night," she squeaked up to Bee. "Bonnie and I ran into each other in the parking lot."

"I'll take them," Bee said. "Jo's makeup is almost done."

Dede scampered upstairs, her chin tucked into the cartoon dinosaur on her sternum. The red patent-leather shoes rubbed together as they swung from her fingertips, making almost as much noise as the stairs. Bee took them by the ankle straps and thanked Dede for making a special trip to help Jo.

When the front door closed behind Dede, Bonnie's jaw dropped. "It's true? You're letting a girl take her clothes off in your grandparents' home?"

"It's not their home," Bianca said. "They once lived here. Lita's home is my house."

"Oh, it's *your* house now," Bonnie said, acerbic. "I see. Well, Little Miss Square Slice, *that* room is the office in *your* business."

"That room is empty," Bee snapped back. "I can't rent it out. I can't convert it. Am I just supposed to light the candle and sweep out the cobwebs?"

Bonnie's lips pressed together into bloodless anger. "It's not right, Bianca."

"I didn't realize you were such a prude, Mom. Was that not your butt crack in *Inked* magazine?"

Bonnie glared at her. "I was displaying the art on my back, Bianca, and making money for this shop. That article brought in a lot of customers."

"That was art, but my friend wanting to reclaim some of her sexuality from the infantilization of living with her parents is what?"

"None of our business and does not belong *at* our business."

"It's upstairs. We aren't open just because you're taking a special appointment—and barely on time, by the way. This isn't about business. This is about you not wanting anyone inside your dad's house!"

"Don't talk to me like that, Bianca. I am your mother and one of the artists of this business. You need to think like a professional and—"

"And what, Mom? Promote our work? Advertise for us like you do?" Dumping the red heels on the floor, Bee pulled the shirt over her head, frizzing her hair in defiance. "How about I get some professional pictures taken of some of our art?"

Dripping in inked rose petals and rubies below the cups of her bra the word *Boria* connected to the crescent-moon curve of her underbust by delicately drawn lace.

"I'm very proud of Dede's lacework," Bianca said to her mother, voice clipped. "I've been neglecting my duties by not advertising her strengths. I have thigh tattoos to match, but I wouldn't want to disgrace the family by having pictures taken in a bra that doesn't match my chonies. Now, when your appointment is over, please lock the front door after you're done sanitizing your station. Cruz has a ten o'clock session there tomorrow. Excuse me."

COMPLETED ITEMS

- ✓ TP Bianca's house
- ✓ Perform onstage
- ✓ Get belly button pierced
- ✓ Redo the yearbook prank
- ✓ Eat the giant sundae at Frosty's
- ✓ Host a dinner party
- ✓ Pose like a pinup girl

TO BE COMPLETED

- ◯ Surf the Point
- ◯ Have a glitter fight
- ◯ Get stoned
- ◯ Try everything on the menu at Days
- ◯ Do a keg stand
- ◯ Play hide-and-seek in public
- ◯ Break something with a sledgehammer
- ◯ Climb the giant anchor on the boardwalk (and survive)
- ◯ Get a high score at the boardwalk arcade
- ◯ Get a pet
- ◯ Learn an entire dance routine
- ◯ Have a bonfire
- ◯ Eat breakfast at midnight
- ◯ Dig up the time capsule

BIANCA: If you don't have Easter plans, you're welcome to join us for Family Dinner tonight at 5:30. Autumn & Flo are coming!

JO: Thanks for the offer, but I have to pass. I quietly bulldozed my dad into cooking tonight.

BIANCA: How do you bulldoze quietly?

JO: Since I've been back, my dad hasn't cooked. He makes salads and sandwiches at the store but zero cooking at home.

So I noticed it. Out loud. A couple times. And so today he is barbecuing, Mom got a nap, and I'm getting ribs. Everyone wins.

BIANCA: You're a Capricorn, aren't you?

JO: I don't know what my birthday has to do with this.

But yes 🐐 💪

twelve

AUTUMN

The spring-break carnival—a PTA fund-raiser slash *please don't get so bored that you try meth* stopgap—spanned the inside of the main building, including the gym. The setup looked the same as it had for as long as Autumn could remember: every inch of wall space packed with all-ages games, G-rated dares like "hot coals" made of Lego bricks, and water-bottle flip contests. Complimentary coffee and lemonade flowed all day, depending on one's just-add-water preference. Tinny pop music blasted out of the speakers Autumn and Flo had helped carry in at sunrise.

"Spin the wheel, win a piece of candy!" Autumn called to a passing group of carnival goers, her barking only slightly louder than anyone else's. So much for all those vocal-projection lessons.

The candy wheel might not have been as exciting as one of the skill games, but Autumn counted herself lucky not to be running one of the more thankless booths—like being in charge of rotating kids in and out of the bounce house at the other end of the gym.

The line was already starting to wind in front of the emergency exits.

"Spin the wheel, win a piece of candy!"

"Two tickets for a miniature candy? You scammer, that's like a dollar per piece!" said Jo, appearing with a fistful of tickets and—to Autumn's surprise and delight—Bianca.

"Is it a carnival if you aren't being ripped off?" Bee asked, arching one of her dramatically drawn eyebrows.

"It's a fun-size candy, which is bigger than a mini and you know it!" Autumn jumped down off her stool to scoop Bee into a hug. "What did I do to deserve a tag-team visit from both of my favorites? Bee, you've never surprised me before!"

Normally, Bee texted a preface to every phone call. That was still an improvement from college when she would email Autumn to let her know that there would be a text notification before she left her dorm two doors down to knock on the door. She'd never shown up unannounced to anything a day in her life. She needed more invitations than a vampire.

Bee laughed in her ear as Autumn swished the two of them side to side. "Surprise, sweets!"

Autumn stepped back but kept her hands on Bee's shoulders. "How did you slip away?"

"Birdy is taking Lita to get a pedicure. We had a nail-clipping incident this morning that almost tore our family apart, but, good news, hi, I'm free!"

"We ran into each other in the front yard," Jo told Autumn. "I told her I had to stop for cash to get in and she flashed me a twenty."

Autumn's heart soared. Her dream of her friends being friends was coming true.

Next stop, three-part harmony!

"So, this is the spring carnival?" Bee asked, caught up reading the banner over every station. She tucked in her elbows as a gaggle of kids ran by on their way to the Frisbee and football toss. "It is so much more popular than I imagined. And more indoors. I was picturing the last scene in *Grease*."

Autumn beamed at her. "Because you are my friend and you are perfect."

"I can't believe you've never been to the spring carnival before!" Jo said to Bee.

"Believe it!" Bee said with a laugh. "While you guys were playing laundry-hamper Hungry Hungry Hippos—we passed it on the way in, I have to go back—I was being quiet and out of the way somewhere. Or secretly listening to Lita's records with headphones on. If only I'd known that I would be forced to hear 'Black Magic Woman' every morning for the rest of my life, I could have spent my time on something worthwhile."

Autumn had known in the larger sense that Bianca hadn't really participated in any extracurricular fun things when she was a kid. There were very few town events that Autumn could name that Bee had attended. Imagining tiny Bianca, alone and friendless, made Autumn want to cry. More so because she could perfectly picture baby Bee, in the too-tight French braid she'd worn through high school and pristine white tights. It wasn't that she hadn't liked Bianca when they were kids. She'd just never noticed her at all, which felt like an even greater sin. If Autumn could change anything about the past, she would tell her younger self to take a chance on the prissy kid who spent recess staying clean and practicing penmanship.

Not that she thought her younger self would have been able

to slow down long enough to listen. Baby!Autumn had only been interested in things that could make her a Broadway starlet or seem cool to Flo.

Jo stood on the toes of her gray suede loafers, scanning the handwritten signs over the many booths.

"Is there an age limit for the bounce house yet?" she asked.

"No way!" Autumn said. "PTA invested in the deluxe bouncer for sober grad nights. It has a two-thousand-pound weight limit. Just wait for an adult jump session. They happen every nine minutes. Or whenever a Pitbull song starts, whichever comes first."

"Bianca." Jo turned to Bee, breathless with excitement. "We have to bounce. I took a class at an inflatable gym once. It's so fun."

"I don't know if I'm wearing a bounce-house bra." Bee rubbed one of her straps through her sweater.

"And I don't think my mattifying foundation will hold up." Jo laughed. "But I'm gonna try!"

Over Bee's finger-waved hair, Autumn could see Pat Markey charging toward them. Her stomach sank down to her red glitter sneakers. Pat never charged toward her with good news.

"Good morning, Jo, Bianca," Pat said pertly. Her recall for past student names put Autumn to shame. Autumn had to check her roster before second-period freshman drama every day. There were simply too many Kaydens and yet no one *looked* like a Kayden. "Aren't you both lovely today?"

"Thank you, Mrs. Markey," Jo and Bianca intoned. Autumn tried not to look down at her flannel shirt. It was never warm enough in Sandy Point for the clothes bought in Los Angeles. Standing near Bee's immaculate hair and makeup and Jo's expensive fabrics made her glitter sneakers seem costume-y.

"Miss Autumn," Pat said with syrupy softness. She still hadn't gotten the hang of calling Autumn by her surname. "There was a coffee spill over on the floor where your Broadway Club is setting up for their performance. I told you that putting them in the main room would be a problem. Now, I don't know where the custodians are, they're so busy today. If you could be a dear and—"

"Autumn, do you have the keys for the custodial closet? Or a mop?" Jo asked, popping the *P* at the end of the sentence pointedly to stop Autumn from running to clean the spill.

Autumn pressed hard into the balls of her feet. She thought she could hear the glitter crunching. "No. I parked next to our head custodian Jim this morning. I know he's on campus—"

"Great!" Jo said. She squinted a sarcastic smile at Pat. "Then, Mrs. Markey, you should track down Jim the head custodian. Is the Broadway Club safe in the meantime?"

"Y-yes," Pat stammered, visibly unnerved. It was rare for her to fail at forced delegation. "I'll go check the front office and see if Jim has his radio."

"Bye, Mrs. Markey!" Bianca said cheerfully.

Jo whirled on Autumn. "Don't let that vest beat you up! You're not her personal complaint department!"

I kind of am, Autumn realized. She took all of Pat's complaints, whether they were about the theater, the PTA, or Autumn's classes being too loud on the other side of the accordion wall.

"It's a PTA event," Autumn said. She jammed a miniature Snickers in her mouth and chewed sadly. "I'm the staff liaison."

"So you have to go mop the mystery puddle?" Jo asked.

"She doesn't have real authority over you, does she?" Bee asked. "She can't fire you or give you an F?"

"I'm sure she hasn't forgotten how many Fs she gave me. Algebra was *not* my subject."

"It wasn't hers either," Jo snapped. "She's a fucking choir teacher."

"She hates all of my ideas," Autumn said. "I didn't think she hated me in high school. But maybe that's why she and Mr. Hearn cast me as Ado Annie and not Laurie. She doesn't think I'm pro- tagonist material."

"You were too funny not to be Ado Annie," Jo comforted her. "The rest of that show was boring as hell."

"Speaking of people who hate us, Jen G just walked in with her kids," Bee said.

Jo snuck a glimpse. "Yikes. They sure got her head size, huh?"

"Huge noggins," Bee agreed.

"People watching is the best part of spring carnival. Wait until you see the crowd of mommies that follows Flo around." Autumn giggled. She shooed her friends away. "You two go have fun! The Broadway Club performance starts across the gym in forty-five minutes!"

An hour if I have to find a mop, she added silently.

"We'll meet you there!" Jo promised.

"I'll set a reminder on my watch," Bee said.

"God help us. More beeping." Jo laughed. "Come on, Bianca. You've never played shoe-box Jenga, and we are going to fix that!"

An hour later, with the carnival in full swing, the gym filled to fire code. Autumn turned the candy wheel over to Glen from the science department. As she walked across the gym, she imagined herself in the opening number of *Beauty and the Beast*. There went Jen G with a scowl like always. The same old homemade soap for sale. Dr. Wiley was doing a victory dance beside the rubber-duckie race. Diane, the president of the PTA, had her face painted like a butterfly as she sank shot after shot at the football toss—her twin giants screaming her on shouting "QB MOM! QB MOM!"

Between the palatial bounce house and the selfie booth full of floating picture frames, there was an empty patch of gym floor that had been roped off after the spill. The sign overhead designated it *Dance Party Central.* Against the back wall baked goods were stacked for the impending cake-then-cookie walks beside the plastic Party City top hats Autumn had paid an exorbitant shipping fee on. Her four-person Broadway Club was outside, warming up away from the prying eyes of the audience that was starting to assemble in front of the empty booth. Including Bee, Jo, and Florencio, who had a stuffed snake—the grand prize for library mini golf— wrapped around his shoulders.

"Hello, I love the spring carnival," Bee announced, handing Autumn a sleeve with two hand-warming pretzels.

"A convert!" Autumn exclaimed. She tore off a piece of pretzel with her teeth. The salty carbs provided a nice contrast to her bellyful of chocolate and caramel.

"There was an unforeseen tragedy at the fishbowl toss," Florencio said.

"Yes," Jo scoffed. "And that tragedy is that I am fucking garbage at throwing a Ping-Pong ball."

Flo gestured toward a passing family with small children on their way to the Craft Corner. "And watching your language around kids."

"Oops." Jo covered her mouth and snickered. One of her fingers was splotched with paint. "Everyone, please meet my replacement very first pet, Rock Rockamore."

In her palm was a rock hastily painted pale blue. Above a red marker smile—with U-shaped tongue—it had googly eyes resting on top of hot-glue blobs.

Autumn squinted at it. "Is it supposed to resemble Grover from *Sesame Street?*"

Jo gave an approving nod to the rock. "Grover is the best Muppet, so Rock Rockamore and I will take that as a compliment."

"You're going to say its full name every time?" Flo asked her archly.

"Don't be bitter because I didn't use your Rock the Rock Rockson idea, Coach."

Flo pushed up his sleeves. "I should get the rest of the coffee cups out of my car. The beverage station was looking low when we came in."

"But the Broadway Club performance is about to start!" Autumn said.

"I'll catch the dances when Jo posts them!" Florencio said, bounding away from them, throwing deuces over his head.

"What a fucking Boy Scout," Jo said. "Is his trunk just a huge emergency kit or what?"

"You're kidding, but he literally has a bug-out bag packed for every season in there," Autumn said.

Jo snorted in disbelief. "He is so his father's son."

Autumn couldn't have agreed more. "Try telling him that, would you? He won't listen to me."

"There she is!" Autumn turned in time to see Ginger Jay skittering toward her with arms outstretched, stiletto fingernails wagging. "Our little triple threat! Is that Autumn Kelly or Bob Fosse?"

"I consider myself more of a Gwen Verdon type— Oof!" Ginger's red-lacquered nails clacked together as she enveloped Autumn in a squashy hug.

Ginger Jay was all intense eye contact and zebra-striped poly-ester. She considered her pop of animal print to be her townie signature, adorably unaware that everyone in town thought of her as the puppet alter ego from her old ad campaign. She smelled like the height of suburban class: a Macy's perfume counter and retinol cream.

Towering over most of the crowd, the Chief adjusted the sleeves of his flannel. Autumn noticed, in horror, that his blue checks matched her own. Instead of casual cosplaying Dorothy, she was dressed as her dad. Mortifying.

"Sorry we're late," the Chief rumbled. Birdy liked to say that Chuck Kelly was one of few men who had a mustache sound, even without the look. *The Chief's got a voice that could fight a bear.* He searched around, obviously scanning for Florencio. His nostrils flared as he looked down at Autumn with hazel eyes that mirrored her own. "We didn't miss the show, did we? Where's your mother?"

"She went to spend Easter with Aunt Fred," she said. She looked back at the door. "Flo popped out for just a second. I'm sure he'll be right back."

"I'm sure," the Chief parroted. He looked down his long nose at Jo and narrowed his eyes. "That's not little Jo Freeman behind you, is it? Where are your curls?"

"Heya, Chief Chuck," Jo said. "I've never seen so much of your face before! Don't you miss your flavor saver?"

The Chief touched his bare upper lip. "It's been a cold spring, I'll tell you that for free. Now, who do we have to bribe to get this show on the road?"

"Psst! Miss Kelly!"

The Broadway Club, in their matching black T-shirts and light-weight jazz shoes, were standing in a stiff line behind the velvet rope, doing their best to wave and whisper at Autumn without drawing the attention of proud parents and fellow students in the audience.

Autumn excused herself. She gave the signal to the kid at the bounce house and the music paused.

While the Broadway Club scrambled to look casual in their places, Autumn tapped on the cakewalk microphone. Her voice boomed out at the crowd.

"Hello, Point High Privateers! Yo-ho-ho!"

There was a return "Yo-ho-ho!"—although the loudest voices came from the club members lined up in tableau behind Autumn.

"I am Miss Kelly, the drama teacher here at Point High."

There was a hoot from the crowd.

"This year we have a new club on campus for students who love to perform but don't want to wait for Mrs. Markey and me to make up our minds about the fall musical."

"*Hadestown!*" someone in the crowd shouted. Probably a Kayden.

"The Broadway Club is here to perform a couple of numbers we put together in just a few weeks of meeting after school. Any Point High student is welcome to come hang out with us after school Tuesdays and Thursdays onstage in the auditorium to learn Broadway dance numbers and sing harmonies or just talk about the joyful expression that is musical theater—"

Behind her, a throat cleared. Autumn was hogging center.

"And with that!" She clapped her hands together in a half bow. "Let me introduce to you, for the very first time: the Point High Broadway Club!"

The canned music kicked in, forcing the folks in the bounce house to jump around to the faux-Motown sound of the *Hairspray* karaoke track Autumn had trimmed in GarageBand. She hurried out of the way, skirting the audience and sneaking in between Bee and Jo as the Broadway Club exploded into song and dance, introducing themselves as "The Nicest Kids in Town."

Pat would never in a million years let Autumn stage a John Waters musical on the main stage.

The Broadway Club nailed the synchronized fan kicks in "9 to 5" and no one dropped their hat during "One" from *A Chorus Line*. At the last trumpet, the club hit their final pose, clutching the brims of their plastic top hats with perfect Fosse extension.

The crowd applauded, which caught the attention of the rest of the carnival goers and inspired them into applauding, too. Autumn stuck her fingers in her mouth and whistled, the loudest expression of her joy she could muster. The Broadway Club was swarmed by parents with bouquets and friends with video.

"Wow, they're really good," Jo noted, clapping along with the crowd. "I am not going to be able to go from zero to *A Chorus Line*."

"It's just a little back, step, pivot, step," Autumn scoffed. "Easy peasy."

"We've done it, Bianca," Jo said. "That's everything spring carnival has to offer us. Unless you want to go back and join the line for band room *Rock Band*."

Bee shook her head. "Birdy would be so sad if I played *Rock Band* without him. We fell in love crushing 'Bohemian Rhapsody.'"

"I wish we'd done this together in high school." Autumn sighed. "I have to go back to the candy wheel. I want to play with my friends!"

"In high school, what would you guys have done next?" Bee asked.

"Go home, terrorize Florencio if he was around," Autumn said, searching around the gym for any sign of her brother. "Instead of hiding from his dad like a loser."

"I feel like spring carnival was the beginning of an entire week of sleepovers," Jo said. "As long as neither of us was leaving town for Easter, we'd just go from my house to Autumn's house and back again until our parents got sick of having an extra kid around."

"I didn't sleep anywhere that wasn't my house until the first night of college," Bee said. "I was such a scaredy-cat."

"Seriously?" Jo asked. "What about vacations?"

"We never went anywhere." Bee shrugged. "I probably slept at my grandparents' apartment above the shop once, I just don't remember."

"What if," Autumn mused, starting a thought that she hadn't had time to formulate, "we had a sleepover? The three of us?"

"In my parents' house or your studio?" Jo asked in a monotone that suggested she didn't like either idea.

"Neither," Autumn said, hoping thousands of dollars of improv classes would help fan an idea into a proposal. "A girls' weekend. Just the three of us."

"I couldn't get away for a whole weekend, Autumn." Bee frowned. "Not right now, not without a ton of notice—"

"But that's just it!" Autumn said, verbally tap-dancing faster. She felt like she was eight years old, performing a one-woman show to try to get her parents to look at her and only her. "We could stay here! In town. In a vacation house. I've never stayed in Waterfront Cove. Have either of you? Bee, you'd be as close to home as you would be at work. Just on the other side of the hill."

"Where are we going to get a vacation house?" Bee asked slowly.

"It's not tourist season yet," Jo said.

"It's the start!" Bee said, counting problems on her fingers. "It depends on what surf groups are coming through town, what the weather for the next month looks like, whether or not the Tillamook Creamery scheduled their beer and wine weekend at the same time as the kite festival—"

"I'll go ask Ginger!" Autumn blurted. "Ginger Jay owns vacation houses. I'll see if she has an open weekend coming up. You guys can go through whatever else on the list you want to tackle that weekend. We could definitely cross off eating breakfast at midnight. And we could play all the sleepover games we used to!"

"I'm in," Jo said. "Bee?"

"Okay," Bianca said, nodding more and more resolutely. "Find a weekend and I will spend the night. But it has to be within city limits. Not even one exit up."

"I promise to keep you out of Rockaway Beach," Autumn said.

Bee lowered her gaze to the floor. "It's not that I wouldn't like to go somewhere farther, it's just . . ."

"We get it," Autumn said quickly. "You need to stay close to home. Just in case Lita needs you."

"In case anyone needs me," Bee murmured.

"Miss Kelly!" Eden exclaimed, bouncing toward them. "Those dances were so awesome! Why don't the seniors get a dance break in *9 to 5*? That's from our showcase, isn't it?"

"I had planned to use it for the Senior Showcase, but we cut it for time," Autumn said delicately. It didn't feel right to rat on a fellow adult. Wren was always saying that the faculty were supposed to present as a unit. Like parents getting paid to keep their shit together.

Unfooled, Eden stuck her hands on her hips. "You said that the Broadway Club learned it in a couple weeks! We have hella time before the Senior Showcase! Like a month!"

Autumn had rehearsed entire shows in less than a month. In college, she had stepped in to play Shelley in *Bat Boy: The Musical* halfway through tech week. Theater made anything possible. That was the magic of it.

Except.

"We'd have to ask Mrs. Markey," she said.

Jo and Eden made identical faces of annoyance, although neither of them seemed to notice the other. Bee laughed.

"We're co-directing the Senior Showcase," Autumn stressed. "But if you want to come learn the dances on your own time, you're welcome to join Broadway Club."

"With the sophomores?" Eden scoffed. "No offense, Miss Kelly, but I don't think so."

"Jo is going to come learn a dance with us for the list!" Autumn said. She turned to Jo.

"Jo is definitely not that good of a dancer," Eden said. When Jo shot her a dirty look, Eden's shoulders came up to her ears. "What? We all saw the video of you dancing at karaoke."

"Rude!" Jo said.

"But true." Bee giggled.

"You should come learn the dances with me, Eden," Jo said. "It could be fun."

Eden chewed on her lower lip, looking pleased but determined not to show it. "I guess it could be."

"And you ran out on the last list item you helped with," Jo said, playfully swatting her sister on the shoulder.

"Yeah, because I didn't need to watch you make out with the new VP," Eden said. "But, whatever, I'll think about it."

"I already drafted an introductory email telling their parents that they were going to study with my new dance captain," Autumn told Jo after Eden left to rejoin a group of friends. "I'll just leave out the part where you have two left feet. Let's hope none of them follow the Throwback List. Or maybe let's hope they do?"

"You're utterly ridiculous," Jo said.

"And you are so competitive that with a group of fourteen-year-old experts *and* your sister, you will work a billion times harder than if it was just you and me."

"That is"—Jo started to argue, but rolled her eyes instead—"probably true."

COMPLETED ITEMS

- ✔ TP Bianca's house
- ✔ Perform onstage
- ✔ Get belly button pierced
- ✔ Redo the yearbook prank
- ✔ Eat the giant sundae at Frosty's
- ✔ Host a dinner party
- ✔ Pose like a pinup girl
- ✔ Get a pet

TO BE COMPLETED

- ◯ Surf the Point
- ◯ Have a glitter fight
- ◯ Get stoned
- ◯ Try everything on the menu at Days
- ◯ Do a keg stand
- ◯ Play hide-and-seek in public
- ◯ Break something with a sledgehammer
- ◯ Climb the giant anchor on the boardwalk (and survive)
- ◯ Get a high score at the boardwalk arcade
- ◯ Learn an entire dance routine
- ◯ Have a bonfire
- ◯ Eat breakfast at midnight
- ◯ Dig up the time capsule

JO: What do I bring to a dance class? A water bottle? A snack?

AUTUMN: A can-do attitude and clothes you can move in!

BIANCA: I require photographic evidence of this casual moment, Jo.

I do not believe you own cozy clothes.

JO: B, I am home alone while my entire family is at work or school. I now take off real pants the second I walk in the door. I'm in sweatpants ALL DAY.

thirteen

JO

The following Monday, delighted to escape her parents' day off, Jo drove to Point High with Safeway Starbucks drinks for her and Autumn.

During her tenure as Point High's student yearbook photographer, Jo had spent a lot of time cataloging mush-mouthed stage readings of *Our Town*. It was almost a relief to be here to learn a dance from fourteen-year-olds, rather than listening to yet another George blather on about ice cream sodas.

The collection of Oregon Shakespeare Festival posters that had dominated the walls ten years ago had been replaced by the Broadway posters from the Kellys' Main Street house and overlapping anchor charts covered in Autumn's energetic handwriting. Vocabulary words, sentence diagrams, theater-history timelines, all written on gigantic white lined paper.

"You have list walls!" Jo observed proudly when she—and her first official visitor's pass—had entered Autumn's classroom. She clutched her heart. "And some of them are alphabetical?!"

Autumn laughed. "Am I literally watching you re-fall in friend love with me?"

"You knew what I was like when you invited me here."

"I did!" Autumn beamed. "I can't wait for you to see the organization system for my script library. But first: What are you doing *this* Friday night?"

Jo racked her brain. "I want to say nothing, but I feel like you're going to tell me that's wrong?"

"Correct!" Autumn slapped the top of her desk. She poked wildly at her phone screen. When she held it up, Jo saw a Tiffany-blue box of a house overlooking the ocean. "That, my friend, is the fanciest vacation rental in Waterfront Cove." Autumn swiped through photos of the interior. "Professional gas range, two bathrooms, four bedrooms, so we could have one just for coats or séances or something! And there's a hot tub!"

"For serious?" Jo hadn't had a sleepover in years. It also—to borrow a phrase from her sister—actively bummed her out to think about baby Bianca Boria never staying away from home. And while a hot tub overlooking the ocean wasn't exactly the same as sleeping bags in the Main Street living room, it definitely wasn't worse.

"Ginger Jay sent me the key code and everything," Autumn said, tossing the phone on top of a pile of quizzes. "I told Bee at family dinner last night. You should make her a sample packing list. She's only ever made sex-date suitcases. Very different."

"Way fewer clay face masks than a sleepover requires," Jo said.

"Fewer, but not none!" Autumn tittered. She checked the accordion wall and lowered her voice. "Speaking of sex dates, how are you and Wren? Are you going to see her while you're here?"

"We've only spent one night together," Jo said, feeling disloyal mentioning sex with Wren in Wren's place of work. Even if Point

High had once been the place where most of their fooling around happened. They were adults now. Adults who had sex in a prep kitchen and then pulled over on the way to Forest Grove just to make out. Jo couldn't casually explain how the drive to Wren's apartment had taken forever, how every King Princess song on the stereo felt like it was about them. Her skin felt hot as she tried to scrape the words together. "I texted her that I was coming to campus today, but I didn't hear back from her."

Wren's reply had been an auto-responder.

> **WREN:** This is W. Vos. I am currently in a disciplinary hearing and am unavailable until 5pm. Please refer PHS business to my email queue. Go Privateers!

Jo had never had enough power at a job to put an away message on her phone. It was an impressive power move, if needlessly formal.

"Don't take it personal! Wren never checks her texts when she's in a meeting. And she's always in a meeting. She barely has time to eat while she's here," Autumn assured her.

"Oh, I know. Wren was a workaholic even before she had a job," Jo said, comforted nonetheless.

"She's a woman with a plan," Autumn concurred. "Now, I hope you're ready to dance, because it's time for you to pay—with sweat!"

Thus Jo was surrendered to the sophomores on the undressed stage in the auditorium. Three hundred empty teal seats stared at them from the audience.

"Jo, meet the Broadway Club," Autumn said with an introductory arm-swoop. "Orin, Ellen, Ayden, and Kayden P, this is my friend Jo—"

"Kayden G," Kayden G corrected.

"They are going to help you learn one of the dances from their spring carnival performance," Autumn explained to Jo.

"If you're not a strong dancer, I would go *9 to 5*," Ayden told Jo.

"Are you Eden's sister?" Ellen asked Jo.

"Isn't it obvious?" asked Ayden.

"No," Ellen said. "She looks way less like Zoë Kravitz than Eden."

Jo reflexively touched her own cheek, unsure if she was being insulted or not. Who didn't want to be a Kravitz?

Orin broke free of the pack and stepped toward Jo, examining her without reserve. He sank his weight to one leg and crossed his arms. "If you had been allowed to take headshots when you were here before spring break, would you have excluded the non-seniors?" he asked.

"Um, no?" Jo guessed.

"Good," Orin said with an officious nod. "Go ahead and take one of the plastic top hats stacked stage right."

"No way," Jo said. She looked at Autumn. "I was offered *9 to 5*."

The sophomores collectively groaned. "But *Chorus Line* is the more impressive dance!"

Jo stood her ground. "I need an underhand pitch, please."

"And I need fewer sports metaphors coming from you," said Orin. "Miss Kelly, would you please cue up '9 to 5'? Jo, you can watch us do it once and then—"

A metal side door opened in the audience, the sound of it like the opening of a safe. Sunlight flooded the entrance, a natural spotlight following the line of teens now walking up the aisle.

Beside Jo, Orin, Ayden, Ellen, and Kayden G gasped.

"The seniors," Kayden G whispered in a reverent susurrus.

At the front of a group of her peers was Eden, who gave a wave that was mostly sleeve.

"You said we could come learn the dances you cut from the Senior Showcase," she told Autumn. "Is that okay?"

Autumn hesitated for a moment, checking over her shoulder like she expected the bogeyman to leap out from behind the heavy black curtains. But she turned back an instant later, face bright. "Of course! Come in, come in, come in! We've barely even stretched!"

The seniors shuffled onstage.

"I'm glad you made it," Jo told her sister.

Eden rolled her eyes to her friends but stood next to Jo.

The dance break jammed into the middle of Dolly Parton's classic was, at least, slower than the rest of the song. It mostly involved what the kids kept calling "heaven hands," which Jo knew to be shoulder presses.

It took half of their allotted dance hour for the group to master the step-clap jazz square and sugar-stepping that composed most of the routine, which meant that they'd started to rush by the time they got to the tricks. When Jo almost punted Kayden G offstage during a misaimed fan kick, everyone was granted a water break.

The seniors took turns stretching each other's arms behind their backs.

Jo stood up. Stretching teens looming over her was creepy. Like an old PE nightmare.

"It's coming along," Orin said with the pre-disappointed weariness Jo's mother had when anyone else offered to cook. "But I don't know if Jo will be ready to be filmed by our next meeting. It's only the day after tomorrow."

"I promised that I would practice at home," Jo said, taking a surly swig from an old Q-Co water bottle she'd found deep within her parents' kitchen cupboard.

"Practicing only helps if you have all the steps perfect before you leave," Orin said with a matter-of-fact frown.

Cruel, but true. Jo's bones creaked as she set her water bottle on the floor.

"Back to places," Orin called. "Let's take it from the *'get up and work'* breakdown. Five six seven and, straight arms, Jo!"

Jo said goodbye to the Broadway Club when they switched their focus to singing the songs they were dancing. Eden wanted to stay and lend her soprano to the *Chorus Line* harmonies. Jo had no soprano to lend and left.

Alone, Jo walked stiffly across campus, the setting sun stretching her shadow out long on the quad pavement. In the front office, she peeled off her visitor sticker and signed out on an actual pad of paper on a clipboard; lobby software apparently hadn't made it to Point High.

She finished signing the unsearchable paper—she was positive the secretaries would throw it away at the end of the day—when she looked up and saw Wren in navy cashmere that made her eyes look like the sky over the sea.

"I just got your message," Wren said, her shoulder wedged against the wall. She tipped her head, letting all the white-blond locks fall across her eyes. "Can I walk you to your car?"

Jo smoothed down her hair and prayed she was sexy-dewy rather than nasty-sweaty. It wasn't that she hadn't imagined running into Wren here, but none of her idle daydreams had included her edges sweat out.

"Of course," she said, hyperconscious of the office manager and secretaries in the room.

Wren hadn't been much for public affection before Point High was her place of employment and Jo was worried about her own pit stains, so she didn't push for a hug hello. The hair on her arms still rose when Wren brushed their pinkies together in acknowledgment.

The last time they'd seen each other in person was the morning after the dinner party. Whereas Jo found sex with strangers could be awkward and impersonal—clothes put back on immediately after, Ubers ordered—the history between her and Wren had made space for a familiar sensuality. They drank coffee in bed, feet tangled in the sheets. Jo could still feel Wren kissing her eyelids and the tip of her nose to wake her up.

In the intervening week, while Wren spent spring break with friends in Portland, Jo had worried over the dearth of contact between them. Wren responded to texts in five words or less, without the comforting lies of emojis or nonliteral LOLs. The long silences made Jo remember the abrupt shift of the first few months of Wren at Reed.

But now, as they fell into step leaving the office, Wren stayed close enough to her for their hands to graze.

Maybe Autumn was right and Wren really did just hate texting.

"How'd it go with the drama kids?" Wren asked.

Jo rubbed her sore shoulders. "I hope my parents have IcyHot because those children have springs for feet. They could make a killing teaching show-tunes aerobics."

"Not a bad idea. This town could use a gym."

Jo flashed her a smile. "Who are you telling? At least you can run in your neighborhood. I'm too afraid of eating shit on these sandy-ass streets."

Wren held open the door at the front of the school, leading the way down the wide cement stairs. The air was misty and crisp.

"Do I get to see the video of your newfound dancing expertise?" Wren asked. "Or do I have to wait until it goes online with everyone else?"

"Ha! There is no video yet. I'm going to take an extra day of rehearsal," Jo said, tightening her ponytail. A muscle in her back spasmed. Wow, she was so not fourteen anymore. "Wait, do you look at the Throwback List online?"

"I know what Instagram is, Johanna," Wren scoffed. "Although speaking of the list, aren't you worried that the lingerie photo is going to hurt your job hunt?"

The pinup photo ended up being way more of a success than Jo had anticipated, even though a photo of a relatively thin person in their underpants was hardly revolutionary online. Thanks to Bianca's hard work, her skin looked rosy, her eyes looked wider with winged lines, and her glittery belly button was downright adorable.

The comments had been so positive and inspiring, full of people who commiserated with Jo gaining weight while unemployed and applauding her photos being obviously unretouched. An ass with some stretch marks. A visible patch on one leg she'd forgotten to shave.

"Would you not hire someone for having Instagram shots in a bathing suit?" Jo asked Wren as they cut across the lawn near the marquee. An hour ago, the whole street had been filled on both sides with honking parents. The tide had gone out, leaving Jo's Mini alone in the distance.

"It isn't a bathing suit," Wren said. "The caption says it's lingerie. You tagged the brand. It doesn't offend me personally, but it doesn't present you as the most serious job candidate, does it?"

225

"I told you that the orchestra called me in *because* of the Throwback List," Jo said, possibly too sharp. "I'm sorry. Can we backtrack? I thought you were, like, morally opposed to social media. You still call Facebook 'Fakebook.'"

"Well, publicly traded social media companies are morally bankrupt," Wren said, lifting her chin. "But that doesn't change the fact that they're also valid news outlets."

"Doesn't . . . it . . . ?"

Jo found the idea of reading social media without participating unsettling, a digital form of peeping. Jo loved the mini community in her comments, the people cheering her on and sharing their own happiness honeypots, but now she saw all the comments through Wren's inherent judgment: strangers partaking of a false intimacy, leaving their approval in misspellings and meaningless emojis.

Jo's tote buzzed. She reached inside, pushing past her bullet journal to get her phone.

"The orchestra?" Wren guessed.

Jo checked. Gia's name was on the caller ID.

"One of my references." She took the call. "Hello?"

"Jojo!" Gia shouted in Jo's ear. "Where are you?"

Jo winced and turned the volume down. "I'm in Oregon, Gia. Where are you?"

"Can't you hear the ocean behind me?" Gia pouted. "I am talking to your too-cute parents."

"My parents?" Jo repeated. "Are you in Sandy Point?!"

"Yes! How have your parents not had their own post on the Throwback List, by the way? Your dad! Very Denzel."

He wasn't. At best, with the new gray in his beard, Phil was a LeVar Burton. Some people just had to prove they could list two good-looking Black men at the same time, even if the other example was *always* Denzel Washington.

Lo and behold, after Jo drove down the hill, there was Gia at the window seat of the Surf & Saucer. She had the same dye job with new change-of-life bangs. Jo's parents were obviously spying from the other side of the room. Phil was pretending to dust the teapots full of surf leashes.

"They fired you!" Jo exclaimed as she sat down at the table across from Gia to avoid having to hug her.

Gia flicked her bleached-blond hair over her shoulder, eating individual sliced almonds from the top of a scone. "I would have quit, on principle, but I wanted to spend my severance on movers. While the paint dries on my new place, my sisters and I are taking a mini break here. Away from it all. Yoga on the beach in the morning. Blended drinks at Days at night. Totally inspired by you."

"Seriously?" Jo inched her chair away from the table. "You actually came *here*? Because of my posts?"

"Oh, honey. Look at you. You look like I'm going to try to wear your skin. No, no, no. I picked here"—Gia knocked on the table and gestured out to the ocean—"because of you. But it was between here and wherever the *Goonies* house is. Somewhere halfway between home and Portland. My sister—you remember Rachel? She looks like me but older and plainer? Kidding! She's overseeing a team of brand reps for my parents' company right now, and *she* is in Portland—such a thriving bar market. I'm going to do the same thing in Tacoma. Anyway, she and our other sister are meeting me at our vacation rental. We're staying in Waterfront Cove for a couple days, do you know it?"

"I'm familiar," Jo said, not sure whether or not she was supposed to laugh. Did she know Waterfront Cove? Other than having her own getaway scheduled there, once, on a particularly boring weekend in high school, she and Autumn had watched the foundations of the suburb being poured, the two of them making up stories about the displaced ghosts of the demolished Waterfront Cove resort that would surely haunt the town from that day forward. She'd literally watched the cement dry on Waterfront Cove.

"I would love if you came and got a drink with us," Gia said earnestly. Or, as earnest as she could be while breathlessly monologuing. She reached out and took both of Jo's hands in a tight squeeze. "Because obviously I am ready to offer you a job on the spot, but you're going to need to kiss Rachel's ass a little. Mention how thirsty you are for sales goals and networking. Compliment her awful highlights—oh my God, you are not prepared, they got worse. I'll pay for dinner. You come knock it out of the park."

"You want me to come out for, like, a job interview?" Jo asked stupidly. "Over cocktails?"

"I told you that I would take care of you! I never got any reference calls, so I assumed you were still looking for a job?"

Stung, Jo sat back in her chair. A thousand pop-ups cluttered her brain—maybe the orchestra just needed more time, maybe Gia just didn't check her voicemails often enough, she could be sort of flighty about that, maybe Wren was right and the lingerie shoot had ruined Jo's chances to get back on track. Gia had once lost a job for being too fun. Maybe it was Jo's turn.

Out of the corner of her eye, Jo could see her mother sneaking closer, pretending to bus a nearby table. It would have been more convincing if the table had been dirty.

"I'm still looking," Jo told Gia. "Are you sure I'd make a good brand rep? I've never done sales."

"It's exactly what you already do, just a different job title," Gia said, and Jo's mom nodded in agreement before scurrying back to the prep kitchen. "It's talking to people about products you like. You were selling things for the Q. You're selling things on the Throwback List. You could sell boutique spirits. And the money is good. For you." Her shoulders fell as her voice dropped to the least affected it had ever been. "I had to take a pay cut and eat the security deposit on my place. Fucking Devo." She nibbled at an almond sliver like an agitated squirrel. Shaking herself, she gave Jo a strained smile. "Go home and get fresh. Your ponytail is looking ratchet. Meet us at Days at eight. Is it sing-along night?"

"Um, no," Jo said. "It's nineties night."

"So much better!" Gia kicked Jo in the ankle with the toe of her snakeskin mules. "Cheer up, Jojo! Your ticket out has arrived! I mean, this place is adorbs, but you don't want to get stuck in the boonies before the *Goonies*, do you? You came here to kill time. Consider it slayed and move on."

COMPLETED ITEMS

- ⊘ TP Bianca's house
- ⊘ Perform onstage
- ⊘ Get belly button pierced
- ⊘ Redo the yearbook prank
- ⊘ Eat the giant sundae at Frosty's
- ⊘ Host a dinner party
- ⊘ Pose like a pinup girl
- ⊘ Get a pet
- ⊘ Learn an entire dance routine

TO BE COMPLETED

- ○ Surf the Point
- ○ Have a glitter fight
- ○ Get stoned
- ○ Try everything on the menu at Days
- ○ Do a keg stand
- ○ Play hide-and-seek in public
- ○ Break something with a sledgehammer
- ○ Climb the giant anchor on the boardwalk (and survive)
- ○ Get a high score at the boardwalk arcade
- ○ Have a bonfire
- ○ Eat breakfast at midnight
- ○ Dig up the time capsule

AUTUMN: You guys, the seniors showed Pat the new 9 to 5 choreo during rehearsal today. They didn't even tell me they were ready! But they did such an amazing job that Pat agreed to put dancing back into the Senior Showcase!!

JO: Is there still room for me in the back row of the dance? JK, can you imagine my sister's face if I tried to crash her end of high school show? Lololol

I am at Days waiting for a spur-of-the-moment job interview (long story) but I have to tell you guys: the cotton-candy milk shake is equal parts cotton-candy vodka, milk, and ice cream. I have ordered it. Flo says it's going to turn my insides blue.

AUTUMN: I want to drink that!!

BIANCA: I don't trust any job interview that takes place at Days. Johanna, are you safe??

JO: I am waiting for a girl who called my hair ratchet earlier. If she doesn't murder me, I will tell you all about it at the sleepover!

fourteen

AUTUMN

Seafoam Cottage—the name of the vacation listing on Ginger's website *and* the Wi-Fi password—was the perfect setting for a girls' night. Out front, rainbow wind socks fluttered in the breeze. Inside, everything was pastel, soft, and inviting. Birch logs were stacked in the fireplace. Wineglasses were set out on the kitchen island. Ginger Jay had even left them the customary welcome basket of wine and cheese, despite their not being officially booked guests.

Rather than making them go through the vacation-rental website, Ginger had marked the house unavailable for a day in exchange for Autumn doing a week of cleanup between guests over summer break. The busy season. Autumn was more than willing to trade her labor for her friends' openmouthed surprise.

"Wow," Jo said, standing stock-still in the middle of the foyer. "I saw the pictures of the house Gia rented from your stepmom, but this place is too nice to be in this town."

"I have a mom. Ginger is my dad's wife," Autumn corrected lightly as she dropped her suitcase behind one of the low pale-blue sofas. "She says that people always want luxury on vacation, even if it's just knowing that the sheets are better than the ones they have at home."

"Look at these beautiful hardwood floors! And that couch!" Bianca said. "The chandelier is the same color as the outside! Okay. It's official. This place is cuter than Florencio's."

"High praise!" Autumn said with a rush of pride.

Like anyone staying in a vacation rental, the girls' first order of business was to open every door downstairs to see what was behind them.

"Florencio's house is cute?" Jo asked, having located a downstairs bedroom. She reported its ocean view and coral lamp dispassionately. "It isn't just a stack of dumbbells and posters of Rihanna?"

"Oh no. Flo's house is adorable, just a little empty," Autumn said. She looked inside a closet, empty except for wooden hangers awaiting coats.

"Melody wasn't a good girlfriend, but she was a great interior designer," Bee said. "She convinced me to paint my front door blue."

"Who decides to be an interior designer?" Jo asked. "In Sandy Point?"

"No one who wants to stay long," Autumn said. She found the downstairs bathroom and called it out. "But she did do a good job on Flo's house before she disappeared into the night."

"That makes it sound like either Flo murdered her or she *Gone Girl*'d herself," Bee said, closing the door on the water heater. "Melody abruptly broke up with Flo and moved in with another dude in Seaside."

"A taller dude," Autumn grumbled. "So *that* was a whole thing."

Bee and Autumn followed Jo upstairs. Rather, they followed Jo's luggage, a dusty Disney Princess suitcase that Eden hadn't been old enough to find ironically cool yet. When Jo had pulled the bag out of the front seat of her Mini, she'd announced, "Behold the glory of my girl Tiana front and center! My sister is never getting this back."

"Bee, is your house cute?" Jo asked, glancing over her shoulder with one hand on the white railing. "Do you guys have the same layout as us? Two bedrooms upstairs and one downstairs?"

"Yes, but a rat's nest is cuter than my house," Bianca said, giving her watch an anxious glance as though expecting Lita's face to appear and scold her. "My house is Birdy's stuff piled on top of Lita's stuff in a war for bad-taste dominance."

"Where is your stuff?" Jo asked.

"My stuff doesn't take up as much space as theirs. I have one overfilled vanity, most of which I brought in this box." She lifted the metal travel case she was carrying in one hand. "For what Jo's packing list called *makeover montage accessories*. I have lots of makeup and hair product. I have zero feather boas."

"That's totally fine," Autumn said. "I made sure that the kitchen had wooden spoons to sing into. You never know when you'll need an impromptu microphone!"

"Oh, I hope we all impossibly know all the words to the same song that happens to play by accident," Bianca said.

"If I start dancing well, it's demonic possession," Jo said.

"We know," Bee said. "We saw the "Mamma Mia" video *and* the *9 to 5* video."

"Hey!" Autumn protested. "Jo did very well with her heaven hands."

"Yeah, but my face did the sideways thing." Jo shrugged. "All the comments are about how nervous I look. Little do they know my face is naturally awkward as fuck."

On the second floor, the three fanned out again to open doors. Two small bedrooms and a hall bath.

Together, they explored the last bedroom.

"Oh my God, this place has a balcony hot tub and a *separate* Jacuzzi tub?" Bee called from the en suite bathroom. She reappeared in the doorway. "That is so needless, and I love it so much."

"Why don't you unpack in here, Bee?" Autumn said. She opened her arms and spun to show off the amount of space. "I mean, sleeping in different rooms *almost* defeats the whole purpose of the sleepover, but we're all grown-ups and you're entitled to privacy. That said, if anyone wants to bunk down in the living room together, let me know and I will whip us up a floor bed in a jiff."

"We'll keep you posted, sweets," Bee said. "I might sleep like a starfish and fill whatever room I'm in with two years of farts. I have been on my best behavior since Birdy moved in, and it is killing me. I don't have to have the biggest bedroom for that. Does anyone else want to stay in here?"

"I already sleep in an empty room at home. My whole house is a giant empty room," Autumn said. She threw Jo a side glance, hoping for encouragement.

"Oh! Um yeah! You should have this room, Bianca!" Jo stammered to be helpful. She peered into the open bathroom. "After the way Autumn's students and Dolly Parton beat me up this week, I couldn't get down into that tub anyway. It's sunken in. It would be wasted on me."

"And I have to save Jo from the ocean view downstairs!" Autumn said. "You know how she feels about the ocean."

"Hate it," Jo agreed. "Yuck. It'll keep me up all night with its dumb wet face ...?"

"Fine, fine!" Bee laughed. "I will take this room. Thank you, guys."

"Now that we're done with the tour..." Autumn said, gearing up for her prepared welcome speech. She looked around for her suitcase. "Wait. Shit. I left my prop downstairs."

"There's a prop?" Jo asked.

"Remember who you're talking to," Bee said.

Jo nodded. "Of course there's a prop."

Autumn ran downstairs, rifled through her suitcase, and returned with the scroll she'd made with paper and dowels borrowed from the art classroom.

The scroll paper was dented from riding in her suitcase, but thankfully still readable. She unrolled it and held it aloft, like the town crier in *Cinderella*.

"Beloved besties," she began grandly. "We are gathered together here in Seafoam Cottage to celebrate Bianca's very first slumber party."

"This is very elaborate," Bianca said, reaching forward to run a finger down the line of bubbled numbers in ROYGBIV marker. "Did you do this at work? Like, during work hours?"

"I gave up playing sudoku at lunch," Autumn said evasively. She had also avoided grading some pre-spring-break quizzes in order to make the glittery bees around the border. "Can I go on reading the list, please? Ahem, Bee's Very First Sleepover!"

BEE'S VERY 1ST SLUMBER PARTY

1. *Pajamas*

2. *Cocktail hour + snacks!*

3. *Never have I ever*

4. Makeovers

5. Dinner

6. Marijuana!

7. Chubby bunny

8. Charades and/or head's-up

9. Movie marathon

10. Breakfast at midnight

*No phones** or flash photography, please!

**Yes, that includes your watch, Bianca!!

"I can't take any pictures?" Jo asked. "What about just the outside of the building so that I can tag Ginger Jay's company?"

"Tomorrow, in daylight," Autumn conceded, laying the list gently on top of the lacy white bedding. "But the camera stays packed until then."

"What in the fuck is chubby bunny?" Bianca asked with a grimace. She held on to her watch like she'd bite whoever tried to take it off her.

"You fill your mouth with mini marshmallows and see who can say 'chubby bunny' the clearest," Autumn explained. "The most marshmallows wins! But everyone gets to eat a bunch of marshmallows, so no one really loses."

"Didn't someone die playing it?" Jo asked Autumn.

"Someone in the world, yes," Autumn said. "Someone in Sandy Point, no."

"Then it must be safe," Bianca said. She frowned at the list. "The exclamation point after *marijuana* makes you seem like a narc."

"Who could I narc to? Weed is legal in Oregon. I hope low-dose sour-apple gummies are good for everyone. I can't sacrifice my lungs for the list—sorry, Jo—so I had Florencio pick out edibles that shouldn't make us disassociate from our bodies."

"Is that a thing that happens?" Bee asked, alarmed.

"Hardly ever!" Autumn clapped her on the back. "Let's get through step one! It's not a sleepover until you're in your pajamas."

"Thank God." Bianca squirmed out into the hallway and came back with her luggage. "I am in the pinchiest bra."

"Is this the non-bounce-house bra?" Jo asked with a curious glance.

Bee put her makeup case on the shell-shaped velvet chair that matched the plush blue headboard. "Possibly?"

"Bianca, we have to work on your underpants game," Jo said.

"But this is my lucky red bra," Bee said, plucking at the band and attempting a low-key adjustment that fooled no one. "I bought it for my first Valentine's Day with Birdy."

"The *first one?*" Jo shrieked. "Are you wearing a two-year-old bra right now?"

"Three-year-old?" Bianca said in the most sheepish squeak Autumn had ever heard from her.

"Bianca, no!" Jo cackled. "Your bra should not be in preschool! Love yourself! The bra has been commemorated. It's time for it to go out to pasture."

"During makeover hour, I will let you search the internet for a comfortable—reasonably priced—bra in my size. But I want to hear five glowing reviews before I agree to purchase," Bee said. "Now everyone clear the room, please. We have to get through step one before moving on to cocktail hour! It's pajama time!"

Heart taking wing, Autumn flew down the stairs. If she hadn't been toting the itinerary scroll, she would have slid down the banister. She didn't unpack in the downstairs bedroom, just used it as an alcove for a quick change from work-jeans to Lucky Charms pajamas.

When they were kids, she and Jo would have both slept in baggy T-shirts. There was a brief period in high school when Autumn wore exclusively novelty boxer shorts as pajamas—and sometimes to school; it wasn't her proudest phase.

If she'd known she was going to end up a teacher, she would have refrained from attending school with the Grinch on her butt. Who knew how many of her coworkers pictured her as a freshman in Dr. Seuss boxers?

Maybe that was why Pat treated her like she didn't have two brain cells. Autumn promised herself that if any of her students ever came back to Point High, she would do everything she could not to hold their teen selves against them.

Autumn and Jo met up in front of the welcome basket. Jo got to work uncorking the wine. From the grocery bags Autumn had brought in from the car, she set out the bounty of sleepover snacks. Ruffles and ranch dip, peanut M&M'S, many kinds of Cheeto and Dorito, cookies, microwavable brownies, and, of course, a quantity of light beer only Bee could be excited about.

Cheese pizzas and liter sodas would be delivered during make-over hour. Autumn had already put the order in, an old Cindy Kelly sleepover trick. Pizzas would appear out of the blue right as hunger set in, as if by providence.

It was, Autumn recognized now, a happiness honeypot.

Bee appeared in a fluffy blue Stitch the alien union suit, complete with long ears on the hood. A row of white plush teeth appeared to be swallowing her bumper bangs.

"Oh my God!" Autumn cooed. "You are the actual cutest person alive."

"It almost makes me forget about all the fart talk that preceded this," Jo said.

"I've never been so comfortable," Bee said. She struck a pose and her sleeve fell away from her wrist, exposing the pale bracelet of her watch tan.

Autumn couldn't believe it. She'd written the party rules down almost as a joke, never believing that Jo or Bee would adhere to them.

Seeing Bianca untethered to her smartwatch was enough to make Autumn want to scream in delight. But she knew better. Any sudden movements would send Bee running back to check all of her alarms. A distracted Bee was a happy Bee.

Autumn thrust a glass of wine into Bee's hand. "Let's take this bottle outside and see the hot-tub deck."

"After you, Stitch," Jo said, following Bee to the french doors leading to the back deck. She glanced at Autumn over her shoulder. "Please stop me from yanking Bianca's tail."

"Don't you dare touch my tail!"

"But it's so squashy and round!" Autumn snickered.

Outside, the ocean lolled under the mostly set sun. Gold light spilled over the empty stretch of private beach held at bay from the suburb by a strip of black asphalt where Waterfront Covers walked dogs and strollers.

Above it all, standing in a faded yellow glow at odds with the spring chill, Autumn, Bianca, and Jo sipped Fred Meyer merlot next to a modestly sized hot tub that no one was in a hurry to climb into.

"Kudos to your father's wife, Autumn. Even the welcome-basket wine is good."

"It must be," Autumn said. "Because Miss Bianca didn't even ask if I got any Miller High Life."

"That's Mrs. Bianca," Bee said with the squiggly smile she got when drinking. "High Life is the champagne of beers. And I am the champagne of ladies."

"That's why there is a case in the fridge," Autumn said. "I thought about making themed cocktails for each of us. Like Jo's parents do with the lunch plates at the restaurant."

"*Restaurant* is a strong word. It's more like a gift shop that serves sandwiches," Jo said with a haughty scoff. "What goes into a Jo cocktail? Don't say mushroom tart!"

"I already had it all planned out. We're not the same kind of liquor, and it was going to be way too expensive. Everyone can be drinkable cheap red wine and light beer," Autumn said. She paused and took a sip. "If we were cocktails, I would be frozen rosé because I may be basic but I am refreshing. Jo would be something that looks savory but is really made of syrup—a rosemary old-fashioned. Bee would be a dirty Shirley Temple because she'd really rather just drink light beer, but if you put enough grenadine and rum together, she will consume it."

"Wow. I've never felt so seen," Bianca said, touched.

"That was like a magic trick," Jo said.

"The magic of theater casting!" Autumn laughed.

Jo set her elbows on the railing, watching the ocean like a sea captain hunting for land. "Who looks at all that and thinks *I wanna go out there?*"

Autumn looked over at her. "You really don't want to surf, do you?"

"I'm dreading it!" Jo groaned. She rolled the stem of her glass between her thumb and forefinger. "When my old mentor was here earlier this week, she found out that everyone in my family surfs except me and put the idea into my mother's head that me learning to surf could be a whole family thing. Mom, Dad, Eden, and me. In the ocean together. Now they're all stoked at the idea of being included on a list item, and I don't know if I should be an asshole and tell them that I didn't actually invite them. Gia did."

"Is this the same Gia who invited you to a job interview at Days?" Bee asked, hopping up to sit on the edge of the empty hot tub. Her tattooed feet swung off the ground. "The night of the cotton-candy milk shake?"

"Oh," Jo said, visibly deflating a bit. "That. Yeah, she was in town with her sisters and she had me meet up with them for drinks. Their family owns a liquor distribution company. Gia's older sister runs their main sales team. In Portland. And she offered me a job."

Clammy tendrils of anxiety dampened the edges of Autumn's happiness. Jo had been back for barely a month. It was too soon for her to be rushing away again.

"Liquor distribution?" she asked, keeping her voice bright and bubbly. Betraying no sign of disappointment. Jo deserved a million job offers. "That's pretty different than the job you went to interview for in Seattle?"

"It would be a different career track, that's for sure." Jo sighed. "The sales team get small salaries and big commissions. There are weekly goals and seasonal products to push and a hierarchy of who gets to wear what kind of polo that I didn't really follow, which all sounds kind of terrible, actually."

Bianca tittered. "So then why even consider it?"

"Because it's a real job," Jo said. "The first job I've been offered since I got fired three months ago. And Gia said the orchestra hasn't called to check on my references, so I don't know if I can keep hoping for that. Wren thinks it's because of the pinup pictures."

"Your boobies have the power to repel work?" Bee asked.

"I guess," Jo said. "I didn't even know she was following the list, and then all of a sudden she was talking about how being in my underwear online was going to hurt my hire-ability. She said it made me look like an 'unserious candidate.'"

"Those seem like very Wren priorities," Bee said. "She's like an Oregonian impression of a New Yorker. No nonsense and blunt as hell."

"*Blunt* sounds mean," Autumn cut in quickly. "Brusque, maybe."

"Fancy blunt," Jo said. "Much better."

"Do you think she could be jealous?" Autumn asked. "You guys just reunited and you're showing off your ta-tas for the 'gram."

"I doubt it's jealousy. We've only spent one night together and the morning after she used the phrase *we'll see how it goes* about twelve times. Which is fine. I could be moving again any minute. It's not like we'd be able to keep seeing each other if I'm in Seattle," Jo said. "And she really just doesn't seem to understand what I'm getting out of the list."

"Just because she doesn't understand doesn't mean it's bad," Bee said. "If she's going to stay mad about how you choose to present yourself to the world, she's not worth your time."

Jo gave an unconvinced nod as she sipped from her glass. "She's Wren. She doesn't have time for grudges. She made her disapproval clear. I disagreed. She's coming to have a glitter fight on Sunday afternoon. We might get Thai food after."

"Thai food?" Autumn asked. "You're going back to Forest Grove again?"

"Wren wasn't into the idea of people seeing a school adminis-trator on a date," Jo said.

"It's not like she's a pastor," Autumn said, confused. "Our con-tracts don't come with a morality clause."

"They don't?" Bianca asked with a wicked smile. "Then why have you been totally celibate since you moved back from LA, Autumn?"

"J'accuse!" Jo gasped, pointing her wineglass at Autumn. "Never have I ever gone two years without having sex."

Autumn drained her glass. "I'm gonna need to refill for this game."

"Let's break into the cheeses!" Jo said.

Bianca hiccuped. "And the face masks!"

The pizza delivery kid was kind enough not to mention that the drunk women who answered the door at Seafoam Cottage were midway through a makeover montage. Autumn's nose strip was starting to harden, Bee sported an old-school baby Bianca Boria French braid, and Jo was wearing a decorative tiara found on a bookcase.

They ate on the floor around the coffee table. The compli-mentary wine was gone. They cracked into Bianca's beer. Autumn appreciated its lack of depth. In LA, she had gone through an expensive beer-snob phase during which she pretended to love bitter, artisanal, *expensive* beers rather than the fruity garbage of her heart.

"Bianca," Jo said, chomping and exhaling in an attempt to eat a molten slice of extra-cheesy cheese pizza. "Was Birdy the first guy in your . . . beehive?"

"Splort!" Bee choked into her beer. "Spare me the sex euphemisms, please. We're grown-ups. He has a dick. I have a—"

"Magic cavern," Autumn interrupted with jazz hands.

"And no, Johanna, Birdy is at the bottom of my scroll. In college, I was what the kids call easy. I sowed my oats. Porked my pies. If you catch my drift."

"Oh, I caught it." Jo laughed. "You porked your oats out before you settled down with Dr. Birdy. So why don't you want kids?"

Bee made a sour face. "Not you, too, Jo. Aren't you supposed to be hip and metropolitan?"

"I'm just Oregon beach trash like everybody else here," Jo said.

"Must I worry about kids right this second? I'm not even thirty yet. I have time. We're not repopulating the world here."

"Tell that to your in-laws," Autumn said.

"You had to know when you married into a family that size that he'd want kids," Jo said.

"I knew," Bee sniffed. "And I thought I wanted them, too, but—I don't know how to explain it."

"Do you want to draft a pro/con list about it?" Jo offered.

Bee shut her eyes. "I don't need a pro/con list."

Autumn set her hand on the watch tan line on Bee's wrist. "Because it's about Lita?"

Bianca offered a weak nod. "Because it's about Lita. She's my responsibility. I moved back here literally just to take care of her. Even working in the shop is supposed to be second to making sure she's okay. And she's not. She's angry and she's sad and she's lonely, and that's all my fault."

"Bee," Autumn interrupted. "No, that's not fair."

"But it's true!" Bee said. "I've done everything to her that she did to me when I was a kid. I leave her at home when I go to work.

I tell her not to answer the door if someone knocks because she'll buy literally everything she has enough cash for. She's not allowed to use the stove because she forgets about it and sets shit on fire, so I make all her food. I do her hair in a style that doesn't fall out easily." She pointed up at her French braid. "I swear to God, if she asked me for a prom dress, I'd probably get it from Thrift Town, just like she did for me. If I can't be a better mom than this for Lita—whom I love and owe everything to—then how could I take care of a whole new person?" Her voice broke, letting out a wave of tears. She exchanged her slice of pizza for a wad of thin napkins that she shoved in front of her face. "I'm scared of having a baby. I'm scared of getting a *dog*. I don't want to fail at anything else because it feels like I'm already failing at everything everyone wants from me." She flinched apologetically at Jo and Autumn. "Almost everyone."

"Bianca, you have to tell Birdy how you feel," Autumn said, choked at hearing her friend's confession. She'd never imagined Bianca as a poor parent—to grandparent, dog, or human child. Bianca didn't fail at anything. Just set her expectations so high that only a superhuman could reach them.

"Birdy seems like a good guy," Jo said, reaching over and rubbing Bee's back. "He'll understand."

"He'll understand." Bee sniffled. "But he'll be so sad."

"As sad as this?" Jo asked, ducking her head to make eye contact. "As sad as you? Why does he get protected from this, but you get to be miserable?"

"I don't want to be high maintenance," Bee said meekly. "I already wear a lot of makeup and do my hair for at least half an hour every day, and we live with my family and—"

"You go on vacation with his family!" Autumn said. She was reminded of elementary school and the way she used to shake Jo by the shoulders, shouting *Be nice to my friend!* when she caught Jo being too mean to herself. Maybe it was time to bring Tough Love Autumn back. "Everyone has their shit, Bee. Feelings aren't high maintenance. Self-care isn't high maintenance. You just have emotions and a stressful life. It's normal to have a stressed reaction."

"I'm sorry," Bee said, dabbing her damp face. "I shouldn't be crying at my first slumber party."

"What do you think slumber parties are? Crying couldn't go on the list because it's unpredictably timed but never fails. Someone cries and then apologizes for ruining the sleepover by crying," Autumn said.

"I once cried at a sleepover because I brought the wrong pajama bottoms," Jo offered encouragingly.

Bee pushed the tears away from her cheeks with the heel of her hand. "I haven't scheduled enough time to cry in ages."

"Maybe you need to cultivate a life where you don't have to schedule your feelings," Autumn said.

Bee blew her nose into a new wad of napkins. "I hate Birdy's new office."

"The one he's so pumped about?" Jo asked.

"It's Dr. Banns's bungalow," Autumn said. "The one with the bush."

"Oh, I wouldn't want to pay for the landscaping there," Jo said.

Bee's head fell back and she sobbed at the ceiling. "It ruined our honeymoon, and I'll always hate it for that. I just wanted to have one experience that was, beginning to end, exactly the way it was supposed to be. Engagement party, rehearsal dinner, wedding, reception, honeymoon. But no! We had to put it off. And now I'll never get it back. All for an office that has a funny smell and needs a new roof!"

"Will it get him more business?" Jo asked.

Bee sniffled. "Probably."

"And could you reschedule your honeymoon?" Autumn asked.

"Someday. Maybe." Bianca scratched her bare wrist with the pad of her thumb. "I should check my phone, make sure he's okay at home with Lita. My mom was going to stay late after dinner, just in case."

"No way, Bee. This is the farthest you've been from your phone in forever," Autumn said, leaping up. "Let's break into the sour-apple gummies. And the breakfast food."

They agreed to turn off the lights in the kitchen rather than confront the tower of empty beer bottles and dip jars, the pancake batter spilled across the counter. The fireplace put out twice as much light as the TV. The snap of logs and torn pages of Jo's bullet journal scrawled with midnight wishes was almost as loud as the pastel Technicolor of *My Little Pony: Friendship Is Magic*, a show they had put on ironically but genuinely got sucked into around episode three.

"I want to lie on our backs in a circle like the Baby-Sitters Club," Autumn said, leading by example. Pushing aside a decorative chair, she backward dove onto the floor.

"Did they lie on the floor a lot?" Bianca asked. She slipped down the couch to the carpet next to Autumn. "I was a Royal Diaries kid."

"Fake diaries were my shit." Jo landed on the floor on the other side of Autumn, hands clasped behind her head. "I thought for sure that they found a bunch of real diaries and printed them. I kept such a detailed record of fourth grade, in case someone wanted to print it with a silk ribbon. Then the librarian pointed out the authors' names on the title page, and my whole world was ruined. Now my journals are shopping lists and encouraging quotes I heard during workouts."

The ceiling stared back down at them with a dozen glowing LED eyes and a wicker-fan-blade nose.

"I'd read your fourth-grade diary, Jo," Bianca confessed to the ceiling face.

"Page one," Jo intoned. "Today they announced the honor roll. I got an award, but Bianca Boria got ten. How has Bianca Boria gotten ten? Got ten?"

"Bianca Boria-Birdy," Bee corrected. "Three *B*s. I would have sobbed if I got three Bs in school."

"We did it," Autumn cheered. "We're stoned."

"Quick, someone go get Jo's camera and take a picture of her for the internet."

"Noooo!" Jo howled, hiding her face behind a nearby throw pillow that had *Beach Life* embroidered across the front.

"Shh!" Autumn demanded. She found her legs propped up on a nearby couch arm. "Listen to the ocean. It sounds like your heartbeat."

"Weed makes the world feel knowable," Bianca said with a pleased sigh.

"Guys," Jo said, over the heartbeat of the ocean.

"What?" Bee said. "I was listening to the ocean."

"We are stoned! I want to go check it off the list." Jo peeled her body upward in a gradual crunch. "I should celebrate more when I finish something, not when I post something."

"I told you that," Bee said.

"You were right," Jo conceded, tiptoeing over to the pile of purses on the window seat overlooking the ocean. Her hair hadn't recovered from the tiara. Wisps of it had frizzed up like antennae, making her look a little bit more like the girl Autumn remembered. She took a journal out of her tote and started scribbling.

"Jo, stop doing work!" Bee declared. "It's time to upgrade this sleepover to full snuggle."

"Yes!" Autumn cheered, pouncing on Bee's feet. "We can be a human centipede of friendship!"

"Okay," Jo said, reluctantly putting her journal away. "But I'm keeping my blanket. My toes are freezing."

Lying on the floor in front of the couch, they pulled the pillows and throw blankets into a loosely assembled nest and puppy-piled together. Autumn made a show of snuggling up to Jo's surprisingly uncomfortable clavicle.

"'There were three in the bed and the little one said,'" she sang.

Bee grumbled somewhere near her knees, "'Roll over!'"

The girls rolled in a wave in the other direction. Feet up, head resting on the hip of the girl ahead. On the TV, the ponies planned a Galloping Gala. Outside, the ocean sang them to sleep.

Autumn felt her eyelids starting to close.

I can't fall asleep yet, she begged her brain. *Not when we're finally in harmony.*

"What if?" Jo's voice was sudden and clear. "What if I turn the sales job down and I never get another one? What if I end up stuck working for my parents again?"

"Oh no," Bee said drolly. "Not that. Anything but the family business."

"I don't like tea," Jo said. "I do not drink hot anything. I drink to be refreshed or inebriated but never warmed. I think it's gross. Like drinking bathwater."

"What an odd duck you are," Bianca said, craning her head to look past Autumn at Jo. "How do you live without coffee?"

"It comes iced as long as I go to the Starbucks inside Safeway," Jo said. "My parents have never sold anything I liked, though. Not used clothes or dead people's dishes or ocean-themed paintings. I spent so much of high school trying to convince tourists to buy bad paintings of the ocean in a gallery without one abstract! I like my art to make me work a little harder." She wrapped herself tighter inside the chunky knit blanket she'd claimed. "I don't fit in with my family. I love them and I appreciate them, but it's like I got every recessive personality gene. It was easier to be somewhere else than not fit in where I'm supposed to."

Autumn gripped Jo's wrist. "You fit in here."

"I fit in *here*, in the friendship centipede," Jo said, motioning up the line of them. "But eventually I'll have to get up. Sleep in a bed. Pay rent. You know, regular grown-up stuff."

Autumn sighed. "I wish we could have had this sleepover at the Main Street house. Like the old days. On the floor in the living room."

Jo smiled. "Flo trying to ignore us on his way to the kitchen—"

"But ending up talking to us, like, twenty minutes anyway like a dork—"

"Was the living room green?" Bee asked in a sleepy voice. "I never got to see the Main Street house."

"Nothing was green until you hit the dining room," Jo explained. "Then it was just an explosion of green from floor to ceiling. And the kitchen! The fridge, the stove, the tile, the walls, the cupboards! It was buck wild. You've never seen anyone commit to decorating so hard. No wonder Flo tried to marry an interior designer."

Autumn loved hearing Jo's description of her childhood home. Her memories felt like well-loved quilt squares. Knowing that Jo hadn't forgotten, even when she'd distanced herself, was salve on a long, deep wound Autumn had been carrying. She nuzzled her head into her friend's arm.

"Thank you for still being you," she said.

Jo gave her a pat on the top of the head that also could have been a tap-out. "Couldn't stop if I tried."

Bee yawned. "Someone put another log on the fire. It's getting cold, but I'm cozy."

"Then we should get all the blankets," Jo said.

The doorbell rang, cheery chimes that seemed deafening in the midnight hush. All three girls craned their necks toward the shadowy foyer.

"No fucking way," Jo said. "That's the beginning of a horror movie."

"Or a romantic comedy," Autumn said, springing to her feet. "I'm prepared to be meet-cuted, universe!"

"As long as it's not with a hatchet!" Jo called after her.

But when Autumn opened the door, it wasn't a meet-cute. Just her bad luck, it was her brother. Once again, she was stuck in someone else's movie.

"Florencio!" she cried. "How did you even find us?"

"Why aren't any of you answering your phones? I need Bianca," he growled. Wild-eyed, he pushed past Autumn, into the house.

"Bee?" Autumn half asked, half called to the next room.

Trailing behind him, she noticed that he was dressed in his

Days uniform. A haze of fry oil seemed to follow him. Autumn caught a whiff as he hit the lighted hallway.

"Did you drive up and down the street looking for our cars?"

"I called Ginger on my way here," he said tightly.

"You called—"

Flo strode into the living room and raised his voice. "Bianca!"

"What's wrong?" Bee was rushing forward, the ears of her pajamas flopping.

"We couldn't reach any of you! I need to take you to the hospital."

Bee skittered behind him. "What happened, Flo? Is it Lita's heart? Is she going to be okay?"

"Lita's fine. She's with your mom." Pausing halfway out the front door, he explained. "It's Birdy."

BIRDY: Hate to bug you guys, but I'm on my way to Tillamook County Hospital. Someone tell Bianca to check her voicemail?

fifteen

BIANCA

Bianca raced ahead of Florencio. Distantly, she heard her friends' voices. Autumn calling after her. Jo racing behind with an armful of her possessions.

Bianca was buckled into the front seat of Flo's car before he made it to his door. Birdy was hurt. Birdy had never been hurt before. Not here. Back in Ohio there were stories of trees he fell out of as a child, cars crashed, the ridiculous game he and his brothers used to play where they threw an aluminum baseball bat at each other.

He'd never been hurt since he'd become Bianca's.

"He called me himself to come get you," Florencio said, sticking the key into the ignition ten times slower than Bianca would have if she could have driven, if she were sober, if her thoughts weren't floating out of reach. "Since none of you were answering your phones. Are you okay?"

"No, Florencio," she said, staring out of the windshield as they left well-lit Waterfront Cove for the shadowy sleepiness of old town

Sandy Point. She was surprised to find her lap laden with the shoes and jacket she'd left next to the door in the vacation house. "My husband is in the hospital and I am dressed like Stitch the alien and I'm on drugs."

"Oh, right," Flo said. "You guys were eating edibles tonight. It's not working if it isn't keeping you calm."

"It *is* keeping me calm," Bee said. She put the shoes on her feet. Tied the laces. "That's what is freaking me out. I'm not a naturally calm person, Flo. I want to access the depth of my emotions right now."

"If you were going to the ER with a panic attack, what would they give you?"

"I don't know," she huffed. "A tranquilizer?"

"Well, you tranq'd yourself, Bee."

She reached up and held on to the ears on her hood. It was soothing, the way she used to rub the ears smooth on her childhood stuffed rabbit. "I don't think I would buy that sober, but thank you."

"Do you really think I would leave the house in this if it *weren't* an emergency?" Bianca snapped at the nurse inside the hospital who told her how adorable her pajamas were. She hugged her coat closed—or as close to closed as it could be over the onesie. "Please just tell me where my husband is."

When she got to Birdy's room, she found him with his leg up in a splint, one leg of his jeans cut away. His skin was ashy gray.

"Honeybee," Birdy said, wincing as he tried to rise to greet her. He fell back. "Ow, shit. The painkillers aren't strong enough for that." Interlacing their fingers instead, he gave her a brave little soldier smile. "I'm sorry I ruined your girls' night. It's really nice to see you. I FaceTimed my mom in the ambulance, and she said not to bug you—"

"Baby, what happened?" Bee asked, pushing the hair away from his face.

He squinted at her. "See, when I tell you, you're going to overreact—"

"Robert Birdy."

"Please, Robert Birdy is my father. Call me Dr. Robert Birdy." He grinned at her as best he could. Pain made him hiss as he leaned forward. "I fell down the stairs."

"You what?!"

"Inside voice, honey. You're at Autumn levels."

Bee struggled to regain control of her volume. "What do you mean you fell down the stairs? How? Why? Just to make me the most scared you could?"

"I stepped down wrong. Wasn't paying attention and had an armful of laundry."

"You were doing the laundry?" she asked. "It's the middle of the night."

"Your mom told Lita she could wear a particular shirt in the morning without realizing it wasn't clean. I had time to wash it. It wasn't a huge deal. But since I was doing a load anyway, I brought our hamper down, too. My sciatic nerve pinched and my knee pitched forward and, uh, turns out that I go wherever the knee goes. Landed on my shin and broke it."

"It's broken?" Bee reached out as though to touch the splint and thought better of it. She reached up and ran her nails through Birdy's hair. He tipped his head toward her touch.

"Oh, it is very broken," he said, eyes closed. "Learned that the hard way when I tried to stand up to let in the EMTs. The doctor says it'll be healed in time for swimsuit season. In the meantime, rest and pain management. I'll stay home with Lita for at least two weeks. It'll give me a chance to catch up on all those Santana concerts I've seen thirty seconds of."

Bee pressed her forehead against his temple. If she could, she would put on a stethoscope and listen to his heartbeat until it lulled her to sleep, promising signs of life. "I should have been home with you. I shouldn't have left you home alone with Lita."

"Lita's fine. Your mom pulled up at the same time as the ambulance."

"The sleepover was a mistake. What if it'd been more serious? What if you'd hit your head?"

"Bee, take a deep breath. We're okay. Where's your watch?"

"I—I must have left it in the vacation house."

"It's okay," Birdy said soothingly. "Jo can bring it by tomorrow. Any chance you brought the car?"

"Florencio dropped me off. He couldn't get ahold of us, and then I was too stoned to drive myself. My car is back at the beach house. I told Flo to go back to sleep."

Birdy steepled his fingers and winced. "This is awkward. I also got a ride here. Expensive taxi, many sirens."

Bee held out her hand. "I'll call my mom with your phone."

How could we be the parents? she thought, stroking his hair. *We're the kids.*

It was excruciating getting Birdy in and out of Bonnie's car without the help of his right leg or anyone close to his height. Twice Bonnie offered to call and wake up her skinny fiancé before Birdy literally put his belt between his teeth and sat down in a hurry.

Bianca had barely come through the front door when Lita was flying at them, worried hands flapping as fast as her words.

"Mano, mano," Lita said, hovering around Birdy as he limped toward the couch. "My friend, are you okay?"

"I'm okay, Lita," Birdy said. He wagged a finger at her. "But you should be asleep, young lady."

"How could I sleep? I didn't know if you were alive or dead. ¡No sé nada! Nobody called me!"

"I don't have my phone, Lita," Bee said, gesturing to her jammies. "I left everything at the sleepover. I have shoes and a coat."

"Birdy has his phone," Lita snapped. "He called your mother! You couldn't call me?"

"I didn't think of it, Lita," Bianca confessed guiltily. She took Lita gently by the elbow, steering her toward the hallway. "I'm sorry. Let's go back to your room. Birdy's right. You should be sleeping."

She threw an apologetic look at Birdy, who didn't notice. His eyes were closed, one leg awkwardly propped on the couch cushions.

Lita shuffled furiously down the long hall toward her bedroom, talking so fast her tongue tangled like tape ribbon.

"I couldn't help my friend, Bianca. He was laying there, just like me, just like when I fell and Cruz came and found me. But I couldn't pick him up. I couldn't move him. I had to stand and watch."

"You did the right thing," Bee assured her. "You called Mom. And Birdy sent Florencio to come get me, so everything is fine."

"Everything is not fine," Lita said, stopping defiantly in the doorway of her bedroom. "What happens if he is hurt again? What if you aren't here? Where were you?"

"I was with Autumn, remember? I told you that I was going—"

Lita interrupted with a stamp of her foot. "You should have been here. You should have been helping. You should have seen— You can't know how it felt, muñeca. It was so scary and then everyone left and I didn't know ... I had a right to know if he was okay!"

"I'm sorry, Lita," Bee whispered. "You did have the right. We really messed up."

"Yes. You did."

Bee crawled into bed behind her grandmother, holding her shoulders until her agitated breathing turned to sure snores. Then she climbed out of bed, cried in a bathroom, and got to work.

During the single-digit hours, rather than collapsing into an exhausted puddle in fuzzy pajamas, Bianca rearranged the downstairs for Birdy to live in. The dining room table into the TV-less living room. The couch went in front of the TV with space for Lita's rollator. Most—but not all—of Birdy's man-cave paraphernalia came downstairs. A broken leg didn't require anyone else looking at that *Warcraft* tapestry.

Around dawn, before Lita's first wake-up alarm but not long after Birdy had fallen asleep with an Xbox controller in his hands, Bee took a shower. Changed out of frivolous pajamas into efficient clothes with many pockets. Hair up in a clip. Brows on in a rush.

She emailed the shop to tell them she wasn't coming in.

At nearly noon, after a knock on the door that startled everyone, she spotted Jo in the peephole. To Bianca's sleep-starved brain, it might as well have been weeks since the sleepover. Since midnight, she had sweated and cried and in general lost so much saline that her body might have accepted a mug of seawater easier than it choked down a fifth cup of coffee. Her eyes felt like hot golf balls shoved inside an old paper bag.

From her lateness, Jo must have hung out at the vacation-rental house until the bitter end of their rental period. Bianca was too tired to feel jealous, but she recognized that later she would file this information away under the headline *Things Autumn and Jo Did Without Me.*

"It's Jo," she told Birdy and Lita.

"Hi, Jo!" Birdy called from the couch now residing in their dining room.

"Who?" Lita asked so bluntly that it made Bee cringe. She couldn't even blame it on the brain injury. Lita had never been great with names.

"It's Jo from next door," Bee told her patiently. "Phil and Deb's daughter."

"Oh," Lita said, showing zero signs of recognition even as she waved politely.

"Hi, Mrs. Boria," Jo called back. She lifted the luggage off the porch and passed it to Bee. "Here, Bee. Your makeup case had a very restful night on a mermaid bed. And I didn't even consider stealing that cool ergonomic eyeliner you brought to the pinup shoot."

Bee hoped her mouth was smiling because her eyes were too tired. "It's from Fred Meyer. Don't rob my makeup case."

"From the many, many phone calls and texts we missed last night, Autumn and I put together what happened. Is Birdy's leg okay?"

"Snapped clean in half!" Birdy answered loudly from the dining room.

The noise made Bee's temples throb. She strapped her watch back on. It needed charging, but it didn't matter. "He'll be home for a few weeks. He's devastated, as you can see."

"Drop by for a co-op game sometime, Jo!" Birdy called.

"Hush, mano," Lita chided. "You're shouting."

"Fortnite! Warhammer!" Birdy whisper-shouted. "You name it!"

"I know things are sort of in flux right now," Jo said to Bee diplomatically. "But can I still put you down for public hide-and-seek for the Throwback List? We can tailor the time and place to fit your needs. Just around the neighborhood or down at the boardwalk on your lunch break. I want to get as much done as I can while I'm waiting to hear back on my job interviews. Autumn loses access to the Main Street house on May first. And since digging up the time capsule is supposed to be last, that only gives us three weeks to catch up...."

Jo was nervous-rambling, but Bianca didn't have time to soothe another person's feelings.

"We'll see. I don't think I'll have a lot of leisure time coming up. Thanks again for dropping my stuff. I'll see you when you and Wren do your glitter photo shoot on Sunday. Okay?"

"Okay," Jo said.

Bianca closed the door.

AUTUMN: Wren seems unclear about what a glitter fight is.

JO: I really don't understand where she could be confused. What could be clearer than glitter + fight?

BIANCA: As long as she remembers what time to show up tomorrow. I'm sorry to rush you but I have to have the store's alarm set again by five so I can cook dinner.

sixteen

JO

On Sunday morning, Quandt Corporation's social media accounts were all emptied to make room for the HeartChart announcement. Every social media campaign Jo had ever professionally written and designed had been erased from existence.

And then she got a form rejection email from the Seattle City Orchestra, thanking her, in not so many words, for wasting her time and getting her hopes up. Her youthful exuberance hadn't been enough to get her back on track.

She drafted messages to the group chat, but every version felt too whiny in comparison to the Birdys waiting to hear from an orthopedic surgeon.

She went into Days even though she wasn't scheduled to take pictures and found herself faced with the brunch rush. For the first time since she'd come home, she clearly spotted two tourists sitting next to the window, even though the view was only the matching Wolcott Furniture and Mattress Emporium.

Jo was relieved to see Florencio was behind the bar, stirring electric-blue drinks in tall glasses. She sat herself at the nearest stool and propped her elbows up on the counter. "You're in early today, Coach!"

"I'm here for the tips. Brunch is the perfect intersection of tourists and kooks," Flo said. He plopped maraschino cherries into the blue drinks and passed them to a barback before steering back to Jo. "You don't have your photography rig with you. Can you take pictures without your big umbrellas?"

"I *could*, but the lighting would be worse," Jo said, sticking her tongue out at the tease. The umbrellas were in her car, ready for the glitter-fight photo shoot. "I'm not here to take pictures. I'm here as a regular customer. A townie customer."

Flo set his beefy biceps on the bar, leaning in just close enough that Jo could smell something piney on him. Maybe it was the pomade that made his black hair so glossy. "As a townie, you should know that cotton-candy milk shakes aren't available on Sundays. We usually run out of the blue milk on Saturday nights."

Jo recoiled, remembering chugging cotton-candy mistakes with the Nicotera sisters. "I never want to drink cotton-candy anything ever again. My morning has already been shitty, and I have a list-item date with Wren in two hours. Give me"—she paused, taking a sobering breath—"a Sandy Point shake, hold the pineapple. It's the last thing on the menu I haven't tasted."

"Do you want the sand dollar that comes with?" Flo asked. "I know you hate everything that comes out of the ocean."

"Keep your sand dollar. But I will take an order of totchos, please. Extra jalapeños on the side."

"One Sheet Load for the lady," Flo said with a wink.

Jo rolled her eyes at him. "You like the names here too much, Coach. We have to get you a real job."

"I've got a real job with the school district," Flo reminded her. "It just doesn't pay anything. The education system is broken."

As Jo waited for her order and Flo went to blend her booze shake, she started scrolling through her phone, only to realize that she didn't know what news she could hope to find there. It wasn't like the orchestra was going to call back and change their minds. She could either wait for an official offer from Gia's family or she could keep applying.

If Gia had told her about a liquor sales job in Portland the day she'd been laid off, Jo would have dropped everything to go. No questions asked. Back in Palo Alto, Jo would have done anything for a life preserver.

She didn't want to drop everything and leave now. Not when she was so close to finishing the Throwback List. That was one silver lining of not getting the job in Seattle. And she and Wren wouldn't have the looming threat of her possibly moving two hundred miles away keeping them from moving forward in their rekindled romance. A picture of the two of them sprinkled in silver glitter could make a delightful first couple photo.

If they decided to go back to being official.

Not to brag, but Johanna Freeman often went on to date people she had sex with.

She smoothed out her bullet journal on the bar. In the next two weeks, she still needed to:

○ *Surf the Point*
○ *Do a keg stand*
○ *Play hide-and-seek in public*
○ *Break something with a sledgehammer*
○ *Climb the giant anchor on the boardwalk (and survive)*

- ○ *Get a high score at the boardwalk arcade*
- ○ *Have a bonfire*
- ○ *Dig up the time capsule*

After yesterday's stop by Bianca's house, Jo was fairly sure that her social circle was about to shrink again. When she saw Wren today, she'd drop a hint that she was ready for an invite to meet the Portland queer-professionals group Wren was in. From Wren's stories about them, they mostly drank craft beer and talked about the Trail Blazers.

The basketball team, not queer historical icons as Jo had naively hoped.

Dating as adults was so different from dating as teenagers. Other than a fuller scope of Wren's biography, playing the game before gave Jo absolutely no leg up on it now. Instead of stealing short bursts of togetherness between classes, they saved up conversation for days at a time. Wren's disinterest in texting meant that Jo spent more time wondering what she was doing than knowing for sure. It saved Jo the trouble of having to seem busy when she was really sitting around her parents' empty house while everyone else was out at work.

But it was slightly aggravating when Jo rushed out of Days to make it to the boardwalk parking lot on time and there was no Wren and no way of knowing how late she was going to be.

Rather than wait in the parking lot, staring at the ocean, Jo went into the Salty Dog and let Bee usher her upstairs to set up her lighting equipment.

Bianca was jittery as fuck, double and triple checking that Jo would be careful and clean up meticulously and let herself out and jiggle the handle three times on the upstairs toilet but only twice downstairs. When Jo mentioned family dinner that night, as she'd sworn to Autumn she would, Bee didn't warmly issue her an invitation—as Autumn had sworn she would.

"Sunday," Bianca said. "Dinner. Sunday family dinner. I still need to go to the store."

She jabbed her watch so hard Jo was surprised it didn't crack in half like an egg. Shortly after Bianca rushed out, Wren strode in.

Wren kissed Jo hello not quite on the bull's-eye, already mid-rant.

"Look at this place!" she said, gesturing up at the ceiling, one side of her mouth curved to frowning. "This is ready-made rental space. Why aren't you living in here instead of with your parents?"

"It's Bee's dead grandpa's apartment," Jo said. "She said she wouldn't want it to be living space for nonfamily members."

"She's letting you rent it out for this, though," Wren said. "It could be any number of things this town doesn't have. Weren't you complaining about the lack of a wine bar here?"

"Here meaning the Oregon coast itself," Jo said. "I wasn't saying Bianca should open a speakeasy over her tattoo parlor."

"That's exactly the sort of shit that might get more people to visit this town. Instead of catering to the nouveaux riches of Waterfront Cove, someone should take a chance and open something interesting. A speakeasy. A bottle shop. A good barber. Bike rentals. Anything."

Jo blinked twice. "That is . . . literally everything in your neighborhood."

Perplexed, Wren cocked her head. "Yes, Johanna. I like my neighborhood. That's why I live there."

Jo breezed over to the desk and retrieved the bags of glitter she made—in the driveway, at her mother's request. "Here is your pixie dust. We should take off our shoes so that we don't track anything off the tarp. It'll brush off your socks."

"Remind me the point of this one?" Wren asked, frowning at the bag in her hand.

"It's a glitter fight," Jo said. She stepped out of her shoes and set them on top of the desk. Then, finding that disrespectful to the desk, the floor. "It has no point. It looks pretty."

Grudgingly, Wren rested her back against the wall and unzipped a boot. Her long legs were sculpted in skintight maroon jeans. "Wasn't that why you did the pinup pictures?"

Jo thought of what Autumn had said about upgrading to new teeth. The pinup shoot hadn't fixed her relationship with her body, but it hadn't hurt. At least now she knew she wasn't too scared to stand in front of a camera in her best underpants.

"The lingerie photos were for my self-esteem. This is aesthetically charming." Wren didn't seem convinced, so Jo bloated the idea. Explaining things to Wren could make her feel like a robot, redacting all lines of emotion from her code and replacing them with endless philosophical hypotheticals. "It's to capture beauty in the frivolity of life through the fragmented lens of unrecycleable bits of shimmery plastic. Okay?"

That last word might have been sharper than she intended, but Wren accepted it with a nose twitch.

"We're gonna do everything on top of this tarp so that we don't track glitter all over Bianca's store. I don't need her stress-cleaning after us. She's got enough on her plate right now. I'll frame you in the shot and then set the timer to jump in myself. We'll do one glitter throw per shot sequence. You hit me, I'll hit you. We'll do one at the same time, then freestyle until we're out of glitter."

"That's it?" Wren asked. "Doesn't sound like it'll take long. I drove almost two hours to get here. On my day off."

"I know that," Jo said, feeling wounded. It would be nice if Wren thought she was worth driving to see, regardless of how long. But that wasn't practical. You couldn't ask Wren to be impractical. "I had a not-great morning, too. But after we're done, we can go to the Thai place you wanted to try. It's early enough to reclaim the day from the shitter."

Wren glanced at her phone. "We'll see how it goes. I don't know if I want to wander around covered in glitter. Let's see how well it *brushes off.*"

Devo Quandt, Jo's old boss, used to quote her back to herself in meetings in that same tone, suspiciously highlighting buzzwords in order to undermine her. When Wren did it, she wasn't standing on Jo's shoulders to feel tall. Terse was just baked into her backbone.

Knowing that didn't always take the sting out of being mocked.

Jo imagined what Autumn would do. Relentless in her pursuit of a good time, Autumn would put on a smile and double down. Even if it meant ignoring pesky things like hurt feelings.

"Ready!" Jo said, smiling twice as wide. She bounced up and down twice, psyching herself up. Music would be helpful for mood setting, but she didn't want to reignite the argument they'd had after the dinner party about Jo's Spotify subscription contributing to the collapse of the music industry.

"Three, two, one!" she counted down cheerfully, sprinting toward Wren, and into the frame. "Glitter me!"

An audible sigh from Wren preceded the first fistful of glitter flying at Jo's face.

It was awful, immediately. Glitter hit like the finest ground sand, ricocheting off her cheek and toward her nose and eyes. Instinctively, Jo panicked and turned away, her brain already playing the headline of her obituary on BuzzFeed: "Woman Asphyxiates on Glitter for Social Media; Dies."

The camera cheeped, alerting her that the burst of photos was done.

Struggling not to scream *This was a mistake!*, Jo checked them. Unsurprisingly, the camera had only caught the truth of how miserable it had been. Disdain creased the captured lines of Wren's brow, lips, and button nose. The glitter looked like a punishment.

Jo cleared her throat. "Um . . . you don't look like you're having a good time."

Wren's lips disappeared in a frown. "Maybe because I don't particularly want to throw things at you?"

Jo bared her teeth in a threatening smile. "Should I be more annoying to inspire you? Do you want to hear about how I got rejected for the orchestra job and drowned my sorrows in Days' brunch?"

"Time-out." Wren's lashes fluttered as she processed. "The Seattle job rejected you? Did they tell you why?"

"Nope; it's just not my destiny to reinvent the image of Pacific Northwest classical music. It's fine. It wasn't a scene that, like, screamed Jo Freeman." She set the camera back on the tripod, refocused the view. "Ready for round two?"

Wren cracked her neck. "Fine. Hit me."

The camera blinked a warning countdown as Jo leaped back into the frame. Glitter sank in under her fingernails as she pinched inside her bag. She slid forward on the tarp, moving to sprinkle Wren while stealing a kiss. As the stream of glitter started to fall, Wren yanked her head back. The apartment echoed with the sounds of her slapping the back of her skull until the metallic dusting was out.

"Fuck, Jo. I don't want this shit in my hair. I have plans tonight. I can't have this craft disease stuck to my scalp."

Jo tried not to show her surprise at being double-booked. She wanted to ask what Wren's plans were but was afraid of prying. Should she not have assumed they'd spend more of the day together after the photo shoot?

And just how late were Wren's other plans if she was two hours away from home?

"Sorry," Jo said tightly. "We should have established more ground rules. No hair. Maybe don't aim directly for my eyes?"

Wren looked at her upside down as she continued to rake out her undercut. "I don't want to kiss on camera. It's disingenuous. We're not a couple."

"It's a picture, not a U-Haul!" Jo said with a disbelieving laugh.

"It's a picture that you want to broadcast to thousands of people on the internet."

"Oh my God, Wren," Jo growled, throwing up her hands. "The internet is not a mythical place where shit goes wrong. It's a communication tool, not the lost city of Atlantis. This list is a scrapbook, nothing more."

Wren dragged a hand over her eyes. When it came away sparkly, she snapped it toward the wall in irritation. "It's a public forum, and has an international audience. If you had a public scrapbook where you wanted to hang a lock of my hair, I'd say no, too."

"Because that would be fucking creepy!"

"As opposed to pretending to have fun for the amusement of strangers?"

"Could you concede on anything? Ever?" Jo snapped.

"Yes!" Wren shot back. "But first you need to score on me."

"Conversations don't have a score!"

"Everything can be scored, Johanna," Wren scoffed, scratching her hair back into place. "And if the orchestra people turned you down, then you should be begging that friend for the liquor sales job. Take it and quit when you find something better. Portland is civilization. The list is for fun. It doesn't have to be perfect. It doesn't have to be done exactly the way you planned. This little photo shoot was too couple-y from the start. It implies a level of commitment we don't have. You should have done this with your friends, and I should have said something earlier. I didn't want to hurt your feelings, but if your feelings are hurt anyway—"

"This has been you *playing nice*?" Jo asked.

The switchblade flick of sarcasm didn't touch Wren. She opened her arms like Jesus at the Last Supper, always the magnanimous martyr.

"I can take pictures of you throwing glitter around if you want to keep faking a smile, but I'm going to bow out of the rest being on camera. It raises a lot of questions that are, frankly, premature."

Jo felt like she was waking up in the middle of a boxing match. She didn't even have her hands taped up, yet there were her metaphoric teeth knocked against the metaphoric wall. "Because you don't like that I post on social media? Something that has been completely and utterly normal for the last two decades?"

Wren strode calmly over to her boots. She sat down on the edge of the desk to put them back on. "No. Because when you first came back here, you were talking about immediately moving again. You wanted to find a new job, a better job. And if we were going to open the discussion on the two of us becoming something more official, it would be conditional on you becoming the kind of partner who was more challenging, career-wise."

"Ouch," Jo said. What was she doing dating a vice principal? Hadn't she had her fill of efficiency-starved administrators in the real world? "Are you saying this because I'm not good enough to work for the orchestra? Am I not cultured enough for you and your Reedie friends?"

Wren hopped down from the desk, almost toppling the red candle. "It's not about culture, Jo! It's about *drive*. I am on track to hit my career goals by thirty. Are you?"

Knockout. Jo staggered backward before roaring forward. "I said ouch! Take the hint. We don't have a safe word! I get it, Wren. You don't have to rub it in. I'm not as good as you, *and* I'm not good enough for you."

Shouting was beneath Wren's dignity. She lowered her voice to infuriatingly reasonable. "I already fell in love with your potential. Ten years ago. You're not proving to be a safe bet."

Jo flung her arms out. "There's no such thing. Gambling is inherently risky. I've seen *Guys and Dolls* one million times, thanks to Autumn, so I should know!"

Wren looked perplexed. "Why are you shouting about musicals right now?"

"Because you hurt my feelings, and I'm waiting for an apology!"

"I'm sorry, Johanna." Wren blew out an exasperated breath. "This just isn't going to work. Not the way I think you want it to."

"Wanted," Jo bit off. "I'm twenty-six years old, Wren. I'm too old to chase people who don't want me back."

"I don't want to be chased," Wren said. She met Jo's eyes. "I should go."

Jo agreed.

Making for the door, Wren looked back over her shoulder. She had never looked back at Jo before. Jo wondered what kind of last look she cut, glitter stained and flushed from the fight.

"We don't have to go back to not knowing each other," Wren said crisply.

Jo opened her mouth—to say: *not now* or *maybe later*—but everything felt like too much of a promise, another open end, so instead she said the stupidest thing she could think of:

"Byezers, Wren."

Wren left without question.

Jo cleaned up the glitter mess in a daze. Rolling the tarp to trap the glitter inside, she wasn't quite sure she should cry. Wasn't sure she could. This sadness was ten years old, the regrets well trod. Jo and Wren had never found a way to say a fulfilling goodbye. Not in an email. Not in person.

The real pain was in realizing that Wren was an old favorite song she couldn't feel as deeply as she used to. Expecting the same notes to play a new tune made her feel foolish.

She carried her lighting equipment downstairs, scanning the shop for Bianca. She could use someone to cuff her on the chin and tell her Wren wasn't shit.

"She'll be back to set the alarm," said the very pretty tattoo artist who was showing off pictures of her baby to a client. "But she had to run to the store."

"Sounds like Bee," Jo said, surprised at how disappointed she was. "Always running."

She drove home with the windows down, letting the noise of the ocean shush her thoughts.

When she pulled up in front of her parents' house, she nearly took off again, just to forestall the questions and the reopening of a fresh wound. But the lure of unglittered clothing was too strong and her bladder too weak. She trudged up the driveway. The door swung open before she could put her key in the lock.

Any other day, it would have been odd to see Autumn waiting for her inside her parents' house. Today, it was magic.

"Thank God you're here," Jo said. "Today fucking sucked. Careful, I'm covered in glitter."

"I could use some sparkle," Autumn said, throwing her arms around Jo's shoulders and squeezing tight. "Bee canceled family dinner this week. Your parents kindly took me in so I wouldn't have to sit in front of her house like a creep while I waited for you to come home. I don't have a car right now."

"Wren told me that I'm too much of a loser to date," Jo said.

"What a jerk," Autumn said. "If you're a loser, I'm a loser."

"Is that from *The Notebook*?"

"Sort of."

Jo stayed in the hug. Like a too-hot bath, hugs with Autumn were nice once you adjusted to the pressure. "Autumn, she's not wrong. I failed at everything I tried to do."

"That's not even sort of true," Autumn said. "You got laid off from one job."

"And I didn't get the orchestra job."

"Fuck Seattle. It's too far away anyway."

Two throats cleared. Phil and Deb were hovering in the open door. Jo wasn't sure if they had subconsciously dressed in matching Patagonia sweatshirts, but they certainly were wearing them at the same time.

"Everything okay, you two?" Deb asked, eyes full of gentle blue concern. "You stood like this when they killed all your favorite doctors on *Grey's Anatomy*."

Rag-doll floppy, Jo frowned at her parents. "Rough day."

"Very Monday-like for a Sunday," Autumn agreed. Her eyebrows went up in surprise when she whacked Jo in the shoulder and released a spray of silver glitter in the air. "Do you want to hit Days' happy hour?"

"As you can see, I'm in sore need of de-glittering. Never let me try to do something that whimsical again, you hear me?" Jo shook out the end of her ponytail. Despite her best efforts, it was shimmering. "If you're down to wait half an hour, we can go to Days. I had totchos for breakfast, but mozz sticks and milk shakes could be dinner."

"Why don't you guys eat here?" Phil said. "Eden's off with her friends, so we don't even have to worry about remembering to call Autumn Miss Kelly."

"Hotcha!" Deb clapped her hands together. "We can have a game night, like when you two were little. Before Eden came along."

Eden's birth being referred to as an eventuality now was particularly funny when Jo thought about how blindsided the family had been at the time. Eden came along and got right in the way of the plan to turn 180 Boardwalk Avenue into a beer taproom. Deb hadn't been able to do tastings to pick a menu, so the store sold consigned clothes for another few years.

"You aren't going to trick me into learning Bunco," Jo said, tracking glitter into the house.

"No, not Bunco. We can play penny poker. Autumn, do you remember the rules to Texas Hold'em?"

Autumn closed the door behind her with a flourish. "Is the Chief a ginger?"

"Like his father before him," Deb cheered.

"Okay!" Jo laughed. "But Dad is dealing. Don't think that I've forgotten Mom's light fingers."

Her mother gasped. "Johanna Jordan! I have never cheated a day in my life."

"Tell that to my piggy bank," Autumn said. "You know how many erasers I didn't buy at the Scholastic Book Fair because of you?"

"Are we playing no limit?" Deb asked.

Jo's dad thrust a finger at her. "In this house we live without limits."

"That is from *Westworld*." Jo groaned. "Ugh, I hate that I know that."

"It said *fight* right there on the list. No matter how much glitter you put on it, a fight is a fight," Deb said, tossing a handful of pennies into the pot. After many years of being grifted at penny-poker night, Jo had learned to sit to the left of her mom so she could see her raises before not after. "You should have brought someone you wanted to fight with. Your sister would have been a great candidate. Dad, maybe. But not someone as serious as Ms. Wren Vos."

"I really don't want to talk about the glitter fight. Or Wren," Jo said as best as she could with a lollipop tucked into her cheek.

"She's just trying to psych you out, Jo," Autumn warned. "Because she's got nothing in her hands."

Deb tossed another lollipop at Autumn. "You wish, Pippi Longstocking. I'm coming for your pennies."

Poker night had a minimum buy-in of two cents, and everyone

got a Dum Dum so that Jo had a shot at a poker face. When she was little, her nervous laughing had been a real expensive problem on penny-poker nights.

"Come on, Jojo bean," her dad said from behind his cards. "How bad could it have been?"

Setting her cards facedown—and making sure her mother wasn't peeking at them—Jo fished out her camera. She displayed the abysmal glitter shots. A picture of her taking a spray of silver to the face was the unanimous favorite.

"That is the one!" Deb cackled. "That is the face of someone who realized some things aren't as fun as they look."

"God, it did seem like it was going to be fun," Jo said. "In the moment, I was so much more scared of getting something in my eye."

"Sounds like sleeping with an ex to me," Deb said.

"Mom!"

"What? Eden's not here. Am I supposed to pretend like you don't have sex? You were named after a romance novelist, Johanna. Now bet, because Miss Kelly and I are gearing up for a showdown."

"You're on, old woman!" Autumn said, with a loud suck on her lollipop. "I've got more credit card debt to pay off than you've got pennies."

"Weird flex, friend," Jo said.

"I am keeping everyone on their toes with radical honesty!" Autumn said.

Phil tapped the side of his nose. "It's better than the night she decided to play in character as Oliver Twist. You almost lost your open invite to this house after that accent."

Autumn gasped. "One, I was the Artful Dodger, and two, yes, that accent was a crime against England."

"England? Our ears were right here!" Phil said, punching the table with a laugh.

"Wasn't Mrs. Markey the musical director when you were in *Oliver!?*" Jo asked Autumn.

"Oh my God! She was!" Autumn squealed. "Could she really still hate me over a bad performance from freshman year?"

"Pat Markey only says the nicest things about you at Bunco!" Deb said. "But I remember that accent, Autumn, and it was worth holding a grudge over."

The table fell out laughing for so long that Phil accidentally spilled his seltzer and flashed his cards.

It took a while of searching inside herself before Jo realized that what she was feeling was contentment. She wasn't clawing at the walls, searching for an escape, or scrawling lists of how to get away. In this moment, she felt a total absence of dread.

But her life was supposed to be about more than fitting in with her family.

Wasn't it?

COMPLETED ITEMS

- ✔ TP Bianca's house
- ✔ Perform onstage
- ✔ Get belly button pierced
- ✔ Redo the yearbook prank
- ✔ Eat the giant sundae at Frosty's
- ✔ Host a dinner party
- ✔ Pose like a pinup girl
- ✔ Get a pet
- ✔ Learn an entire dance routine
- ✔ Get stoned
- ✔ Eat breakfast at midnight
- ✔ Try everything on the menu at Days
- ✔ Have a glitter fight

TO BE COMPLETED

- ○ Surf the Point
- ○ Do a keg stand
- ○ Play hide-and-seek in public
- ○ Break something with a sledgehammer
- ○ Climb the giant anchor on the boardwalk (and survive)
- ○ Get a high score at the boardwalk arcade
- ○ Have a bonfire
- ○ Dig up the time capsule

FLORENCIO: The keg has been ordered. You guys better show up to drink it. Sunday @ 8.

BIRDY: I can't wait! I can't wait to leave the house and see the sky!!!!

JO: You feeling okay, bud?

BIRDY: I will be. On Sunday. When I see the SKY.

FLORENCIO: You can't drink on your pain meds, dude.

AUTUMN: The sky is pretty!!

seventeen

BIANCA

After a long morning of Birdy playing a cartoon farming game for Lita's amusement, the TV in the dining room now broadcast one of Lita's many soaps.

Birdy was deep in his phone, his *Zelda*-green cast propped up on an airport neck pillow and a dining room chair. From her position among the displaced furniture in the living room, Bee could only assume he was continuing the game he had just stopped playing on the television.

"Oh, it's them," Lita said, with a dismissive puff at the opening credits. "We can talk during this one."

"Did I ever show you a picture of my long hair, Lita?" Birdy asked. "All through high school, I had beautiful Kurt Russell hair."

Lita leaned over to him. "Why did you cut it, mano?"

"Long hair AND an orthodontist? That screams pervert. I've got to pay the bills here!"

"Not right now you don't," Bee called from behind her laptop. A relic from her college—as evidenced by its forever crooked *Go Beavs* sticker—it wasn't good for much these days. It could run Excel, so Bianca had booted it up to review their budget.

A two-thousand-dollar calculator, Bianca could hear Tito saying. It was a blessing that she never had to explain to him how much cell phones cost now.

With Birdy's office closed for a month so that he could be off his broken leg, all the bills were weighing on Bee more than usual. They had enough in savings to not fall to pieces immediately—but what if all of Birdy's redirected clients fell in love with the orthodontist in Rockaway Beach? Right before he moved to a bigger and more expensive space?

The Salty Dog's mortgage was too high for the amount of business they took in through the majority of the year. They would make more money if they charged rent on the artists' stations instead of commission on their tattoos.

But that wasn't the way Borias ran a shop. Borias put artists first and money second. Even if they starved.

"We'll be fine," Birdy said.

"I know we'll be fine. I'm doing the math to make sure we'll be fine," Bee said sharply. "It would be easier to be fine if we could go without some subscriptions. Why do we have three music-streaming services?"

"Because music is everything good in the world," Lita said, swatting at Birdy as she waited for him to back her up. "Oh, I want to hear this part. Shush, shush."

"If thirty dollars is going to make or break us, honeybee," Birdy said in his peacemaker tone. "Aren't there some clothes with tags on them in the closet you could return?"

"I will get right on that for you, Birdy. What was I thinking owning multiple dresses? I don't have anywhere to go." Bianca slammed her laptop closed and got to her feet. The only good thing about Birdy's broken leg—and there were zero other upsides—was that it gave her exclusive use of the second floor. The stairs were too narrow for Birdy to maneuver with crutches. She had been getting in a lot of good private cries this week. "While I'm at the shop today, please remember to call and tell the Sand Bar that you are not coming in to play your set this month."

"What?" Birdy twisted around, watching her escape toward the stairs.

"This is too much talking during the show," Lita complained.

"Read the closed captions, Lita. That's why we turned them on," Bee said, careful to keep her voice from being too snappish. "Birdy, there is no way I am driving you to and from the Sand Bar's happy hour so you can play Dave Matthews covers for an hour. That doesn't make sense. What if a patient saw you out? Your Yelp review would tank. Then how would you pay for the new office? If you can't work, you can't play."

His mouth pursed into reluctant acceptance. "Does that mean you're rescinding my invite to the keg party at Flo's?"

Bianca marched back into the dining room. "There is no way we're going to that."

"Why not?" Birdy asked. "I RSVP'd in the group chat!"

"So what? You're injured. I'm tired."

"You have days to rest up!" Birdy protested.

"Flo is right. You shouldn't drink on your painkillers. It's stupid dangerous."

"Then I won't take them! Or I won't drink." He grinned, reaching out to brush his thumb over Bee's wrist. "Whichever helps here."

She hugged her laptop to her chest defensively. "The last time I went out partying, you got hurt."

"I'll be with you!"

"Increasing the likelihood of you getting hurt again."

"You're a gorgeous fatalist woman, Bee. Please let me go to the fancy party. Give me a reason to be clean."

"Go to the party!" Lita shouted. "Just shut up about it! You've talked through my whole show!"

Freed from lunch duty by Birdy's ability to heat pizza bagels, Bianca went into the shop early to catch her mother and ask her to watch Lita the night of Florencio's kegger.

Bonnie was already wrapping up her special appointment, one of many local surfers who hadn't grown out his side-parted corporate crop. The Salty Dog got a lot of business from surfers who had recently been labeled kooks by the cool kids. Surely spending four sessions on a *lost at sea* fake Sailor Jerry back piece would convince people he was no newbie.

Counting ATM-stiff twenties, Bonnie met Bee at the counter as the door banged not-quite-closed behind the kook. Her hair was loosely tied back with a piece of leather that upon closer inspection turned out to be a necklace.

"Geez, Mom," Bee said, hopping onto the chair next to the register and popping open the drawer for Bonnie's deposit. "All that hair and you can't remember a hair tie?"

"Ha ha," Bonnie said, focused on the bills as she split them, sixty–forty. "Unlike you, Miss Thick Crust Pizza, I would never tear out my hair for vanity. The leather is gentler than those rubber bands you use."

"Gentler for you, maybe. I'm sure the cow who used to wear that skin would disagree."

The diamond of Bonnie's engagement ring winked at Bee from its position twisted into the space between her mother's fingers.

"Do you want me to get you a spacer for that ring? It's too big."

"Pick, pick, pick," Bonnie said, swatting at the air like Bianca was a fly buzzing in her ear. "Let me live, Bianca. Fuck. I know you're the boss, but you're not *my* boss, muñeca."

Yes, I am, Bianca thought but did not say. She moved out of the way of Bonnie shoving twenties into the register.

Mo shuffled in, head dwarfed by noise-canceling headphones. The door caught a breeze and swung back, hinges screeching, into the framed shop rules.

"Door's broken," Mo called back without turning. Bobbing along to whatever was blasting in their headphones, they danced into their station.

Bee ran around the counter and wrenched the door until it latched.

Winded, she turned back and found her mother digging keys out of a hideous purse that had been intended for people a fraction of her age. Bianca considered dying of embarrassment as she imagined her mother toting a bag that clearly said *Netflix & Chill* on it around town. Fishing her wallet out of it. Intentionally carrying it incoherent-saying-side out.

But the purse—and the deeper lecture about how to google meme references—would have to wait.

"Oh, Mom," Bianca said casually. Low pressure, sunny voice. "Could you come hang out with Lita Sunday night?"

Head tipped back, Bonnie threw up her arms. "Who could have

seen this coming?" she loudly asked the ceiling. "Bianca needs a favor!"

Bee crossed her arms, self-hugging hard to keep from skittering off to a corner. "Mom, please. This isn't for me. It's for Birdy. He's been cooped up, and he just wants to go down the hill to Flo's house after family dinner. We need you to do bedtime duty."

"She's a grown woman," Bonnie said, keys jingling against her knuckles. "Does she really need to be tucked in?"

"Are you going to stay up with her when she gets too anxious to wind down and refuses to sleep alone?" Bee dug her nails into her elbows. Lita wasn't a grown woman; she was an old woman. The difference wasn't just hours already clocked but her health, her cognition, her emotional age. Bee didn't know why her mother didn't know this when she had so clearly seen it up close.

Bonnie's lower eyelid vibrated. She had labeled it a stress twitch, but Bianca was pretty sure it was eye strain from working without glasses. Bonnie was young to have an adult daughter, but no longer young for her industry. Especially when trends were swinging toward smaller needles and delicate lines.

Bonnie swept the twitch away, dragging the pad of her finger over her deepening crow's-feet. "I'm sorry, Bianca. I have plans this weekend."

"Mom!"

"It's not for me. It's for Tony," she parroted Bianca, the impression dopey and mush-mouthed. "Sunday is Tony's son's birthday. We're going down to Coos Bay to see him."

Bianca's mouth fell open. "Coos Bay is hours away! When were you going to tell me?"

"I'm telling you right now. We'll probably stay for a few days."

"But what about family dinner? What about Lita?"

"I have more than one family now, muñeca," Bonnie said with a withering look. "And I thought you weren't hosting dinners while your husband was injured."

Bianca had sent off a blanket cancellation of all plans over the weekend. Written on her watch after Jo had reminded her that she had responsibilities—other than rescheduling all of Birdy's appointments, rearranging furniture, and making crack-of-dawn trips to Fred Meyer—the message had come off Wren Vos brusque.

"What if I had needed your help and you were just gone?" Bianca asked her mother. "Why wouldn't you tell me earlier so that I wouldn't make plans counting on you?"

"Why would you promise away my time without consulting me?" Bonnie snapped. Bee checked to make sure that Mo was wearing headphones. Bonnie had no qualms with public disputes. They were easier for her to win. "I have my own life, Bianca. Not just making yours easier."

"Easier?" Bianca hissed. "You think *this* is easy?"

"Do you call me to chat?" Bonnie asked with a regal wave of her hand. "Do you take me to lunch or come see me and Tony? No. You only call when you need me to sit with Lita. Drive Lita somewhere. Pick you and Birdy up from the hospital in the middle of the night."

"When," Bianca growled, "between running your father's store and wiping your mother's butt would I take *you* to lunch?"

"Bianca!" Born with her father's pop eyes, Bonnie went from naturally scandalized to cartoonish prig with one blink. Her chest puffed, she minced in an offended circle. "It's my turn to do the girlie romance stuff."

"There's nothing inherently feminine about falling in love, Mother."

"When you came home to live with Lita," Bonnie said, planting the tip of her index finger in the tender underside of Bianca's upper arm, "you called me almost every night so you could see Birdy, talk to Birdy, think about Birdy. When you were going out every weekend until late-late-late, who was home with Lita then? Me! When you went home to meet his family, who was home with *your* family? Me! When you were planning a wedding— Have you even congratulated me on getting engaged, Bianca? Did you send a card that I didn't see? I've never been married before. How would you have felt if when you got engaged, I said nothing?"

Bianca's eyes stung with hurt tears. Nothing made her cry faster than being wrong. "Because *I* am the kid! It was my turn to fall in love and get married. You and Tito and Lita kept me like an indoor dog until college! And in college I was working to pay my own way because you never gave me a college fund!"

"A college fund? That money was the roof over your head in high school. Grow up, Bianca," Bonnie said, unmoved by the sight of her daughter's tears. She dumped her heinous bag on the counter. "Haven't you figured out that parents are just people, too? We didn't map out life just to disappoint you. You think I wouldn't rather have found love before my child? You think I didn't spend my whole life and yours waiting for someone to be my partner? We don't choose when we hit our milestones. We don't have all the answers. We make do."

Bee let the tears leak down the sides of her face, rivers and lakes of mascara and eye shadow pooling. That's what she got for bothering to get dressed today. "If you don't have all the answers then why do I have to run everything by you?"

"What are you talking about?" Bonnie asked, not looking up as she rummaged through the detritus of her bag for a tube of beeswax balm, undoubtedly made by a middle-aged white woman who smelled like palo santo.

"You and Lita," Bee explained. "You check my work. I have a degree in business management and literally ran a store for three years, which is more experience coming in than anyone else who ever managed this place. You really do think I'm just a stupid baby doll. You double-check my bank deposits and run my artists. Lita plans flash events behind my back."

"I know you think you learned the whole world making pizza and going to college, but we're your family, Bianca. We check on you—"

"No. No, you run me," Bee said, shaking her hands in the air to keep the ball of the conversation in her court. "You gave me your shop, your mother, Tito's rules. And I'm just supposed to keep it all running. Then what?"

"Then what...what?" Bonnie asked, exasperated.

"After I do everything on the Bianca Is a Good Daughter list—like running the shop, taking care of Lita, propagating the species—then what? Do I just wait for you all to die? You know I'm not actually a doll, right? No matter how much you call me muñeca, I'm not a toy! I'm a person!"

"I'm not going to stand here and listen to you talk like this," Bonnie said. "You're not making sense. I'm sorry if *all of a sudden* you just hate the nickname we've been calling you since you were a little baby—"

She tried to storm past but Bianca got in her way, too hungry for information to stop now.

"I'm not being mean, Mom. I'm asking you a serious question. If you're all making do and I'm doing whatever you throw together, then what's the long-term plan? What happens if Lita needs more in-home care than we can give? What happens if she needs a nurse? What happens if she already does? What happens when she dies and you die and I have the shop and the house? Is that when I get to change the paint? Is that when Birdy can get a dog?"

"Don't be selfish," Bonnie said, frustration making her extra dismissive. As though she could wave away all of Bianca's bullshit with a roll of her eyes and flick of her wrist. "There is more to life than paint and dogs."

"Is there?!" Bianca shrieked. She was tired of being waved away. Questioned but never answered. She tugged at the sides of her hair. "If I have a kid, will they also have to do all this, too? Because if I have to tell my daughter that the hideous, chipped, *cheap-looking* paint on the front door is so precious to this family that covering it up is the same thing as spitting on Tito's grave— then I fucking swear that I will never, ever, ever bring another person into this world!"

"Good!" Bonnie shouted back. "You're not ready if you're throwing tantrums like this."

"You throw tantrums all the time and yet I have to buy *you* a Mother's Day card! What happens when you're as old as Lita, Mom? Did you even think about the fact that you're going to ask me to do this twice? What happens when you fall down?"

Purse in hand, Bonnie broke for the door. The necklace in her hair rippled in the breeze she made. "When you are ready to apologize, you can call me."

"You'll be waiting."

Bee marched upstairs. She could see Mo in their stall, eyes focused determinedly on the ocean outside and certainly not on the owners' screaming match. Bee owed them a raise. If only she could afford it.

After the glitter fight with Wren, Jo had moved the shoji screen over the window again. Long shadows crept across the scuffed floor. The hardwood could use refinishing. There were deep-carved grooves where Lita and Tito's bistro table and chairs had been—the wrought iron wasn't meant for indoor use but Lita thought it was too beautiful to be left outside.

Rather than feeling sad about the fight, Bianca was electrified by the possibility of living a different way. She had never considered how well formulated the decisions that laid the track of her life were.

Bianca had grown up in a world where the rules were literally posted on the wall, framed for customers, quoted from artist to artist. Laws were debated before ratification, not after—at least, that was what *Schoolhouse Rock!* had taught her.

But life wasn't an oversimplified—if musically genius—seventies cartoon.

Some of the rules were arbitrary. Some of the rules were guesses thrown out in an attempt to stop a fight, like Birdy asking her to return her honeymoon clothes. Some of the rules were built on prejudice, like Tito telling Bianca to put on a one-piece. There were rules for vanity (Bonnie's unfashionably long hair with sad scraggly ends) and rules for self-preservation (Lita's sleep schedule). If the rules were changeable, then Bianca would be changeable.

What if all her life needed was a fresh coat of paint? What if she could preserve what was precious and still move forward?

As expected, the red candle was lit on the desk. It was a fresh candle from the supply in the kitchenette cupboard. Bonnie hadn't trimmed the wick. It bloomed into a smoky mushroom cap, tangling black threads into the air.

Back when everyone in town called him Captain Kelly, the

Chief used to come to Sandy Point Elementary once a year to talk fire safety.

"And remember," he'd say, mustache quivering with smoldering ginger intensity. "Never walk away from a candle. You turn your back and it could burn you up!"

Bee had thought about it every day since Bonnie had showed up with a crate of glass pillar candles from the dollar store.

"You wouldn't thank us for burning the place down either, would you?" Bee asked Tito, giving him one last chance to protest.

He didn't.

She blew the candle out.

BIANCA: Have you guys found a sledgehammer yet?

AUTUMN: We can borrow one from the Chief!

JO: I was thinking about breaking open a Bratz piggy bank I found in my room. It swishes like there might be paper in it.

BIANCA: I have a better idea

Can you meet me at the Salty Dog early Saturday morning?

And maybe bring the Chief's truck?

AUTUMN: Hell yeah, mystery item!! I'll call Dad!

eighteen

AUTUMN

The Chief's truck was triple the size of Autumn's Saturn, and the squeaking suspension bounced up and down the road. Autumn tried to make the most of it by singing "Surrey with the Fringe on Top" on the short drive from Waterfront Cove to the Freemans' house, where Jo was waiting for her.

"Watch out for the sledgehammer on the floor!" Autumn warned as Jo took a second try at climbing up into the cab. "I didn't want it sliding around in the back."

"Good looking out!" Jo puffed, setting her feet neatly on top of the hammer as she reached back for her seat belt. "I could hear you coming from three blocks away."

"My singing or the engine?"

Jo laughed. "First one, then the other."

"If you'd like to join me in whistling a happy tune to make the ride more fun, there's a pitch-pipe app on my phone!" Autumn pulled the gearshift and the truck lurched forwardly with slightly less grace than intended. "Whoops!"

Jo not-so-covertly tightened her seat belt. "Do you really have a pitch pipe? You aren't planning an elaborate a cappella coup against Mrs. Markey, are you?"

"No way. A cappella is so ten years ago." Autumn snorted. "But Pat is very territorial about the Point High piano—"

"There's only one?" Jo asked.

"I mean, yeah. A piano isn't something we can just tack onto the Staples order," Autumn said. She held her breath as the truck pitched over what she prayed was a pothole. "If Broadway Club wants to learn music at the same time as Pat's afterschool choir, then we have to use a pitch pipe."

"Broadway Club must be going well. Eden has been step-clap, step-clapping all over the place. Which was mildly embarrassing while we were waiting for a table at the new Mexican restaurant in Tillamook."

"Aww, inappropriately rehearsing in public is a theater-kid milestone. She'll treasure that forever." The Broadway Club had tripled in size since the seniors had dropped in to learn 9 to 5 with Jo. They mastered the spring carnival routine so quickly that Autumn had ended up teaching them the rest of the dances she had planned for the Senior Showcase. "Eden and her friends brought the finished dances to Pat all on their own. It wasn't even during my class period! They told her that they wouldn't do the Senior Showcase if it didn't actually showcase all of their talents."

"How dramatic of them," Jo noted.

Autumn beamed. "They are my babies with whom I am well pleased. We have four official dance numbers in the Showcase. Five if I can figure out what to do with 'It's a Grand Night for Singing,' the most boring song ever written."

The boardwalk came into view, each storefront like the false front of an old Western movie set. When Autumn was little, she would try to hoard all the Lego bricks so that she'd have enough to do a full replica of the boardwalk. The buildings were just so perfectly storybook square and brightly colored set against the blue-gray endlessness behind them. Flo always ended up needing bricks to make more towers or swords or whatever. She wondered if there were any Legos left in the Main Street house. With the truck, she could definitely rescue more boxes before the dumpster deadline.

"What do you think Bianca wants to smash this morning?" Jo asked, tapping her toes against the head of the sledgehammer. "I didn't think she was that interested in participating in the on-camera stuff."

The boardwalk parking lot was fairly full, which made the process of turning into it much more dangerous than Autumn had anticipated. She slowed down to a crawl and started hunting for two spaces next to each other. "I assume she really needs something smashed? Like a mug she hates."

"Or the prom-queen crown so we can show Jen G?"

"Oh, I hope it's that one!" Autumn giggled.

The truck squeezed tight into a space and a half. Autumn set the parking brake just in time to see a red door approaching the side view mirror, possibly closer than it appeared.

"Is that the front door to the shop?" Autumn asked Jo as the red door bobbled to a stop in front of the tailgate. She repeated the question when she jumped down from the truck and darted forward to help Bee heave the door into the truck bed.

"It was!" Bee said, not seeming to notice the help. "I just had a new one installed that will actually open and close. This is going home, where it will be safe from the seawater. Things can be precious or they can be functional, but I am tired of treating functional things preciously. Jo, do you think your dad would help me mount this on the wall at my house? The way they have the surfboards up at Surf & Saucer?"

"I can ask him," Jo said.

"Great! Follow me in," Bee said, dusting off her hands. She stopped short, checking first the heavy sledgehammer Jo carried and then Jo's footwear. "Good, you got my message about closed-toed shoes. Bring the sledgehammer and your camera!"

The three of them walked into the Salty Dog through the new glass front door. Bee lovingly stroked the gold handle. "Isn't it gorgeous? It latches clean every single time."

"Doors are supposed to," Jo said.

"Around here, you'd be surprised!" Bee said.

She started up the stairs. Autumn and Jo tripped over each other in an attempt to keep up.

Inside the room upstairs, however, there was nothing out of place other than the nostril-ringing smell of fresh paint. Bee herself was spotless, if underdressed—by Bianca standards—in sneakers and black overalls, leading Autumn to assume that Bee had paid someone else to do the painting. Which was good. Manic wall painting could lead to manic paint huffing, something firmly warned against at the spring carnival.

Bianca passed out filtered face masks. "From Florencio's emergency kit," she said. "So you know it's good."

Autumn strapped on her mask and looked around the room. "What are we gathered together to smash, Bee? Is it metaphorical?"

"No! We're getting rid of the kitchenette!" Bee said, motioning to the back wall. "All of it! The cabinets, the counters. I hired a permanent-makeup artist and I'm turning this whole upstairs into an aesthetician's studio. I'm abolishing the no-permanent-makeup rule! Instagram has really blown up the demand for microblading. The girl I hired even has me considering it. I do spend a lot of time on my brows. Scabby eyebrows during the healing week in exchange for three years of perfection? By the time I get the chair up here, I'm sure she'll have me sold. I haven't told Lita about my plan yet. She's going to try to disown me, but then I'll call her bluff and go back to business school!"

"Or phlebotomy school?" Jo offered.

"Ha!" Bee gave an uncharacteristically maniacal laugh. "Wouldn't that just be the pie at the bottom of the sundae if I redecorated this entire place and then went back to community college? That would show my mom for running off with no notice."

Autumn and Jo shared a silent moment, confirming that this was new information to both of them.

"Your mom took off?" Autumn asked in a voice that sounded soothing-casual rather than worried-accusing, which is how she felt.

"Oh yeah, Mom's going out of town for a while and didn't tell me. And then yelled at me about it. That's why I'm asking Flo to move up the keg party. I need to be home in time to put Lita to bed. Who says I can't have it all?" Her watch chirped, and Bee swiped the alarm away before gesturing to the longest wall in the room. "This will be mirrors and mood lighting. Over there will be a little retail corner. We never have a place to put out the aftercare product we sell."

As Bee described the aesthetician chairs she had ordered and the mural two of the shop's employees were planning to paint downstairs in tribute to her grandfather, Autumn looked around the room, seeing it bloom through her friend's imagination. It was definitely going to be awesome. Bee had waited a long time to take full control of the shop.

"I'm done babysitting this place," Bee announced. "This is my shop, and it's going to look how *I* want it. I'm tired of waiting for other people to make the rules. This is my place! I make the rules!"

"Just like Taylor Swift said!" Autumn grinned. She loved seeing Bee fired up and passionate about something again. It felt like a glimpse of College!Bee, the girl who had talked for hours and hours about how meaningful she found making pizza.

"That's right!" Bee cheered. "We're the grown-ups! It already happened!"

"Do you want me to take before and after pictures of the room?" Jo asked Bee, taking her camera out of its case. "Or pictures of you smashing the cabinets?"

"No." Bee skittered away like Jo was going to start paparazzi-shooting her to death. "*I* want to take a picture of *you* taking the first swing. For the Throwback List. If you hadn't needed this room for the list, I never would have thought about fixing it up!"

"Oh," Jo said, eyes rounding with feeling. "Bee, that's so nice. I'm so glad that my annoying need to borrow your space inspired you to use it more yourself!"

"You totally inspire me to do more for myself!" Bee laughed. "I'm wearing a comfortable and sexy new bra, thank you for asking!"

"Oh my God!" Jo dropped her camera back into her bag, flung her arms around Bee's shoulders, and jostled the two of them in an excited hug. "I'm so proud of you!"

Autumn couldn't contain herself. She threw herself onto the end of the hug, squeezing both her best friends at the same time.

"I'm finally redecorating the shop and my new bra earns a group hug?" Bee said in a constricted voice.

"Friendship is magic!" Autumn cried. "Friendship centipede!"

"Stop referencing that poop movie!" Bee begged.

"Okay, okay." Jo shimmied out of the group hug. "Let's wreck this kitchen."

Properly attired in the safety gear the Chief had provided—goofy goggles and Ginger Jay's gardening gloves—Jo picked up the sledgehammer with both hands. From the other side of the room, Bee and Autumn watched through the camera's digital display as Jo took a practice swing like she was using a baseball bat.

"Don't crack your head open!" Autumn called to Jo, wishing she'd brought helmets from the Main Street garage.

"Aim downward!" Bee coached.

"I got it!" Jo said. She squared up to the cabinets and brought the hammer down hard. The slam shook the walls, scaring a storm of seagulls from the window. The cupboard stood strong. Jo geared up for her second swing.

"Wait!" Bee cried.

Jo flinched so hard that the sledgehammer dropped loudly to the floor. Autumn jumped aside with a squeal.

"This moment requires music," Bee said. She pulled her phone out of the wooden desk—a rare sighting of something she couldn't delegate to her watch—and put on the Rolling Stones. "You Can't Always Get What You Want." Everyone took a second to get loose, humming and swaying along to the music.

Jo took the second swing, cracking the bottom out of the cabinet. Wood shards exploded onto the countertop. She pumped her fist in the air. She held the sledgehammer out to Bee. "Next!"

"Get it, Bee!" Autumn cheered.

"I was never very good at hitting baseballs or piñatas," Bee said. "But maybe it's easier with your eyes open?"

With her knees bent and a panicked cry of "You get what you need!" she brought the hammer down on the cabinet, noisily pulling down one side. She lifted her knees in a victory jig.

"Bring it all the way down, Autumn!" she said, passing the hammer.

"Then we can start figuring out how to break the counter." Jo snorted. "Do we think it's glued or bolted to that wall?"

When Autumn had gone to borrow the sledgehammer from her dad, she hadn't imagined using it herself. Throwback List items were supposed to spotlight Jo. Even in writing it as a teenager, Autumn had known that the list was about convincing her über-practical friend that there were things in life that couldn't go on her Stanford application.

She took up the sledgehammer. For years, she had let herself believe that she'd failed in being the right friend to Jo. Growing apart had tarnished some of Autumn's happiest childhood memories, making her doubt their validity.

Seeing Jo bring joy to Sandy Point through the Throwback List gave Autumn those happy memories back.

Here, in the endless possibilities of a room on the brink of transformation, Autumn could feel every version of herself rocking out in tandem. Baby bucktoothed Autumn, college unfortunate-haircut Autumn, present day Autumn in an oversize Patagonia hoodie she'd found on Main Street.

She squared up with the lopsided counter, taking a moment to really feel being in exactly the right place at the right moment—with her two favorite people, trying something for the very first time.

Swinging the hammer from her shoulder in an arc, as though she were hitting a carnival bell, she misjudged the angle, missed the cupboard, and cracked the laminate counter in half.

"Good problem solving, Autumn!" Bee giggled. "But maybe we could go back to getting one piece down at a time?"

"I'm strong as heck, but I can't aim for shit!" Autumn said. She passed the hammer back to Bee.

The three of them spent the morning singing and sweating and laughing over the crack and thud of demolition.

Who knew a hammer could be a honeypot?

COMPLETED ITEMS

- ✓ TP Bianca's house
- ✓ Perform onstage
- ✓ Get belly button pierced
- ✓ Redo the yearbook prank
- ✓ Eat the giant sundae at Frosty's
- ✓ Host a dinner party
- ✓ Pose like a pinup girl
- ✓ Get a pet
- ✓ Learn an entire dance routine
- ✓ Get stoned
- ✓ Eat breakfast at midnight
- ✓ Have a glitter fight
- ✓ Try everything on the menu at Days
- ✓ Break something with a sledgehammer

TO BE COMPLETED

- ○ Surf the Point
- ○ Do a keg stand
- ○ Play hide-and-seek in public
- ○ Climb the giant anchor on the boardwalk (and survive)
- ○ Get a high score at the boardwalk arcade
- ○ Have a bonfire
- ○ Dig up the time capsule

JO: It finally happened, guys. Jen G bagged all of my shit upside down. She broke the chips I'm bringing to the kegger.

AUTUMN: Aww! You're a real townie now!

BIANCA: Are we the Anti Jen G club or is Jen G the Anti Us club?

JO: Did you get stoned without us?

BIANCA: I wish! What happened to the rest of the gummies?

JO: 🫤

AUTUMN: They help me sleep!

BIANCA: Yeah but they could be helping ALL of us sleep

JO: Share with the class, Autumn Breeze

AUTUMN: Autumn Breeze sounds like an air freshener. What a bananas thing for parents to do to a baby

I ate one of the gummies

nineteen

JO

Bee and Birdy bowed out of going to the boardwalk arcade before everyone was scheduled to go to Florencio's. Bianca swore up and down that they would join everyone when it was time to tap the keg.

"Shouldn't we have tapped the keg before we came down here?" Jo asked the Kelly siblings, scooping a handful of tokens out of the change converter—*where you win every time!* as Phil Freeman used to say. "I might be better at air hockey a little tipsy."

"One, you are never going to win the high score at air hockey," Flo said. "Two, don't be the drunk guy at a place for kids. It's a bad look."

"He's only saying that because I accidentally got too drunk at Knott's Berry Farm during last year's Birdy Bash," Autumn explained to Jo. "Turns out that beer is still beer even when it tastes like juice! Lesson learned!"

"But how many kids lost out on a nice day to you and Bianca puking purple on a log ride?" Flo asked drolly.

"You are such a fucking dad sometimes." Jo laughed and cuffed him on the shoulder. She thought about playfully mussing his hair, but that might cross the line between fun shit talk and actual fight. She wasn't sure if the hair stood up on its own or if, like Wren, Florencio spent twenty minutes each morning with blow-dryer, texturizer, and pomade.

High Tide USA Arcade was a wood-walled antique on the boardwalk, two doors down from Jo's parents' store. In California, Jo had been to movie theaters with better arcades than High Tide USA, but none of them had High Tide's grimy indoor carnival unstuck-in-time vibe. Like KDEP radio, High Tide USA boasted the best of the eighties, nineties, and today—a crowded collection of recent-to-this-century electronics and classic wooden box games that could barely keep score in blinking yellow pointillist digits.

"I have a high-score battle plan," Jo told the Kellys.

"Was there any doubt?" Flo asked.

"I'm going to hit the oldest game in every corner of the arcade," Jo said. "Skee-Ball, mini basketball, and shitty old gun games are my best bet, I think."

Autumn rubbed a crinkled dollar bill against the side of the machine, a move Florencio had taught them when they were just unsupervised kids let loose on the boardwalk.

"And if that doesn't work?" she asked.

"I will take down the *Dance Dance Revolution*," Jo said.

"Ha!" Flo said. "People devote their lives to the *Dance*. You can't defeat *DDR* on a whim."

Autumn giggled and stole Jo's phone out of her tote, easily swiping past her passcode and protests. "I am setting an alarm on your phone. We're meeting Bee and Birdy at Flo's house at three thirty."

Flo posted an elbow up on the token machine as he scooped

coins into his pocket. "Like that totally well-known saying 'it's always three thirty somewhere.'"

"Don't be mad because you're hosting a midday rager," Jo said. "Day drinking is a respectable pastime."

"I know it's early." Autumn sighed. "But if we want to see Bee and Birdy, they need to be sober and home by eight."

"But until then we rage," Flo said, pretending to Hulk out. Veins snaked through both his forearms. How was he keeping his arms so jacked without a gym in town? Jo wanted to ask but was sure he would tease her so hard he'd forget to answer the question.

The three of them made their way past the admissions booth onto the play floor. A group of passing kids hollered when they saw Flo, chanting "Coach Kelly" until he excused himself to play a round of foosball against one of his star middle school wrestlers.

"This is why you don't roll up to an arcade drunk," he said knowingly to Jo and Autumn.

"You gotta be sharp to beat a child at a child's game?" Jo asked.

"Don't you know that eventually the younger generation inherits the whole world out from under you?" Flo snorted. "Like when your sister kicked your ass in the *9 to 5* dance."

"Ew, rude! Get out of here, Coach!"

It took forty-five minutes for Jo to uncover her hidden talent as a digital fisherman as she racked up the high score at a bizarre rod-and-reel game called *Bass Trolling*. She was so proud of herself when the screen burst into the final win screen that she refused to put the fake fishing pole down until Autumn and Florencio—back from losing at foosball—took pictures of her backlit by the giant golden *HIGH SCORE* screen.

Jo walked out of the arcade a winner.

"If you like digital fishing, you should definitely come with us for the next Birdy Bash," Birdy said as his crutches wobbled in the gravel in front of Flo's shiplap matchbox house at precisely three thirty. "We're heading to the Dave and Buster's resort the week before Thanksgiving. It's supposed to be out-of-this-world bonkers. Like Vegas but no one cool would ever ever go there."

"Keep selling, man, because I am definitely buying." Jo laughed.

Florencio's house was so deep into the forest side of town that the trees blocked out the view of the beach.

"I can't believe you bought a house downhill. You can't see the ocean," Jo said, taking in the mostly gravel front yard.

"You don't even like the ocean!" Flo said.

"*I* don't," Jo said. "But people do."

Florencio looked offended. "You think I'm people?"

"I did until you bought a house in the flats like a real townie weirdo."

The house was rectangular, two hallways coming off the living room like wings. The walls were pin-pricked, evidence of where picture frames had been recently torn down, nails and all. Had the pictures been of Flo and Melody or impersonal beach art like Freeman Fine Arts once sold? College textbooks and a surprising number of sci-fi paperbacks were the only signs of personality in the place.

Flo and Autumn were busy bickering about who was going to move the pony keg into the backyard.

Autumn finally won by shrieking, "Let people help you!"

She and Flo each took a handle of the keg and waddled it to the backyard. Jo popped open the freezer and found it packed with homemade meals in labeled Tupperware and three bags of ice. She claimed all the ice to save Bianca the trouble. Bee seemed busy helping Birdy maneuver down the single cement stair.

Arms loaded down, Jo joined the group in the surprisingly unfinished backyard: a circle of wood lawn chairs around a firepit so obviously DIY that it was fair to call it a pit but not quite a feature of the house. Evergreen trees blocking out the neighbors and the ocean. Wild grass that wasn't quite a lawn. A plain aluminum grill that Autumn was filling with charcoal briquettes. The squat keg was sitting close to the side of the house.

"For support during your handstand," Autumn explained.

"Don't you remember what Wu-Tang said?" Flo asked.

Jo dropped the bags of ice on the ground. "'Cash rules everything around me'?"

"You're a dream girl." Flo snorted, shaking his head. "No, 'protect ya neck.' During the headstand. You can rest your legs up on the wall."

"Autumn," Birdy called. "Could you help me drag this cooler to use as an ottoman?"

"Sure thing!" Autumn gazelle-leaped across the yard like she was crossing the stage at the opening of *The Lion King*.

"Show-off!" Jo shouted after her. She tore open a bag of ice and poured it around the keg's base. "It's a nice place, Coach. A little bare. I didn't peg you for a minimalist."

"Oh yeah?" Flo swept a hand through his hair, making it stand up extra tall. "How did you want me pegged, Jo?"

Jo cut her eyes at him as her nails split open another bag of ice. The cold was a relief. It kept her cheeks from burning. "Do you ever worry about someone just coming by and picking the whole place up while you're at work? That used to happen to real tiny houses in Silicon Valley. I mean, that's what happens when you ignore a human-rights crisis like homelessness. . . ." She trailed off. She had definitely lost this round of flirting.

She was losing a lot lately.

"Flo," Bianca said, unknowingly bailing Jo out as she appeared at Flo's elbow with her dark-penciled brows pulled together. "I brought a case of frozen taquitos for appetizers. Can I pop them in the oven, or should I use your microwave?"

Flo sniffed. "I'm between microwaves. Autumn was starving to death without one. You can use the oven. You know where the cookie sheets are."

"You do?" Jo asked Bianca. Then, to Flo: "You have cookie sheets?"

Bianca stuck her index finger into one of Flo's dimples. "Flo used to host family dinner once a month so Lita could have a change of scenery. He's used to me barging into his kitchen. We're cousins from different islands."

"Colonized by the Spanish, ignored by the US government," Flo agreed.

"And now everyone assumes we're Mexican." Bee giggled.

"The keg is High Life for you, mana," Flo said.

Bianca held her heart in a swoon. "You shouldn't have, mano!"

"I had to make sure you wouldn't wuss out of helping us drain this thing," Flo said. "We're starting with plenty of time for you to sober up."

"I'm not getting drunk," Bee said seriously before bowing her head in regal acquiescence. "But I will have a drink or two."

"Totally fine," Flo said, holding his hands up in surrender. "When you go into the kitchen, will you put the onion dip on the counter?"

Bee gave a thumb's-up over her head as she went back inside.

"Cindy Kelly's famous church dip?" Jo asked, excited. "I haven't had that since Autumn's graduation party!"

She checked her chin to make sure she wasn't drooling. Caramelized onions had once represented the height of luxury to a young Jo Freeman, who had been brought up to believe French onion soup only came from white-tablecloth restaurants on trips to see Grandma. Her parents had never been home long enough when she was a kid to lovingly cook down onions for an hour. Certainly not just to make dip.

Reclaiming her position at the grill, Autumn stuck her tongue out. "Tell me Mom isn't cooking for you, Flo. And us by extension."

"It was Mom's recipe, but I did all the work," Flo said with a defensive grunt. "I can stir onions in a pot."

"If you say so," Autumn sang. She stacked briquettes into a pyramid. With sooty hands, she pointed toward the kitchen door. "It'll go perfectly with the only bag of Doritos to escape the slumber-party junk-food massacre. It was hiding in the back of my trunk."

"It can't be as broken as my Jen G chips," Jo said.

"You only brought Doritos?" Flo asked his sister. "We can't have hot dogs without buns, Autumn!"

"Hot-dog buns?" Autumn repeated, eyes wide with panic. "Did you tell me to bring—"

Florencio cracked up, shaking his head. "Too easy!"

"Shit-ass!" Autumn chucked an unlit piece of coal at him.

The grill was starting to smoke. Oregon didn't smell like home until something was on fire. Smoke and sand and sea, the whole world in a deep breath.

No one questioned when Jo started setting up her tripod in front of the keg.

"Let's do this," she announced when the shot was framed to her liking. "I'm not trying any amateur acrobatics with light beer already in my belly."

"Despite its pale color, High Life is technically a pilsner," Birdy said. "The light is a different— You know what? No one cares. I apologize! I haven't had this much fresh air in a whole week. It's going straight to my head."

The Kelly siblings came to Jo's aid with the handstand.

"I could carry her weight by myself," Flo said.

"It's not a keg wheelbarrow," Autumn said, grabbing Jo's right leg. "It's a keg *stand*. Her legs need to go straight up."

"I swear, if you chant *chug* I'm gonna throw up in your yard," Jo hissed at Florencio, doing her best not to picture him holding her legs like a wheelbarrow here in front of God and the Birdys.

Up she went. Or down? She nearly went over. Her arms trembled, from nerves and strain and the freezing rim of the keg biting into the heels of her hands. The end of the keg tap appeared in her line of sight, bumping into her chin. She opened her mouth; Autumn popped the faucet between her lips.

"Did we consider how to clean this?" Bianca asked.

"Clorox wipes," Jo tried to say with her mouth full. Plastic clacked against her teeth.

"Chug!" Autumn said.

"Drink!" Flo cheered.

"Imbibe quickly!" Birdy added.

Jo did not drown in beer, but she could definitely see her stupid BuzzFeed death headline for this stunt as well—"Grown Woman Dies Upside Down; Forgot to Breathe." She tapped out as well as she could while keeping her balance and the Kellys righted her.

As she staggered away, her feet took her in a dizzy circle, the same way she used to feel when she and Autumn would hold each other's hands and spin underneath the endless blue skies of idyllic childhood.

Jo did not throw up, but she did sit down hard. Her designated Adirondack chair was in front of the lopsided fire pit. The circle of gray pavers filled with flames waggled in front of her eyes for a whole minute before she could belch and say, "Someone pass me the camera. I gotta make sure I never have to do that again."

Hot dogs, church dip, and frozen taquitos eaten and beer starting to feel like a chore, the group pulled on jackets and sat around the fire pit. With the sun faded behind the trees, the fire was twilight's bright star.

Autumn gave a victorious cry as she successfully hacked into the speaker system, replacing the campy rap of Florencio's workout mix.

"What the fuck is this?" Florencio asked, frowning up at the mounted speaker.

"The Baz Luhrmann *Romeo and Juliet* soundtrack," Jo responded into the head of her most recent beer. She licked the foam away from her lips. She smiled at Autumn. "It's one of the top-five all-time favorite Autumn Kelly albums, dude."

"You don't recognize 'Young Hearts Run Free,' Florencio?" Birdy asked. "It's a classic."

"Lita would surely disagree. She's anti-disco, like anyone still cares," Bee said, gulping down the ice water Flo had poured her. It felt too early to be sobering up. Day drinking was a tricky mistress.

"Lita feels about disco the way hipsters—I mean..." Birdy gave a fake cough. "I'm sorry. The way Wren feels about wrapping things in bacon."

"Oh my God," Bianca said, leaning toward Jo. "How is Wren?

I haven't thought about your handsome ice queen in days! Is she still creeping on your social media without an account?"

"There is no more Wren," Autumn said, plopping herself down next to Bianca with a new cup of beer. Clear plastic because Florencio insisted that only children drank out of red Solos. "In a *she's mean and wrong* way. Not in a *she's dead* way."

"We decided not to go forward with a romantic relationship," Jo told Bianca. "I'm too much of a loser for her."

Jo tugged at her wool collar. Everyone else was cozy in flannel or fleece and all she had was her sandstone J.Crew coat. Her life in California had included far fewer cold-weather hangs. No one in Palo Alto would be outside in weather cooler than sixty.

If her wrists and neck couldn't get warm at the same time, she would have to resort to borrowing one of Florencio's many uniform hoodies. Luckily everywhere he worked branded him in printed sweatshirts. There had to be extras in the house.

"Wren was unnecessarily mean about it, though," Autumn said, pausing to drink. Tiny rabid bubbles were left in the corner of her mouth as she smacked her lips. "So we're mad at her."

"We are not," Jo said, putting her palms as close to the fire as she dared. She was sure her Brazilian blowout made her extra flammable. "My feelings do not affect the feelings of the group. That's culty."

"That's family," Bianca corrected from behind her water cup.

"I'm not mad at Wren," Jo stated, for the group record. She hadn't considered that it needed stating. "I'm mad that she was right about me. Like, I'm not on track to hit my goals by thirty."

"That's not true. You landed that keg stand beautifully!" Birdy said.

"You are getting real close to the end of the Throwback List," Flo said, holding his beer loose between his knees.

"How did you guys decide that you were doing the right job?" Jo asked. "What makes a career *your* career? What makes a job the right job?"

"The paycheck?" Autumn guessed.

Florencio made a buzzer sound. "Stop trying to buy your happiness, Autumn. It's why you can't replace your car."

"To replace my car, I still have to buy something," Autumn said petulantly. "So, money can fix some of my problems but not all of them? Pfft, ya burnt, Flo!"

"Birdy, why are you an orthodontist?" Jo asked. "Did you ever know another orthodontist or were you just like *fuck everything else, I love fixing a goof-ass smile?*"

"There's also option three: secret sadism," Autumn guessed.

"I've told you many times, Autumn, I am not the dentist from *Little Shop of Horrors*. I'm not a dentist at all," Birdy said, taking a sip of water for every sip of beer. To Jo, he explained, "My mom was a dental assistant when I was a kid, so I grew up in dental offices. I think the tech is neat and saw how impactful the work was and knew it was for me."

Jo scowled up at the sky as stars started fading into view. "Ugh, not helpful. My parents can't commit to anything long enough to be useful to my career aspirations. They've never sold anything I liked." She bit the inside of her cheek, realizing that wasn't quite true. "I guess I wanted to work in an office because my dad used to. Before he fell in love with my mom and the ocean, he worked in finance in Seattle. I used to think he was so stupid for cashing out his 401(k) to buy the store. I mean, I continue to worry about how they'll ever retire, but . . . they're happy. I have so many questions about how they live their lives, but they seem to have found something to love in selling tea and surfboards."

"Maybe they just like being together," Autumn said. "And work is second."

"You could try doing the opposite of whatever they do," Bee said, leaning closer to the fire. "They sell tea and surfboards, so you could sell iced coffee and snowboards."

"Not quite opposite enough," Jo said.

"Have you thought about doing wedding photography?" Florencio asked. "It's expensive as fuck, so I'd imagine the pay is okay."

"I'd need a portfolio. I've never shot a wedding. I'd need to find someone to apprentice under for a bit. I don't know how long I can put my parents through having me at home. Not long enough to do an unpaid internship."

"We could host a fake wedding!" Autumn gasped. "Totally stage it with people from the town. On the beach. A white dress. Some fancy angles and your website skills? It's a recipe for success!"

"My mother is getting married," Bianca said as though the information was also a surprise to herself. "I'm sure she wouldn't have a photographer unless it was someone free. We'll be lucky if she even puts on a dress without wrinkles."

"Bonnie still isn't speaking to you?" Autumn asked Bianca, voice heavy with concern.

"She heard about the renovations. I don't know which of the artists snitched on me. Or maybe it was Lita. Mom called me, super pissed. I told her that if she didn't like it, then she and Lita could fire me and figure out how to pay the bills on the house and the shop."

"Bianca!" Autumn gasped. "That's so huge. Good for you!"

"Only if they don't take me up on the firing thing," Bianca said.

A laugh bubbled up in her throat. "Because she and Lita sure as hell aren't talking to me. If Birdy weren't home, I would be starting to believe I was a ghost."

"In my experience," Flo said, tongue wedged into the corner of his mouth, "when people aren't talking to you, it's because you made a choice without them. They give you silence when they feel silenced. When you're working toward the same goal, then the truth doesn't hurt to hear." He squinted into his beer with one eye and swiped a fleck of ash out of the foam.

Jo's coat pocket vibrated. She checked the caller ID.

Gia.

Shit.

"It's official. I'm crying uncle," she said in the too-loud voice that slipped out when she was trying to pretend to be a functioning human being. "Florencio, may I please borrow one of your many, *many* sweatshirts?"

Flo gave her a smug smile from the keg. "Sure thing. You can wear whatever's in my closet."

"You're too kind," she said, getting to her feet.

"And yet not kind enough to go get it himself," Autumn noted, passing her empty cup to Flo.

"It's fine," Jo said, rushing for the door before anyone activated Flo's inflated sense of gallantry. "I'm gonna rifle through his medicine cabinet, too."

"It's many kinds of allergy meds!" Autumn warned.

"And suspicious amounts of lotion!" Bianca added.

"Oh my God," Flo said, reproachfully holding Autumn's cup out of her reach. "I can't invite you people anywhere!"

Jo slipped inside, answering the call but waiting until she was out of sight of the backyard before putting the phone to her ear.

"Hi, Gia, I'm so sorry," she whispered, tiptoeing into Flo's bedroom. She had to fumble for the light switch. When the room finally flooded with light, she caught her reflection in the mirrored closet doors.

"You have been avoiding my texts!" Gia squawked in her ear. "You gave us a clean piss sample, so I know we have your interest. Have you been on a bender since? Because, girl, I have been there before."

For all the things Sandy Point didn't have, there was a diagnostic lab next to Fred Meyer. Not submitting a sample would have been as definitive a choice as just saying no. To count as a maybe, she had to submit her urine. It wasn't like she had anything to hide. She'd been to the spring carnival and knew meth-free was the way to be.

"No, really, G, it's just been sort of a—"

"It's okay. I get it. Going into sales isn't what you were expecting. But, Jo, I really think you could be great at this, okay? I have seen you grow from that gawky intern in an Old Navy blazer to a marketing powerhouse. You could be using that in the field. Not just thinking up slogans and giving goody bags to influencers. Actually talking to people. Trying new things. Haven't you been happier since you've been doing your list?"

"Yes, but—"

"And aren't you running out of list to do?"

Jo gulped. There were fewer than ten items left on the list. She had been so focused on getting things done, she hadn't realized how few remained until someone had commented, asking what she would do next.

There was no plan for after the list. May 1 would come and go, and all of her friends would still have jobs and families and responsibilities. What would Jo have when the Throwback List was over?

"This could be your next big thing," Gia continued. "I want you. Rachel wants you. Here's what we're offering." She listed a number that made Jo sit down on Florencio's blue plaid duvet. "Full medical, dental, vision. You make your quota in the first month and we'll write you a signing bonus that will pay off your car, Jojo. I'm serious. If you want this, you need to say yes right now."

"Yes," Jo breathed.

"Good girl. Call Rachel to set up paperwork. I'm texting you her number riiiight now. There."

Jo hung up the phone, stared at her reflection in the closet doors. Mirror-Jo had guilty eyes and one hand fisted in the comforter. Her pineapple necklace wiggled as she gave a dry swallow. She grabbed the first hoodie she found in the closet.

Outside, the world kept spinning. Jo meant to open her mouth, tell her friends that she had made the decision to change her life and move to a new city. But Autumn had another beer waiting for her and Florencio was mid-story, explaining how many of his wrestlers cried the first time they got pinned and the ways he was trying to normalize it for them.

Jo sat down in her chair, toasty warm in a sweatshirt that only fit because Flo wore it baggy, her coat draped over her knees like a blanket.

Was this the feeling that led her father to cash out all the money he had, all those years ago, when he decided to choose the smaller life of a small town? Why had she never asked him before?

About two logs swallowed by the fire later, the party had wound down much further than the keg. Bianca's watch gave a sleepy chirp.

"Look, Elton John gets a lot of heat," Birdy slurred. "But 'Can You Feel the Love Tonight' is the best song ever written. People don't know because they don't know the best version isn't the one *in* the movie."

"I know, big guy," Bee said, rubbing circles on his chest. "That's why we played it at our wedding."

"Should have played the live version. Biggest regret of my life."

"You've lived a blessed life, man," Flo said.

"Time to go. I need to put Lita to bed," Bianca announced. She helped Birdy to his solid leg.

"Damn, I wish I had my guitar," Birdy said. "I could play 'Can You Feel the Love Tonight' and convince you all it's the greatest."

"Next time, Birdy," Autumn promised.

"I love him so much," Bianca told the group with a shake of her head. "But I will never fix his taste in music." She gave hugs all around. "Autumn, you want a ride?"

"Yes! I am so tired of walking." Autumn bounded for the car, seemingly more happy to be invited than to be off her feet. "Good night, friends!"

"Good night!" Jo called back. She looked at her own car and then back at Flo. "I'm not sober enough to drive yet."

"Glass of water?" Flo offered. "Or another beer?"

Jo accepted the latter. She didn't have work tomorrow.

But she had a job. A new job. A new career.

She sat down on the chair next to Flo, in front of the waning light of embers in the pit. It wasn't the first time they'd been left alone, but there was no activity to drive them, no bar between them. Insects buzzing and the whisper of the ocean blended together into a comfortable white noise that kept the lack of talking from feeling like silence.

Flo pushed his sleeves up, warming the art on his arms. There were pictures of his tattoos on Bianca's website. Apparently, both his and the Chief's Celtic knot work had been done by Bee's grandfather, the Salty Dog himself. After he died, one of the other artists finished the left sleeve and worked on the Filipino iconography of his right arm.

Jo's curiosity finally spilled over. "What kind of person gets nature-versus-nurture sleeves?"

Flo shook his head and rested his chin in his palm. No one pulled off semibashful like Florencio Kelly. His whole face crinkled with the joy of it. "Just your average transracial adoptee with internet degrees in child development and friends who own a tattoo parlor."

"Internet degrees, huh?" Jo asked, curling up the best she could in the slant of the Adirondack chair. "Is that how you managed to never leave town?"

"That's how," Flo said. "I spent some time at Tillamook Bay, thought I would get into the fire program, do the job—"

"Fight fires instead of starting them," Jo said, indicating the dying embers in the fire pit.

"Exactly," Florencio said. "But it turned out that I liked being able to focus on school without spending all of my free time training. So, I switched majors and transferred to OSU's distance learning school. I got to work part-time and go to school from home. It was a good system."

Jo combed her fingers through her hair. "You never got tired of living here? Don't you get tired of people asking where you're really from?"

Flo picked up his beer and took a swig. "You mean do I get tired of people expecting me to speak Spanish when I'm Asian? Sure. Who likes racism?"

323

"And there being no Filipino community for you here?"

"Not here in Sandy Point, maybe, but there's the Filipino American Association in Portland. It's like a community center. I volunteer there over summer break, help out with the Fourth of July barbecue and the annual fund-raiser feast. I met my ex there."

"Melody the interior designer was Filipina?" Jo wondered why Autumn hadn't mentioned that. Did she not realize how much deeper Flo's hurt would be losing not just a fiancée but a connection to his culture?

Flo bobbed his head, staring into the fire. "Second generation. Her mom taught me how to make lumpia and pancit bihon, let me practice my Tagalog outside of Rosetta Stone."

"So you can finally sing along with all of those Pinoy novelty songs you used to make us listen to?"

He snorted and shook his head. "Diaspora will make you starve for crumbs. Turns out the lyrics to 'Basketbol' by Viva Hot Babes aren't much deeper than you'd assume."

Around the keg, the ice was turning to slush, wetting a ring into the broken grass. Jo tried to remember who Florencio had packed into the Kelly house back in the day. There had never been a single best friend the way that Jo and Autumn had each other, but Flo had made up for that in quantity. Dudes from the wrestling team, girls from honors classes, anyone who lived up Main Street and into old town.

"Where did all your bros end up?" she asked idly. "You used to be king of the jocks."

"No one under five-eight has ever been king of the jocks, Jo."

"Not everything is about your height, Florencio."

Properly shamefaced, he sipped from his cup. "My bros are

mostly elsewhere. Joe Roscoe is in Washington. Puckett moved to Coos Bay, has kids. Jon Chung works for the Creamery."

"And you would never associate with a filthy cheesemaker?"

"Remember how you're unemployed and I work two jobs, seven days a week?" he asked. Jo's skin went cold as she remembered Gia's voice. She huddled deeper into the hoodie. "When I'm not working, I have to prioritize my people. I keep an eye on my mom now that she's alone. I feed Autumn because she usually blows all of her money on premade salads instead of making them herself and then can't figure out why she can't afford dinner."

"And it's your job to fix all of that."

He frowned at her. "It's someone's job, and no one else is doing it."

"All that nobility is going to burn out someday; then what will you have?"

"Happy loved ones, I hope."

She rolled her eyes and was surprised to see the moon overhead. "You're impossible."

"I'm very possible."

Jo held eye contact with him as she took a drink of cold beer. "You talk too fast to be sincere, you know that? It really ruins the effect."

Flo's Adirondack chair groaned as he posted an elbow on the arm, the subtle shift in weight bringing his canary-eating grin close enough to ruffle her. "You're giving me line readings now? You want to tell me how to talk to you, Johanna Freeman?"

"Ew, get my full name out of your mouth, Coach. We're nick-name people."

What would it be like to kiss Florencio?

She had wondered before, obviously. Flo was the kind of

good-looking that she'd run her hands over, scan into her memory, and relive often. A tactile attraction that, sure, included supposition about the crush of his lips on hers.

Can he still pin someone in under ten seconds?

Jo hadn't wrestled Flo since they were both scrappy skinned-kneed kids on the boardwalk. But since then, they had never been closer than a dap. They didn't even hug hello.

She got to her feet. "Come on."

Flo looked up at her, curiously. "Where are we going?"

"To climb the anchor."

"Now?" Florencio padded behind her, slowing down only to set his beer on the mailbox as they passed by. "Why?"

"Because," Jo said, marching determinedly away from his house, "I am in the mood to do something stupid."

Elsewhere in the world, restaurants were still open and bars were thronged and music was playing. In Sandy Point, where everything shuttered by eleven, the night was quiet except for the ocean. The boardwalk was pitch-black all the way from Frosty's to the Salty Dog. Even the streetlamps were off to deter visitors from walking the beach at night.

"So this was possibly a question to have before I started climbing," Jo said, hugging the top of the anchor and peering at the cement below. "But how did you climb down when you did this?"

"I used rope," Florencio called up to her. "I could walk back and get some from my bug-out bag?"

"Don't you dare dive into your personal rope collection for me, Coach," Jo huffed. She adjusted her weight, hoping to swing one

leg down the way she'd come up. Instead, her butt fell into noth-
ingness. "Ow. Fuck."

"'She's beauty and she's grace,'" Florencio sang, taking this
inopportune moment to remind Jo that he was Autumn Kelly's
brother.

"Be helpful!" Jo grunted, struggling to pull herself up with her
forearms. "Or at least encouraging!"

"Okay," Flo said. "I encourage you to climb down now."

"I'd love to, but, um, surprise! I can't."

"What do you mean you can't?"

"I mean I have been trying to come down this entire time,
Florencio. And now I'm pretty sure I'm stuck."

"Really?"

"If I weren't, would I have handed you my camera and then
curled myself up into a painful crunch up here?"

"Oh. Fuck."

"Yeah."

"And you really don't want me to try to get rope?"

"So you can lasso me down?" Jo said, feeling shrieky. "Get me
a ladder, Coach! We're adults!"

"She says, from atop a piece of public art. I don't have a ladder, Jo."

"But you have a house!"

"An empty house! You've seen it!"

"Fuck! Flo! Help me get down!"

"Hold on! Goddamn it, I have an idea." He pulled out his phone,
swearing at it the entire time and kicking sand off the sidewalk.

Ten minutes later Main Street lit up with burning red emergency
lights and wailing sirens. The Sandy Point fire engine rumbled to a

stop at the exact corner of Boardwalk and Main. The Chief leaped down off the truck.

"Dad," Flo said with a nod.

"Son," the Chief said. He squinted up the anchor. "Is that little Jo Freeman? You know, we get this call a couple times a year, but you must be the oldest person I've had to fetch up there."

Jo waved. "Heya, Chief Chuck! I'm honored that you rode the truck for me. This seems frankly beneath you. Isn't this intern work?"

The Chief smiled up at her. "Can't think of a call I would have rather received. Be up there in a jiff."

COMPLETED ITEMS

- ✓ TP Bianca's house
- ✓ Perform onstage
- ✓ Get belly button pierced
- ✓ Redo the yearbook prank
- ✓ Eat the giant sundae at Frosty's
- ✓ Host a dinner party
- ✓ Pose like a pinup girl
- ✓ Get a pet
- ✓ Learn an entire dance routine
- ✓ Get stoned
- ✓ Eat breakfast at midnight
- ✓ Have a glitter fight
- ✓ Try everything on the menu at Days
- ✓ Break something with a sledgehammer
- ✓ Do a keg stand
- ✓ Get a high score at the boardwalk arcade
- ✓ Climb the giant anchor on the boardwalk (and survive)

TO BE COMPLETED

- ○ Surf the Point
- ○ Play hide-and-seek in public
- ○ Have a bonfire
- ○ Dig up the time capsule

FLORENCIO: Chief had to rescue a kitten out of a tree

FLORENCIO: Wait sorry no my bad

It's a Stanford grad stuck on a statue

😄

BIANCA: OMG, Jo, are you okay?!

JO: I'm fine. Don't climb under the influence, kids.

AUTUMN: That should be my spring carnival booth next year!

BIRDY: Why aren't we congratulating Jo? Fuck yeah, Jo! You climbed the anchor and a fire ladder!

twenty

AUTUMN

Choosing where to play public hide-and-seek was surprisingly difficult. Autumn's first three ideas were rejected automatically. The park, for being too obvious and too full of people they knew with kids. Bianca didn't want to do anything unprofessional on the boardwalk. And Jo was sure Jen G would call the cops if they sneaked around Fred Meyer too much.

They settled on the last free community space, one of the only buildings in town that didn't want to sell them souvenirs: the Sandy Point Public Library.

The brick crown jewel of old town, Sandy Point's library was one of the few Carnegie libraries opened in Oregon. Autumn, Bee, and Jo drove in separately and parked in a row. Jo's white Mini. Bianca's red hatchback. Autumn's green Saturn, which only stalled once on the drive over. Autumn imagined them as a gang of popular girls with unofficially official parking spots all over town, walking in tandem like the leads in a movie. Bianca's camera-ready swirling

French twist with clipped-in fake flower and Jo's clattering kitten heels made them more Pink Ladies than Plastics.

"Jo!" Autumn shouted the moment Jo climbed out of her Mini. "Tell me literally everything about getting stuck on top of the anchor right now!"

"I can't believe you got stuck." Bee giggled, adjusting the Hawaiian hibiscus clipped into her swirling chignon. "That's literally why I never tried climbing the anchor."

"It was cold," Jo said, brow furrowed in thought. "And embarrassing. Yeah. That about covers the whole spectrum of the night."

"Did Florencio call the Chief directly?" Autumn asked.

"I don't know," Jo said. "I was stuck in the air at the time. Flo just swore a lot, made a call, then *boom*. The Chief was there, rescuing me. It didn't seem like a Dad favor, honestly. It seemed like a perfectly reasonable use of emergency services that my parents are going to make fun of me for literally every day until I die."

"Did Dad and Flo, like, talk or hug or express all the feelings they've been denying? Looked they 'red or pale, or sad or merrily? What observation mad'st thou in this case of his heart's meteors tilting in his face?'" Autumn stopped, took a deep breath, and forced herself to speak slowly—and not in Shakespeare. "Sorry. My freshmen are working through *Comedy of Errors* right now."

"No, it's good." Jo snorted. "Quoting Shakespeare makes you sound well-read."

"As opposed to quoting musicals?" Autumn asked.

"They're pretty equally esoteric," Bee said. She paused, touching Autumn's elbow. "When do you need to be back at work, sweets? I told the shop I'd be in by two."

"I put in for a sub because I was supposed to have an appointment with Birdy to check on my new toofers," Autumn said. She tapped on her front teeth with her fingernail. "I just didn't tell work that my appointment was canceled when Birdy broke his leg. The sub can deal with the juniors butchering commedia dell'arte. I need a break. I'll go back for Broadway Club rehearsal."

The three girls fell into silence as they crossed the library threshold.

The Sandy Point library considered itself lucky to be open and asked for very little. The carpets were the same hideous maroon installed around the bicentennial. The bookcases were lined up like dominoes from different packs—short mixed with tall, walnut and redwood and pine. Midweekday and post-story-time, it was unpopulated except for people sitting at the community computers.

"Oh my God," Jo whispered. "It's exactly the same."

"You had doubts?" Bee asked.

"Hide-and-seek huddle," Autumn whispered as they crowded together in the first aisle of nonfiction. A DOS manual loomed over Bianca's elaborate hairdo. "Ground rules. We're going to play three rounds, so everyone has a chance to be It. No hiding inside of a bookcase so we don't get kicked out—"

"Or get maimed by falling books?" Bianca said.

"Exactly," Autumn said. "And no hiding outside. We have to stay *in* the library."

They agreed on a count of sixty before the hunt began. They were adults and inside, so running was definitely out. Besides, part of the game was to pretend to be looking at books the whole time. Autumn was sort of counting on one of her beloved, dyed-in-the-wool nerd besties starting to read and forgetting to hide.

Using playground rules—oldest first—Bianca took her turn as It, letting her watch do the countdown for her as Jo and Autumn strode casually and quickly to find hiding spots. Jo bent to pretend to tie her—unlaceable—shoes behind a permanent collection of Nehalem grass and cedar baskets, a very good hiding space as it faced a blank wall.

Autumn lay down flat on her stomach, pretending to search for something that had rolled underneath a study table. She pulled the chairs in front of her body, caging herself and hopefully blending into the musty carpet. She was starting to worry about whether or not lice could live in flooring when Bee found her.

"I can see your shoes, Autumn. You're It!"

Sitting on the floor back-to-back with an armchair, Autumn stared blankly at her phone for sixty seconds. After a full minute of torturing herself with windows into more interesting lives than her own on Instagram, she murmured, "Olly olly oxen free!" which had been part of the neighborhood hide-and-seek rules on Main Street. She wondered if Jo had the same reflex.

There was no polite way to interrogate someone about what they did and did not hold sacred about your shared past. Autumn had been shocked to find out that Jo had a lasting fondness for church dip, a stinky sour-cream blob that Autumn found delicious until the second she got the smell stuck in her nose and then it was dead to her for years. Putting it on hot dogs had been, admittedly, pretty damn genius of her brother.

Autumn wasn't sure what Jo thought about Florencio, if she'd noticed the dopey way he looked at her. What about being alone with him for five minutes had sent Jo running for the top of the anchor on Sunday night? The picture had gone up on Instagram before Autumn had even been home long enough to floss the onions from her teeth.

Autumn checked behind a shelving cart full of DVDs and underneath a low table. When in sight of the circulation desk, she picked up a prop—*Code Name Verity*; oh no, suddenly there was a very high chance of weeping—and studiously pretended to read the first page before spotting the wooden tree in the children's section.

When they were little, Florencio used to go to the library for tutoring and Autumn would play in the tree, sticking her face in the cutouts meant for story-time puppets. She had put on many one-person shows in that puppet tree while the librarians told her that the tree was to be shared with everyone. As Autumn had been reminded many, many times as a child, the puppet tree could hold four children. Or one adult.

She changed course, sauntering toward the tree as she pretended to look elsewhere. Between bookcases of picture books. Behind rainbow beanbag chairs. She got lost staring up at the wall. They still had the Little Orphan Annie *Read!* American Library Association poster. Her whole life she'd coveted that poster. It belonged in the Point High drama room. Or above her bed.

She recognized Jo's low murmur coming from inside the puppet tree. She crept closer.

"Yes, thank you for calling me back. I'd like to make an appointment to see the furnished loft you have listed. The studio, that's right. I'm not in town, actually. I'm moving from the coast, so I can't be there today but would—"

"Moving?" Autumn gasped.

Jo was curled fetal against the interior wall of the puppet tree, her hand cupped around her phone. Eyes wide and trembling like a scream queen, she looked up at Autumn, found. "I need to call you back again. I'm so sorry."

The phone dropped into her lap and she scrambled to her feet, hitting first her spine and then her face on the low ceiling of the puppet tree.

"Shit, shit, shit," she whispered.

"Ma'am!" scolded a passing librarian. "Do you mind? This is the children's section."

"Sorry!" Jo whispered back, holding her hands up. She winced and touched her bruised forehead.

"Outside!" Autumn hissed. In a loud whisper she called for Bianca, who unfolded herself from behind a love seat near the computer creeps. Autumn motioned toward the front doors with two fingers, like a flight attendant.

"What do you mean you're moving, Jo?" Autumn asked the second she hit cold, less bookish air. She turned and walked backward down the entrance ramp. "Where are you looking at studios that aren't on the coast, Jo?"

"Stop saying my name like that," Jo said, staring straight ahead at the parking lot.

"Did you say she's moving?" Bianca asked, bring up the rear. She held on to the flower in her hair as she jogged to catch up to Jo. "You're moving?"

Jo stopped at the bottom of the ramp and folded her hands together on top of her stomach. "I took the sales job with Gia's family. In Portland. I start a week from Monday."

"A week!" Autumn couldn't believe what she was hearing. Her eyes had barely adjusted to the daylight, leaving spots in her vision. "A week, as in one?!"

Jo grimaced. "It's more like a week and a half. This weekend I'm looking for a place so that I can be in on May first. I don't want to spend rent on a place I'm not in."

"May first?" Autumn repeated. She was going to lose her best friend and the house on Main Street on the same day. She imagined Jo riding out of town on a dumpster full of memories.

Bee hung back on the ramp, looking stunned. "Jo, that's so soon."

"You said you didn't want to work in sales!" Autumn protested, feeling younger and younger with every word. "At the sleepover, you said!"

"I didn't have a lot of choice after I didn't get the other job!" Jo said with infuriating composure. "What was I supposed to do? I've already been here for over a month. I can't just do nothing and wait for the perfect job to fall into my lap!"

"Oh, so spending time with us is nothing?" Bee asked.

"I didn't say that!" Jo said. She leveled a threatening finger at Bee. "Don't project your shit onto me, Bee. I didn't cancel your honeymoon."

Bianca stepped toward her, growling, "Excuse me?"

"But we haven't finished the Throwback List!" Autumn said with a hitch in her throat. She couldn't tell if she was going to cry or scream. "There's so much left to do!"

"Not enough to turn down a job," Jo said firmly. "My parents want to do the bonfire as a goodbye party—"

"So you told your parents but not us," Bee said.

Jo threw up her hands. "It's been a couple of days! It all happened so fast—*is* happening so fast. As long as I can get in to see these furnished apartments and repack my clothes and—"

"When were you going to tell us?" Autumn asked. Her eyes felt hot. She hated how reasonable Jo was being, as though this were just another to-do list, not a stomping out of the sprout of their renewed friendship. "How long were going to keep it a secret that in a *week* you won't even live here anymore?"

"This is exactly what I was knew was going to happen! I told Birdy that Jo was going to blow into town for a couple weeks and then bail—" Bee stormed past them, toward the parking lot. She pulled the keys from her purse and jangled them in her fist at Jo. "I can't believe I pushed my whole schedule forward for you. You didn't want real friends. You wanted to just waste time with the townies before you ran back to your real life! Well, fuck that! Waste someone else's time, Johanna. Some of us are living our actual lives here. Not staging it for Instagram."

The color drained from Jo's face. "That's not fair, Bianca! I don't have to live here to be friends with you!"

"Of course you don't," Bianca said, batting her lashes with beatific innocence. "Because here you are. Not being a friend. I'm going to work. Autumn, I will call you when I can, but this week is very full of doctor's appointments for Lita and Birdy."

She got into her hatchback and roared out of the parking lot, music blaring against the closed windows.

"She doesn't deserve this," Autumn said, watching Bianca peel around the corner. She turned back to Jo. "You suck, you know that?"

Jo shivered in her coat, pulling the collar closer to her neck. "Wow, Autumn, real mature."

"Suck my butt, Johanna Jordan Freeman! You just hurt my best friend's feelings *and* my feelings. And when we have to tell Birdy and Florencio, it will hurt *their* feelings! Because these people actually like you! All of us have gone out of our way for you, for your list! Do you understand that? Do you care? You weren't just killing time here. You were part of the friendship centipede and now you're just blowing it all up for no reason!"

"I didn't come here to stay, Autumn, you knew that!" Jo said. "I'm living in my parents' house. My whole life is in boxes in the garage. What did you expect me to do? Find an apartment here?"

"Would that be so awful?" Autumn asked as an image crystallized in her mind: a two-bedroom house, maybe in the flats near Flo, filled with Jo's ridiculously gray-scale belongings and the green piano and all the dishware from Main Street. Autumn had lived with many people, but never with either of her best friends. She hadn't thought to wish for it.

"It's not the plan," Jo said, the pin in Autumn's dream balloon.

Autumn folded her arms in a regal posture, hoping it would help to keep her from crying. "All of the plans you've ever made brought you right back here, Jo. Think about that!"

Autumn left first.

Blinking away tears, she drove and found herself at work, more out of habit than anything else. The substitute had her class in the auditorium, the students practicing their scenes on the stage, which should afford Autumn just enough time to sneak into her classroom for the quizzes she'd been putting off grading. She could while away the hours between now and Broadway Club slamming back free staff-lounge coffee.

The moment Autumn opened the door to her classroom, though, she knew she had made a mistake. The accordion wall was open, exposing the mess of music stands the last choir class had left on Pat's side of the room. Pat herself was sitting at her piano—in case there was any doubt it was hers, she had inscribed her name in Sharpie on the side—rifling through papers.

"Oh, Autumn!" Pat said, looking up. "There you are! You have been gone all day!"

"I'm not officially here," Autumn said. "I was supposed to be at the orthodontist. I'm picking up some quizzes—"

"Good! Then you have a moment to chat!" Abruptly standing, Pat scooped up a folder from the papers piled atop the piano and hugged it to her vest. "I heard what you were saying about the fall musical. About the transformative power of playing a juicy part and how the students deserved to have an audience they can really impact."

"Yes!" Autumn said, for once not having to force a smile at Pat. "Transformative Power: The Adolescent Brain Onstage" had been the title of her thesis. "If we give the students a safe place to express the scope of their emotions, then they'll be less likely to engage in riskier behaviors—"

"Exactly," Pat said warmly. "So, I went ahead and I found the perfect show for the fall musical. It's called *Bully Away!* It's a musical intended to teach schoolchildren kindness and active anti-bullying techniques."

Autumn blinked twice, but the words didn't resolve themselves into something sensical. Pat thrust the folder into her hands. It was teal and had a logo crowded with animals wearing clothes.

Bully Away! A Musical with a Message!

Today was starting to feel like bizarro world. Autumn wanted to go home and put her head under the covers.

"I'm sorry," she said weakly. "Doesn't this look a little bit young for high schoolers?"

"Autumn!" Pat's laugh was the ice-pick twinkle of the bell she used to control her classroom. "It's very obviously for children. Our students are going to rehearse and perform the fall musical for the elementary school. That way they are guaranteed a captive and impressionable audience and the elementary school can stop hiring that ridiculous local clown. Everybody wins!"

Autumn hot-potato'd the folder back to Pat. She couldn't trust herself not to tear it to pieces. "I don't want to work on an anti-bullying play, Pat. This isn't what the drama program is about. The students are supposed to be learning what it's like to work on a professional-scale production. For a lot of kids—onstage and in the audience—it's the closest they'll ever get to Broadway."

"Well!" Pat huffed, hugging the folder as though she could cover its virgin ears. "If you don't want to participate, you could bring back staged readings. You must remember that Mr. Hearn's charming readings of *Our Town* every year—"

"No one wants to do *Our Town*. No one wants to *see Our Town*."

"Not with that attitude!" Pat chastised with an exaggerated frown.

"How will we convince the students that they want to dress up like a—is the skunk on the cover also a scientist? I mean, come on! Was this literally the musical directly next to *Bugsy Malone* in the bad-idea musical catalog or what?"

Pat stood as tall as she could, forcing her neck to extend out of her turtleneck so she could be a full five-three. "The rights are purchased, regardless of whether or not you agree to participate in the production."

"You bought that?" Autumn asked.

"If you had bothered to look—" Pat sighed, displaying the inside of the folder. Backing-track CDs, a thin script, pictures of children wearing felt animal costumes and preaching against bullying.

"Oh. Oh no," Autumn said. She tried to imagine showing pictures of those costumes to the Broadway Club. They would eat her alive. Before they all left the program. And if no one signed up for the drama program, Point High definitely wouldn't need a drama teacher. She'd end up teaching speech or, worse, PE. Sharing the school gym with her brother might actually kill her. "Did you buy this with the drama funds?"

Pat gave an imperious sniff. "That's within my purview as the senior co-chair of the theater."

"That title doesn't mean anything! I am the drama teacher! That was the funding for *my* program!"

"And that is where you are wrong, my dear! This was supposed to be *our* program," Pat said, elocuting hard enough to send spittle flying dangerously close to Autumn's face. "You came in and didn't want to make a single compromise. You've never been a classroom teacher, but, oh, you're the authority on the theater. You choreographed the entire Senior Showcase behind my back, pretending that it was just a harmless little side project! You have kept secrets and undermined me this entire year, but you will not push me out of my department, Miss Autumn Kelly. I will not let it happen. I will not be dismissed by anyone, but particularly not a former student. I watched your very first audition. You can't go off into the world and then march back in here like you're someone else. I hired you, and you may work beside me or against me. It will not change the course of my life one bit."

With no trace of irony, she held out the *Bully Away!* folder.

Autumn took it.

COMPLETED ITEMS

- ☑ TP Bianca's house
- ☑ Perform onstage
- ☑ Get belly button pierced
- ☑ Redo the yearbook prank
- ☑ Eat the giant sundae at Frosty's
- ☑ Host a dinner party
- ☑ Pose like a pinup girl
- ☑ Get a pet
- ☑ Learn an entire dance routine
- ☑ Get stoned
- ☑ Eat breakfast at midnight
- ☑ Have a glitter fight
- ☑ Try everything on the menu at Days
- ☑ Break something with a sledgehammer
- ☑ Do a keg stand
- ☑ Get a high score at the boardwalk arcade
- ☑ Climb the giant anchor on the boardwalk (and survive)
- ☑ Play hide-and-seek in public

TO BE COMPLETED

- ◯ Surf the Point
- ◯ Have a bonfire
- ◯ Dig up the time capsule

AUTUMN: I know we're fighting but my day got worse

I'm sending you the link for the show Pat bought for the fall musical

BIANCA: I'm sorry are those 8 year olds in animal pajamas?

JO: Why is the skunk a scientist?

AUTUMN: I accidentally started a war

JO: I know the feeling

AUTUMN: A fight isn't a war

BIANCA: But for the record, it's still a fight

JO: I'm sorry that I didn't tell you I took the job.

Talking about it meant thinking about it more and figuring out all of the steps. I just wanted one more fun day with you both. Maybe that sounds selfish but it's the truth.

The only way I can prove that I want to be friends with you is to keep being friends with you, no matter where I live.

My parents want to turn the bonfire into a goodbye party on the beach in front of the Surf & Saucer this Saturday. I'd really love it if you guys would come and invite your families.

I appreciate that you've let me into your lives and I'd like a chance to celebrate that.

If not, then I'll let you know the next time I'm in town.

BIANCA: I'd like time to process before I make a decision.

AUTUMN: Me too.

JO: 👍

twenty-one

BIANCA

After a long afternoon of doctor's appointments, Lita fell into a surly nap in the armchair she had demanded be moved beneath the Salty Dog's former front door. She hadn't barked more than food orders at Bee since the door came home last week. Asking for a chair was practically a hug.

For the first couple of days after Phil Freeman had bolted the door to the wall, Lita tried avoiding Bianca altogether, taking her pills only when Birdy handed them to her and shuffling out of the room when Bee came downstairs. Eventually Lita wanted to bathe, and Bianca was the only person around to help her into the tub until Bonnie came back from Washington.

The Boria women had begun a battle of haughtiness that completely dampened the brief euphoria Bee had experienced in wresting full control of the shop. Now there was only the churning panic of needing it all to work. The new aesthetician had to succeed. They had to make enough money for Bee to pay down the first line of credit she had ever opened under her married name.

In the silent wall between her and Lita and Bonnie, Bianca could sense not just the expectation of her failure, but her family's hunger for it.

Is that how the Chief had felt when Florencio refused to acknowledge him? Like every unspoken word was a curse?

In the alarm-free time before dinner, Bianca told Birdy that she'd be back in time to heat leftovers and got in her car.

Jo's apology texts and bonfire invite were sitting in her phone, waiting to be analyzed. And while Birdy had plenty of opinions on the matter—he wanted to overnight Lita a new outdoor walker so she could go to the beach party—his wasn't the opinion Bianca wanted.

She drove to Autumn's tiny house. In the matted-down lawn that was nearly a driveway, Autumn's car and beach cruiser were parked beside each other.

Before today, going to the spring carnival on a whim was the closest Bee had ever been to dropping in on anyone. Usually, she liked to give lots of room for people to say that they needed time to be alone. Alone time was her most prized possession. And increasingly rare.

Second-guessing her plan to casually drop by, she started tapping out a text warning on her watch when she looked up and saw Autumn standing in the doorway, face scrunched.

Bee got out of the car. "Hi, sweets."

"Hi," Autumn said.

"I thought you might want company. Yesterday seemed hard for you."

Autumn let out a sigh of relief. "I was afraid you were going to say someone was dead. You never drop by."

"It was an impulse. I went with it. I regret it," Bee admitted.

"Do you want to go get a latte at Safeway Starbucks or do you want to watch soothing TV?"

"TV. I'm still marathoning *My Little Pony*, and I'm almost through season three. But maybe we should go to your house. You don't want to sit on my bed-couch."

"We'll sit on the floor," Bee said. She needed a break from her house. With Lita and Birdy home basically all day, every day, the air was starting to taste like everyone else's exhales. Lita didn't want anyone letting the heat out by opening a window.

Autumn's shoulders slumped as she led Bee into the cottage.

The single-room house had always been snug with wood paneling and a general lack of square footage, but now cardboard boxes and odd bits of furniture crowded the room. Autumn's bed didn't have a frame, but beside it there was a solid oak coffee table with a checkerboard top and a brass floor lamp with a tasseled shade.

"What is all this?" Bianca asked.

"A couple things from Main Street." Autumn sniffled. "I wanted to save some stuff before the dumpster deadline."

"You don't say," Bianca said. She moved aside a covered dish that looked like a cabbage to get to the precarious stack of boxes beneath. Inside the top box were T-shirts, soft with age. Bee shook one out by the shoulders so that she could read the logo. *"If You're Not Front of the Pack, the View Never Changes.* Autumn, there's a dog butt on this shirt."

"Those were the Chief's!" Autumn said, snatching the shirt from Bee and folding it neatly into a Marie Kondo square. "He was going to send all of these to Thrift Town."

"Oh no, not the dog-butt shirt?" Bianca said, lips pulled back in a grimace as she looked at the many, many other folded slogan

T-shirts in the box. "Shirts? Why are there are multiple shirts about being a big dog?"

"That was Dad's style back in the day. Back when he was the Captain," Autumn said. She stashed the butt shirt with its brethren, then, with a shove and a pull, folded the box closed, hiding the rest of the dog slogans. "He doesn't wear shirts that say things now that he's married to Ginger."

"Is that a bad thing?" Bee asked. "I've been trying to convince Birdy to stop wearing inside-joke gamer T-shirts basically since the day we met."

"It's not bad. I'll just miss them," Autumn said. She gestured vaguely to a corner where a white sewing machine was crushing a box labeled *St. Paddy's Decorations*. "I was thinking about making a memory blanket out of them."

"So you could have your own big dog quilt?" Bee asked.

"This stuff is from my childhood, okay?" Autumn said. She put the cabbage back on top of the shirt box. "It's nostalgic for me."

"Just because it's nostalgic doesn't mean it's good. Or that you need it," Bee said.

Autumn crossed her arms. "Are you talking about the shirts or are you talking about Jo?"

"I was talking about the shirts, but since you brought it up, fine, let's talk about Jo."

After walking around the boxes, Autumn sat down on the edge of her bed. "You don't want to go to the bonfire party."

"No!" Bee said, glad to see they were on the same page.

Autumn picked up a fluffy throw pillow and held it in her lap. "Because Jo screwed up and doesn't deserve a second chance."

"I don't have room in my life for liars, Autumn. If Jo doesn't want us to know her business, then she doesn't want us to be her friends—"

"You mean the way you never told me that Birdy canceled your honeymoon?" Autumn asked. "The way I had to find out because you mentioned it in passing in front of everyone?"

A verbal trap! raged Bianca's inner child. *How could you not see that coming, stupid?*

Bianca backed up, calves running into the checkerboard coffee table. "You were busy! With Jo, I might add."

"You literally sleep in a watch that can text me on command, Bee!" Autumn said with an incredulous laugh. "You just didn't want to talk about it. You still don't!"

"Why should I talk about it? It's already done and decided!" Bee said. She clenched her hands until her nails bit into her palms. "But, yeah, it still hurts and it still makes me sad. I told you that at the sleepover!"

"And I heard you," Autumn said gently. "So, what I am asking you to imagine with me is that maybe—even though the way she showed it sucked—maybe Jo actually is sad about leaving. Enough to leave in sort of a shitty way. With no notice. Where we can't talk her out of going. Or she can't talk herself out of going."

"You only want to assume the best of her because of the childhood best-friend thing," Bianca said tightly. "Your special bond. It's based on a sunk-cost fallacy, you get that, right? Just because you've put in the hours doesn't mean that your friendship is infallible."

"It's definitely one hundred percent fallible," Autumn said. "We all are. But, yeah, because I have known Jo for a long time, I'm going to acknowledge that she fucked up and try to move forward. That means believing her when she says she's going to try harder next time. Because I want to make space in my life for more people. The world has to be bigger than five people."

Bianca sat down on the other side of the bed, mostly so that she could buy time as she mentally counted the people in her life. "There are at least a dozen people I *have* to deal with."

"Don't count your employees."

Shit, Bee thought. *Another verbal trap.*

"Bee, if you say no pets, no babies, no new friends—that's so much denying yourself. And it's denying other people an amazing person to know. I want to be able to make new friends and introduce them to my super-awesome bestie because she's one of my favorite people ever born. But that means you have to be willing to give people a shot."

"It's easier when it's brand-new people," Bee said, letting her gaze wander to the photo taken at last year's Birdy Bash at Knott's Berry Farm. The Birdy family was so wide and ever expanding; Bee had found her first two Bashes to be wholly overwhelming, drowning in a sea of noise and endless Code Red Mountain Dew. Having Autumn with her was like bringing a piece of home, even though she hadn't yet moved back to Sandy Point. "You and Jo already know everything about each other. I'm always having to catch up."

"If you want brand-new people, friend, you are in the wrong place. As far as new friends, I can give you Jo or Jen G. Or Wren, but I don't think you'd like that."

"She's—" Bee inhaled. "Not my favorite. I definitely would rather keep Jo than Wren. Has Wren helped you out at all with Mrs. Markey's animal show? Does a vice principal have the authority to cancel a play?"

"You can't cancel a play for being a bad idea. The baby-bullying show will go on whether I want it to or not. The money's been spent." Autumn dropped her face in her hands. "This would never have happened to Mr. Hearn."

"Mr. Hearn probably wouldn't have snuck five dances into the Senior Showcase without consulting his co-director," Bee said.

Autumn looked up at her, aghast.

"I'm sorry! I thought we were doing tough love today!" Bee said. "You took control away from Pat, so she took control away from you. You both think the only way for you to win is for the other to lose. You're just . . . in each other's way."

Autumn flopped across the bed backward. She stared up at the ceiling as her hair wagged against the floor. "When I moved back here, I thought I would know what to do. I thought I would finally be an expert at something. My theater. My town. But I'm not. It wasn't supposed to go like this."

"Then you'll have to find a new way to go," Bianca said. "And maybe take some of these boxes to Thrift Town."

BIANCA: We'll see at you at the bonfire.

JO: You're coming!

BIRDY: Wait until you see the all-terrain rollator we got for Lita!

I just got plain old crutches

AUTUMN: Awesome! I miss Lita!

BIANCA: First we have to see if she can actually get from the parking lot down to the beach

She seems excited to try

As in, she would like to try right now while we are having dinner

FLORENCIO: Should I bring church dip or beer to this send-off party?

JO: Both, Coach! Duh. It's a party!

AUTUMN: Even if it's the sad kind.

twenty-two

JO

"You're really overthinking it," Eden said, standing over the eerily headless body laid out on Jo's bed. "You're literally just going to float on a piece of wood in the ocean. It's not brain surgery, Jo."

"Brain surgery has a lot less risk of sharks and drowning," Jo said, poking at a neoprene arm. It smelled like an unwashed yoga mat. "Bianca's grandma had brain surgery, and she's fine!"

Eden threw her hands up. "Look, you must have wanted to surf once because you wrote it on your stupid list."

"I didn't write it," Jo protested. "It's in Autumn's handwriting. I have zero curiosity about the briny deep, thanks. There are fucking dinosaurs in there."

Deb appeared in the doorway, half invited, half eavesdropping in the way only mothers can. "But cute dinosaurs. Like whales and silly seals."

Jo glared at her mother. "If everything in the ocean was an herbivore, it wouldn't change the fact that you can *drown* in there."

"You could drown in the bathtub!" Deb snorted. "You could

have fallen off the top of the anchor when you climbed it, too. Cracked your head wide open and never set foot on a surfboard."

"God, Mom. That's so morbid," Eden said.

Deb held her hands up. "Life is unpredictable! That's all I'm saying."

"Fine!" Jo said to preemptively block out any more talking. "I'm putting on the wet suit."

Before getting into the water, Jo had assumed the caption for this list item would be something along the lines of *A beautiful communal moment between myself, my family, and the infinite cradle of the sea.*

Five minutes in, she knew her post would actually start with the phrase *Today I let the ocean beat the living shit out of me.* She had no natural balance or grace to keep her planted to the board; the surf leash meant that she couldn't lose her board, but it could fly up and smack her in the nose. And she still couldn't cross this idiotic exercise off the list.

"You got this one, Jojo!" Phil shouted, pointing back at the incoming foamy white surf.

Chin up, Jo kept her belly pressed flat to the deck. Behind her, waves rushed, growing from high to higher than her head. They caught the board, carrying it toward the beach.

"Stand up, Jo! Don't forget to goofy!"

Knees wobbling, Jo got to her feet, taking her southpaw stance. When they were done, she really needed to talk to her family about the stupidity of surf jargon. They could call this position *goofy* all they wanted, but it was a left-foot warrior two pose and she knew it.

Her ankles started to quiver. The board went forward as Jo's balance faltered to the side. Ass into the water and then under. Salt water irrigated her nose and brain. The inside of her skull ached. When she got to shore, she threw up a mouthful of the ocean.

"Okay," she called to her family. "I'm done now."

"One more wave!" Eden called. "You got the hang of it now!"

"Yeah! One more!" Deb agreed, shaking both arms over her head, the same way she did when she wanted to stay up late with one more episode.

Jo thought about the price of the wet suit and board. Jo's parents had special-ordered her a board through their vendor at the Surf & Saucer. It was gray and made Jo feel like she was riding a shark.

Jo blew the water out of her nose, squared her shoulders, and marched back into the ocean before, once again, being blitzed back to the sand.

"I get it," she told her dad, lying on their boards on the beach. "But that doesn't mean I have to do it again."

Phil turned to face her. "Ever?"

Jo scrunched her nose. It felt like there were sand castles stuck between her tongue and her brain. "Anytime soon," she said.

"Hot dog! I'll take it!" Deb cheered, kicking her French pedicure around in the sand. When she looked at Jo, her eyes crinkled at the corners like a paper fan set to flapping. "It's not never, bean!"

"Or a list of why it sucked," Eden agreed. She pulled on thick wool socks and slid her feet into slides, somehow making the combination high fashion. Youths made everything look cool. Jo sometimes thought about Autumn's boxers fad and how weird it was that instead of her being mocked, other girls had gone out and bought novelty boxers to wear as shorts under hoodies.

With a scowl, Jo noted the wet ropes of her hair. Her blowout couldn't fight seawater. It only kept her curls from exploding to their fullest potential. Spirals of water dripped around each tendril.

"I feel like kelp," she grumbled.

"Like you wanna eat it? Because we could go to that fish place in Oceanside. The one that used to be a titty bar."

"Dad!" Eden said. "You have two daughters. Could you try for, like, a modicum of feminism?"

"I'm very sorry, Eden Ellison. The former palace of erotic entertainments—"

"Phil, pass the sunblock, please. Not all of us have the gift of melanin."

"My hair is frizzy!" Jo said over everyone. "I need conditioner and a flat iron, stat."

"Oh please," Eden said. "All of your subscribers are going to be like, *You should wear your hair natural all the time, OMG we stan a queen, blah, blah, blah.*"

Phil found the huge beach bag Deb had spent predawn expertly packing with surf day essentials. From within, Phil produced the sunblock and tossed it to Deb for a reapply.

"Your curls are beautiful, Jojo," he told his eldest. "There's no law that says you have to get rid of them."

Jo motioned to his glistening scalp, reflecting the weak sun. "Tell that to your scalp!"

"Hey, you know men lose their hair because of excess testosterone," Deb purred, rubbing sunblock suggestively over her cheeks.

"Ew, ew, ew." Jo shuddered. "I am so glad I am moving out of your house."

"Me too!" Phil joked, delighting himself. Snickering, he said, "Kidding. You're always welcome at home."

Bringing Deb one hundred Mother's Days' worth of joy, the lunch picnic marked the first time every Freeman ate their namesake Surf & Sauce combination plate at the same time. Under great duress Jo admitted that the mushroom-and-onion tart was her favorite of the four dishes. She ate all of it and the side of chickpea feta salad.

When Deb and Eden went back into the water for one last ride, Jo hung back with her dad. He cleaned up the to-go containers. She triple-checked to make sure her camera was safely wrapped in plastic and cushioned in towels.

"Dad, do you ever regret leaving your salaried job?"

Phil's wide brow furrowed, taken aback but not mad about it. "I had to quit that job to keep your mother. She wanted out of the city. I wanted her. I don't regret a thing."

Jo sat back down on her board. She wrung her hands together until the knuckles popped. Her dad sighed, knelt in the sand beside her.

"If you are looking for the meaning of life, I haven't found it. What I have found is that the most fun thing about being alive is the scariest damned part. You get to be whoever you want to be. Once you figure out who that person is. The guy I was back in my suit-and-tie days, up in Washington." He wiggled his spine into a straight line and deepened his already deep voice. "Philip John Freeman the Third—yeah, the whole name every time—he couldn't have been your dad, Jo. He couldn't have been anybody's dad. My priorities changed, and that changed how I fit into the world."

"Did leaving the job change your priorities? Or did you just decide to be a new person?"

He sat back on his heels, turned to the sea. "Well, first I fell in love with a bossy white girl. You know how that goes."

"I have been there," Jo said. "They'll wreck your shit."

Deb beamed and waved from her board. They waved back.

"Mine, thankfully, can run a business. And has emotions," Phil said. "We learned quick that there's less room to fail when your name's on the door. There's no coworkers or shareholders to cover your ass. Just you and your family and the world. And that's the second thing, we had you and your sister. Having kids means different priorities."

"No more cigars on penny-poker night."

"Yes, that is probably the very smallest way things changed. But also being ready to drive twelve hours to get my daughter out of her apartment before she's evicted. Opening the store on a Sunday when Eden wants to throw a cast party in there. Gotta stay alive. Gotta stay healthy. Gotta not lose the house when tourism rates tank."

"Normal adult shit," Jo said heavily.

"Normal adult shit," Phil concurred. He got to his feet, only the hard set of his jaw betraying the creakiness he felt. He extended a hand to Jo and pulled her to her feet. "If your shit isn't here, Jo, that is okay. If you want to go out there and sell booze or HeartCharts or fun on the interwebs, then do it. But do it all the way. That's the only way you'll know whether or not it's got the potential to make you happy."

Happy had never been Jo's goal. She had lists for productivity and lists to kill time and lists for shopping and lists for chores.

Or was the Thowback List her list for happiness? What did that mean when she was so close to the end?

She picked up her board and started psyching herself up to carry it back up the steep stairs to Jetty Avenue. The trek down had involved her almost being dragged to her death twice.

"Thanks for moving my shit from California," she said to her father.

"I wasn't fishing for that, but you're welcome. When you get that signing bonus, you can hire movers to get the shit out of my garage. When you're ready."

"When I'm ready," Jo said, staring out at the ocean. "That's a good idea, Dad."

"A compliment for your father? Don't strain yourself before your big party!"

COMPLETED ITEMS

- ⊙ TP Bianca's house
- ⊙ Perform onstage
- ⊙ Get belly button pierced
- ⊙ Redo the yearbook prank
- ⊙ Eat the giant sundae at Frosty's
- ⊙ Host a dinner party
- ⊙ Pose like a pinup girl
- ⊙ Get a pet
- ⊙ Learn an entire dance routine
- ⊙ Get stoned
- ⊙ Eat breakfast at midnight
- ⊙ Have a glitter fight
- ⊙ Try everything on the menu at Days
- ⊙ Break something with a sledgehammer
- ⊙ Do a keg stand
- ⊙ Get a high score at the boardwalk arcade
- ⊙ Climb the giant anchor on the boardwalk (and survive)
- ⊙ Play hide-and-seek in public
- ⊙ Surf the Point

TO BE COMPLETED

- ◯ Have a bonfire
- ◯ Dig up the time capsule

twenty-three

AUTUMN

When Autumn went to use her key at the red-and-white house on Main Street for the last time, she found the door already unlocked. Her mother's voice echoed out of the dining room, loudly detailing the contents of the china hutch to someone on the phone.

"You used to love those Precious Moments figurines! You gave me about a million of them!" Cindy Kelly complained to the person on the other end of the line. Aunt Fred, from the sound of it. "I suppose I could check to see if they're worth anything on eBay. . . ."

"They aren't. They're just porcelain Funko pops," Autumn piped in as Cindy hung up the call. "Cute but not valuable."

"Well, you never know," her mother said in syrupy singsong as she swept Autumn up in a squeeze. "Hello, my baby."

"Hello, Momsie." Autumn buried her nose in her mom's crisp hair. In the dim light, Cindy Kelly's hair was a shock of white, no longer the faded blond of the woman in the Sears portraits. Although the hairspray use was about the same. "I didn't know you were going to be here," she said. "I'm supposed to meet Jo."

Her mom's shoulder twisted in a delicate, put-upon shrug. "The May-first deadline was for everybody. And here we are at the end of April."

Autumn gestured at the things accumulated in the dining room: a pair of skis, a Big Mouth Billy Bass, her parents' wedding china, a freestanding carousel horse. "Couldn't you just tell Dad not to throw away—"

"The Chief can throw away whatever he wants," Cindy interrupted. "It's time for us to take what we want and let go."

A knock on the front door made Autumn's mouth shut.

"Hello?" Jo called, poking her head in. Her face was haloed in soft brown curls.

"Your hair!" Autumn exclaimed. "There's my friend! You look like high school Jo."

"Please," Jo said, clutching invisible pearls as she fully entered the room. "I am not wearing an outfit color-coordinated to flip-flops. My hair did not like spending the day in salt water, so I'm letting it rest before I flat-iron again."

"Little Jojo!" Cindy cried, bum-rushing Jo into a mama-bear hug. "I can't believe I'm seeing you again on the day before you leave!"

"Oh! Hi, Mrs. Kelly!" Jo said, wobbling from the force of the hug. "Are you coming to the bonfire tonight?"

Cindy looked faux-offended. "Of course! Who else would make the church dip?"

"Florencio's dip isn't bad," Jo said tactfully.

"Oh well, speaking of, guess who was just here?" Cindy Kelly asked, holding her hand up to signal how conspiratorial she was being. Autumn had never been able to direct her mother away from overacting.

Jo opened her mouth, possibly to actually name the obvious guess, which was not what Autumn's mother wanted.

"Who, Momsie?" Autumn asked.

"Florencio came to pick up a few things," Cindy said. "At the same time as your father."

"And did they both stay?" Autumn asked.

"They did!" Cindy grinned. "They cleared out all the surfboards and camping things from the garage! They weren't chatty about it, of course. They have a lot of healing to do, but it was more talking than I've seen them do in years."

"All because Jo got stuck in the anchor," Autumn said proudly.

Jo gave a nervous laugh. "Happy to help?"

"I'm glad Dad and Flo are talking again," Autumn said, glancing over her shoulder at the furniture still piled up in the living room. "Do you think they'd move the green piano to the theater for me?"

"It wouldn't hurt to ask. Try tonight at the bonfire. The Chief loves to look magnanimous at parties," Cindy said. She caught Jo in a second surprise hug. "Have fun digging in the yard! We'll see you down on the beach for your big party!"

"I don't know who she means by *we* now," Autumn said under her breath as she and Jo made their way to the backyard. "It used to mean her and Dad, but I think she's keeping it all for herself."

Jo snickered. "The royal we suits her. We don't question the creator of the Henrietta casserole."

In the backyard toolshed, alongside a dead Weedwacker and mystery cans of paint, they found two cobwebby shovels. Most likely the same shovels they had used to bury the time capsule in the first place.

Without the doghouse to mark the spot, Autumn walked from the back porch forward ten paces and Jo walked five paces from the back fence. The white decorative rocks made walking slippery and loud, every step a crunch or a crack. Where they met in the middle, they planted their shovels.

The sound of rusted shovels breaking the rocks set Autumn's teeth on edge, making her dig faster to get to the noiseless dirt.

"We couldn't have buried it that deep," Jo said. "We were little kids. We were still wearing clothes from Limited Too."

"You're right," Autumn said, taking a digging pause. "We're probably digging in the wrong place. It's hard to tell without landmarks."

They went to the back porch, touched their fingertips to the door.

"Ten paces forward," Autumn said.

They counted their steps. Stuck their shovels in the ground. Turned over a foot of dirt and nothing. They tried again from the fence. Autumn slammed her heel into her shovel, burying the blade entirely in the earth so that she could flip over a pancake of dirt and rocks. No sign of the buried tackle box.

"Maybe we were taking smaller steps because we were shorter," Autumn said, counting her steps from the fence again. She stuck her shovel in the dirt at random. "Or maybe we were taking much bigger steps assuming we'd get taller. Who the fuck fills a yard with rocks anyway?"

"They are a lot less flammable than grass," Jo said.

"Don't take the rocks' side!" Autumn snapped, carving another pit in the ground. Dirt and rocks rained down in a noisy mess beside her. "They're ugly and impractical and getting in our way! This is it. The end of the list. We waited years and years to dig up this time capsule and today it's—"

It's time to take what we want and let go, she thought, and glanced back at the house, almost expecting to see her mom watching through the blinds to see the realization land.

Autumn stopped digging and looked up at Jo. "Do you remember when all of my dad's shirts had dogs on them?"

"The big-dogs shirts?" Jo asked. "The ones that said, like, *Top Dog* or *Last Dog* or whatever? Those were, like, all he ever wore. Why?"

Autumn shook her head. "Some things just feel more real when you're not the only person who remembers them. Can we take a digging break?"

"I thought you'd never ask!" Jo threw her shovel aside and cracked her knuckles. "Why don't we go back inside and check all the rooms to make sure nothing cool gets left behind?" She surveyed the many holes they'd made. "We can always come back for the time capsule later. The house isn't sold yet. And if whoever buys it has any sense, they'll get rid of all these stupid fucking rocks and we can ask to look for our time capsule. I bet you fifty bucks that a townie buys the place anyway."

"Fifty bucks and one time capsule," Autumn said. "I'll take that action."

BIANCA

It seemed like all of Sandy Point had come down to the beach. The Salty Dog closed early so that all the artists could join in the party around the bonfire, where the party had already started with Phil Freeman's surf-bros and other shop owners from the boardwalk. Dez and Dede introduced the shop's new aesthetician to Deb Freeman's Bunco group.

Standing near the fire with her parents, Jo sipped a can of La Croix. Her hair was curly again and pulled away from her face. Autumn boinged the curl behind her ear.

Lita refused to be pushed from the parking lot, using her new all-terrain wheels to walk surely up the planks of the boardwalk, then down to the sand of the beach. She wore her favorite glittery leggings and one of the few sweatshirts she had that hadn't once belonged to Tito. She tipped her face up to the sky like she could feel the sun's warmth through the spring chill in the air.

It was a party for Jo, so the mess of fresh clams and crabs that normally came with a beach bonfire was replaced with camping food like hot dogs and s'mores. When Chief Chuck and Ginger Jay arrived, they brought a bushel of artichokes. Cindy Kelly brought onion dip. Florencio brought a party platter of hot wings, compliments of Alfie Jay and the Days morning crew. Eden and her friends showed up in a shrieking, giggling mass, approaching Autumn like she was a celebrity.

It didn't take long before Lita started holding court and telling her favorite stories.

"You were at Woodstock, Mrs. Boria?" Jo asked.

"Lita, Lita. Everybody young calls me Lita," said Lita, already moving on to the next part of the story. "I was just a little New York punk, younger and shorter than Bianca is now."

"Thank you for not saying thinner," Bee said.

"That would be a lie," said Lita. "At the time, my husband, Manny, was off on a boat."

"With the navy," Bee clarified to the small audience Lita had amassed.

"Who is telling this story, Bianca?" Lita rolled her eyes. "You see how she pecks at me like she's the mama now? Anyway, anyway, I was living with my hippie friend Tina. She walked with loose hips, like Miss Autumn. She was so fun. But, not so smart."

Autumn pointed accusingly at her brother. "Don't say a word."

"I'd never." Flo snorted.

"We showed up late," Lita continued. "To Woodstock! Day two! I was so mad. I had put all my trust in loose-hips Tina, and she got the day wrong. But we were there in time to see my love. Santana. A once-in-a-lifetime concert!"

Jo poured wine into plastic cups for those inclined as she told the story of finding out that it was illegal to drink on the beach in California. Bee ran back to the car to get Lita's coat and then again to get her own.

Above them, the sky went dark-water blue, reaching out to the sliver of sunlight on the horizon. Sparks flew off the bonfire, zinging past surfers bragging to the owners of Frosty's about today's chop.

At seven thirty, Bee's watch cheeped, reminding her that it was Lita's bedtime. She looked across the bonfire to where her grandmother was with Mo and Cruz, clutching both of their hands as they knelt beside her, as if paying tribute.

Bianca would never admit it to Bonnie or Lita, but this was something that Square Slice Pizza could never have taught her. The intersection of business and family, how love and art could hitch lives into bowline knots. How hard it was to accept help even when the thing at stake was the well-being of the people you loved most. Or, worse, yourself.

"Bee?" Birdy said, breaking into her thoughts with a wince on his face.

Bianca rushed to put a hand on his chest. "You okay? Is it your leg? Are you standing too much?"

"No." He chuckled, shaking his head to clear away her concerns. "I've been thinking."

"Is that why you look like you're in pain?" she teased. She swallowed the last of her wine and set her cup aside to unleash a flurry of pestering index fingers in the ticklish spot of his waist.

"Unfair! I can't run away from these pokes." Birdy dug his crutch into the sand and wiggled an inch to the side. "I've been thinking about the new office."

Bee abandoned her poke attack. "I am very aware. You talk about dental equipment in your sleep. You woke Lita up the other night moaning about intra-oral cameras. She thought it was something dirty."

"There are some things I need, but if we leave the office as is and maybe spend a couple days with my parents another time, I was thinking that maybe we could skip Birdy Bash this year. If that's okay."

"Skip Birdy Bash?" Bianca laughed because there was no world in which that sentence wasn't a joke. "Benji and Blakely have already planned your route through the arcades."

Since Birdy's gaming systems moved downstairs, Bee could now hear a third of the conversation that happened during the Birdy Brothers' weekly gaming appointments. The majority of talk seemed to revolve around how hard they were going to party the next time they were all together.

"Most of the games at the Dave and Buster's resort are two-player. My brothers will be fine," Birdy said, unconcerned. "You don't want to wait another year for Hawaii, do you?"

"N-no," Bee said, her heart cautiously alight.

As he turned toward the sunset, Birdy's eyes closed like he could feel the warmth in the fading light. "Between being home for almost two months and changing offices . . . I just don't want to miss our chance. We don't know what's going to happen next. I never thought I would spend more time with Lita than with you, but since I've been stuck downstairs, that's definitely been true. I'm tired of sleeping without you. I don't want to take that for granted again once I get it back. We already took two weeks off work in November. Let's go away and sleep next to each other and not take breaks to hang out with my cousins."

"You want to go on our honeymoon this year? Instead of Birdy Bash? Is this the pain meds talking?"

"Pretty sure this is love talking. But with, like, a heaping side of cabin fever."

Bee stopped his mouth with a kiss. "Let's look at tickets right now."

JO

The fire had been expertly extinguished by Chief Chuck. Jo had hugged more people in one night than she had in her entire life. It felt a little bit like attending her own wake, but in an uplifting way.

She had held on to Autumn and Bee the longest, hoping that they could feel, in the best hug she could muster, how much she treasured this moment.

"Friendship centipede," she said to them.

"That can't be our thing," Bianca said.

"Too late," Autumn said with a giggle that could have been a sob. "We're sewn together by the butts of friendship."

Jo let everyone else leave first. The Birdys hurried to get yawning Lita into the car with Flo's help. Cindy Kelly bragged to Autumn about getting invited to Bunco. Phil and Deb walked up the beach to take the stairs into their neighborhood. Eden caught a ride with the Broadway Club.

Jo looked out at the ocean. *I surfed you this morning,* she thought. *How fucking weird is that?*

"Jo!"

She turned to find Florencio leaning against the anchor. His hands were on his hips, like he was about to ask her to drop and give him twenty.

His mouth flopped open and closed, at a momentary loss at having caught her attention so easily.

"Are you going to climb it?" Jo asked, pointing up at the anchor.

He shook his head. "I just wanted to say that I'm sorry you're leaving town. Days won't be the same without you clogging the bar with milk-shake orders."

Jo smiled. "It's truly the Cream Dream I'll miss most. Do you think I could get an actual TGI Friday's to make it for me?"

"I bet you could talk them into it." He walked down the lawn and put his fist out for a dap.

She dapped him up. Neither of them moved to leave Bee's front yard.

"I've really liked spending time with you," he said. "Getting to know you not as just my sister's friend."

"Oh," Jo said. "Thanks, Coach. Likewise."

"I don't want you to go without telling you that." Florencio huffed a sigh, tugged his hair taller. "That I liked helping with your lists and making sure you didn't die climbing the anchor and seeing you fish electronically. I like seeing you every day or almost every day, even if you're just drinking water and taking up space at my bar. But sort of no matter what I do, I can't vibe you out.

You want to chat me up, wear my clothes, talk about my parents. And I guess there's a chance that you want a third best friend and I'm down for the job, Jo. But I would prefer that it not be platonic because you are a fucking smoke show."

Jo stared at him, stupefied to speechlessness. Her brain was doing its very best, chugging uphill toward the very concept that she was, in fact, being Bridget Jones'd right now.

Florencio Kelly was the one who liked her just the way she was.

"Wait," she said, her voice tremulous. "You've really been flirting with me this whole time? I sort of thought we were keeping our skills sharp."

"Skills?" Flo asked. His forehead wrinkled in offense. "I'm a person, not a whetstone."

"This isn't like a formal flirting arrangement?"

"Where I pretend to be into you and everybody in town knows it?"

"Um..." Jo looked helplessly back toward the parking lot, then back at Flo. "Yes?"

"No. That's not a thing. That would be...like, beyond prank show and into gaslighting."

"A real life ruiner," Jo agreed. "So, this is..."

Flo closed the distance between them. Rested his hand against her hip.

"The opposite," he said.

Jo's breath caught. "The opposite meaning that you actually like me."

"Yes, ma'am."

She set her hand on the nape of his neck, letting her knuckles brush through his dark silky hair. "Even though I call you Coach."

"Even though."

Jo set her forehead to his, momentarily forgetting that they were directly in the center of town, alone with the ocean. The warmth of his skin on hers, the smell of him so close was making her reckless, hungry. She rubbed her nose against his. "Why didn't you do anything before? The night with the keg? Before I climbed the anchor. I get why you wouldn't want to after."

"You were drunk as fuck. I'm not going to hook up with a drunk girl. Tonight you're sober enough for your parents, my parents, and Bianca to let you drive home by yourself."

"Chivalrous."

"Yeah, I'm basically a knight for wanting real consent." He caught her hand and folded their fingers together.

"You were so sure we were gonna have sex?"

"You lose a hundred percent of the shots you don't take."

She caught his mouth, inhaling the surprise on his breath. She kissed him expecting to compare it to other kisses with other people, to flashback to Wren and her recently bruised heart. But kissing Flo was wholly original, wholly here in this moment. Actively holding her and kissing her back and grinning like an idiot about it.

She stroked the squareness of his jaw with the pad of her thumb. "Let's get out of here, Coach."

He smiled against her mouth. "Yeah?"

"I need to be home by sunrise," she said. She kissed him again, once, twice, and nipped at his bottom lip. "I'm moving tomorrow."

- ☑ TP Bianca's house
- ☑ Perform onstage
- ☑ Get belly button pierced
- ☑ Redo the yearbook prank
- ☑ Eat the giant sundae at Frosty's
- ☑ Host a dinner party
- ☑ Pose like a pinup girl
- ☑ Get a pet
- ☑ Learn an entire dance routine
- ☑ Get stoned
- ☑ Eat breakfast at midnight
- ☑ Have a glitter fight
- ☑ Try everything on the menu at Days
- ☑ Break something with a sledgehammer
- ☑ Do a keg stand
- ☑ Get a high score at the boardwalk arcade
- ☑ Climb the giant anchor on the boardwalk (and survive)
- ☑ Play hide-and-seek in public
- ☑ Surf the Point
- ☑ Have a bonfire

- ◯ Dig up the time capsule

AUTUMN: BROTHERFUCKER!

BIANCA: Excuse me?

JO: ?

AUTUMN: My mom saw a white Mini parked at Flo's last night. And this morning!!!!

BIANCA: Oh dang

JO: Okay I don't deny it

Can we be cool about this?

AUTUMN: You humped my brother!

Tell me nothing because he is my brother but also tell me everything in that you are my best friend and I at least require a thumbs up or down to know how to feel about this?

JO: 👍

BIANCA: Not thumbs up enough to stop you from moving, tho

JO: Florencio is many things, but he is not a living wage in the city

BIANCA: No man is

And with that: bon voyage, sweets

AUTUMN: Drive safe! Text us when you get there!!!

twenty-four
One Month Later

BIANCA

"Hotel California" was blaring behind the closed door of the downstairs bedroom, drowning out the lunch alarm on Bianca's watch as she crept inside. Lita was curled up on top of her blankets, already dressed.

"It's lunchtime, Lita," Bianca said, waking her. "Did you have a nice morning?"

Bianca had started what she was secretly referring to as Lita Speed Dating. Different Lita-sitters came in and out of the house at the same time each day to spend their time with Lita however they—but mostly however Lita—liked. Shortly after taking Lita out to the bonfire, Bee had put out an email to all of Lita's people, opening the doors to the house. Lita needed friends—who could be trusted with her schedule and needs—and Bianca needed help making sure that Lita's life felt full.

The response surprised her. Where she had expected obligatory apologies or outright silence, there had been enthusiasm. The artists from the shop, old-timers on the Boardwalk Association, neighbors, Tito's friends and their widows.

People had missed Lita as much as Lita had missed people.

"Yes," Lita said, pausing to yawn. "Dez introduced me to a wonderful new show. *The Real Bitches of LA.*"

Bianca let out a startled giggle. "That can't be the name."

Lita's brow furrowed and her nails went searching for her reading glasses on her bedside table. "No, I think that's it. I had her write it down for me...."

Bee, touched that Lita had made an effort to use her memory notebook—which normally sat around forgotten in a drawer—agreed to program *The Real Bitches* into Lita's bedroom DVR. She sat down on the mattress next to her grandmother and scooped up the remotes.

"I was thinking we could invite Dez and her kids over," Bee said. "You haven't met the baby yet. They could come to family dinner some Sunday."

"That would be nice. It's been a long time since we had company."

Bee stopped laboriously typing into the search bar. "That's not true. Autumn comes over every week. Flo sometimes, too."

"One or two people, but no parties," Lita said with a dismissive twitch of her chin. "Not like the big bonfire on the beach!"

"That was to say goodbye to Jo," Bee reminded her.

"That is not the only reason to have a party! We used to have friends over every weekend, your Tito and I. Noisy parties in the backyard. I think the neighbors did not like us so much then. That was before Phil and Deb. Before you, even. Your mother would dance on the tables and make everybody laugh. She was wild!"

"She's still wild, Lita," Bee said.

"She's young and in love," Lita said with a shrug. "Maybe not that young. But in love. She'll come back when she gets bored. People always do."

Bee was sure Lita was right. Any day now, Bonnie would appear at the shop or in Bee's texts or at the front door with a box of doughnuts. Maybe she would bring with her the family that Tony already had. Maybe she would successfully wring the attention out of them that she could never seem to find at home.

"We'll work on having more people over," Bee promised Lita, programming *The Real Bitches* to record.

"Invite my Cruz," Lita said. "I'm worried about him living over a bar. It's not good for him to be tempted like that."

"I will invite Cruz," Bee promised. "But whenever we have people over, all you have to do is tell me you want everyone out and we're done."

Lita frowned at her. "That would be rude, muñeca. You can't invite people over and then kick them out."

"We can if you don't feel well."

"If I don't feel well, the world doesn't stop."

"But it could."

"What then? You're going to hang the moon on my ceiling?"

"If you wanted."

Bee picked up Lita's hand. Bonnie was normally in charge of taking Lita for manicures. Without her, Lita's nails were unpainted and uneven. The cinnamon-brown skin around her knuckles was rough and cracked. Bee found a tube of hand cream and massaged it into Lita's arthritic fingers.

"When I first came home you were so sick," she said to the palm of Lita's right hand. "We were doing physical therapy every day, remember?"

"Ay, don't remind me," Lita groaned. "I never want to do PT again. It was torture."

Relearning to walk, to speak, to think. Bianca tried her best to keep her thoughts out of that time, away from the Lita so frail that she was almost a stranger. They had been so close to losing her so shortly after Tito. Sometimes it felt like they'd been in free fall since, waiting to crash.

"But you got better," Bee said. She rubbed lotion into Lita's other hand, taking care around the gold band of her wedding ring.

"I got better," Lita agreed.

"But not younger."

"No one gets younger, Bianca."

"Tell that to J.Lo."

"You know I would. I have words for that girl."

"Ask her how she keeps her skin so nice. I'm starting to wrinkle."

"My baby? Never." The tip of her nose pressed to the curve of Bee's temple.

They sat in silence, curled together, hands between them like little girls with a secret to share. Bee could feel how thin Lita's skin was, how close to the surface her pulse.

"Lita, what would you think about being a bisabuela?" Bianca asked, too scared to move, to see the truth in Lita's eyes. "Realistically. Sharing the house with a baby. Sharing attention with a baby. Being around a baby day in and day out."

"Is that why you are in such a hurry to go to Hawaii? So you can have time to get pregnant?"

Bee laughed. "No! Going on vacation is about sleeping in and

379

having nicer weather. This is me asking you if you think you could handle living in a house with an infant. Again. You've already gone through it with Mom and then with me. Do you want to go through it a third time?"

"If you and Birdy want a baby."

Bee pulled back, holding firm to Lita's hands, squeezing them in emphasis. "This house has three adults in it. You get a vote. Not the biggest vote. You don't have veto power on everything. But a baby is officially on the table for discussion, so if you have concerns, I need to know them now. Not later. Not when I'm stroller shopping. Will you think about it for me? Maybe make a list?"

"A list of complaints." Lita grinned, her eyes disappearing into her cheeks. "I will write complaints for you all day. In many languages."

"I can always count on you."

Lita stamped a kiss to her temple. "Always, my girl."

AUTUMN

Pausing behind the closed door of her empty classroom, Autumn gave herself last looks. Smoothing the sides of her cardigan, she wished again that she had a button-down shirt or jacket to make her appear more professional. The blazer her mom had bought her for her initial Point High job interview had been hopelessly wrinkled when she found it at the bottom of her dresser last night.

But she was trying. That had to count for something.

The clock above her makeshift desk turned to seven thirty, marking the beginning of official working hours.

Autumn left her classroom, reciting her list of talking points in her head.

Engagement. Encouragement. Enrichment.

Pulse leaping and fighting the sudden urge to pee—a common reaction to stage fright—she waited until she saw Wren Vos go into the staff lounge and then marched inside.

Before the school was remodeled in the seventies, the staff lounge had been a home ec. classroom. One wall retained the built-in stoves and faded yellow cabinets. At the line of coffee-makers and teakettles, Wren stirred oat milk into her travel mug.

More importantly, Pat was not in the room.

With a confident spine and steady voice, Autumn said, "Good morning, Wren!"

Wren's icy stare was twice as intimidating coming at her side-ways. "Oh. Are you done avoiding me?"

"I haven't been avoiding you!" Autumn lied. "I've been riding my bike instead of coming in with my brother, so I don't have to be here as early. The weather's been nice."

Wren turned around and folded her arms in a movement so swift Autumn wondered if it was a rehearsed bit of principal-ing. "You want me to believe that it is pure coincidence that when I stopped seeing your friend, you stopped meeting me for coffee in the morning?"

"Not pure coincidence, I guess," Autumn admitted. "But not purely planned?"

Autumn had been avoiding the awkwardness more than she had been avoiding Wren directly.

"I'm sorry if you felt like me and Johanna not working out was a reflection on your idea to bring us back together," Wren said, focusing her attention back on dressing her coffee. "I wouldn't have agreed to date her again if I thought it would complicate our working relationship. I hope you understand."

"I don't get it," Autumn admitted. "You lit up when you were talking about Jo!"

"I don't like a lot of people, but I've always liked her," Wren said, with a wrinkle in her forehead that very nearly spelled out the word *duh*. "But I miscalculated how sustainable that would be. I probably could have just tried knowing her again, but... Well, she's also still the first girl I ever loved. And she's so hot."

Autumn let out a surprised giggle. "I mean, the chemistry between you two is enviable."

"Oh?" Wren cocked an eyebrow, then lowered it after a second thought. "Well, it turns out that chemistry alone doesn't make a team. But I'm glad we tried again. I always wondered about her. About what could have been."

"Then I'm glad that I helped you answer that question," Autumn said. Then, remembering herself, she straightened up and pressed the buttons of her cardigan flat against her stomach. "Do you have a second to talk about raising the level of student engagement in the drama program?"

Wren cocked her head and blinked at the subject change. A piece of blond hair fell across her forehead, bisecting the suspicious wrinkle between her fair brows.

"I can find a second," she said. She screwed the top on her coffee cup and stowed the oat milk back in the fridge. "It'll have to be a walk-and-talk. I'm on my way to an IEP meeting."

"Great." Autumn jumped to fall into step beside Wren, making sure to start on the same foot. Mirroring people made them trust you more. It proved you were paying attention to them. "What do you think of a schoolwide vote for the fall musical? Four available shows, age appropriate, no write-ins."

"What will it accomplish?" Wren asked, making a show of adjusting the strap of her leather messenger bag. No doubt it was full of important paperwork, but Autumn couldn't help but remember the beat-up army surplus bag Wren had worn slung across her chest back when they were both students. It had been covered in buttons for bands Autumn still wasn't cool enough to have heard of.

"I want the drama program to feel more supported by their peers," Autumn said, galloping to keep up. "If the whole school has a say in the musical, they'll be more inclined to see and audition for the show." She was talking too fast. Another rookie mistake. She had performed in front hundreds of kids on field trips, elderly people eating spaghetti, and at bars where people did not want to see improv comedy. She could certainly perform to an audience of one. "Normally the fall musical is only open to students who are enrolled in a drama class. Mr. Hearn thought it was the only way to guarantee a full-size cast. But I would like to do a musical that is open to any Point High student as long as they agree to fund-raise a certain amount for the rights to the musical. That way, there's a lot of talk about the show during auditions, during the fund-raiser, and leading up to the weekend of performances. It pays for itself."

Out of talking points, Autumn was starting to panic about which building Wren's meeting was in. Point High wasn't huge and they had already passed the library. Wren continued at a brisk stride.

"I need a chance to build a new program. From scratch," Autumn blurted. "And, honestly? I really, really do not want to co-direct a play for children about bullying with Pat Markey. If it had been pitched in my job interview, I wouldn't have taken the job."

Wren hissed. Autumn had never heard the vice principal have a giggle fit before. She would have remembered that it was sort of...goofy. Wren Vos had a laugh like a squeaky toy. Who knew Wren Vos had a laugh?

"Give me four shows that you can get cleared by the PTA and we'll take it to the next meeting," Wren said. "Unless you already have a fund-raiser in mind?"

Autumn shook her head. "N-no. Cookie dough sales are always popular."

"Once we get the okay from the PTA, you can put the vote out to homerooms," Wren said with a decisive nod. "Nice initiative, Kelly. Bring me more stuff like this and you're looking at a promotion." When Autumn looked confused, Wren explained, "I'm kidding? We don't work at a nineteen forties newspaper. But I like the idea of giving the students a vote. High school should spend more time modeling itself after democracy than prison. Mark the email urgent for me."

Elated, but playing it cool, Autumn nodded back. "You got it, Boss."

"Not your boss," Wren said.

"Not a newsie either, but we've got a bit now."

"A bit. I like it." A sliver of Wren's teeth appeared between her lips, the breath of a smile. "If you're going to secede from Pat, we should look at getting your classroom moved. You don't want to have to hear her railing 'howl, howl, howl, howl' against you."

Autumn laughed. "Was that a *King Lear* reference?"

"I taught it in AP English for two years."

"No way, I played Regan in college!"

"This is my meeting." Wren came to an abrupt stop in front

of the conference room. With her hand on the handle, she turned back to Autumn. She cleared her throat, made clear eye contact, and held out a hand to shake. "Good walk-and-talk, Autumn."

"We should meet like this more often!" Autumn smiled as Wren disappeared into the conference room.

The Broadway Club was going to be so proud of her.

J O

At any of the jobs she'd had in Silicon Valley, Jo never once found herself looking forward to a team-building day, but her new job hadn't given her much time with her fellow sales reps. They only saw one another at a weekly briefing in the cramped conference room attached to Rachel's cowork building. Jo had missed last month's team building—it had been scheduled for the day she moved to town.

Jo was praying that today's diversion would be more fun than her new normal of sucking up to bar managers and wearing either a black or white Nicotera Spirits polo every day—she had not yet earned the blue one. The polos worked on some kind of karate-belt ranking system that she hadn't bothered to memorize.

She could use something entertaining that wasn't texting. She was tired of living inside her phone.

Circling the block in figure eights, Jo ended up parking her Mini in front of a meter and running up four blocks to the gym that was too exclusive to show up on her Gym Class app. Her bag flopped behind her, water bottle banging against the side of her camera bag.

Her new bangs slipped into her eyes. Not pinning them back

had been a mistake. Cutting them had probably been a mistake, but she was trying to embrace them and move on. At least until they were long enough to pin back.

Rachel's gym had just as many spa packages as workout classes. The interior had club lighting, too dark and moody to be practical for the person behind the desk. Jo checked in under Nicotera Spirits and was pointed to the third door on the left.

Most of the sales team were already present, standing in their workout gear inside a dance studio that was at once dark and neon, the way that try-hard spin studios in Silicon Valley had been. It was surprisingly tight quarters, with hardly room enough for the liquor reps and their designer bags.

The other reps were mostly white, thin, and fresh out of college. Jo was the oldest person in the room aside from Rachel and possibly the dance instructor.

Jo hated that she noticed. She was twenty-six—and a half. Was she supposed to stop counting the halves? If every Nicotera rep in the room stayed with the company from today until retirement, they all had over thirty years left. At the end, they would bake going-away cakes for one another and forget who went blue first.

Well. Not Larisa. Jo got the feeling that girl who prided herself on being top sales every week would take all this shit to her grave. A real Jen G type, Larisa had been the only rep who had made sure Jo remembered her name with a too-tight handshake and the collar of her blue polo popped.

"I hear we have some folks who like to drink in here!" said the instructor, very much misrepresenting the liquor reps' relationship to their product. Jo's coworkers whooped in response—so maybe not. Music cued up, surprising Jo with the shrill synthesizers of party-rocking.

"Oh my God, I have not heard this since the seventh-grade dance," gushed one of the reps.

Jo had been at homecoming the year this song came out. Post-Wren, the first time. The year she and Autumn went in matching suits and pretended to be spies in order to kill the crushing boredom of not having dates.

With less than six of them in the room, it was hard to establish a front and back row, but Jo somehow managed to be teacher's-pet close. She tried not to worry about it, to focus on the steps being presented at top speed. She checked Rachel's progress and found her team leader leaning against a wall, answering a text, then waving and mouthing an excuse under the music and making her way to the door.

"Keep the energy up, everybody!" the instructor said, eyes frantic as the reps around Jo started to peter out, unwatched. "You're getting the hang of it now! Let's take it from the top, okay?" She started the song from the top. "Kick, kick, knee, knee! You got this! Elbows up!"

Beside her, Jo's coworkers were taking turns recording each other.

"It's too dark in here. It's making my video grainy."

"Wait, no, show me doing the spin!"

As Jo bounced higher, a phone screen came into her view.

"Jo, you're the queen of Instagram, aren't you?" asked one of the few male reps, aiming the selfie camera at her. "Would you cameo in my Story?"

"Don't stop now!" the instructor begged.

The door opened and Rachel stepped back in, filming herself. "Here we are live at the Nicotera Spirits sales rep day at Shift PDX in the Pearl! Someone show me how to do that Rockette thing in the middle because it's making me look like I've been sipping on too much of that new Nicotera chili pepper vodka, am I right? Eighty-four proof and a World Vodka Award nominee. Let's dance!"

An hour later, no one on the team could replicate the entire dance from beginning to end and left without thanking the instructor, their Instagram stories newly clogged with Boomerangs and water breaks.

Her coworkers shouted goodbye to one another as they separated at the studio door, off to make the most of their free day, now that the hurdle of forced camaraderie was out of the way. Jo found herself the last in the studio. She toweled off her face, caught in the fleeting impulse to scream into the terry cloth. There was a knot in her chest that pulled tighter and tighter as she refused to put pen to paper and release the cons of her new life.

Storming through the lobby, she took her phone out, wanting to unleash a stream of complaints into a text. But she had endured worse office environments plenty of times and survived. She didn't want anyone to worry about her. It was Monday—her parents' one day off, the beginning of everyone else's workweek.

It was so strange to remember that not that long ago, she didn't know how her loved ones spent their time. Now she could picture them perfectly on their ordinary Monday.

She looked up and found three people standing on the other side of the front window, fogging the glass and staring at her. Jo stepped outside cautiously, feeling their eyes follow her.

"Excuse me!" she heard the second she hit fresh air.

"I'm so sorry, this is so awkward—" said a girl with an extreme side part.

Jo opened her mouth, ready to tell the girl that she was not

Meghan Markle. Cutting bangs had not helped her with this question, even though she was in Portland and never near a prince, a bodyguard, or children.

"Are you PhotogFreeman from Instagram?"

"Jo," corrected one of the others.

Surprise momentarily overtook the confusion and fear of being approached by a stranger. She'd also never heard someone say her username out loud. "Yeah, that's me."

"We're huge fans of your Instagram, the Throwback List, everything!" said the third friend. "What are you doing in Portland? Are you starting a new project? A new list?"

"Not yet," Jo said.

"Other than your bu-jo, right?" asked Side Part. "I totally got addicted to bullet journal videos after that post where you recommended a bunch."

"I still have my bullet journal," Jo said. She patted her gym bag. "But all of my lists right now are regular to-dos and work stuff. I'm working here in town now."

"Oh," said Tall Friend, visibly disappointed. "We're doing a doughnut crawl. Ana has always wanted to try every doughnut in Portland, so we decided to help her."

"It's a happiness honeypot!" Side Part squealed.

"What's happier than doughnuts?" Jo asked.

"I'm the Bianca of the group," said First Friend. Jo could not begin to imagine how Bianca would react to a skinny white girl thinking they were anything alike. "These two were besties in high school, but we met in college. Now we're a trio! It's basically the best thing that ever happened to me."

"Everyone needs a crew," Jo agreed. Her voice sounded hollow.

She needed to eat lunch and make work calls. Her to-do lists were full, even if they weren't packed with honeypots. "It was great meeting you all. I need to run."

"Hope you post again soon!" said the Tall Friend, sounding like they didn't believe she would.

The Jo of the group, then.

Jo hadn't posted in weeks. She told her followers it was a hiatus. She knew it was closer to writer's block. She didn't know what came after the Throwback List.

Back in her furnished-by-someone-else apartment, she sat on the couch that smelled like cats. Rock Rockamore sat beside the TV, overlooking the living room she hadn't made a mark on.

Jo checked her phone.

Autumn had a picture taken in front of her house of twenty plastic top hats on a drop cloth in the process of being spray-painted with gold glitter for the *Chorus Line* dance number in the Senior Showcase. The entire Broadway Club was going to perform in the finale, making it the first time underclassmen had been invited to perform in the Senior Showcase, which explained why Eden had a video that was just her and Orin chanting *peripatetic, poetic, and chic* over someone badly beatboxing.

Florencio had a group selfie with his wrestlers at their last practice of the school year. Apparently Flo gave a speech about each of his players at eighth-grade promotion.

Bianca posted a video of Lita seeing the new upstairs office for the first time. Yesterday, the group chat had received the behind-the-scenes photo of Cruz carrying Lita up the stairs, everyone in the shop trailing behind. Lita's verdict was that the new office was very pretty and too fancy to do real tattoos. She was interested in seeing how Bee's new eyebrows healed up, though. So far, microblading seemed like a clean-brow miracle.

Jo wanted to call Bianca and tell her about the "Bianca of the group" white girl, but she didn't know what today's Lita schedule was and didn't want to interrupt. She wanted to hear about how the Broadway Club rehearsals were going now that membership had expanded to almost twenty kids. Their last recording of *9 to 5* had been a blur of heaven hands.

I'd rather be at home, Jo thought, not thinking of an apartment or California.

She got in the car and drove toward the ocean.

♡ ◯ ⊿

PhotogFreeman: Sandy Point, Oregon. A town you could mistake for forgettable. The boonies on the way to the Goonies house. Where the ocean is part of the sky and the trees are taller than the buildings. Where my dreams were written on the walls because people who loved me gave me walls and stars to wish on.

The Throwback List is done. I know that younger me would be proud.

I know now how much of her I carry in my heart. And I know how much of my heart I leave behind when I'm not here. The ultimate happiness honeypot is coming home to the people you love.

And I'm home.

#TheThrowbackList

THE
ACKNOWLEDGMENTS
LIST

Kieran Viola
Britt Rubiano
Heather Crowley
Laura Zats
Hannah Gómez
Leanna Keyes
Lara Ruark
Tyler Torres
Dad & Nil
The Harbor Family
Tehlor Kay Mejia
Elizabeth Flambert
Erin Duffey
Stephen Sondheim